# Carolyn Hart

"If I were teaching a course on how to
write a mystery, I would make Carolyn Hart
required reading."
*Los Angeles Times*

"Carolyn Hart's craftmanship makes her mystery's
Queen of C's—cozy, clever, and chock
full of charm."
Mary Daheim

"Displays the charm and coziness of Christie."
*Chicago Sun-Times*

"Carolyn Hart embodies the spirit of Agatha
Christie more than any other
contemporary writer."
Dean James, author of *By a Woman's Hand*

"Hart creates lively, sympathetic characters
and interesting locales
and maintains a snappy pace."
*Booklist*

## By Carolyn Hart

### Henrie O

DEAD MAN'S ISLAND • SCANDAL IN FAIR HAVEN
DEATH IN LOVER'S LANE • DEATH IN PARADISE
DEATH ON THE RIVER WALK • RESORT TO MURDER

### Death on Demand

DEATH ON DEMAND • DESIGN FOR MURDER
SOMETHING WICKED • HONEYMOON WITH MURDER
A LITTLE CLASS ON MURDER • DEADLY VALENTINE
THE CHRISTIE CAPER • SOUTHERN GHOST
MINT JULEP MURDER • YANKEE DOODLE DEAD
WHITE ELEPHANT DEAD • SUGARPLUM DEAD
APRIL FOOL DEAD • ENGAGED TO DIE
MURDER WALKS THE PLANK • DEATH OF THE PARTY
DEAD DAYS OF SUMMER • DEATH WALKED IN

# CAROLYN HART

# SET SAIL FOR MURDER

**A Henrie O Mystery**

**A V O N**

*An Imprint of HarperCollinsPublishers*

This book is a work of fiction. The characters, incidents, and dialogue are drawn from the author's imagination and are not to be construed as real. Any resemblance to actual events or persons, living or dead, is entirely coincidental.

AVON BOOKS
*An Imprint of* HarperCollins*Publishers*
10 East 53rd street
New York, New York 10022-5299

Copyright © 2007 by Carolyn Hart
Excerpt from *Death Walked In* copyright © 2008 by Carolyn Hart
ISBN: 978-0-06-072408-5
www.avonmystery.com

First Avon Books paperback printing: April 2008
First William Morrow hardcover printing: April 2007

Avon Trademark Reg. U.S. Pat. Off. and in Other Countries, Marca Registrada, Hecho en U.S.A.
HarperCollins® is a registered trademark of HarperCollins Publishers.

Printed in the U.S.A.

10 9 8 7 6 5 4 3 2 1

*To Mary and Bill Price,*
*wonderful companions on our Baltic adventure*

# one

THE telephone shrilled as I stepped inside the house. I was hot and thirsty, intent upon reaching the kitchen and a frosty glass of Gatorade, but, of course, I picked up the ringing portable phone from the move-scarred walnut table in my front hallway. Old reporters never ignore that imperious summons even when the days of deadlines are long past. I glanced at the small screen. Suddenly I was breathless.

Caller ID: James A. Lennox.

This was a call I had never expected to receive, certainly not on a casual summer morning, sweaty and relaxed after a jog on the university track. It was a slow jog at my age, but nonetheless I could still pick one foot up, put it down, take pleasure in exercise.

The ring sounded again. I struggled for breath, punched TALK. "Hello."

"Henrie O." The clear, resonant tenor was still youthful, without the dour droop of age. A dear voice. Once I had welcomed his calls, come to depend upon them, my spirits lifting when he spoke my name. Jimmy Lennox had long been a cherished friend and, once, my lover, but he took one road and I another. This unexpected call loosed emotions I had thought neatly packaged and filed in the past. I was swept by tenderness, unease, sadness, and a sense of foreboding.

I should have answered right away, but how do you respond to an old friend and former lover whose proposal of marriage you declined? The last time I saw Jimmy . . .

"Henrie O, please don't hang up." The appeal was utterly unlike confident, unflappable Jimmy. Lanky, laconic, and clever, Jimmy had become a part of my life with his quick curiosity, wry sense of humor, and lack of pretension.

When I spoke, I spoke with my heart. "I'll never hang up on you."

His appeal and my response held a world of meaning for both of us. I knew Jimmy was upset. He knew I cared for him still, would never be quite certain how much was friendship and how much was love.

Ultimately I'd felt there was not enough love for me to marry him. That decision haunted me still. I missed Jimmy, missed him intensely, but now he was married. I would always care for Jimmy. He'd achieved a measure of fame as a newsman and later as a biographer. In my memory he moved with his usual grace, lithe and lean, with an air of placidity that often fooled his interview subjects into thinking him a trifle slow. That was a mistake.

"What's wrong?" We never minced words with each other. I swept off a calico headband, swiped at my perspiring face. In the mirror above the table, my cheeks still flamed from exertion and my silvered dark hair curled in damp ringlets.

"I don't have any right to call on you. But you're the only person who can possibly help me." He was uncertain, reluctant.

I've never been able to stay on the sidelines when someone I love is in trouble. "What can I do?"

He drew a deep breath. "I haven't talked to you since I married Sophia."

Deep in sleepless nights, I still willed away the emptiness I'd felt upon receiving the wedding invitation. Sophia Montgomery. I remembered her well. I doubt she recalled me. Sophia lived in a blaze of excitement, attention, and achievement. She'd succeeded hugely in documentary films, recording everything from genocide in Rwanda to the shrinking of the polar ice cap. I'd met her when she was in Mexico cataloging the struggle of insurrectionists in Chiapas. Along her way to fame, she'd married an actor and later a financier. Twice a widow, she was now Jimmy's wife. She was now in her fifties, almost fifteen years younger than Jimmy. And me, of course.

I looked again in the mirror at deep-set dark eyes in a narrow face with lines that mapped a lifetime of happiness and sorrow. Not a young face.

I'd sent an elegant cut-glass bowl as a wedding gift. She and Jimmy had married last year at her home near Carmel. The nuptials were a celebrity-studded extravaganza. I'd read about the glamorous guest list in *People*. Clearly, something had gone awry in this celebrated union. "Of course. How is Sophia?" Smart as ever? Intense as ever? Brilliant as ever?

"She won't listen to me. I keep warning her, but she won't listen." Anger warred with despair. "I've got to have help or—"

I felt a twist of irritation. That easygoing Jimmy might end up at odds with Sophia came as no surprise. Sophia had a genius for barreling straight to the destination of her choice, disregarding both approval and opposition. I wouldn't have expected Jimmy to seek me out as a mediator for a troubled relationship. I almost cut in to say I'd left my Ann Landers hat in someone else's closet, but he continued, the words anguished.

"—she may die."

I felt cold. I reached out, turned off the air-conditioning. "Cancer?" Sophia was in her fifties, the age when so many women are struck by that devastating disease. Was she a woman who would not take care, ignored danger signals?

"God, I wish. You can cut it out, right? Even Sophia would pay attention to cancer. When a boulder crashed down a cliff yesterday and missed her by a foot, hey, that's just an unfortunate accident. Accident, my foot. Somebody pushed that boulder and it has to be one of the family."

I shivered in my clammy T-shirt and shorts. I walked down the hall into the cheerful kitchen, with its yellow tile floor, white counters, yellow walls, white kitchen table, and chairs. If I hadn't known Jimmy for almost a half century, known him in good times and bad, I might have dismissed his fear, as Sophia obviously had. But Jimmy was never an alarmist.

I squeezed the phone between my head and shoulder, pulled open the refrigerator, retrieved the Gatorade, poured a huge tumblerful. "Five W's and an H, Jimmy." It was the old journalism litany: who, what, when, where, why, and how? I grabbed a notepad from the counter and sat at the kitchen table, pen in hand.

He didn't waste words or time. "Sophia walks to her office—"

I remembered a pic included in the wedding layout. Sophia's office was a glass and redwood structure on a headland with a panoramic view of the Pacific. Caption: *Filmmaker's Eagle's-Eye View.*

"—at eight o'clock every morning. Not a minute earlier, not a minute later. You could set Greenwich time by her. Yesterday, right on schedule, she's coming around a bend in the trail when a boulder crashes down on the cliff path. It's a hundred-foot drop from there to rocks and high surf. If she'd been hit—" His indrawn breath left no doubt about the outcome.

I pictured a flailing figure tumbling to destruction.

"The boulder didn't hit her." My tone was neutral. Boulders are known to bounce down unstable hillsides in California.

"It would have if she didn't have the luck of children and fools. You know why it missed her?" His voice rose in disbelief. "She has a thing about snails. Sure, gardeners hate them. Trust Sophia to have a soft spot for snails. She's hurrying along the trail because she always hurries and there's a big snail right in the middle of the path. She stopped to watch the snail ooze across. The boulder missed her by a foot."

Children and fools. Or maybe Sophia's angel breathed purpose into a snail. Or maybe Sophia Montgomery still rode the wave of luck that had lifted her to the top. To succeed as the world measures success, it helps to be good, but you have to be lucky.

"I heard the rumble and came out on the balcony of our room. I saw the scar on the side of the cliff where the boulder snagged and bounced and there was Sophia looking down at the water. One more step . . ."

Jimmy was struck by the small distance between life and death. I was focused on the huge leap between accident and willful murder. "Boulders come loose."

"That's what Sophia said. Why then? Why at the precise moment she's walking to her office as she does every morning? I checked it out. I went up the side of the cliff. Pines screen that part of the cliff from the house, making it easy for anybody to get up there and back to the house without being seen. I figured out where the boulder came from. It was part of an outcropping behind a big fir. It looked to me like there were some depressions in a blanket of leaves where somebody could have stood and prized it loose and pushed. I think there were gouge marks where it had broken off. I came back down to the house, tried to find out where everybody was when it happened. Nobody could vouch for anyone else."

*. . . looked to me like . . . somebody could have . . . think there were . . . Nobody could vouch . . .*

I sketched a rugged Big Sur cliff studded with pines and mounds of broken rock. "No real evidence." No clear footprints. No one sighted. Possible scratches on split stone. No alibi for anyone but the hour was early. Nothing definitive to show a police detective. Nothing but Jimmy's dogged conviction.

"You haven't heard the rest. The big why." Jimmy sounded grim. "Sophia might as well be treading water surrounded by barracudas. She's all that stands between her stepchildren and the kind of money you and I can't even imagine."

I drew jagged teeth in the snout of a torpedo-shaped fish aimed at a stick figure.

"They were here, every last one of them. She married Frank Riordan—"

Venture capitalist Riordan had been Sophia's second husband. The first was long dead and long forgotten. I have a good memory, though, and it snagged a name: Joe Dan Holbrook, a short-lived movie actor. After a few less-than-memorable westerns, a fiery car crash after an all-night party in Tijuana—sans Sophia—marked the finale. As I recalled, Sophia was in a Latin American jungle at the time. She didn't make it back for a service, but had his ashes flown down and scattered from a mountain-top. Quintessential Sophia. This was pre-*People*, but the tabloids gave it a big play. My late husband and I had been in Mexico City then and I'd read about it over breakfast one morning.

"—who was a widower with four kids. Not exactly the Brady Bunch. Sophia promptly got them settled in boarding schools. She wasn't the mean stepmother. She was the titular stepmother. Since she never had kids of her own, she didn't have a clue that kids need a personal touch. Frank ran a corporate family and he had never been the all-American dad anyway. The only exception to his board-room rule was Sophia. She dazzled him until the day he died. That accounts for his will, which has him yanking strings in his children's lives from the other side of the grave."

Where there's a will . . .

But this was far afield from an errant boulder tumbling to the sea. I shifted uncomfortably on the wooden chair, aware that I was sticky and damp and increasingly puzzled by Jimmy's call. Almost half the continent distant from California, what could I be expected to do about Sophia and the possibly dangerous Riordan clan? Wasn't it the foolhardy will that influenced him, made him see dark design in a near accident?

Jimmy and I had always spoken frankly to each other, even when truth was not especially welcome. "You need to talk to Sophia, not me. If that won't work, send the guests home. If you can't do that, cause a scene. Announce that you know one of them tried to kill Sophia and any more near accidents and you're going to the police."

"God, I love you." His voice almost held a hint of laughter. "Direct as a bullet and twice as deadly. I'd do it in a heartbeat if that would shake us free of them. But it won't. Thursday we all catch a flight at LAX to London. We overnight at the Heathrow Hilton, then take a Qantas flight Saturday morning to Copenhagen, where we board the *Clio* for a two-week cruise in the Baltic. It's all because of Frank's will. Sophia got a letter from the lawyer. Each heir has been receiving income—subject to Sophia's approval, and that's another story—from a five-million-dollar trust, but this year the oldest child turns thirty. That triggers a provision where Sophia determines whether the trusts should be dissolved and the heirs receive full control."

"Sophia?" It seemed a great deal of power to accord to a not-very-engaged stepmother.

"That's how Riordan set it up. He ran his family with an iron hand and he couldn't give up control even when he was dead." Jimmy's disgust was clear. "If she decides one or all of them would be better served to have the trusts remain in place, there won't be another consideration for ten years and it's up to her whether they get the income during the interim. As for the rest of his estate, Sophia has a life interest. Upon her death, all of it will be divided among the children. Talk about setting up motives for murder! The irony is that she doesn't care a whit about money. Never has. She's made plenty. She puts the income from Frank into accounts for the estate. But she feels she owes it to Frank to try and make the best decisions possible for the future of his kids. She's been crossways with them the last few years, but she decided to invite all of them to take this cruise. Her hope is to smooth things over and at the same time figure out if they're ready to handle big bucks."

"A command performance." It wasn't a question.

"You bet your life."

Or Sophia's.

"Henrie O, I've reserved a cabin for you, got plane tickets—"

"Wait a minute, Jimmy." I sounded stiff. I felt stiff. It wasn't a command performance for me. "There's nothing I can do to help."

"You're the best reporter I ever knew." He spoke quietly but with conviction, a tribute from one professional to another.

That was another lifetime. I remembered old-time newsrooms with the clack of typewriters, unceasing deadline pressure, a heavy fog of cigarette smoke, and front pages hot off the press with ink that smeared. I remembered as well computers and quiet, college-educated reporters who could no longer read type upside down.

My career had spanned both. Newsrooms, whether noisy or quiet, always held a sense of urgency and excitement. I remembered. I'd been good. But I wasn't a reporter now. I didn't teach journalism any longer. I lived the life of a retiree: travel, books, plays, films, family, friends. Friends . . .

"You have a knack. You read people." The plea returned to his voice. "If anyone can spot trouble, it's you. Maybe I'm nuts. I'd like for that to be true. Maybe I'm seeing phantasms that don't exist, but I can't take a chance. Not with Sophia's life. And you'll know. Maybe we'll have a drink one night and you'll tell me to stop seeing monsters under the bed. Look, I've got it figured out." He was cajoling, insistent. "You keep out of sight until we get to the ship. We'll run into each other on the ship and it will be a big deal, bumping into an old friend. I'll invite you to hang out with us. Maybe there won't be any danger, but it has to make things easier, lessen the tension, if we have an outsider involved."

I would definitely be an outsider. Sophia was Jimmy's wife.

"It's a lot to ask." His voice was husky. "I've always felt I can count on you."

Jimmy was my friend. That trumped everything, but I didn't share his confidence. I doubted I could make a difference. I drew the bow of a ship on the pad.

His voice was hopeful. "Maybe you and Sophia will get around to talking about the will—"

I shook my head at this suggestion.

"—and you can encourage her to let them have the money."

"I don't recall Sophia as a let-down-her-hair gal." My tone was dry.

"She says what she thinks and she's going to be thinking about the will. Henrie O, you're coming?" His voice lifted with hope.

"How much does the cruise cost?" A two-week cruise could be very pricey. I don't have a bare-bones budget, but I look for travel bargains.

"That's taken care of." Suddenly his voice was eager. "You'll come, won't you?"

"I can't let you buy my passage." I'd always insisted on paying my share on our holidays.

"I've already done it. Everything's paid for. I don't expect you to pick up the tab here. You're doing this for me—"

If I agreed, certainly my journey would be for Jimmy. Still—

"—and it's like an assignment. Travel expenses included. Henrie O, thank you." Relief and gratitude lifted his voice, restored the timbre I remembered.

Friends . . . Yet my presence would ask more of me than he realized. How hard would it be for me to stand near, accept Sophia's possessive hand on his arm? Harder than he would ever know. Yet the fact remained that deep inside I felt a certainty: if I called on Jimmy, he would come. I could do no less for him, no matter how difficult it might be.

I kept my tone casual. "A Baltic cruise sounds wonderful. Sure. I'll do what I can and maybe together we can lighten the atmosphere."

He rushed ahead. "I'll overnight everything. Tickets and background on the Riordans. Between us, we'll figure it out. I'll see you on board."

*two*

THE huge airliner, dim except for reading lights such as mine, was a capsule of drowsiness as it winged over the Atlantic. An occasional cough or snore, the quiet rustle as a steward moved past, the distant click of shuffled cards were the only sounds in this deep watch of the night. I'd napped, comfortable in the reclining seat. Jimmy had reserved a business-class seat at a window. Now I was wide awake. I looked at the screen that reported the progress of the flight: speed, direction, time elapsed, time remaining, and the—to me—lonely inching of the line marking the plane's journey over emptiness.

I opened the packet I'd received from Jimmy and slid out dossiers with information he had gathered about the family members I would soon meet. A good reporter digs hard before an actual interview. Jimmy had dug well. I started with Sophia. Much of it I knew, some I didn't.

Sophia Montgomery Holbrook Riordan Lennox: 52, b. in Laguna Beach, CA. Father Benton Montgomery, well-known seascape artist; mother Hazel Taggart Montgomery, poet. B.A. in journalism from UCLA. Member women's tennis team. First documentary job with Brittany Films.

Started as an assistant to Joshua Abbott. Twice nominated for an Oscar for best documentary. Married actor Joe Dan Holbrook January 1, 1980. Widowed September 9, 1984. Married financier Frank Riordan June 22, 1990. Widowed March 19, 2000. Married writer James Allen Lennox October 4, 2003. Four stepchildren: Alexander, Kent, Rosemary, and Valerie.

Jimmy had appended a recent interview from the *L.A. Times*. The photo layout contained dramatic pix of Sophia atop an elephant, Sophia maneuvering a lever in a diving bell, Sophia at the keyboard of her computer, fingers flying.

The reporter described her as passionate about poetry ("The imagery in *The Waste Land* touches my soul") and travel ("Everything's different but everything's the same. We all live and love and hope whether in Constantinople or an Andean village or a dusty West Texas town").

I scanned the piece: ". . . a slightly built woman with a mass of blond ringlets, Montgomery exudes a wild and restless energy. Her blue eyes glisten as she speaks in staccato phrases. A thin hand moves in butterfly-swift gestures. The nails are colorless but a top-dollar diamond flashes . . ."

I raised an eyebrow. Jimmy's taste ran more to a single golden band. Did she still wear Frank Riordan's ring? If so, how did Jimmy feel about that? That wasn't any business of mine.

". . . Montgomery is rarely still, hand moving, foot tapping, jumping to her feet to pace. She smiles often, a vivid, infectious smile. Her laughter is throaty, intimate, unaffected. 'Regrets?' Her look of surprise is obvious. 'Who looks back? Why?' She swipes a hand through her curls and looks more windblown than ever. 'Sweetie, who has time? I have projects up to here.' She flips her fingers beneath her chin. 'Who's checking out under-the-counter steroid sales to high school kids who don't have a clue about Faustian bargains? What's happening now with women in Afghanistan? How secure are our borders?' Montgomery claps her hands together. 'As long as I have a camera, I'm all right.' 'You're happy?' For an instant, her sparkle dims. 'Happy? That's a Walt Disney word. I'll settle for busy.' "

Happy? I wondered at the age of Sophia's interviewer. Content. Challenged. Stressed. Engaged. Satisfied. Excited. Despairing. There are many emotional possibilities in life, but rarely does anyone over the age of thirty have the temerity to proclaim happiness. I understood Sophia's answer. I found an interesting passage near the end of the interview: "I believe in the ideal. I've never reached it. None of us do. But we have to try. I'm willing to cut anyone slack if they try. If they don't try, it's sayonara."

If she applied this standard to her stepchildren's lives, Sophia might not be an errant heir's best friend.

A steward paused in the aisle, spoke softly. "May I get you a snack? Some nuts and juice?"

I smiled. "Yes, and water, please." It's never possible to have too much water on a long flight.

When the steward returned, the mixed nuts heated, the orange juice cold, the water icy, I moved the papers on my tray. The nuts were delicious. When I returned home, would I take the time to microwave cashews? Probably not, but I enjoyed the ripple of sybaritic pleasure as I ate. I picked up the dossier on Frank Riordan's eldest son.

Alexander (Alex) Timothy Riordan, 29, b. in San Francisco, CA. Father Frank Riordan, financier; mother Anna Nesbitt, civic leader. Private schools in San Francisco.

Business graduate UCLA, master's in finance USC. Worked two years for WorldCom in Atlanta. Joined two friends in a telecommunications company in China. Failed in December 2002. Next venture involved delivery of hybrid vehicles in Bolivia. Failed in March 2003. Invested in a whole foods restaurant in Berkeley. Failed June 2004. Trying to raise capital for a wireless venture in China. Accomplished mountain climber, biker. Married Margaret (Madge) Louise Brinker 2003 in Santa Monica. He met Madge at a UCLA football game. She was a cheerleader, aspiring actress, sometime model. Madge grew up in Long Beach, father a pharmacist, mother a secretary.

Kent Clarence Riordan, 28, b. in San Francisco. Private schools. English honors graduate USC. Worked as a reporter for newspapers in Pasadena, Long Beach, Santa Clara. Currently teaching as adjunct faculty at a community college in Marin County. Author of several short stories published by online magazines. Triathlete. Competed in Ironman Triathlon in Hawaii last five years. Single.

Rosemary (Rosie) Margaret Riordan, 26, b. in San Francisco. Private schools. Dropped out of Claremont. Spent a year as a singer on a cruise ship. Worked as a waitress in Las Vegas. Two years in Rio with an import-export company owned by one of Frank's old friends. Currently working as a hostess on a dinner cruise ship out of Long Beach. Single.

Valerie (Val) Amelia Riordan, 25, b. in San Francisco. Private schools. B.A. in film studies from UCLA. Working for an independent filmmaker in Los Angeles. Single.

Evelyn Jessamine Riordan, 56, unmarried sister of Frank Riordan. Education degree from USC, taught French in high schools in Long Beach, Pasadena, and San Diego. Joined Frank's household after the death of his first wife to assist with the children. Returned to teaching upon Frank's

marriage to Sophia Montgomery. Came to Carmel after
Riordan was diagnosed with cancer and was there to oversee his care until his death. Still lives in the Carmel house.

That last succinct summary was studded with red flags.
The children had been young when their mother died.
How painful had it been for their aunt to see them dis-
persed to boarding schools when Frank married Sophia?
Where was Sophia when Frank was ill? Why did Evelyn
still live in the house? Why was she on the jaunt to the
Baltic?

I stacked the dossiers, unfolded several sheets of ruled
paper. Even in the dim light, Jimmy's bold, unmistakable
script was easy to read.

*Dear Henrie O,*

*You know what you mean to me, what you have al-
ways meant. You are kind and brave and generous.
You are also smart and tough and persevering.
That's why I know you will find the truth. Maybe
I'm wrong and they're as innocent as babes. That
would be wonderful. If I'm right, the shock will be
enormous. In the best of all possible worlds, I'll be
wrong and we'll enjoy a wonderful holiday.*

*God knows Sophia has managed to upset or
disturb—oh, I might as well admit it—alienate almost all of them. If I can plead her case, her decisions are based on what she feels Frank would
have wished. She isn't motivated by greed or dislike
or jealousy or indifference. She means well, but she
has never been able to empathize. She has a curious inability to divorce abstract principles from
emotional reality. She's trying to do what she thinks*

*Frank would have wished. Frank wanted his kids to be big, tough, take-charge Riordans. That's not who they are. Here's who they are:*

*Alex is the oldest. He turns thirty in November, which triggers the provision concerning possible dissolution of the trusts. He's a little guy who wants to be as big as his dad. You remember Frank, six feet three and built like a bunker. Alex is five feet five and scrawny. He took after his mother, short, redheaded, nervous. He's been in one financial scrape after another, always thinking he's going to hit it big. He lost a bundle in telecommunications. Now he's trying to get in on a wireless boom in China. His wife never met an expensive piece of jewelry she didn't want to buy. Madge is an ice blonde with a frozen heart. No kids. Fortunately. Yeah, I don't like her. All the charm of a viper. Poor Alex. Nobody's ever made him feel like a big guy. We all need to be big guys at home. So like any approval-starved kid, he acts out. Swaggers, blusters, tries to bully, never with much success. If Alex relaxed, figured out who he is, liked himself, he'd be a different guy. He's a good athlete, runs a mile in under five, mountain climbs, shoots rapids. If he'd yank the plastic away from Madge, he'd roll a boulder off his shoulders.*

I wiggled my toes in their airplane fuzzies. What Sophia lacked in empathy, Jimmy had in spades. I grabbed another handful of warm cashews and continued to read.

*I don't have a handle on Kent. I'd never met him until this week. He didn't come to the wedding. He and Sophia quarreled before she and I married.*

*I've tried to find out what happened and Sophia shrugs it off. All she'll say is that anybody who wants to live with a lie is a fool. He'd be likable if he didn't radiate hatred when Sophia's around. He's a good-looking guy, about six feet tall, dark hair, blue eyes, sensitive face.*

*Rosie's a pistol, as we used to say in West Texas. Red hair that glistens like hot lava. Green eyes. A body to lust for. She's a knockout and knows it. She enjoys attracting men and blowing them off. At the wedding, she gave one of the toasts. I still remember it. Throaty voice, flute of champagne held high. "To Sophia and Jimmy. May life reward each of them as they deserve." I looked at Sophia. It's never occurred to her that Rosie despises her. That's when I decided Rosie was a woman to watch.*

*Val drifted around the wedding like a ghost. No smiles. No frowns. She's a redhead too, but with none of Rosie's fire. Val has a soft voice and a face that reminds me of a Minnesota lake on a windless day. Still. Quiet. But you know the water is deep and cold. When Sophia and I came back up the path after the boulder crashed down, Val was standing on the terrace. I yelled that Sophia had almost been killed. Val stared at us, cool as a Mississippi gambler, and said, "It would have been a long way down." I swear she sounded disappointed. She gave a little nod and strolled to a chair and settled down with a book.*

*As for Evelyn, she's an enigma. When we got married, I told Sophia I was surprised that Frank's sister lived at the house. Sophia laughed and told me that Evelyn couldn't make up her mind whether Sophia was a devil or an angel. A devil because she married Frank, an angel because she made him happy. A devil because she insisted the children go to boarding schools, an angel because that made them depend upon Evelyn. A devil because she kept on traveling and working when Frank was ill, an angel because that made Evelyn his companion. Sophia said after Frank died, she asked Evelyn to stay on and that was a plus on the angel side.*

*Sophia said she'd send Evelyn away if I preferred. Frank left Evelyn comfortably fixed so money wasn't a problem. I told Sophia absolutely not, Evelyn was fine, leave her in peace. Everything runs beautifully and I like Evelyn. She's cheerful and good-humored, always saying something positive.*

*That's the happy family. Any one of them might have wobbled that rock loose.*

Any one of them . . .

I pulled out a sheaf of photos printed from a computer. There were several of Sophia but one I suspected was Jimmy's favorite. She stood on a rugged cliffside, likely near her office, looking out to sea, a breeze stirring her golden ringlets, a slight smile softening her ascetic face. Her blue eyes were piercing and eager. The only hint of her eternal restlessness was the almost imperceptible lift of one hand. I wondered if she'd thought of something she had to do or if she was commanding the photographer to hurry. I had no doubt the moment of inaction had dissolved into a flurry of movement. There was work to be done, scripts to write, films to make. Sophia Montgomery was not a woman to waste a moment. How like her to transform a decision about her stepchildren's trusts from a dry legal responsibility into a journey of . . . what exactly? Expectations? Reconciliation? Confrontation?

The five sheets of photos contained a montage for each of the family members with brief descriptions written by Jimmy beneath each photograph. I took Alex's sheet first. In his wedding picture, was he standing especially straight to seem taller? Madge was a beautiful bride. She looked triumphant, excited, pleased. She lifted a champagne flute to her husband but I saw no softening of her features. Where was the love? I could imagine the same expression after a big catch while deep-sea fishing. In the next picture, I felt a vicarious thrill as I looked at the sheer cliff face. Alex's narrow face ridged with effort as he climbed hand over hand up a rope. In an office shot, a beaming Alex shook hands with a much taller man. Alex's expensive chalk-stripe black suit was too big through the shoulders. On a tropical beach, a coconut palm suggested carefree days. Alex slumped in a webbed chair near a swimming pool, zinc oxide on his nose, bare shoulders an unlovely pink from sunburn, blue trunks baggy. He stared forlornly across the pool. His mouth had a sullen set. I wondered what he saw.

I looked at the second sheet. Jimmy had written: *Kent would be likable if he didn't radiate hatred . . .* Unlike Alex, whose features were too sharp, too ferret-like for handsomeness, Kent Riordan was an attractive young man. Moreover, all the photographs reflected a shy charm. In one shot, he strummed a mandolin with a whimsical smile. He leaned against a wrought-iron lamppost, relaxed in a sky blue polo and worn chinos and leather sandals. In a beach scene, he ran barefoot and shirtless with an easy grace, hair tousled, baggy chinos rolled up to his knees, laughing. A studio portrait caught a look of inquiry. Lips parted, he might have been asking a question. In a snapshot, he opened his arms as his sister Rosie ran toward him. They were teenagers, features still not quite set. Their affection was apparent.

Despite reservations, I grinned at the third sheet. Ah yes, I expected that Rosie Riordan was indeed a pistol. Her studio portrait was impudent as the taunt of a street kid, red hair spiky, malachite-bright eyes challenging, voluptuous lips in a seductive droop. Each photo was distinctive. In a sailor suit dress, she looked like a winsome waif. In a gold lamé gown molded to an exquisite figure, she was the eternal enchantress. A snapshot caught her cross-legged on the beach, wet hair plastered against her head, face spattered with mud, industriously excavating a sand castle.

Val's pictures were shockingly different. Val and Rosie both had the same classic bone structure, which they shared with their brother Kent. Only Alex missed out on the Riordan good looks. But Val's expression in a studio portrait was severe, remote, her gaze cool and reserved behind heavy and distinctly unstylish horn-rim glasses. On a movie set, her face was stern as she gestured to a group of men clustered around a camera. The glasses rode atop her head. She wore no makeup. An oversize dingy white sweatshirt hung almost to the knees of loose worn jeans. At a premiere, her black taffeta dress was high-necked and unrevealing. Again no makeup or jewelry. Always, her face was enigmatic, unreadable. One photo told a different story. I reached out and touched it with my finger. In a snapshot obviously taken without her realizing it, Val cradled a huge tortoiseshell cat in her arms, head bent, eyes soft, lips curved in love.

Was Val only comfortable offering love to creatures

without power or expectations? Why was her face to the world as inhospitable as a barbed-wire barrier?

The final sheet made me smile. It would take a curmudgeon or a snob to resist Evelyn Riordan. At a glance, she was untidy, her Riordan red hair straggling from a shapeless, sagging bun, and unstylish, her clothes unimaginative and dated, but in these pictures with her brother's children she was gloriously, unrestrainedly effervescent, eyes shining, rosebud mouth smiling. Beneath the first, Jimmy noted: *Alex's wedding.* Evelyn was shapeless in a pink silk suit, but her face was alight with joy as she threw rose petals. Standing near a Christmas tree, she held out a wrapped package with silver paper and a huge red bow to a teenage Kent. Her gray cardigan drooped, lacking the bottom button, and a hem hung loose, but Santa couldn't have appeared more eager to please. On the beach, she walked arm in arm with a grown-up Rosie. Evelyn was smiling, her face eager as she listened to her niece. The last picture was as far from gaiety as a war-ravaged street from a peaceful country lane. A younger Evelyn was in funeral black. She bent her head against bright red curls as a child clung to her. Beneath it, Jimmy had written: *Don't know whether it was Val or Rosie. Obviously a funeral. Maybe Frank's first wife.*

Suddenly weary, feeling buffeted by other lives and sensing emotional storms with yet-to-be-calculated damages, I swept the photomontages into a stack, slid them along with Jimmy's letter and the dossiers into a folder. I looked up at the line that continued to inch across the small screen. The stewards and stewardesses were turning on lights, moving briskly up and down the aisles, bringing coffee and juice and sweet rolls. It wasn't far now to Heathrow and the true beginning of my journey.

I snapped shut the folder, but I could not as easily will away the memory of faces. Defensive Alex. Sensitive Kent. Unquenchable Rosie. Beleaguered Val. Affectionate Evelyn.

Was one of them the face of a murderer-in-waiting?

# three

AFTER I reached the hotel, I wanted to sleep, but I knew better than to succumb. The only way to overcome jet lag is to fight through the wearying hours following a flight and remain awake until early evening. I decided not to wander about the hotel. The area was too small and the likelihood of encountering Jimmy and the Riordan clan too great.

Instead, I took the train into London. The day was unusually warm for London in August, the temperature in the nineties. I found a small café near Bond Street and drank several cups of strong tea with a scone and determinedly did not think about the trip ahead. At this nadir of energy, I would regret the burden I had accepted. Instead, I spent a cheerful afternoon in Harrods enjoying shopping for my daughter Emily and her family. When all the gifts had been dispatched, I looked at the time with grainy eyes and walked back to the station. It was an effort to stay awake. Once again I traversed Terminal 4 and was too weary to scan the hotel lobby when I arrived.

I went straight to my room. I didn't expect any messages but I checked the telephone on the desk. The message light wasn't lit, which was all to the good. Unexpected messages rarely bring good news. I yawned, took a step toward the bed, then abruptly turned away. I needed to stay awake a few more hours to adapt to the time change. I'd take a hot shower. As I walked toward the bath, a sharp knock sounded at the door.

I looked through the aperture. Jimmy, a haggard Jimmy, was lifting his hand to knock again. I'd not seen him in several years. His hair was more white now than blond, but he was still a commanding figure: tall, well built, with an aura of vigor. I opened the door and knew that I still cared for him, that I wanted him to be the Jimmy I remembered, laughing and eager.

He shot a worried glance up the corridor. When his eyes met mine, I was shocked by the fierceness in his gaze. Fatigue emphasized dark circles beneath his eyes, but fatigue couldn't account for his somber expression.

I stepped back, held the door wide. I didn't try for a greeting. His arrival at my room wasn't according to his plan.

He stepped inside, grabbed my hands, squeezed them, held tight, a bridge over time. "I saw you come through the lobby and I had to talk to you. I've only got a minute. They're waiting downstairs. We're going to have an early dinner." He loosed his grip.

I gestured toward the single easy chair near the small desk. The room was small and seemed smaller now, a rather narrow double bed, a luggage rack, a desk, a straight chair, a cushioned chair, dark drapes drawn across the window, all within a dozen feet. Jimmy was tall and rangy. It seemed odd to have him so near and yet now, as the husband of Sophia Montgomery, always out of my reach. There had been a time when a hotel room spelled laughter and love.

He shook his head, remained standing just inside the

door. "I'll only stay a minute. I want to tell you what happened the night before we left. It may sound crazy, but I think one of them may have tried to poison her."

"Poison?" It is an ugly word for an ugly deed.

His face creased in a worried frown. "Every night Sophia has a glass of cream sherry. I have Scotch and soda. Wednesday, our last night at home, I went down to get the drinks. They are always on a tray on the breakfast bar. Chandelle, our cook, has them ready. I was starting up the stairs and here came Evelyn, hustling down the steps. When she was even with me, she stumbled and knocked the tray loose. Everything spilled. Evelyn was all apologies. She claimed she'd lost her balance."

The tension began to seep out of me. Jimmy had lost perspective. A household mishap was hardly the stuff of melodrama.

He saw my expression. "It sounds innocuous, but if you had seen Evelyn's face, you might understand. She was white as a ghost. I swear she knocked the tray down deliberately. Either she knew Sophia's sherry was poisoned or laced with an overdose of barbiturate or she was afraid that was so."

I blinked, wished I didn't feel stupid from lack of sleep. Jimmy believed what he was telling me, once again saw a near escape from death for Sophia. I tried to focus through the numbness of fatigue. "There's no way death from poison would escape detection. Everyone knows that."

"Maybe it was an overdose of sleeping pills. Who could prove that was murder?" He squinted and I wondered if he saw faces in his mind. "Maybe one of them has to have big bucks. Maybe dislike has turned to hatred. Maybe when the boulder missed, one of them decided to be sure. I tried to persuade Sophia to close it all down, announce to everyone that the trusts are going to be dissolved. She won't listen. Now she's furious with me." He blew out an exasperated spurt of air.

I wasn't convinced. "Evelyn's on the heavy side. She could have stumbled."

"She looks clumsy, but she's athletic." He was emphatic. "She's a former dancer. Ballet. She still practices. Besides, I followed her downstairs to get a cloth to clean up the mess and fix another drink. I found the sherry bottle in the trash, empty. The night before, it was half full. I picked it up and I'd swear it had been rinsed out. Somebody had emptied the bottle and washed it."

I sat on the edge of the bed, struggling to stay awake. "You know what you're saying, don't you? If Evelyn knew the sherry was dangerous, either she doctored it or she saw someone put something in it."

"I asked her."

"What did she say?" I tried to imagine that moment, Jimmy in pajamas, possibly in his blue and white seersucker robe I'd given him one Christmas, standing there accusingly, demanding information from Evelyn. His questions would have been vintage Jimmy: "What was in the sherry? Who put something in it? You? Alex? Kent? Rosie? Val?"

"She pretended shock and horror at the idea. She insisted the sherry was all right. I told her I knew the bottle had been almost half full. She waved her hand as if brushing away some pestering insect, said I was overwrought." Jimmy's gaze was bleak. "I told her, yeah, I was overwrought. I told her murder was a crime. I asked her how was she going to feel if Sophia was killed." He gave a weary sigh. "Evelyn looked half sick. She shook her head, told me everything would be all right, nothing was going to happen to Sophia. With that, she turned and hurried into the hall. I watched her go up the stairs, graceful as a gazelle." His words were clipped. "That's where we are. I'd better get downstairs. Sophia may wonder where I am. But maybe, after we meet on the ship, maybe you can get close to Evelyn. She'll like you. Everybody does."

I would have smiled at that if I hadn't been so tired. Everybody didn't. One of the pleasures of age—my age—was doing and saying what I pleased.

He flung out a beseeching hand. "Evelyn won't tell you the family secrets, but if you get close to her, maybe you'll pick up on which one of them she's worried about. She's going to avoid me for sure." He moved toward the door, yanked it open.

As it closed behind him, I rubbed my tired eyes. A bouncing boulder. Spilled sherry. A loving aunt. Did Evelyn Riordan love one of her nieces or nephews enough to shield a murderer?

I slipped out of my clothes, tossed them on the luggage rack, pulled on a nightgown, moved like a somnambulist toward the bed. Too tired to shower. Too tired for dinner. As I pulled back the spread and sank into the too-soft mattress, I was shaking my head. Evelyn wasn't shielding a murderer. Sophia was alive. But Evelyn might be charting an even more perilous course. What if Evelyn spoke to one of them, said, "I saw you"?

What would happen then?

The gate area Saturday morning was jammed with cruise passengers. The cruise line provided a charter flight on Qantas Airways to Copenhagen, where we would board the *Clio*. I sat with my back to the window overlooking the runway. I held a London *Times,* but it was easy to lower it enough to survey my fellow travelers. Although I didn't think Sophia Montgomery would recognize me, I was effectively anonymous beneath a floppy-brimmed straw hat with cloth ties. Oversize dark sunglasses and the *Times* were added protection. I doubted if Jimmy would know me.

There were about a hundred and fifty travelers waiting to board the plane. It was an attractive crowd, if attractiveness is measured by appearance. This kind of travel doesn't come cheap, so the clothes were from pricey London boutiques, Saks Fifth Avenue, and Neiman Marcus. There was the added, more subtle distinction of good health and rigid diets and the implicit arrogance of people who don't have to ask what anything costs.

I easily picked out couples traveling together, an occasional family group, assorted solo passengers. Sophia Montgomery and her entourage were among the last to arrive. Almost all of the seats in the gate area were taken. That late arrival surprised me. I would expect Sophia to be careless of others' expectations, but I would also expect her to be in too much of a hurry ever to run late.

To actually see them after they had filled my mind for so many hours was almost disturbing. If not disturbing, certainly unsettling. Reading their capsule histories, studying their family photos, had been an intellectual exercise. Now they were standing not far from me, near enough for me to see their eyes, read their faces.

I will confess I looked first at Jimmy. The whiteness of his hair was even more noticeable in the well-lit waiting area. He moved with familiar grace, a tall, lanky man at ease with himself and the world, confident, unpretentious, observant. But, most unlike Jimmy, his face was bunched in a tight frown. He stared out on the tarmac, didn't look toward his wife. Sophia's chin jutted and her lips were compressed. It didn't take a swami to know she was irritated. Her pale blue linen dress was immaculate, her matching sandals the latest style. Diminutive Alex munched on a doughnut and a dribble of sugar dotted his chin. His striped polo was loose and his carpenter pants baggy. He looked even smaller than in his photos since he was flanked by Jimmy and by his six-feet-plus brother Kent. Kent stood a little apart in a navy turtleneck and white jeans and sneakers. He held a paperback and appeared to be reading and oblivious to his surroundings as well as his companions. Alex's wife darted a little ahead to snag a single open seat. Plopping down, she opened her straw purse, pulled out a Tiffany compact, lifted the lid, and painstakingly freshened her lip gloss, the whole of her attention centered upon her image in the small mirror. Her blond hair was upswept in a French twist and her lilac slack suit crisp and fresh, but her appearance lacked assurance, as if she'd thumbed through an expensive catalog and a pink-tipped finger had chosen this and that and the other with the goal of achieving style. Rosie, whose dress was surely more bizarre, had the swagger of a beautiful woman who wears what she wishes with utter authority. Her peasant blouse drooped seductively. Her gypsy skirt was odd, arresting, and suited her flashing beauty. If she had worn a lace mantilla and pinned a rose to her shoulder, she would have fitted into any Spanish village on a Saturday night. As it was, men turned to look and women watched, and Rosie's dark red lips curved in an exuberant smile. There was something primal and direct and unstoppable about Rosie Riordan. The contrast with her sister Val was as striking as that between the blazing noon sun and a faint crescent moon. Val wore a black cotton T, black linen slacks, black loafers. No jewelry. No makeup. Her hair, as Titian red as Rosie's, was drawn into a tight bun. Her eyes were remote behind the horn-rim glasses. She sipped from a Styrofoam cup, her gaze—skeptical, questioning, analytical?—sliding from one to another of her traveling companions.

I wondered if Val's judgment agreed with mine. To me they seemed distinct from the other travelers. I saw no eagerness among them, no excitement over exotic ports of call. They all waited, stiff and silent, as if girded for battle. But no, where was Evelyn? It was Evelyn Jimmy hoped I would come to know. Where . . .

I found her slumped against a pillar near a rubber tree plant a few feet away from the family. One hand nervously fingered the lacy collar of her blouse. The other was clamped so tightly around the strap of her huge cotton purse—a jolly purse festooned with seashells, the canvas a bright orange, a bag meant for a holiday and happiness—that the fingers blanched.

Her face looked old and worn. Of course, I didn't know when the photos I'd studied had been taken, but they could not have been made too many years before, especially the one where she stood by the Christmas tree with Kent. It wasn't the passage of time that had drawn the color from her cheeks, made the muscles flaccid, turned her blue eyes vacant and staring.

I had an uneasy feeling that just before I looked at her, she'd been staring at one of them. If only I'd looked at her first. Would I have seen fright-filled eyes focused on a particular person? Was I imagining that she bore a heavy burden?

Quickly I scanned the group again, looking for a heightened awareness of Evelyn. If one of Frank Riordan's children had twice tried murder and realized Evelyn knew, surely there would be a crackling awareness of her, a tension that would link them. Alex was squirting antibacterial liquid on likely sticky fingers. Kent turned a page of his paperback. Madge snapped shut her compact, dropped it in her purse, and brushed away a speck of lint from her blouse. Rosie's lips curved in an inviting smile and a handsome graying man paused in his conversation with his wife to smile in return. Val brushed back a wisp of hair from her face, her features somber. If one of them was attuned to Evelyn, there was no evidence of it.

Our flight was called. In the swirling movement of boarding passengers, I lost sight of Evelyn's dumpy figure, but I carried with me an indelible image of her pale, strained face.

## four

CHARTERED buses awaited our arrival at the Copenhagen airport. I lagged a half block behind the Riordan party and climbed aboard a different bus. A guide provided capsule descriptions as we drove north through the city to the harbor and Langelinie Pier. Canals were everywhere. Copper spires glistened and gargoyles gazed blindly down from ledges. I have a fondness for gargoyles.

Neoclassical and rococo buildings were punctuated by an occasional modern structure. Bicycles wove in and out of traffic. I glimpsed the turquoise and gold spire of the Church of Our Savior. We passed Amalienborg Palace, the residence of Queen Margrethe II, and, when we neared the harbor, *The Little Mermaid,* the graceful statue inspired by Hans Christian Andersen's fairy tale that speaks always to the young at heart.

Even though several hundred passengers had arrived at once, the scene on the quay was orderly. The *Clio* was a lovely ship, her dark blue hull and white upper decks gleaming in the sun. As I recalled the information in my cruise packet, the *Clio* had been in service for only two years. There were ten decks with an added sundeck forward. In a welcome change from behemoth cruise ships, the *Clio* carried a maximum of 730 passengers. Now her standard fluttered in the breeze and her smiling crew welcomed travelers.

The buses waited to discharge passengers until the previous group had embarked. When our turn came, I joined a line of perhaps fifty inching forward up the gangplank to the entryway on Deck 4. Just inside the ship, each traveler paused to have a photograph taken and was then issued an electronic card to be used each time he or she left or reentered the ship. The card also served as an electronic key to their cabin and for use in charging drinks or shopping on board.

The reception center was on Deck 4, along with the purser's counter. Amid the cheerful, milling throng, I looked at a color-coded pocket map, conveniently tucked into the blue leather holder for the electronic key, and spotted my cabin, 6012. I climbed blue-carpeted stairs to Deck 6. There was a general air of excitement and the good humor of a treasure hunt as travelers sought their quarters. Luggage was piled in the hallways, awaiting the arrival of passengers.

I clicked into my cabin, looked about appreciatively. I hadn't sailed for a number of years. I had expected a cramped box. Instead the cabin seemed spacious. A compact bath was to my left as I stepped inside, a double closet to the right. I opened the closet, noted the safe, picked up a laminated sheet which contained security information, the number to call in an emergency, medical facilities available, hours of operation for the purser's office, and an explanation of the electronic keys, with a note that each key left a record when inserted into a cabin lock. I tossed the sheet back onto the safe and closed the closet door.

Beyond the double bed was a small sofa and coffee ta-

ble. A desk with a telephone sat opposite the sofa. A sliding glass door opened to a balcony, a picture window to
the sea that, with the long mirror on the forward wall,
increased the sense of spaciousness. I stepped out on the
balcony, admired the two comfortable plastic chairs, and
took a deep breath of salt-tanged air. I leaned on the spot-
less wooden railing and welcomed the soft warmth of the
sunshine. Danes too were enjoying the idyllic weather,
strolling on the quay, biking, skating. The harbor on a
summer Saturday afforded continuing entertainment as
the cruise ships arrived and departed.

I paused on the balcony for only a moment. I've spent
my life doing and seeing, seeking and finding, rarely in
repose. I had a ship to explore. Color-coded map in hand,
I started one deck down. The main dining room was at the
stern of Deck 5. A small bar with easy chairs and sofas
offered a cozy corner for prandial visiting. Animated
voices rose as I passed. Then came the shops, clothing
both formal and informal, jewelry, and artworks.

Amidship, Diogenes Bar had the heavy masculine
charm of a gentleman's study with mahogany chairs and
small tables. Nautical paintings hung between huge windows. I passed a painting of Admiral Nelson's HMS *Vic-
tory,* which carried him to his great success at Trafalgar
and to his death. Forward was the main lounge for after-
dinner drinks and coffee and entertainment.

I took a lift to Deck 9 with its public areas for the hale
and hearty. A teenager squealed as she jumped into the
sparkling pool. A muscular young man lounged in the
Jacuzzi and watched her with interest. A foursome had
already settled into bridge in the card room. Signs pointed
to a fitness center, beauty salon, and spa forward, observation deck and informal dining room aft.

I climbed outdoor steps forward from the pool to Deck

10 and the upper promenade. An athletic teenager loped around the track, long hair streaming in the breeze. Two stout ladies walked briskly. At the bow, curving windows provided a panoramic view of the harbor. Comfortable petit point sofas and chairs sat behind small tables, perfect for tea or evening cocktails. A brightly lit enclave contained a half dozen computers affording Internet access. Aft of the promenade was an extensive library replete with reference works, novels, histories, and travel guides. I checked out the main dining room and spotted the *Clio*'s five-star restaurants, the James Beard and the Julia Child.

I returned to my cabin and was pleased to find my two cases in the hall. It took only a few minutes to unpack. I had enjoyed my afternoon exploring the ship and I hadn't spent a minute thinking about the Riordan family. For now, I wasn't concerned about the Riordans. There was nothing I could do until I officially met them. The *Clio* sailed at noon tomorrow from Copenhagen en route to Gdańsk. Jimmy's plan was for me to wander into Diogenes Bar shortly before dinner on Sunday and—huge surprise—old friends would come together. Until then, my time was my own.

I looked forward to this evening. The ship offered an excursion to Tivoli Gardens, the famed amusement park that opened in 1843. I intended to go. I had an instant's hesitation. Sometimes it is unwise to revisit the scene of a special memory. Sometimes the reality of the present destroys a fragile long-ago moment.

I would take that chance.

I tucked dark glasses and a scarf into the pocket of my loose linen jacket in case my path crossed that of the Riordans. But none of that group was aboard my bus—number

12—and there were such big crowds waiting to enter Tivoli that I was certain, should I see them, I could easily remain unnoticed.

The minute I stood on the walk in front of the ornate arched entrance with *Tivoli* inscribed in white Roman letters, I was suffused with happiness. Or rather, as I moved forward, purchased my ticket, and entered the park, I was wrapped in emotions from the past. I was eleven years old when my father brought me to Tivoli. The dark clouds of World War II were forming. Certainly he was aware that the world was poised to explode, but I was innocent of knowledge and foreboding. A widower, my father was a wire service bureau chief based in Paris. I last saw him just before the fall of Paris. I never knew where or when he died. But our final separation was still in our future that summer evening when we came to Tivoli.

I remembered lights and flowers and music and happy faces. This evening, a lifetime later, mimes told a story of love and loss on a stage to my left, lights outlined a turreted building to my right, the path sloped forward, inviting me to return. Red and gold flowers bloomed in profusion. There were, of course, tourists everywhere, camera-laden, backpack-saddled, guidebook-encumbered. There were also hundreds of holidaying Danes, families and young people, many with white-gold hair and fjord blue eyes, just as I remembered from long ago.

My goal was the lake, ringed by restaurants. There was even a restaurant aboard a pirate ship. I didn't recall the huge loop-the-loop roller coaster or a tall tower where riders plummeted down from a platform. I expected they were later additions. But so much was the same. Most of all I remembered the sounds: laughter, the scrape of shoes, cheerful shouts and squeals.

I sat on a bench, watched the streaks of light on dark

water, and listened with my heart. Perhaps it was the
strains of Glenn Miller's "In the Mood" that created an
instant of magic. It was as if my father were sitting beside
me on the bench, his hand on my shoulder, leaning forward to listen. I smelled the mustiness of cigarette smoke,
felt the warmth of his touch, heard his laughter. I saw him
so clearly, short-sleeved white shirt, blue bow tie, and
dark trousers. His summer straw hat rested atop his neatly
folded suit coat on the bench beside him. My lips curved
into a smile.

A little girl pelted past me in hot pursuit of an older
brother holding a bobbing balloon out of reach and my father's presence was gone.

I rose and strolled toward the bandstand, intrigued by
hearing the long-ago swing music that lifted the hearts of
dancers during World War II. The audience clapped as
the piece ended. I felt curiously warmed that Glenn Miller's music still played on a summer evening almost sixty
years after his small plane was lost in the English Chan-
nel during the war.

I was tempted to stop and buy an ice cream cone. My
father had bought me one. No, I would let that memory
remain unchallenged. I was glad I had come. I was wandering back to the entrance, intending a brief stroll on
Stroget, the world's longest pedestrian shopping street,
when I saw Kent Riordan and his sister Rosie. They were
sitting on a bench near the fountain. Her hand gripped his
arm.

I stopped, perhaps fifteen feet away. Kent's features
were a mask of sorrow, eyes downcast, mouth drooping,
expression desolate. Rosie gripped his arm as if she were
holding tight to keep him safe. Her brows drew down in a
straight line. Her lips pressed together.

I passed them, unnoticed in the milling crowd, and

stepped behind their bench, my back to them as I gazed toward the roller-coaster, my head tilted slightly so that I could overhear their conversation. I couldn't see their faces. But, of course, neither could they see mine, should they look.

". . . I never knew anything could hurt this much. I love Heather. I'll always love her, even though—" He stopped, swallowed hard. "If it weren't for you and Val and Alex, I wouldn't have come. I wish I hadn't. I didn't know I could hate anyone as much as I hate her." Kent's bitter words carried the chill of unrelieved fury.

His tone was shocking. For the first time I understood Jimmy's fear. I wasn't quite ready to see a death threat to Sophia, but I realized Jimmy was unquestionably right in sensing hostility.

"Hush, Kent." Rosie's musical voice was low and soft and filled with compassion. "Sophia's not worth hating. She's like a stupid, willful child picking up a piece of pottery, thinking she sees a flaw, and tossing it over her shoulder."

"Flaw . . ."

From the corner of my eye, I glimpsed his swift movement as he swung around to face his sister.

"Is that how you see me? Flawed?" His tone was harsh.

"No." The retort was quick. "That's not what I meant. Never. Not you. It's Heather. Sophia's shrewd, Kent. Somehow she knew Heather—"

I heard his quick indrawn breath. The bench creaked. I turned enough to see him striding away, head down, hands jammed in his pockets, moving fast.

Rosie slowly stood. In the growing twilight, she was young and lovely, her dark red hair bright as a flame in the lamplight. Her face was filled with love and sorrow.

Abruptly, her features hardened and she hurried after her brother. So might Alecto, the avenging Fury, have set out to punish a transgressor.

I shivered though the night was balmy. Had Sophia any inkling of the passions she aroused?

## five

REFRESHED by a dreamless sleep, I was in a holiday mood Sunday morning. I moved through the breakfast buffet, looking forward to the morning of sightseeing in Copenhagen before the *Clio* sailed at one. I'd opted for the informal breakfast area on Deck 9, carrying my choices from the buffet out to a table at the bow. Seagulls circled. Pleasure craft idled near. Weekend sailors waved as they passed. I'd noted Jimmy and Sophia seated at an interior table and carefully avoided passing them. My quick glimpse had been troubling. Sophia's head was bent. She jabbed at a waffle as if poking hay with a pitchfork. Jimmy's face was creased in a tight frown. He looked frustrated. Hurt. Stymied.

I found a table outside on the open deck. I had a quick sharp memory of the night before. Kent's voice had been freighted with hatred of Sophia. Rosie had clearly been angry on Kent's behalf. Now Jimmy and Sophia appeared at odds.

Laughter sounded from a nearby table. An attentive steward smiled as he poured coffee. My spirits lifted. I wasn't going to let the shadow of my purpose on the ship dampen this lovely morning. I had a few hours yet before I would meet Sophia and her entourage. Until then I intended to enjoy the harbor, my breakfast, and the morning excursion.

I love a Scandinavian breakfast and had chosen my favorites from the buffet: smoked salmon, liverwurst, assorted cheeses, and fruit. When I finished, I lingered, drinking coffee. There was no hurry. The first buses would not depart for another hour.

"Madam, I have a message for you." A waiter held out a folded sheet of paper to me.

I thanked him. As I unfolded the sheet, torn from a small pocket notebook, I recognized Jimmy's bold handwriting. Obviously he'd seen me as well. The message was brief: *Your cabin. Three o'clock.*

"Outside, please." I pointed toward the balcony.

The steward placed the tea service on the plastic-topped table. He lifted the silver lid to display the dainty sandwiches—salmon, egg salad, butter—and scones. There was a plate of petits fours for dessert. I had chosen Darjeeling for Jimmy, green tea for me. When Jimmy and I had traveled together, afternoon tea was a highlight of the day. One of the highlights.

When the steward left, I waited on the balcony, the sliding door open, my ears attuned for Jimmy's knock. I heard a familiar rat-a-tat, rat-a-tat, a knock I would recognize anywhere, three rapid taps, a pause, three rapid taps. I pulled open the door.

He gave a nervous, searching glance down the hallway before stepping inside. He was Jimmy, quick-moving, intense, vigorous, yet different from the man I thought I knew well. As the door shut, he looked down at me, his face unsmiling. His words were hurried. "I only have a few minutes. I told Sophia I was going up to the promenade. Look"—he pulled a small notebook from his pocket, tore out a sheet, wrote quickly—"here's where everybody is. We're on this deck at the stern, port side. Sophia and I have an end suite, 6088. Evelyn's in 6086, Alex and Madge in 6084, Kent in 6082, Rosie in 6080, Val in 6078."

I doubted I would visit any of them in their cabins, but I took the sheet as he held it out.

"Let's connect after the Captain's Reception. It starts at six-thirty, then we plan to go down to Diogenes Bar for a drink before dinner. Why don't you stroll into the bar about seven-thirty?"

I looked at him soberly. "Sophia looked furious this morning."

"Yeah." Jimmy's assent was brusque. "At me. At the Riordans. At the universe for not running on Sophia time."

I raised an eyebrow.

Suddenly his wry grin was there, the sardonic, unflappable Jimmy I knew. "Maybe it's reality time for me. Sophia's—" He looked suddenly uncomfortable, a man not eager to explain a new love to an old. He was also a man who had spent his life scraping through dissemblance to the base vein of truth. He and I had been too close to lie to each other. He shrugged. "Sophia's what you see, vibrant, arresting, unpredictable, fascinating. And"—his eyes were suddenly sad—"incapable of seeing anyone else's viewpoint. She thinks I'm trying to tell her what to do." He tilted his head, looked faintly surprised. "You know, I guess she's right." His tone was thoughtful. "I'm telling her to ease off, kiss the money goodbye, give these people their lives. I told her the money belongs to the Riordans, let them have it. She told me in a voice like ice granules that the money belonged to Frank. I told her Frank was dead. She told me I obviously had no sense of honor. On that happy note, I told her I was going to take a walk and slammed out of the cabin. If we were back in California, I'd walk right out of her life." His voice was hard, his eyes hurt. "But she's my wife. I have to protect her." He stared down at me. Without warning he pulled me close, held me in a fierce embrace. "I don't deserve your help in taking care of her. Sophia for sure doesn't."

I felt the warmth of his touch even after the door closed and he was gone.

I walked numbly out to the balcony. The silver tea service glistened in the sun. I sat down. Tea for one, not for two.

I studied my reflection in the broad full-length mirror on the forward wall of my cabin. The sleek silver crepe dress was simply cut, a bateau neckline and Empire waist, and a stylish flared three-tier skirt. A garnet necklace and matching earrings added color. I smoothed back a curl of my silvered dark hair, which I'd pulled back into a French twist.

My expression was a trifle rueful. I wanted to look my best, not perhaps for the most admirable of motives. I was going to see Jimmy and Sophia. I had no intention of appearing old and frumpy in comparison to her. I grinned at the mirror. All right. Reality was reality. Possibly old, but never frumpy. I'd earned every wrinkle on my face and saw them as indicators of a long life fully lived, not always as well as I would have wished, but as well as I had been able to manage. One of the nuggets of age is the realization that, save for the purposefully evil, everyone does the best they can, a conclusion both mitigating and chilling.

I tightened an earring and picked up my silver evening bag. As my cabin door closed behind me, I paused for a moment. Oh yes, the stairways and lifts were to my right. The carpeted corridor was well lit but had the cavernous aspect peculiar to a passageway on a ship. I was getting accustomed to the gentle rock beneath my feet. Other passengers, too, wobbling a bit as they got their sea legs, were on their way to the reception or dinner or drinks. I didn't hurry. It was a few minutes before seven. I would attend the captain's party for a few minutes, then go to the bar as planned.

The party was on the pool deck. The dark-haired captain was impressive in his white uniform. He and others of his staff mingled with the guests, women in pastel dresses, some chiffon, some silk, the men in dark suits and some in black tie. He smiled when we shook hands, and I introduced myself.

"Mrs. Collins." An engaging smile softened his formal appearance. He had an angular face with piercing blue eyes and a blunt chin. "Welcome to the *Clio*. I'm Captain Wilson. I hope you enjoy our cruise."

"I've enjoyed everything so far." Everything but my silent observation of Kent Riordan and his sister in Tivoli. "The tour this morning was excellent."

"What did you find most interesting?" He looked at me intently, as if he truly was interested in my reply.

My answer was immediate. "The queen's birthday tapestries." The magnificent modern-day tapestries depicting a thousand years of Danish history from the Vikings to modern times were created to celebrate the queen's fiftieth birthday in 1990. The seventeen Gobelins hang in the Royal Reception Chambers of Christiansborg Palace. The brilliant colors were a reminder that old tapestries bedecking museums and castles once were fresh and spectacular in their beauty. "I was especially taken by the Gobelins of the present and the future."

His smile was sudden and genuine. He looked like a small boy with a fistful of agates. "My wife is Danish and we spend our shore leave there. They say *The Little Mermaid* is Copenhagen's greatest treasure. She is very fine, but the queen's tapestries can't be matched anywhere." He gave my hand a firm squeeze, then turned to the man behind me.

I stood near the port rail sipping fruit punch and observing the passengers, some stylish, some dowdy, but all affluent and for this moment secure and happy in a very insecure world.

It was easy to find Sophia Montgomery. She was vivid in a lobster pink sleeveless silk dress with a drape neck. Her smile flashed. Her light laughter invited everyone to laugh with her. She was the center of an admiring throng. She exuded star quality. A distinguished-looking man in a boxy jacket and kilt beamed down at her. Jimmy was smiling too and looked like the Jimmy I knew, affable, interested, kindly.

My gaze slipped past them, rested on Alex and Madge Riordan. The contrast could not have been greater: Sophia's effervescence, Madge's pinched face and thin lips.

Careful to keep my head averted from Jimmy, I drifted close to Alex and Madge. ". . . the most beautiful necklace I ever saw. You're disgusting not to get it for me. You know my card's full."

Alex shot a hunted glance toward Sophia. "Don't make a scene, Madge."

His wife tossed her head, slapped her hands to her hips. "I like to make scenes. Maybe I'll go up to Sophia and tell her she's turned you into a miser. I can tell everyone here"—she flung out a thin hand with bright red nails—"that you're under her thumb and she's a bitch. How would she like that?"

His hand shot out, gripped her arm. "Shut up. Don't alienate her. She'll cut us off."

Madge yanked her arm free, rubbed the splotches on her skin. "Look what you've done." There was surprise as well as anger in her voice. She stared at him, blue eyes wide. "Don't ever touch me like that again. If I'd known when I married you—" She broke off.

Alex's thin face sharpened. "Known what? That the money was in trust?" His eyes were dark with pain. "You thought I was rich. Is that why you married me?"

Before Madge could respond, Evelyn thrust herself between them, burbling, her high-pitched voice determined. "Wasn't it fun today? I've never seen so many shops. Didn't you love Caritas Fountain? All those vendors! Did you know that's where the old central market was? Just think, three hundred years later people are still making and selling things in little open-air stalls. Of course, most of the goods now come from factories, but still, it's such fun wandering around and finding the most interesting . . ." She gripped each by an elbow, maneuvered them toward the doorway.

I heard Rosie's light musical voice behind me. "Bless Evelyn. She's still galloping to the rescue. Kittens from treetops when we were kids. Poor Alex from his bitch of a wife now."

I half turned, saw Rosie and Val.

Rosie was breathtakingly lovely. Champagne embroidery swirled in a diagonal swath down her black crepe dress. Titian curls were piled high atop her head, emphasizing her fine bone structure and graceful neck. Chunky faux pearls alternated with gleaming topaz in her earrings, necklace, and bracelet.

Val's unrelievedly black dress was beautifully cut, sleeveless with a surplice vent. She was, in her own remote, distant manner, as lovely as her sister. But it chilled me to see that her jewelry, a double strand of jet beads, was black as well, the black of an abandoned well or lonely country lane at midnight.

Val's expression was faintly sad. "Poor Evelyn. She tries to patch up our lives, but even she can't save us from the ogress."

"Speaking of . . ." Rosie's Titian curls nodded. "We're being summoned."

Sophia held up her hand in a graceful gesture, the queen gathering her retinue.

I moved behind a clutch of passengers, stepped to the starboard rail. I rested my elbows and looked down at the water and the wake of the ship. I would have enjoyed staying where I was, watching the sun sink in the west and splashing the sea with gold and orange. That luxury, that freedom were not to be mine.

I swung about, moving in the preordained pattern Jimmy had devised. In a few minutes I would walk into Diogenes Bar. Would my appearance there spell a difference in the lives of those I had been watching? Or—and I felt a sudden misgiving—in my life?

I took one step, then another. It was too late to question my course.

## six

MUSIC and laughter flowed from Diogenes Bar. Glasses clinked. Bass voices boomed. Treble voices lifted. The room spread on both sides of a central bar. Mirrors behind the bar made the room look much larger. Rich dark wood glistened from polish. Large leather chairs and smaller upholstered chairs ranged around tables of varying sizes. Heavy brocade curtains with a red and gold pattern framed windows. The early evening summer sun still blazed, spilling golden swaths inside. Almost every seat was occupied.

I had only taken a few steps when I heard my name.

"Henrie O!" Jimmy's voice rose in amazement. Suddenly he was there, gripping my hands. "I can't believe it. Halfway around the world and here's a face from home."

I looked up, my eyes widening. "Jimmy, what a wonderful surprise."

He shepherded me toward their table, talking all the while. "Sophia, look who's here."

I swung toward her with a conventional smile.

Sophia stared, her face quite still, her eyes brilliant and hard as sapphires. I'd expected a quick inventory of memory. My face should not be familiar. We'd met twice before many years earlier, once at a National Press Club dinner in Washington when my late husband Richard was honored, again in Mexico City when she received an award for her film on monarchs. I had been there on a holiday, recalling the happy years spent there with Richard and our children, Emily and Bobby.

Yet Sophia Montgomery recognized me immediately. She knew exactly who I was and what I had meant to Jimmy. I read that knowledge in a penetrating gaze of grave inquiry.

"Henrie O Collins." She spoke my name without hesitation. Her voice was cool. Her lips curved in a slight smile. "What an amazing coincidence. That's how life is. Filled with coincidences." Her tone was light, but implicit was disbelief in this particular coincidence. "It's nice to see you again. I'm sure we'll run into you during the voyage." She looked down at her watch, then turned toward Evelyn, in effect dismissing me. "Let's go in to dinner, shall we?"

Jimmy still held my arm. His grip tightened. "Of course we'll see her." He sounded abrupt. "We have a lot of catching up to do." He nodded toward Sophia but spoke to me. "You'll join us for dinner tonight."

Sophia's trill of laughter was one of chagrin. "Not this evening, Jimmy. Henrie O, I know you'll understand." Her smile was artificial. "We're having a family conclave. It would be boring for an outsider. We'll look forward to another time. And now"—Sophia was on her feet—"let's be on our way." Sophia walked past as if I were invisible. She didn't look toward Jimmy.

I felt the tension in Jimmy's tight grip. Before he could move or speak, I said softly, "Let it go. I'll see you tomorrow."

Sophia was already at the doorway. The rest of the group straggled past me. Evelyn flashed an uncomfortable smile. "How lovely for an old friend of Jimmy's to be on the cruise." Rosie swept me with a look of frank interest. Kent's expression was shy but friendly. Val offered a polite nod. Alex gave me a meaningless smile. Madge appeared amused as she looked from Sophia to Jimmy.

Jimmy's hand still gripped my arm.

"Better catch up." I nodded after them.

Jimmy frowned. "I can't believe this." His tone was both irritated and stunned. "I've never seen Sophia treat a friend of mine like this."

"Go on, Jimmy. This is no time to quarrel with Sophia. We'll work things out. I'll talk to you later." I gave him a nudge.

When he was gone, I moved away from the large table where they had sat and walked to the bar. I slid onto a stool, ordered a rum collins. I rarely drink rum. Was my choice prompted by a quick recollection of our years in Mexico? I took a sip, willed away other memories.

It was time for cool, calm thought. Sophia's immediate recognition of a woman she'd only met twice in a life overflowing with names and faces and contacts and subjects was surprising. Moreover, I sensed that she knew more about me—about Jimmy and me—than he had likely revealed to her. Yes, he would have shared the truth of our relationship, but not much more than that fact.

I picked up a vase-shaped container of mixed nuts, poured them into my palm. I welcomed the infusion of energy and saltiness to offset the sweet rum, and considered Sophia's knowledge. Had she investigated Jimmy's past before marrying him? That augured a cool appraisal that would not be a welcome revelation to Jimmy. I wondered if Jimmy too would conclude that Sophia must have hired a private detective to compile a dossier on him.

Whatever the explanation, she knew me and she didn't

believe for a moment that my presence here was a matter of chance.

I once again chose a Scandinavian breakfast. The *Clio* arrived at Gdynia, the port for Gdańsk, at 8 A.M. Jimmy had indicated the Riordans, as a group, were taking the nine-thirty walking tour. A ticket for that tour was included in my travel packet. I rather doubted I would be welcome to join them.

The salmon and cheese were excellent, the coffee so-so. I was once again sitting outside and enjoying the sea air. I'd had no word from Jimmy last night. That didn't surprise me. I imagined Sophia was keeping him on a short leash and he'd had no opportunity to contact me. Certainly he couldn't use the cabin phone in her presence to ring me up. Perhaps I'd arrive on the reception floor a few minutes before departure for the tour and watch for their group and—

"May I join you?" The throaty voice brimmed with confidence and a hint of deviltry.

I looked up. Rosie Riordan's gorgeous hair was loose this morning, brilliant and burnished as polished copper. Once again, her attire set her apart. Her V-neck green silk blouse had an unusual crocheted trim at the throat and sleeves, a demure style that emphasized her sensuality. White capris emphasized a perfect figure.

"I'd be delighted." Passengers on cruises are encouraged to join other travelers, but I didn't think I had been selected to expand her circle of acquaintances. Rosie's first words made that clear.

"We almost met last night. But Sophia wasn't having any." She put down her tray and slipped into the seat opposite me. "I'm Rosie Riordan." She looked at me with amused curiosity. "I can't pass up visiting with a woman our supercilious Sophia is determined to ignore. As they say, there has to be a story there. In the best of all possible worlds, she'll see us together this morning." Her lips curved in an impudent grin.

I grinned back. Rosie's charm was hard to resist. "Henrie O Collins."

She slathered whipped butter atop the richness of a flaky croissant. "How do you know our marvelous Sophia?" Although her tone was pleasant, the darkness in her eyes made the adjective decidedly unflattering.

I curled a piece of salmon around a dollop of cream cheese. "I barely know Sophia. Jimmy is an old friend."

"Aha, as my less-than-sainted late father would have remarked." There was a flash of grim humor in her eyes. "From there it's an easy jump to Sophia's quite amazing determination always to be the only prancing horse in the center ring." Rosie added a swath of strawberry jam to the croissant, took a huge bite. She ate, licked a straggle of jam, and beamed at me. "Please join me for dinner tonight. My siblings will be happy to welcome an old friend of Jimmy's."

I laughed. It was as if I'd known her for years, not moments. I liked Rosie, liked her frankness, her infectious good humor, her disdain for niceties. In other circumstances, I would have been pleased to seek her friendship. Now, I was willing—for Jimmy, not for Sophia—to use Rosie's reckless nature to burrow into her confidence. "And to gig marvelous Sophia?"

"Yes indeed." There was no mistaking the enmity toward Sophia. Rosie lifted an eyebrow. "Do I shock you?"

I finished my last bite of salmon. "Families can be challenging."

Her whoop of laughter turned heads at other tables on the deck. Many smiled in appreciation of youth and beauty on a lovely morning as the sun splashed down, turning the sea a glittering cobalt blue.

I smiled, too, but felt a twist of sadness at the bitter gleam in Rosie's eyes that belied the laughter. No one as young and vivacious and gloriously effervescent should carry such a heavy burden of anger.

"Families . . ." Rosie dropped the remainder of her croissant on her plate, absently brushed butter and jam and crumbs from her fingers. She looked at me with a thoughtful, appraising gaze, abruptly nodded. "You're truly Jimmy's friend?" There was the faintest inflection of uncertainty.

"Yes." There was no doubting my sincerity.

"Okay, consider the dinner invitation canceled." Her shoulders lifted and fell in a resigned shrug. "I'm sorry. That sounds rude." Her grin was rueful. "I don't mean it that way. Look"—she hitched her chair closer to the table, leaned forward—"I'd love to have you horn in on Sophia's dinner, but that isn't fair to Jimmy. I'd be delighted for Sophia to turn her energetic micromanagement skills on you and Jimmy, but Jimmy's a good guy. Why he married her I don't know—"

I did. Jimmy wanted a wife and a home. I'd turned him down. He'd ended up with Sophia, who had great charm and magnetism when she chose to exert them. Jimmy deserved happiness. If I could help him find it, keep it, I would do whatever I had to do.

"—but he did. Of course, Sophia's bright and famous and she can be fun. At least that's what her press kit claims. But Jimmy's been decent to us. He's even tried to help us out in the current mess."

I refilled my coffee mug. "What's wrong?"

Rosie gulped the last of her orange juice. "You don't really want to know the saga of the ripped-off Riordans."

"Sure I do." I kept my tone light.

"It all goes back . . ." She gazed out across the brilliant water, but she wasn't looking at the ocean. "We had a great mom. Five kids. Alex, Kent, me, and Val and Vic."

I managed to keep the surprise from my face. Vic? "A big family."

"Big. Mostly fun. Loud. We like noise and excitement. Or some of us do. We ran the gamut. Show-off Alex. Seeker Kent. Sassy me. Serious Val. Sensitive Vic. Mom laughed a lot. She thought we were all wonderful. That's nice, isn't it?" She gave me a direct, sweet look. "To have a mom who loves you just the way you are. Dad . . . well, Dad had standards. He was Frank Riordan. You may have heard of him." She might have been describing a distant acquaintance. "He was his generation's Midas. He always prevailed. You did it Dad's way or you didn't do it. But he pretty well left us alone. Mom took care of us. If she hadn't died . . ." She blinked, looked down, then managed a bright smile. "But she did. Even then, everything went on pretty well. Evelyn came to take care of us. Dad's sister. She was the one in the billowy lavender dress last night that looked like something out of a thrift shop. And it was new." Now her laughter was soft, affectionate. "I bought it for her. Evelyn can make an Armani gown look like a bathrobe. Evelyn's no fashion plate and she can be spacey and a worrier, but she's as loyal as a little toy dog. Sometimes I feel like she's stood still in time, that she still sees us as kids and wants to fight our battles. It almost killed her when Dad married Sophia and Sophia persuaded him we'd do swell away at boarding schools." There was a look of remembrance, a forlorn, lost expression. It hardened into disdain. "Sophia's pitch to Dad was clever." She frowned. "To give the devil her due, maybe she believed every word of it. She told Dad she knew he'd miss us but he needed to give us space, let us have a chance to grow up without dealing with a stepmother. Of course Dad didn't care where we were, but this plan made him feel noble. He was looking out for our future, giving us independence."

"I see." I thought I did. Sophia didn't want the distraction of a houseful of teenagers. Perhaps, as Rosie reluctantly said, Sophia saw no problem in dispatching kids to boarding schools and thought they'd be happier away.

"Maybe it would have turned out all right if Vic—" She broke off. "You'll have to forgive me. More than you ever wanted to know about the life and times of the Riordan kids. Anyway, I'd better leave you to your coffee. It would be fun to pull Sophia's string, but not at Jimmy's expense." She pushed back her chair, rose.

I spoke swiftly. "Oh, I expect I'll see you at dinner."

Rosie stopped, her hand on the back of the chair. She looked down at me, startled.

"I've known Jimmy for a long time. I imagine he'll insist." I was certain he would. I didn't know if that would be a good thing.

"I love it!" Abruptly, she was serious. "Only if it's your choice. I'm pretty sure Sophia won't play that game. You might warn Jimmy. See you around."

She surged across the deck, young and vibrant, attracting the attention of every man she passed. I liked Rosie Riordan, but that liking didn't blind me to a forceful personality, a rebellious attitude, and a curdling resentment of Sophia Montgomery and the havoc she apparently had wreaked in the lives of Frank Riordan's children. Havoc, indeed, that Sophia might now be compounding as she determined who might or might not receive control of what most of us would consider quite a fortune.

I took a last gulp of coffee and glanced at my watch. I had a little over an hour before the tour left for Gdańsk. As I walked through the interior restaurant, I glanced to my left where I'd seen Jimmy and Sophia breakfasting yesterday. Sophia was there, leaning forward, pointed chin on folded hands, face impassive as she listened to Alex Riordan. Alex was a picture of misery, blinking nervously, expression both placating and petulant, shoulders defensively hunched. Arms folded, Madge stared at her husband, her disappointment evident. Jimmy was absent. I wondered where he was.

But I had very little time and much to do. I hurried on. I carried with me a snapshot of Alex, his discomfort painful to recall.

I was the only person at the bank of computers tucked into an alcove of the spacious observation room on the bow of Deck 10. I logged on, gave my name and cabin number for the charges, and Googled for Frank Riordan's obituary. I clicked to the *L.A. Times* story, scanned to survivors: "... predeceased by his parents, Harold and Janet Riordan, brother Thomas, and daughter Victoria Elaine ..."

Victoria Elaine Riordan. Rosie mentioned Vic. Her sister.

Jimmy had made no mention of another child. He may not have known. Of course, he was focused on those present in the Carmel house when the boulder bounced down the hillside. I understood his preoccupation. Still, we needed to know everything possible about the family. I decided to find out what had happened to the deceased sister. I found an obituary in the *San Francisco Chronicle* on August 20, 1991.

### Victoria Elaine Riordan

Victoria Elaine Riordan, 12, died August 17 in Carmel, CA. She was the daughter of Frank McNair
Riordan and the late Anna Nesbitt Riordan. Victoria
was born April 11, 1979, in San Francisco . . .

The PA system came on: "Passengers disembarking for
the late morning tour of Gdańsk are invited to come at
this time to the reception center on Deck 4."

Quickly I scanned the rest of the obituary, her school,
her activities—

. . . Vic loved poetry, especially "Annabel Lee" by
Edgar Allan Poe. She collected seashells and painted
rocks. Her favorite rock was in psychedelic colors
and she named him Aladdin. Her favorite book was
*Little Women* . . .

I forced myself to continue reading. My son Bobby was
eleven when he died in a car accident. Bobby loved
Chapultepec Park and red and gold balloons and his favorite book was *The Three Musketeers*: Athos, Porthos,
Aramis, and, of course, the swashbuckling hopeful mus-
keteer, D'Artagnan. My eyes were dry but there are always tears in my heart.

. . . and her favorite singer was Mariah Carey. Vic
loved the ocean.

She is survived by her father Frank and stepmother Sophia, her brothers Alex and Kent, her
sister Rosalie, her twin sister Valerie, and her aunt
Evelyn. A funeral mass will be . . .

I wondered if Vic had been ill or if her death was accidental. No matter the reason, Vic's death would mark her twin forever. No wonder Val was withdrawn and defensive, her gaze remote. She'd been hurt to her core.

The PA system sounded again. I wanted to reach the reception area before the Riordans. I needed to hurry, but I found a small address book in my purse, thumbed through it to an old friend's name. Margaret Brown had been a star reporter for the *Long Beach Press-Telegram* for many years. If information was available in California, she would find it. I found her e-mail address. As the final call came over the PA, I typed a quick message, sent it off.

It was only as I logged off that I noted the date. August 16. Vic Riordan died thirteen years ago on August 17.

## seven

WHEN I reached the reception area, passengers were moving through the security system and disembarking for the waiting buses. I didn't see Jimmy or any of the Riordan family. It was, of course, an orderly and mannerly group, so I couldn't edge ahead of the long line. Each passenger's electronic key was scanned, logging in the departure time, and identity checked with the photo made upon embarkation. A cheery tour assistant reminded passengers to carry their passports and electronic keys because both would be needed to return to the ship.

The day was lovely and a small band on the quay played Dixieland jazz to welcome the visitors. I realized Sophia's entourage had likely already cleared customs and departed on an earlier bus.

The long drive to Gdańsk from the shipyards at Gdynia where we disembarked passed drab, undistinguished buildings that looked like relics of the Cold War, a reminder of Poland's long domination by Russia. Graffiti was everywhere, an indication of poverty and anger. Gdańsk itself, the heart of the old Hanseatic League, was light and lively and beautiful, full of bustle and cheer. It reminded me of Williamsburg since it was a restoration of long-ago glory.

Most of the old city had been destroyed in bombing raids during World War II. Now tourists thronged everywhere. Perhaps the restored old town in its way was more true to the past than extant buildings. The re-created structures shone in bright colors and gilt, much as they might have appeared five hundred or seven hundred years ago. Our group entered through the Green Gate. We walked to St. Mary's Church, which was built between 1343 and 1502 and is reputed to be the largest brick church in the world and can accommodate more than twenty thousand worshipers. It suffered some war damage but in the main the church is as it has been for hundreds of years. The altar is a re-creation of a triptych of *The Coronation of the Virgin,* but the fifteenth-century astronomical clock is original to the structure.

I scanned the tour groups for a familiar face but saw none. I relaxed and devoted my attention to our guide, following her outdoors and down a narrow cobbled street into the main walkway of Dlugi Targ and the old town square with the restored sixteenth-century merchant houses. The guide explained that taxes were paid on the basis of the width of each townhouse. Three windows wide, the tax was so much. Four windows, and it was more.

I broke away from the group to pause at the famous Neptune Fountain, a tribute to the maritime glory of Gdańsk. I've tossed coins in fountains from Rome to Mexico City to Singapore. I scrounged in my purse for a fifty-cent piece. I believe in paying a substantial tribute to the fountain gods, thereby lifting my incantation ahead of the penny petitioners. My coin pinged on Neptune's trident and splashed into the water. And my wish? *Neptune, see our voyagers safely—*

"Henrie O." The light high voice was full of cheer and warmth.

Startled, I swung about.

Sophia Montgomery walked toward me, a hand uplifted in greeting, her smile dazzling.

I called out a friendly hello and wondered what accounted for her transformation from dismissal to welcome. Jimmy was a few feet behind her. He looked cheerful and relieved.

Sophia reached me, held out her hand. "How lovely to see you this morning. Please come and lunch with us. You and Jimmy have so much catching up to do." Her tone was eager. "I want you to meet Evelyn, my second husband's sister. Evelyn makes home sunny for Jimmy and me."

Evelyn and I murmured hellos as we crossed the cobblestones to an outdoor café. Pigeons fluttered near the tables, alert for crumbs. Red and blue umbrellas offered shade from the noon sun. After we were seated and awaiting our orders, Sophia prompted Jimmy and me to recall old times. I determinedly kept our recollections to the days when Richard and I and Jimmy and Margaret had been young and happy in Mexico City.

When the food arrived, Sophia poured spicy paprika sauce over a potato pancake. Evelyn murmured happily as she nibbled at a raspberry kolaczki, the flaky crust open at both ends to show the succulent filling. Jimmy cut a large slice of babka in half, offered a piece to Sophia. I splashed thick yellow cream into coffee black as asphalt.

Sophia shook her head. "I have quite enough. Henrie O, you need more than coffee. Jimmy, give half your cake to Henrie O." She gestured to a waiter, spoke crisply in Polish, and in a moment a plate was before me.

Although I dislike having food thrust upon me, I was willing to nibble at the cake, a delicious vanilla lemon, in light of Sophia's amazing turnabout from our meeting in the bar last night. She chattered with good humor, expressing regret that the rest of the family wasn't with us. ". . . But they're young and would rather sun on the pool deck than look at a church. Now they've missed seeing these townhouses as a burgher would have seen them five hundred years ago. Don't you think our cities would be brighter if we had buildings in red and gold with gilt trimming?" She didn't pause for a reply. "But you'll have a chance to meet everyone tomorrow night. We want you to join us for dinner."

There was no hint of the strain so apparent at her breakfast with Alex. Both she and Jimmy were in high spirits. Evelyn too appeared cheerful and relaxed.

I didn't know why Sophia was ladling out charm, but I looked forward to catching Jimmy alone for a moment and discovering the reason for her sea change.

I savored the delicate flavor of the cake. "So you speak Polish." It was an inconsequential comment.

Sophia grinned. "Not really. I know a few phrases. I can ask for a plate, order a meal. Otherwise my Polish runs to *tak* and *nie* and *prosze* and *dziekuje*. I picked up a little bit of the language when I was here to do my documentary on Lech Walesa."

Why was I not surprised? One of the great stories of bravery in modern times was Lech Walesa and his shipyard union defying the might of Russian rule. In fact, I recalled a dramatic prize-winning film made perhaps ten years after that historic confrontation. It was in black and white, a stark reminder of the contrast between freedom and oppression. That very likely had been Sophia's film. Her blue eyes, glinting now with eagerness and enthusiasm, reflected a penetrating intelligence.

She was suddenly frozen in thought, a fork midway to her mouth. "I wish I'd bought those postcards of the

Solidarity Monument. I want to send them to the crew on that film. Jimmy"—her smile was beguiling—"please go back to St. Mary's for me. There's a postcard kiosk right by the main doorway. Get me a half dozen of those cards."

Evelyn chimed in. "Jimmy, would you get one for me? I want to send it to our neighbor." She turned toward me, eyes glowing. "Mamie Thompson—her maiden name was Kowalski—was so excited when she was able to come back to Poland and visit Gdynia. Her daddy worked in the shipyards."

Jimmy took a last bite of cake. "Be glad to." He flashed a cheerful smile and pushed back his chair.

I lifted my mug of coffee and drank. I was thoughtful as I watched his tall figure stride away. Jimmy might think Sophia wanted postcards. I had my doubts. Moreover, there were a dozen stalls not twenty feet away here on the square and that particular card would surely be available.

Sophia continued her bright, animated chatter. "Coming back to Gdańsk was one of the reasons I wanted to take this trip. It's been more than a dozen years since I've been here. The transformation is remarkable." She bathed a piece of pancake in the sauce, looked at me intently. Her tight golden curls glinted in the sunlight. Her blue eyes were searching. She was a remarkably well-preserved woman, especially for a blonde, but her face looked lined and tense. "Henrie O, what brought you on this particular cruise?"

The sting in the scorpion's tail. The gaff. The zinger.

I don't like to lie. Our stop in Copenhagen had brought my father near to me. He loved to quote Shakespeare in a rich baritone, and I had a sudden clear memory of his laughter on a long-ago day when I told him indignantly that Sister Marie Celeste had made me sit in a corner for an hour because I'd told her, when asked, that I hadn't eaten lunch because the soup tasted like old socks. He'd quoted: " 'While you live, tell truth and shame the devil!' " He'd taken me to a little tea shop and bought me two French pastries. As a nine-year-old, the moral lesson for me had been a bit muddled. The truth got me in trouble, but it also earned a sweet reward. Since then, I've followed Mark Twain's wry self-description: "He told the truth, mainly."

However, I could not tell the whole truth without Jimmy's consent. I gave no hint—at least I hope I gave no hint—of the thoughts tumbling through my mind. My smile was casual. "My particular interest is the Hermitage. It seemed a lovely way to see the Impressionist paintings." This was true, if not all the truth.

"When did you decide to come?" She put down her fork, made no pretense of eating.

I added a spoonful of sugar to the coffee, still strong despite the thick cream. "I don't live on a schedule. It was a last-minute decision."

A sleek sable eyebrow made a perfect, skeptical arch. "That's rather extravagant. Booking early saves almost half the cost. I sail on the *Clio* at least twice a year and always book six months in advance. Of course, there are even more discounts for return travelers."

Now I was revealed as a financial nitwit as well as impulsive.

Evelyn shot me an embarrassed glance. "Oh, but it can be so exciting to do things on impulse."

"There are always wonderful last-minute bargains. Cruises will give a deep discount to fill those empty cabins." This was quite true. I made no claim that I had done so. I gave Sophia an admiring smile. "I would think there might be even greater discounts for such a large party. Let me see, you and Jimmy and your children—"

"Stepchildren." Her face creased in uncertainty. "Sometimes I feel that I don't understand them." Abruptly, she was wry. "Sometimes! Make that most of the time. Frank was such a strong man. The children don't seem much like him."

My gaze was admiring. "It's wonderful that you are close enough to them to take a family cruise. You read so much these days about dysfunctional families, and here you are with your stepchildren on a grand cruise. I think you—" I stopped, looked past her, feigned shock and surprise. "I can't believe it! That looks like an old friend." I was pushing back my chair, scrambling in my purse for some bills. I dropped them on the table, smiled at Sophia and Evelyn. "Please excuse me. Tell Jimmy I'll see him later. If I hurry, I can catch up with her . . ."

I was on my feet and rushing across the square. I walked fast though there was nothing Sophia could have done to stop me. But this was simply a respite. I had to talk to Jimmy.

I skirted clumps of tourists and was likely out of Sophia's sight. I took no chances. At the river's edge, I hurried up to a matronly woman with a cruise-ship tag on her handbag, calling out, "Louise! Is that you?"

A good-humored face turned toward me. "Not unless you're Thelma."

We laughed. I introduced myself, exclaiming over her resemblance to a friend. We strolled across the bridge toward the tour buses, and I wished I had nothing more on my mind than rhapsodizing about the colorful restoration of old Gdańsk.

I relaxed on my balcony as the *Clio* pulled away from the dock, en route to Tallinn, Estonia. We would be at sea tonight, tomorrow, and tomorrow night, arriving in Tallinn Wednesday morning. I'd brewed a cup of green tea. I savored the light fresh taste and the vivid red of the sun dipping to the west. I held the note from Jimmy that I'd found slipped beneath my door upon my return.

*7:15 A.M. Monday*

*I'd hoped to catch you before breakfast. Sophia began her interviews with the Riordans today. She set up the schedule at dinner last night. That's why she put off having you join us. In fact, she—*

I took a sip of tea. No, Jimmy. That's not why, but that's what she wants you to believe. I could imagine her surprise when Jimmy accused her of rudeness and her artful disclaimer. ". . . Sorry if I seemed unfriendly. I wanted to speak with the children. It would have been awkward with anyone else present. We'll definitely include Henrie O . . ." Sophia was clever.

Or, I forced myself to consider honestly, was I the one who saw an affront where none was meant? Sophia had a specific goal for this journey. It could easily have dominated her thoughts.

*—wants you to be part of her birthday dinner tomorrow night in the Julia Child restaurant. I've made the reservations and you'll receive a formal invitation from the restaurant. I'm feeling more positive. Sophia doesn't seem as hell-bent on grilling the heirs—*

Jimmy had not been at breakfast with Sophia and Alex. Alex had looked strained and defensive.

*—with an eye to Frank's standards, standards which anybody would have trouble meeting. She started this morning with Alex and Madge. She's doing Kent tomorrow, Rosie Wednesday, Val Thursday. However, she's almost perfunctory about it. That's good. Now she seems more interested in the trip. Of course, she has a long history with Gdańsk and is excited about the tour today. I'm going to do my best to keep her distracted. She's really apologetic about last night, hopes you will understand. I said you were unflappable. She wanted to know all about you.*

Oh, Jimmy, what did you tell her?

*I told her you and Richard and Margaret and I hung out together in Mexico City and that our kids had a great time together. Remember how we used to go to Chapultepec on Sundays? Sophia said she remembered Richard. Everything seems to be settling down, although—*

Sophia had asked questions when she already knew the answers. Clearly Sophia was playing a private game of her own. Instinct told me that she was suspicious of my presence on the ship. I felt sure she would continue to pursue information about my travel plans. Jimmy would likely dismiss my concerns, insist that I had misread her inquiring gaze last night. He would point to her friendliness in Gdańsk and the invitation to her birthday celebration as proof she held no animus toward me.

*. . . tell truth and shame the devil!*

All right. Jimmy might not agree, but I owed him the facts as I saw them. I was convinced that he and I needed to explain my presence, tell Sophia that I was here because he was worried about her safety.

*—the Riordan kids aren't exhibiting any enthusiasm for the itinerary. They turned down the tour to Gdańsk. Sophia blew it off, which surprised me. You'd think they'd have a little appreciation for the trip. Sophia's paying the bill. Val's been doing room service in her cabin, claims she's working on a script. She didn't say a word at dinner last night. Alex is a jerk. He likes to poke if somebody can't poke back. He kept leaning on the young waiter last night, made him so nervous he knocked over a glass of wine. It got all over Madge and you'd have thought she was drowning in carbolic acid. Rosie talks a mile a minute, trying to cover up Val and Kent's silence. Kent's the one who worries me. He won't look at Sophia. There's something about him that makes me think about a time bomb, ticking, ticking, ticking. Evelyn beams at everyone. She'd been drooping around like Lady Macbeth and now she's her usual fluttery, genial self.*

*If this keeps up, it's going to be a long trip. You don't know how it peps me up to catch a glimpse of you. Have I ever told you you're a rock? That's a compliment, by the way.*

*We're at sea all day tomorrow. Let's meet on the promenade during breakfast. Say seven-fifteen.*

Sophia breakfasted with Alex and Madge around seven. I suspected that's when she would meet with Kent in the morning. Jimmy was allowing himself plenty of time to reach the promenade while Sophia was occupied with Kent. He didn't say so but I connected the dots.

Perhaps Jimmy sensed that Sophia was fencing him in.
Or he was simply exercising caution.

> *Maybe between now and then you'll bump into
> some of the Riordans, waggle your antenna, pick
> up on the danger signals.*

> *Yours—Jimmy*

I was afraid Jimmy saw me as a human dowsing rod,
tipping not to water but to evil. I had no such confidence
in my abilities.

# eight

I glimpsed my reflection in the mirrors outside the formal dining room. I felt elegant in a white silk blouse with a dramatic black floral print and black georgette slacks. The print was repeated on my silk slippers. Earrings and a necklace of oversize glass pearls added glitter.

All of the passengers drifting toward dinner were perfectly coiffed and groomed, some in bright colors, others in dependable black. Similar scenes had unfolded for more than a hundred and fifty years on luxury steamships. At this moment somewhere in the world, children died of starvation, bombs exploded to maim and kill the innocent, hurricanes destroyed everything in their path, but the loveliness of this moment was as real as wars and plagues and heartbreak. Pleasure and beauty are as valid as pain and ugliness, and when I am fortunate enough to enjoy the former, I do so.

I was seated with another solo woman traveler from Brisbane and a charming couple from Lancashire. Our conversation was pleasant, desultory, the latest tennis scores, the PM's rousing speech in Parliament, the curious beauty of amber. ". . . Who would think fossilized pine tree resin would end up being made into jewelry? . . . "

I chatted and let my gaze rove. Jimmy, handsome in a

tuxedo, lifted a glass in a toast to Sophia. Silver beads in the design of seashells decorated her black chiffon dress. They sat at a table for two and didn't look as if they had a care in the world. I thought it was encouraging that they were dining without the others. Possibly Sophia had relaxed her insistence upon interaction with the heirs, and that was surely better for everyone. Perhaps she would be satisfied with the breakfast meetings.

I spotted some of the Riordans at a round table on the opposite side of the room. Rosie and Val were absent. I made another survey of the dining room to be certain. I didn't see the sisters. Throughout the courses, I unobtrusively watched the foursome. Evelyn and Kent sat opposite Alex and Madge. If a prize were awarded to the glummest table, theirs would have won handily. I never saw a smile. Kent stared down at his plate, eating mechanically. Madge wriggled and flounced and frowned while Alex looked increasingly morose. But it was Evelyn who puzzled, then worried me. Her genial good humor of the afternoon was gone. She talked to Kent, her face imploring, one hand outstretched as if in appeal. He never looked at her, but his face grew stonier and stonier.

For dessert I chose cheese and fruit. The Lancashire couple each had bananas Foster. Our Australian tablemate waved away dessert, murmuring something about a few laps in the pool before bedtime. I hoped the water was heated.

At the Riordan table, Alex and Madge elected to have another drink. Kent shook his head at dessert, folded his arms, and continued to look intractable. Evelyn slumped wearily against her chair.

I made my farewells, indicated a hope I would have the opportunity to visit with my new acquaintances again. I avoided walking near the Riordan table. It wasn't my plan that Evelyn should see me now. Once outside the dining room, I considered my options. Evelyn's cabin was aft, so she might take the lifts near the dining room. I mingled with a crowd in the far hallway where I had a good vantage point to see the departing diners.

Evelyn came out of the dining room alone. She glanced toward the lines at the elevator, moved past, obviously choosing to walk to the lifts on the far side of the shops.

I moved quickly to reach the shops before her. The arcade was open. Amber jewelry glistened on a table outside the first shop. I loitered, admiring a pendant with the golden glow of fresh honey. I was fingering a double-rope necklace when I saw Evelyn. She appeared worried and abstracted, face furrowed, eyes blank.

True to Rosie's affectionate description, Evelyn looked as though she'd shopped at a rummage sale, though I suspected this dress too was new. The gown, in fact, was lovely, cupid pink floral lace overlay silk organza. The haphazard effect resulted from green jade earrings that looked bilious above the pink, a rainbow-striped scarf draped around her neck, scuffed black flats, and a woeful face.

"Evelyn." I hailed her eagerly. "I was hoping I'd run into you." There was just a hint of a lonely traveler hoping for companionship. "They're playing forties tunes up on 10. I was thinking about an after-dinner drink. Will you join me?"

As I smiled at her, Evelyn came back from a long distance, forcing herself to see me, her worried frown slipping away. She blinked several times, her kindly face concerned. "A drink?" Obviously she'd intended to return to her cabin. Her face was a rapid study in conflicting emotions, underlying uneasiness and abstraction, automatic good manners, empathy. Kindness prevailed. "I'd love that."

We talked about our day in Gdańsk as we walked to the lift. When we got out on 10, the deck was less stable beneath our feet, the ship obviously encountering heavier seas. At one especially pronounced lurch, I lost my balance, flailed toward the wall. She was quick to catch my arm, stabilize me. I realized she had excellent balance, and I understood why Jimmy believed that she'd deliberately upended the tray with Sophia's sherry. Evelyn was unlikely to stumble walking down stairs.

We settled at a table near the bank of windows looking out over the bow with an unobstructed view of open ocean. The cheerful late evening summer sun of the northern latitudes splashed the sea with vivid colors of the sunset. A chanteuse in a silver lamé gown offered a throaty version of "Smoke Gets in Your Eyes." The backup trio played with energy but, happily, kept down the volume.

A rosy light spilled down from a wall sconce, emphasizing the tracery of smile lines on Evelyn's milk white skin. She looked like what she was, a pleasant middle-aged woman with worries and fears and hopes. Although her eyes held the echo of laughter, they also held sadness.

We sat in a companionable silence, enjoying the music, sipping our drinks. She ordered a Scotch and soda. I chose an apricot colada, a frothy mix of dark rum, apricot brandy, and vanilla ice cream. Self-indulgent, yes, but I was on a holiday. Ostensibly.

Our conversation began desultorily, fanning out like ripples of the tide washing onto the beach with no particular direction, leaching sand here, dropping a shell there. My objective was simply to encourage Evelyn to see me as a friend. I hoped to maneuver her into a discussion of her nieces and nephews, but only if they came naturally into our conversation. The music played on, "As Time

Goes By," "O Sole Mio," and "Pistol Packin' Mama." I realized that Evelyn was eliciting a rather full biography of me.

". . . and after my husband's death I was a freelancer for a while, then ended up teaching journalism at Thorndyke University in Missouri. Now I'm fully retired, though I still write an occasional article. I travel quite a bit." Funny, how truth can tell so little, revealing nothing of Richard's death in a fall from a Hawaiian mountainside and my struggle to find light and grace in life alone and the chilling moment when I realized Richard's death was murder. As for being retired . . . well, surely it was time, but I would have enjoyed teaching an occasional class if another crime hadn't forced an end to my association with the university. It was a reminder that what I shared with Evelyn and what she shared with me might be true but far from the whole truth.

I spooned a thick clump of ice cream from the colada. "That's certainly enough about me. Now tell me all about this wonderful trip you are making with your family."

She brushed back a straggle of faded red hair. Her face was suddenly forlorn. "Oh, this trip. I wish—" She broke off, shook her head. Tears glistened in her eyes.

"What's wrong?" My voice was gentle.

She swiped a hand across her eyes, managing to smear eyeliner and leaving a streak down one cheek. "I shouldn't get upset. But I haven't been sleeping well and I feel so helpless." She hesitated, asked bluntly, "Are you a great friend of Sophia's?"

"I met her twice many years ago." I looked directly into blue eyes that wanted something of me, but I wasn't sure what. "Jimmy's my great friend."

"Oh." She sagged back against the chair in disappointment. "I was hoping you could help." She clasped her hands together, began to twist them round and round. "I don't know what to do."

"Would you like to tell me about it?" I steeled myself against a wave of pity. Yes, I felt sorry for Evelyn and her pain, but if one of the Riordans had a murderous heart, Sophia had to be protected.

"There's nothing you can do. I thought if you were Sophia's friend, perhaps you could talk to her. I'm worried about what she may do. You see, she has control over whether the children receive their inheritance, and Sophia doesn't understand them. She's tried to force them into a mold of what she thinks Frank would have wanted, and that's not right. I've tried to talk to her, but Sophia says I'm not impartial. Of course I'm not impartial, whatever that is!" Evelyn looked indignant. "I know them. They're wonderful kids. I came to take care of them after their mother died. They're good kids—"

They weren't kids. Not anymore. Yet I understood her cry. They would always be children to her.

"—but Sophia's never understood them. Oh"—Evelyn sighed heavily—"I have to admit Sophia's tried, but she looks at everything rationally and people aren't rational, not when they're in love or afraid or discouraged or hurt."

Evelyn might not be articulate, but she understood the human heart.

Evelyn turned her glass on the coaster. "Worst of all, she thinks she's doing what Frank would have liked. She's judging them against his standards. Frank expected everyone around him to excel, but it mattered to him if you tried hard. If he were here, he'd see that they are doing the best they can. That's all you can expect of anyone. I know Alex has made some foolish investments and he doesn't listen to advice very well, but it's because he lacks confidence. He's like the Scarecrow in *The Wizard of Oz*. He needs someone to prop him up. It will be so easy for Sophia to decide he can't be trusted with the money. But Kent's right. It's their money."

Evelyn massaged one temple as if it ached. "I'm afraid Kent's going to make Sophia furious. Dear, sweet Kent. He's been hurt, deep inside, and the pain eats away at him like acid. I begged him tonight to go ahead and meet with Sophia in the morning, keep everything pleasant for his brother and sisters. He's furious with Sophia. He said she doesn't have any right to be their judge. But Frank put it in his will that Sophia can decide. Now Rosie"— affection lifted Evelyn's voice, shone in her eyes—"no one ever puts Rosie down. As for Val . . . Oh, I'm so worried about tomorrow." Evelyn looked at me uncertainly. "I didn't mean to burden you with this. Please forgive me."

"Perhaps everything will work out." A positive approach sometimes turn lemons to lemonade. Often enough, lemons are lemons and the taste bitter. "I'll be glad to talk to Jimmy. Perhaps he can persuade Sophia."

A soft smile curved her lips. Her eyes shone with hope. "That would be so kind of you."

I stepped into my cabin, felt the floor moving beneath my feet, braced against the wall for a moment. I felt a little queasy. I don't know whether it was the apricot colada or the swift hug Evelyn had given me as we parted. She was buoyed by the possibility that my intervention with Jimmy might change Sophia's attitude. I shouldn't have given her false hope. Nothing Jimmy might say would be likely to sway Sophia, but tomorrow I would urge him to try.

I walked forward and saw an envelope on the bed along

with tomorrow's ship program. The envelope wasn't sealed. It contained a printout of a lengthy e-mail message. I smiled. Margaret Brown had come through, as old reporters always do.

I undressed, slipped into a cotton gown, washed my face. I settled on the small sofa and began to read.

Dear Henrie O,

What are you doing on the Baltic? How does a kid's death in CA figure in? I expect a blow-by-blow when you get home. It was fun to get your e-mail, first time I've received one from a ship at sea. Ah, the wonders of the cyberworld. It's great for snoops, but I liked life better before I felt like a fly snagged in a sticky web with no place left to hide.

I enjoyed digging until I nosed out the story. Sad one. Don't know how much you know about the circumstances. Valerie was one of a pair of twins, youngest children of Frank and Anna Riordan. Five kids in all. Their mother died in 1988. Frank's sister Evelyn came to live with him and take care of them. The kids were devastated, but Evelyn kept them on track, busy all the time, every sport and extracurricular activity possible. Got this from the housekeeper, who thinks Evelyn hung the moon. "Nicest lady in the world and she didn't try to take their mother's place but she's like a good warm hen, cluck-clucking around the kids, keeping them warm, making them feel safe." Then, as far as the kids were concerned, their world came to an end. Frank married Sophia Montgomery in 1990. You remember Sophia, don't you? Top-notch documentary filmmaker, but about as maternal as a warthog. Although I suppose mama warthogs might take umbrage. Anyway, the bridal bouquet had scarcely been tossed when those kids were shipped off to boarding schools. Sophia did relent and let them come home for the summer. That would be the summer of '91. The housekeeper said they were set to go back to their boarding schools and Rosie had pleaded with her dad to let the twins live with Evelyn. Rosie told him they were too little to be away at school and Evelyn would be glad to have them. According to the housekeeper, Sophia convinced Frank that was nonsense because the school said they were well adjusted, happy children and a change might not be in their best interests. You'd think Frank could also figure a change might not be in the school's best financial interest, plus Sophia was the one who'd advised they be sent away to school and any change would make her look like she'd been wrong. Sophia does not take kindly to being wrong. Frank listened to Sophia, of course. The housekeeper said the kids were packed up and ready to leave the next day. Sophia had a fancy party for them, clowns and a mariachi band and a piñata for each kid. The housekeeper said Vic looked like a little thin ghost. She wouldn't open her piñata, took it upstairs with her. In the morning, Vic was nowhere to be found. They looked everywhere in the house. It was Val who found the piñata at the edge of the cliff, crushed and broken like someone had stomped on it. Val looked down. Vic's body was crumpled on the rocks, the water lifting it up and down. The death was listed officially as an accidental drowning. But everybody knew what had happened. During the night, Vic slipped out of the house, carrying that piñata. At the edge of the cliff, she smashed it and everything in it to pieces, and then she jumped.

No wonder Val was withdrawn and remote. A cauldron of anger and bitterness bubbled within her. Now Sophia had planned a party for tomorrow evening, the anniversary of Vic's death.

I had to tell Jimmy.

My dreams were somber, dark as a stormy day. Waves curled high to crash down upon sharp black rocks and the small body that moved with the water though life was gone . . .

## nine

WALKERS and joggers moved briskly around the promenade, an oblong track that overlooked the pool deck. A massive woman in a blue swimsuit and yellow swim cap bobbed up and down as she swam the breaststroke across the small pool. It was cool enough on the promenade that I zipped up my windbreaker. I finished my coffee—I'd breakfasted early—and dropped the Styrofoam cup in a waste bin. I leaned on the dark wood railing and looked out at the sparkling ocean, the water the deep blue of a northern sea. The breeze stirred my hair, tugged at my slacks.

*Vic loved the ocean.*

That brief sentence from the twin's obituary chilled me. I'd dreamt of her end, and now as I looked at the glistening blue water, riffled with whitecaps elegant as lace, sadness swept me.

"Henrie O." Jimmy's tone was ebullient, the hand on my shoulder warm and living and strong.

I turned toward him, still picturing sharp black rocks and roiling surf, glad to overlay that image with the reality of tall, rangy Jimmy, the breeze stirring his white hair, his face alight with pleasure.

His smile fled. "What's wrong?"

Dear Jimmy. So quick to see and care. That came as no surprise. He had always been attuned to me. I felt a twist of pain. If I hadn't turned him down . . . I cared for him, more than I had realized at the time. I'd felt there wasn't love enough and a man deserves a wife who is wholly and unreservedly and passionately in love with him. Yet now I knew that I loved him more than Sophia ever would, and I knew that he must never guess how I felt. Where to start?

"I've been learning a lot." I needed to tell him about Vic. I was sure he didn't know the sad story or he would have included it in his information about the Riordans. No one could know that history and not realize its impact on the present. If he knew, he would see at once that Sophia's birthday dinner tonight should be rescheduled. Moreover, it was essential that we tell Sophia why I was here.

*. . . tell truth . . .*

I looked at him gravely. "After you went to get the postcards, Sophia quizzed me about this trip. She wanted to know when I booked. Jimmy, she not only knows we were lovers, she thinks that's why I'm here."

He was stunned. He stared deep into my eyes. I knew that he read certainty in my gaze. He turned a little away from me, staring out at the bright blue sea. He'd asked me on the trip because he felt I had a knack for reading people. Now that very quality was either lacking or unhappily accurate. His words were thoughtful, considering. "If she suspects us of being lovers now, she has no trust in me."

I wished for a reply to help him, but Jimmy would have to sort out his feelings about Sophia's suspicions. "We need to tell her exactly why I'm here, that you've called on me to—"

"What an excellent plan. Although, of course, the wife

is always the last to know." Sophia's voice shook. The sun glinting on her blond curls gave her an aura of youthfulness, but there was nothing young about her face, bleak with despair and hurt.

Jimmy scowled. "Don't say anything you'll regret, Sophia. Henrie O's here to help me protect you because you won't admit you're in danger."

Startled, she gave me a quick searching look. "Protect me? How?"

I hoped I could defuse this moment. "Jimmy called me after the boulder almost hit you. He asked me to come on the trip to see if I could help him figure out who pushed it. And who might have put poison in your sherry. It was"—I enunciated clearly—"the first time I had spoken with Jimmy since we parted, long before you and he married. When we arrived at Heathrow, it was the first time I had seen him since then."

I looked into her brilliantly blue—and suspicious—eyes. Our gazes locked, hers uncertain, mine unwavering.

She lifted a shaking hand to shield her eyes from the sun and slowly turned to Jimmy. "Why did you call her? You have plenty of friends. You know policemen and lawyers and detectives. Why her?"

Jimmy's face was unguarded. He looked toward me. "I knew she would come."

It wasn't the answer Sophia wanted. She stood frozen.

"Sophia." His tone was insistent. He moved toward her, a good man with a kind face, and looked into her eyes. "You are my wife. I don't want you to die."

Sophia drew in a quick breath. The tight muscles of her face loosened. She shook her head. "You're serious, aren't you?"

"Deadly serious." He reached out, grabbed her hand. "And Henrie O can help us."

Sophia held tight to his hand. She gave me a not-quite-convinced look, but slowly the tension eased from her body. "It's crazy. Nobody tried to kill me. Jimmy thinks Frank's kids want money at all costs. I don't believe that. I'm amazed he convinced you. I'm afraid you've traveled all this way for no reason. I don't think one of Frank's children is trying to kill me. For one thing, I don't intend to restrict their income even if I don't dissolve the trusts now. They've gotten along very well on that income—"

I understood her conclusion, but apparently it hadn't occurred to her that the prospect of total possession of a substantial sum of money might make the income seem paltry in comparison. As Kent had told his sister, it was their money.

"—in the past. Moreover, how can I be in danger on the ship?" She gestured down toward the pool deck. Early sunbathers occupied the front row of deck chairs. The breaststroker continued to bob back and forth across the pool. Stewards carried trays with coffee and juice. "There are people everywhere and Jimmy is with me in the cabin. I'll decide what to do about the trusts and wire the lawyer before the trip is over. What could possibly happen?"

I looked at the populated deck. Sophia was right. There were always people everywhere.

Jimmy nodded reluctant agreement. "It seems safe enough. Besides, I may be wrong. Maybe that rock rolled on its own. Maybe Evelyn stumbled. Maybe. But it's passing strange we've never had a bouncing boulder before. Stranger still that the rock came down precisely at eight o'clock when you were on the way to your office and the house was full of people who'll be a lot richer if you die. The point is that I don't believe in coincidences. You didn't think it was a coincidence Henrie O was on this ship. You were right. I don't think it's a coincidence that boulder almost killed you. I think somebody pushed it. Evelyn. Alex. Madge. Kent. Rosie. Val. It had to be one of them. But"— and he looked at her eagerly—"there's an easy solution. Give them their money, announce it tonight, turn this into a real holiday, tell them the trusts will be liquidated."

Sophia drew herself up, slim and straight, the lift of her chin imperious. She reminded me of a cat, elegant and certain. "I won't be intimidated. Or cajoled. Frank wanted me to do what was right for his children. I intend to fulfill my responsibility. Although they certainly aren't making it easy. If I weren't terribly patient, I'd simply e-mail the lawyer that the trusts should continue in force. I certainly may do that for Kent. He stood me up this morning. You might tell him since you feel so strongly about their inheritances"—her glance at Jimmy was sardonic—"that it would be in his best interest to show up tonight." She turned and walked away.

Jimmy shot me a look of frustration. He made a helpless gesture with his hands and hurried after Sophia.

I watched them go, feeling both irritated and uneasy. Sophia refused to believe she might be in danger. Sophia—

"Who does Jimmy think he is, accusing us of trying to do away with her?" The sharp, waspish voice startled me. "That's what I want to know."

I looked around to see Madge Riordan's petulant face. Spiky blond hair was fashionable above the soft pink of a mini-cable sweater. The pink was echoed in anchor appliqués down the outside seams of white slacks. Young and well dressed, she would have been attractive except for the hardness in her eyes and the droop of a discontented mouth.

I didn't find Madge appealing. I was tempted to warn her that a mean spirit would leave an indelible imprint by the time she was forty and all the king's horses and all the king's beauticians would be to no avail. Instead, I raised an inquiring eyebrow. "Do you often eavesdrop?"

Madge wasn't fazed. Her thin lips curled in a derisive smile. "Only when necessary. What's Jimmy up to? Why is he trying to convince Sophia somebody pushed that boulder?"

I met her angry stare. "As you heard"—she appeared oblivious to insult—"he doesn't believe in coincidences. Why did that boulder come down—and just the one boulder—at precisely the moment Sophia was walking to her office?"

Madge gave a disdainful shrug but her eyes were uneasy. "That's silly. Coincidences happen all the time. Anyway, at least Jimmy's on the right track about the money. It's ours, not hers. Who's she to decide whether we get it?"

"Sophia's simply trying"—I felt a certain irony in finding myself defending her—"to do what Frank Riordan wanted. It might work out if his children made an effort to get along with her."

"You got that right." Madge's face was glum. "I told Alex to keep his mouth shut about his deals. He always has great ideas about how to make money. At least *he* thinks they're great." She was clearly not into the role of supportive spouse. "He won't listen to anybody." Her resentment was apparent. "This latest one's *sooo* bogus, a Brazilian who's got a plan on how to corner the wireless market in China. I told him to play it cool, tell her he was thinking of going back to school. That always sounds good. And what did he do? He starts drawing on a napkin, explaining how he's going to take the five mil and use it to get a ten-mil loan and then he and Eugenio would set up shop in Beijing. Of course, she wanted to know all about Eugenio and a business plan and what bankers and what investors and whether private or public and about a hundred questions Alex couldn't answer."

"Maybe Alex can tell her he's been thinking about her questions and they've made him realize the plan would need a good deal more work." I doubted this approach would salvage Alex's situation, but it wouldn't do any harm for Madge to see me as an ally.

"Maybe Sophia will turn into a fairy godmother. I don't think so." Madge's tone was discouraged. "Sophia thinks Alex is an idiot. If that's not bad enough, Kent didn't show up this morning. I was sitting across the room, keeping an eye on her. I thought maybe I'd see how Kent did with her, and if she was in a good mood, Alex could talk to her, explain he'd had some second thoughts like you said. Alex wouldn't roust his rear out of bed. He knows he messed up, but his motto is never to let on that he's not the smartest guy around. I told him what I thought—"

Her voice was shrill. I wondered if Alex had burrowed his head beneath his pillow, lain there unmoving, defeated and defensive.

"—and I slammed out of there and came up by myself. Instead of Kent schmoozing her into a better mood, he blew her off. She gave him ten minutes. I mean, you know how queens are. You better not be late. Ten minutes was all she was willing to wait. She threw down her napkin and got up without eating a bite. I wondered what she was going to do. I thought maybe she'd go bang on Kent's door." Madge brightened. "I thought maybe that wouldn't be a bad deal. If she got really mad at Kent, maybe she wouldn't be thinking about Alex. She was so mad I didn't have to worry about her spotting me coming along behind. When we got almost down to our deck, Jimmy was heading up the opposite stairs, looking over his shoulder to make sure nobody was noticing him. That got her attention all right." Madge's giggle was knowing. "It was like watching a cartoon character and the little balloon above her head. She wanted to know where he was going. She hurried down and went to the other staircase. I came right along behind. We ended up here." She looked around the promenade, shading her eyes. "She stood over there"—Madge pointed—"and watched you two like a hawk looking at a couple of rats. For a minute, when she busted up your twosome, I thought maybe we were all off the hook. If Jimmy was screwing around on her, she'd be too furious to care about the Riordans. No such luck. Instead, Jimmy's got her thinking about us again. If Alex weren't such a fool, she'd probably give him a thumbs-up. Like I told him, Sophia wants to feel sure none of them are going to run through the money or act stupid with it. You know, gamble or do drugs. But now she thinks Alex is a financial idiot, and who knows what she thinks about Kent. He's such a fool. All he had to do was have breakfast with her!" Madge planted her elbows on the railing and stared moodily out at the water.

I remembered Kent's bitterness at Tivoli. "Why does Kent hate Sophia?"

Madge's face wrinkled in a puzzled frown. "Nobody talks about it. She had something to do with his breakup with his girlfriend. But so what! He can pick up five million dollars if he plays it right. All he has to do is suck it up and be nice to her on this trip."

Obviously Madge would have cheerfully breakfasted with the devil for five million dollars.

"His girlfriend?" I didn't like asking. It felt like a betrayal of a nice young man with a sensitive face. I could hear Kent's anguished voice against the background of laughter at Tivoli: . . . *I didn't know I could hate anyone as much as I hate her.*

"Yeah. Kent fell like a ton of bricks for this floozy he met at some bar. Heather was a bartender. He thought she was wonderful, working there nights after a sales job all day so she could make enough money to take care of a younger brother. She and the kid brother had lit out from someplace in Kansas, ended up in San Francisco. Kent was talking about marrying her and Sophia said his father would be appalled at his marrying somebody from nowhere and a lower-class background." There was no sympathy in Madge's voice. Kent and Kent's life didn't matter to her, not unless his actions impinged on what she wanted for Alex.

"Jimmy didn't tell me about Heather." There was no reason for Jimmy to have mentioned Heather, but I was confident Madge in her utter self-absorption wouldn't bother to wonder at my comment.

She yawned. "Heather's history. She's probably picked up another hunk with money by this time." Her shrug was dismissive. "Heather was pretty." Her tone was grudging. "She seemed kind of like a sweet kid."

I was puzzled. "Why would breaking up with Heather make Kent mad at Sophia?"

"That's what I asked Alex and he told me to mind my own business." She tossed her head in irritation. "Ever since he broke up with Heather, Kent's refused to have anything to do with Sophia. He's mooned around like a kid. That's stupid. There are plenty of fish in the sea. Kent needs to get over it, find somebody else."

I stared at her. Find somebody else. Pick another card out of the deck, never mind that your heart is crushed.

She was truly puzzled. "He's good-looking. Why

doesn't he pick up a girl on the ship? I wish Alex and I had found somebody for him. If he had a new girlfriend, he'd get over being mad at Sophia. Instead he's ticked her off. And there may be a big bust-up tonight. Anyway"—her brows drew down in a frown—"you tell Jimmy to stop all this stuff about one of us pushing a boulder down the cliff."

I logged on. I started, stopped, deleted, knew the clock was ticking on the charges. E-mails have a lot in common with shouts from a soapbox. You'd better be sure you don't mind who's listening. Finally, I typed fast, knowing I wouldn't want this message seen, yet determined to find out what I could.

Dear Margaret,

Kent Riordan, younger son of Frank, had a girlfriend named Heather. She apparently worked as a bartender. I know, needle in a haystack. See if you can find out her name, get as much personal info as possible, including close friend or confidant. Particularly interested in circumstances of Kent and Heather's breakup. Thanks, Henrie O

I logged off. I stopped on my way out to get a squish of hand sanitizer. Any keyboard used by the public was sure to be rife with more germs than I cared to contemplate. Containers of the antiseptic liquid were scattered about the ship, a reminder of the viruses that often waylay sea-borne passengers and create headlines cruise ship directors hate to see.

I wished the cleansing liquid could sanitize my somber mood. I'd dealt with one unhappy episode and now I needed to deal with another. I hadn't had time to tell Jimmy about Vic, but I doubted Sophia would respond cheerfully to any further intervention by me. Yet I felt compelled to do something. I understood sorrow and I foresaw nothing but pain if Sophia expected a cheerful celebration on this date.

Why a party tonight? Of course, it was her birthday. Had Sophia so dismissed Vic's death from her mind that she didn't recall the date? Or, worse, was she blind to enduring grief?

Whatever her reasoning, the dinner should be rescheduled. Someone needed to talk to Jimmy, ask him to intervene. Rosie Riordan would be the best person to ask.

# ten

I called Rosie's cabin. No answer. I started at the top of the ship, checked the sundeck, then returned to Deck 10. I strolled past the computer area to look over the scattering of leather chairs and small tables that faced the huge windows at the bow, affording a panoramic view of the sea. Only a few places were taken, a woman knitting, her hands flashing with grace, an elderly man in a shabby tweed jacket and baggy trousers studying the morning news digest compiled by the ship personnel.

I took the promenade to the stern area and stepped into the library. Every chair was taken. There was the hush of good manners, only an occasional rustle of sound to mark the turning of pages. Had I truly been on a holiday, I too would have browsed the collection of histories, travelogues, and guidebooks.

I returned to the promenade and walked down a curving outside staircase. Swimmers splashed in the pool. The deck glistened from a recent wash. The informal dining room aft was closed except for the coffee and tea bar. Rosie wasn't in that short line. The hamburger stand near the pool hadn't opened yet for lunch. Most of the wooden tables were filled with lounging travelers enjoying the fresh air.

I scanned the ranks of deck chairs on either side of the pool. Despite the brisk breeze, hardy sun lovers lay supine, eyes closed, bodies glistening with lotions and oils. Toward the end of the last row of chairs on the starboard side, Evelyn was cocooned in a blanket. She held a book, stared down at it, her face somber. I watched for a moment and she never turned a page. I crossed to the port side, though I doubted Evelyn would look up. She had withdrawn behind the book.

The forward area was divided among a card room, spa, fitness center, and beauty salon. In the fitness center, Kent was working out on a treadmill, back glistening with sweat, muscular legs striding fast. When I stepped into the beauty salon, I heard Madge's sharp voice: ". . . Cut a little more off the back . . ." A haughty blonde leafed through a fashion magazine as a manicurist worked on her other hand. At the spa, I told the smiling attendant I was looking for Rosie Riordan, she'd said something about a body wrap . . . The answer was swift: "No, ma'am, Miss Riordan hasn't made an appointment yet."

I took the lift down to Deck 5 to check the remaining public areas, the shops and Diogenes Bar and the rather remote deck chairs on either side of the ship. I made a cursory trip to the reception lobby on Deck 4, then took the lift to Deck 6 and walked swiftly to my cabin. Apparently Rosie Riordan was not spending this lovely sunny day at sea taking advantage of the ship's amenities.

The steward had already serviced the cabin, the fleur-de-lis-patterned spread, white against a soft blue, in place on the bed, fresh towels in the scrubbed bath, bottled water on the desk. I glanced at the phone. It was my last hope of contacting Rosie this morning. I was thoughtful as I brewed a cup of tea. I would have only a few words to persuade her to meet with me. I had to get her attention, get it and hold it. I hoped Jimmy would understand what I was about to do. Since Madge had overheard our confrontation with Sophia, it would not be long before all the Riordans knew why I was on board. Possibly an awareness that they were under suspicion might provide protection to Sophia.

Whether that proved true or not, whether Jimmy approved or not, I was determined to make an effort to respect Vic's death. It wasn't any business of mine, but I knew only too well, now and forever, the sorrow of the soul as another year is marked. I didn't understand why one of the Riordans hadn't spoken up. Evelyn seemed to be on good terms with Sophia yet she'd remained silent. Should I go up to the pool deck, ask her to speak to Jimmy?

I almost turned to go, then shook my head. I didn't want to ask Evelyn to give a message to Jimmy. Evelyn seemed too indecisive to interfere. Rosie would have no difficulty if she agreed to help me.

It seemed odd that apparently none of the Riordans had asked Sophia to reschedule her birthday dinner, but I couldn't see why they would object to Jimmy making that request.

Even self-centered Madge was worried about tonight. I was sure Jimmy would agree that every possible effort should be made to lessen the strain between Sophia and the Riordans. An excellent start would be to move the party to tomorrow night.

I sipped the tea, wished its warmth could dissipate the chill I felt. Maybe it was time to admit to myself that I had a hunch. Hunches are nothing more than the subconscious fluttering of a warning flag. Hunches are ignored at our peril. It was as if I'd heard the distant crack in snowy stillness and knew an avalanche threatened. I could not in good conscience stand aside, do nothing.

I found Jimmy's note where he'd listed the cabin numbers and dialed Rosie's cabin again. No answer. I hung up without leaving a message. Rosie might be anywhere on the ship, perhaps in someone else's cabin. I was sure she was not with Sophia and Jimmy. Was Jimmy still trying to persuade Sophia to dissolve the trusts to remove any possible motive for her death? Or had Jimmy and Sophia settled for an uneasy truce, Sophia mollified that I was no threat to her marriage yet stubbornly dismissive of Jimmy's fears? Evelyn was quite likely still staring at her unread book. Madge was in the beauty salon, Kent on the treadmill. Alex? He was probably still in bed, avoiding the world. Val? What would she be doing on the anniversary of her twin's death? I pictured her sunk in sadness in her cabin. That's where Rosie was. I dialed the cabin number.

"Hello." The voice was tight and grim.

"Rosie?" I wasn't certain.

A pause. "Who is this?"

"Henrie O Collins. I need to talk to you about Vic. I'm in Cabin 6012." I hung up.

Within minutes there was a sharp knock on my door. I opened it, stood aside for her to enter.

Rosie hesitated at the threshold, her gaze sharp and questioning. Despite the plainness of a navy turtleneck and age-faded jeans, she could easily have graced a fashion runway and captivated everyone in the audience. The spill of light in the entryway brought out the fiery shade of her Titian curls, but illuminated too the purplish shadows beneath her eyes and the sadness of her face. One hand fastened tightly on the doorjamb. "What about Vic? How do you know about Vic?"

I gestured toward the balcony. "Please come in. Let me tell you what I know. And why."

"This isn't a good day to talk about Vic." She spoke slowly as if every word cost effort.

"I know. I understand."

Her eyes flared in disbelief. "Do you? I doubt very much that you understand, Mrs. Collins." Her tone was bitter.

"Please come in." I wished Evelyn were there to wrap Rosie in her arms. I couldn't provide the comfort she needed. "I want to help. Perhaps I can help."

Rosie's lips twisted. "That would take a miracle you can't provide."

"Give me a chance. That's all I'm asking." I met her gaze.

Perhaps she saw echoing sadness in my eyes. She moved past me, lithe and lovely except for the hands clenched in tight fists.

On the balcony Rosie stood straight as a sentinel, her face guarded.

I stood too, the two of us facing each other on that gay balcony, both of us a world away from the arching blue sky and dark blue sea. I started at the beginning with Jimmy's call. I told her everything, his conviction some hand shoved a boulder down the cliff at Sophia, Evelyn and the sherry, my reluctant acquiescence, the dossiers Jimmy provided—

A bright flush stained her cheeks. "You're a spy. You must have laughed when I accosted you at breakfast."

"No. I enjoyed our breakfast—"

There was no answering warmth in her face.

"—but I didn't forget why I was here. I continued to gather information about your family and I learned about Vic. I'm sorry."

"Sure you are." Her voice was hard. "Everybody's sorry when a kid dies. Being sorry doesn't matter." Her eyes glittered with unresolved pain.

I held her gaze. "I know that. My son was eleven when he died in a car wreck on a winding mountain road in Mexico. We were on that road because I'd insisted we go to a festival in Toluca."

The anger seeped from her face. "Okay. You hurt. I hurt. Val hurts. But why do you want to talk about Vic? Would it help if I asked you about that car wreck?"

I pushed away the memory of headlights sweeping around a curve. We'd had so much fun at the fiesta. I'd bought Bobby and Emily straw animals, hers a hen, his a donkey. Bobby was alive until . . . "I don't want to talk about Vic. I want to talk to you about tonight. Why haven't you or Evelyn spoken to Sophia—"

"Don't be a fool." Rosie's face hardened. "I'd rather die. Sophia would be graceful, but she wouldn't cancel the dinner. She'd turn it into a remembrance of Vic, probably ask each of us to make a tribute. Come, sisters and brothers, stand up and talk about Vic. Remember her that summer, big lost eyes in a thin face. That last night she ran upstairs, like a ghost, running away because nobody helped her. Not her dad. Not me. Not Val. Not her brothers. Nobody."

Tears streamed down Rosie's face. "Do you think we ever want to hear Sophia say Vic's name? Not now. Not ever. Do you hear me?" Her voice shook. "That would be worse, worse than going to the dinner and seeing Sophia. She killed my baby sister. Damn Sophia's selfish soul to everlasting hell, she killed Vic." Rosie turned and stumbled across the balcony to open the sliding door and blindly rushed through my cabin.

As the door closed behind her, I had my answer. Sophia's party was fated to happen.

I felt restless and out of sorts after lunch. I wandered up to the pool deck and leaned on the railing. I'd warned Jimmy that I was unlikely to meet the Riordans and pinpoint a potential murderer. I'd learned what I could about them, enough to know that Sophia was more than simply a threat to the lifestyle of Frank Riordan's children. Dangerous currents swirled beneath the dark surface of that relationship. Quick-moving, quick-thinking Sophia, absorbed in her own hopes and dreams and projects, had only a cursory understanding of Frank Riordan's children.

I understood both too little and too much. If one of the Riordans shoved a boulder or poisoned a bottle of sherry, I had no inkling of the hand behind the deed. I felt useless. I saw no way of making a difference for Sophia or Jimmy or the Riordans. Oddly, my greatest contribution might be the fact that Sophia was exceedingly wary of me. My presence might distract her from concentrating on the heirs and further alienating them.

If I couldn't do anything more, it was time to put them out of my mind, take pleasure from the steady course of the ship, the ripple of waves, the fresh scent of the sea.

A hand gripped the railing beside me. "I have to talk to you. I've looked everywhere for Jimmy." Evelyn Riordan's voice shook. "Madge heard Jimmy say one of us pushed that boulder down the cliff and poisoned the sherry. That's wrong, I swear it is." Her eyes were wide and strained.

It hadn't taken long for Madge to report the fruits of her eavesdropping. "Jimmy can't get away from the fact that the boulder came down the hill at the exact moment Sophia was walking to her office."

Evelyn was imploring. "Jimmy's made a mistake. Boulders crash down all the time. For all we know, other boulders crashed down earlier when no one was around. The hillside is always unstable."

I watched her carefully. "The night before you came on the trip, you bumped into Jimmy—"

She interrupted. "So I stumbled and the sherry spilled! Is that a crime?"

I didn't take the bait and become defensive. I looked at her steadily. "Maybe you were preventing a crime."

"I lost my balance on the stairs. It was an accident. Jimmy mustn't make these absurd accusations. Henrie O, you know him so well. Please talk to him. He has to see that he's imagining danger that isn't there. Sophia knows better. I just talked to her." Evelyn looked uncertain. "I don't know whether to tell you . . ."

I waited.

"Oh dear." She looked perplexed as a child, afraid to speak and afraid not to speak. "Oh dear. I suppose I should. Sophia found out from the purser that Jimmy paid your way. I don't think she's pleased."

I doubted indeed that Sophia was pleased. "He paid my way because he was afraid for Sophia. I came because I'm trying to help out an old friend, and I can't afford this kind of travel." I waved my hand at the gleaming brass and shining whiteness of the *Clio*.

Evelyn looked distraught. "Afraid for her . . . It's absurd to accuse the children of plotting murder. Not one of the children has ever been mean or violent. Never. But"—she took a breath—"since there isn't anything to it"—her face brightened—"everything will work out. We'll enjoy the trip"—she didn't speak with conviction—"and all go home and everything will be fine and that will prove Jimmy's wrong." Abruptly her face crumpled like a deflated ball. "Once we get past tonight, everything will be better. Oh, the poor dear children." She turned away.

I watched her go, her gait slow. She carried memories and fears with her, but she was convinced that Sophia faced no danger. Was she right or did she remember young faces and voices in the years before Sophia came and Vic jumped?

I started up the steps to the promenade and realized a steward was looking at me curiously. I wondered how much of our conversation he had overheard.


Julia Child would have enjoyed the decor of the restaurant named in her honor. It was styled after a formal French salon. The diners were elegant, the women in gowns and cocktail dresses, the men in tuxedos.

Our table was at the stern, a choice location befitting Sophia's stature as a well-known traveler on the *Clio*. The headwaiter knew her. His attitude was admiring without being familiar. *Would Mrs. Lennox want her favorite wine, the Hermitage Jean-Louis Chave Blanc? The menu tonight offered Polynesian specialities, but if there was anything else Mrs. Lennox preferred . . . Would Mrs. Lennox have a request for the musicians? . . .*

The attentiveness of the waiter and his assistant as they served the courses and the beautiful music and cheerful soft-voiced chatter of other diners contrasted with the glum mood at our table. Meager conversation came in spurts and rushes with interludes of strained silence. Evelyn voiced concern about the effects of global warming. Alex pontificated that temperature fluctuations had to be considered over a span of centuries and industries didn't need any more crippling regulations. Madge wondered why the ship didn't have a style show instead of boring old lectures. Rosie, her face pale and drawn, spoke only when directly addressed, answering in monosyllables. Kent stared at his plate, pushed the food about, ate little. I talked about my eagerness to see the old medieval town of Tallinn, our destination tomorrow.

There was one empty place. Val wasn't present. It was Rosie who had looked defiantly at Sophia when the waiter came to take our orders. "Val's not feeling well. She didn't want anything to eat."

Sophia had raised an eyebrow, looked out at the placid sea. "Perhaps she should take some Dramamine."

Rosie made no reply. Her hand tightened on the stem of her wineglass.

By the time the entrées arrived, Jimmy was doggedly describing the prospects for the Yankees in the playoffs and whether Jeter or Rodriguez should be MVP. Twin spots of color stained Sophia's smooth cheeks. Her glittering gaze moved from one Riordan to another, Evelyn in a shapeless taffeta dress with a shoulder strap that kept slipping, Alex with a smear of hollandaise on his chin and a heavily laden fork, Madge smothering a yawn with carmine fingernails, Rosie's lovely face forlorn in a swath of apricot light from the setting sun, impassive Kent crumbling a roll into tiny pellets.

Sophia looked hurt, her expression brittle, likely interpreting the strained atmosphere as dislike toward her. I didn't glance at Jimmy, but I felt his tension.

". . . His on-base percentage is better than Jeter's but Jeter had that magnificent play . . . "

"Here's the party!" The drawl was thick, the voice low and husky. Val walked toward our table, hand outstretched, finger pointing. She walked with great care, swaying though the floor was steady, the sea calm. Her brilliant red hair hung in a soft cloud around her face. She wore no makeup and looked young, young and vulnerable and drunk. A white cable sweater hung almost to the knees of her jeans. Loose thongs slapped against her feet as she walked.

Evelyn quickly rose. "Val, I'll come with you—"

"Keep your seat, Evie." Val pushed against Evelyn's shoulder. "You can't break up the party." The singsong words slurred. "After all, it's the golden girl's birthday, isn't it?" She bowed toward Sophia, righted herself with difficulty. "Sophia celebrates another year." Val's lips trembled. "Another year." Tears trickled down her cheeks. She made no move to wipe them away.

The headwaiter, face impassive, moved quietly toward Sophia. "Madame, can I be of assistance?"

Sophia waved him away. Tight lines ran from her nose to the corners of her mouth. "Sit down, Val, or return to your cabin. I don't know what prompted this, but we'll talk about it tomorrow."

The headwaiter and several servers moved between our table and the rest of the room, unobtrusively screening our table from view. The pianist played Debussy's Arabesque no. 1. Diners talked, unaware of the drama at our table.

Val placed her hands on the back of Evelyn's chair, braced herself. "You don't know what has prompted this." She enunciated each word. "August 17."

Sophia touched the collar of pearls at her throat. "I'm

well aware that it is August 17. It happens to be my birthday. I'm sorry if that offends you, but I'll understand if you choose not to join us." Her tone was icy.

"You don't remember. How about that. Out of sight, out of mind." Val pressed shaking hands against her cheeks. "What difference did it make to you that Vic jumped off the cliff?"

The silence at our table was crushing, a weight of sorrow pulsing with anger. More shocking than the welter of emotions was the dawning comprehension on Sophia's face. Her eyes widened, her color faded, her lips went slack.

I felt pity for Sophia. It was clear beyond doubt that she had not remembered the date of Vic Riordan's death.

Jimmy was bewildered. "Vic?" He looked from Sophia to Val.

Val's hands dropped, closed into fists. "You've got a lot to learn about Sophia, Jimmy. She's number one, bigger than life, the only one who counts. You don't know about Vic, do you? Sophia never told you, did she? You've lived in my dad's house and you don't know. You worried about a boulder crashing over the cliff. That's how Vic died. My twin sister. She jumped to her death on the rocks because Sophia was making her go back to a school she hated."

Sophia looked stricken. "The school said she was fine, that she was making a good adjustment."

Val wavered on her feet, but her eyes, haunted, angry, implacable eyes, never moved from Sophia's face. "Did you ever ask Vic? You didn't bother. After all, what does a kid know about where they should live. You told Dad everything was fine. Who cares what a little kid says? They get over things, right? But Vic gave up. She went out and jumped and you're having a party tonight."

"Tonight . . ." Sophia's words came slowly, barely above

a whisper. "I knew it was August. I didn't mean to be un-kind. I hadn't forgotten." She lifted a shaking hand in appeal. "I've put it behind me, tried never to think about it. That's what I've always done. I can't let bad things pull at me or they'll bring me down. I didn't mean to hurt any-one."

Val's face was unforgiving. "That's your problem, So-phia. Maybe you don't mean to hurt anyone, but you do. You sent us away." The words ran into each other. "You didn't think about how we felt, how hard it was. And you've never stopped leaning on us. You convinced Dad that Alex was a fool about money. That's one reason Dad made that will. How can Alex ever learn if he doesn't get to try? You look at us like we're dogs in a show. Who gets a ribbon? Who gets disqualified? Judge Sophia will say."

A flush stained Sophia's cheeks. "Your father had con-fidence in my judgment. He knew I—"

"That's right. Financier Frank respected the lady. Let the peons bow in homage." Val couldn't quite articulate "homage." She lifted her arms, made a derisive bow, lurched, and would have fallen except for Evelyn's quick clutch of her arm.

Val shook free of Evelyn. "Sophia the All-Knowing. Have you got a Love-O-Meter tucked in your pocket? Did you hold it up and see how it registered when you decided to buy off Heather? Why don't you tell us how you know better than anybody who we ought to marry? You didn't care that Kent loved her. You just went to see her without a word to anybody—and for sure not to Kent—and of-fered her money to drop him."

"Let it go, Val." Kent's face ridged with misery.

"I won't let it go. I want to know how Sophia's so smart." Val cocked her head and stared at Sophia.

Sophia snapped, "Heather wasn't suitable—"

Val flung out a hand toward Kent. "You got it, Kent? Now we know what happened. Heather wasn't suitable."

"All of us know a young woman who's a bartender"— Sophia's voice was cold, definite—"couldn't fit into Frank Riordan's family. The fact that she took the money shows that I was right about her."

Kent's chair banged to the floor as he jumped up. He flung down his napkin and strode away, almost barreling into a waiter with a heavily laden tray.

Val rubbed a tear-streaked cheek. "You got it right there. Heather took the money. And broke Kent's heart. But he would have married her and been happy if it weren't for you. Now you're going to see if we all measure up to some mythical standard you've invented. All-Knowing Sophia." Abruptly her face crumpled. "What does any of it matter? Take the money and burn it. Money can't bring Vic back. Nothing will ever bring Vic back. Oh God, I should never have come. I want to go home. But we don't have a home. You took Dad away and you took our home away and you didn't even remember Vic." Val turned and moved unsteadily away.

Evelyn came to her feet. "Val, wait. Val, baby, I'm coming."

"I didn't remember." Sophia's lips trembled. "I didn't mean to upset anyone. I'm terribly sorry."

Rosie carefully folded her napkin. "You can say you're sorry. I hope it makes you feel better. But it's too late, Sophia. Years too late." She pushed back her chair, hurried after her sister and her aunt.

Alex shot a worried, uncertain look at Sophia. "I guess Madge and I'll be on our way." He stood, pulling his wife to her feet. "Yeah. It's too bad. Vic was a good little kid. If I'd known . . . I'd gone to the movies with some guys. I didn't know. Poor little kid. Such a long way down." He rubbed at his eyes. "Come on, Madge." He grabbed his wife's arm.

We three were left, Sophia and Jimmy and I. The protective screen of waiters dispersed. Our waiter began to remove plates without a word.

Sophia huddled in her chair. She looked at Jimmy, her gaze shocked and forlorn. "They hate me. They all hate me. I thought it was best for them to go away to school after Frank and I married. They could be independent."

Independent. Bereft of their home. Exiled, as they saw it, from their father, separated from their aunt.

Jimmy said nothing. Nor did I. Between us and Sophia there was the gulf that she couldn't bridge. We'd had children. We'd made mistakes, many mistakes, some grievous, some that could never be remedied, but neither of us would have blithely sent bereaved children away from their home.

"The school assured us Vic would be fine, that they'd work especially hard with her." Sophia's tone was beseeching.

Jimmy reached out, took her hand. "Let it go, Sophia. You can't change the past. What you need to do now is think of the future."

"They hate me . . ." She was wounded, struggling to understand.

I doubted there were magic words to help Sophia, but perhaps any words were better than none. I said gently, "They're struggling with grief."

"But it was so many years ago." Sophia looked bewildered.

Once again Jimmy and I were silent. He and I have both had losses in our lives. It doesn't matter how many years ago a death occurred, the pain remains forever. There can be peace, but there can never be forgetfulness.

I looked at Sophia with pity. She'd never cared for anyone enough to mourn. That might be the saddest judgment that could be made about another human being.

Sophia lifted her chin. She spoke with a flash of defiance. "I certainly wish I'd remembered, but surely they understand I didn't deliberately ignore the date. Why, if I'd thought, we could have had a memorial dinner for Vic. I wonder if I should plan something special?"

I could hear Rosie's bitter words: . . . *Come, sisters and brothers, stand up and talk about Vic* . . .

This wasn't any of my business, but I hoped to prevent an offer that would simply make matters worse. "Sometimes it's better to let sleeping dogs lie."

"I'd say the dogs are howling." Her tone was caustic, her eyes hurt. "I always meant well for them. I don't know what Frank would want me to do."

Jimmy looked at her gravely. "Don't think about it tonight. Tomorrow will be a new day. You can get off to a fresh start with them."

"And they"—Sophia was unsmiling—"with me."

# twelve

I greeted the morning on my balcony, grateful for the end of restless sleep threaded with unpleasant images. I shaded my eyes from brilliant sunshine. The ship was docked and I looked out on a medieval town with shining steeples and spires and red-roofed houses guarded by massive gray stone walls. The modern city to my left was a fascinating contrast.

Even though I knew Tallinn was one of the most extraordinary medieval quarters in Europe, I wasn't expecting this glorious scene. Five hundred years ago, an observer might have studied the town from the deck of a wooden sailing ship and seen very much what I was seeing now.

I refused to burden the sparkling day with recollections of last night's aborted celebration. I didn't plan to make any effort to connect with Jimmy or Sophia or the Riordans. There was nothing I could do to assuage the pain of the Riordan family. This morning I intended to be a traveler and experience the magic of the past.

I held to that resolve through breakfast, still fascinated by the old town awash in sunlight, and through the short drive on the tour bus to the thick walls and immense High Hermann Tower. The tower was a survivor of many turbulent lifetimes and military occupations. This morning the Estonian flag fluttered at the top of High Hermann as it had daily since 1989, several years before the last Russian troops withdrew.

We entered Upper Town and I admired the ornate exterior of Alexander Nevski Cathedral, still a bastion of Russian pride. Tourists thronged the cobbled streets. Walls of narrow old townhouses glowed pink and gray and gold in the sunlight. We climbed up and down stairways and curved through narrow passageways in a sprawling castle, a reminder of the inconveniences of regal living in medieval times: steep steps. It was a relief to return to the sunny outdoors. On an August morning, the ancient walls and streets were cheerful and welcoming. Most magnificent of all was the view from the square on Citadel Hill. A hundred feet below stretched Lower Town, the shops and homes of long-ago well-to-do merchants. A steep staircase led down but I declined to continue with the group, settling instead on a stone bench to look out over Lower Town. Behind me shops and cafés bordered the square. I had an hour before our bus departed for the ship. I might stroll down the steps. I might in a moment get a cup of coffee at one of the cafés. Or I might simply savor the sun and the peace.

"Henrie O."

I came back from long ago, from imagining a world I'd never known—Teutonic knights, canny burghers, ladies in fine lace, bone-chattering winters, smoky interiors, and the desperate struggle to live another year—to look up into Evelyn's eager face. She pointed at the space beside me. "May I join you?"

I smiled a welcome, patted the bench. "It's a lovely view."

She surveyed Lower Town with a cheerful smile and

settled comfortably beside me. "It's a wonderful day." She sounded positively ebullient. "I'm glad I ran into you. I wanted to tell you how much I appreciate what Jimmy's done."

My surprise must have been evident.

"Oh"—she sounded faintly embarrassed—"I supposed you and he kept in close touch. That is"—she wriggled uncomfortably—"I know you are good friends and I'm sure you'll have a chance to talk to him and I don't usually see him except when Sophia's around and I didn't want to say anything in front of her so please tell him he's made a world of difference."

"Good." I hadn't the faintest idea what she was talking about.

"Of course, I've always liked Jimmy. I felt he was way too—" She broke off in confusion. "Anyway, he has the best interests of the children—"

It grated on me every time she called the Riordan siblings "children." They were in their mid-to-late twenties. Young, yes. Children, no.

"—at heart. In fact, he's worked a miracle."

"Miracle?" I was startled.

Evelyn brushed back a straggling red curl. "He came around and talked to each one of us, except Val, of course. She isn't feeling well." Her eyes defied me to define Val's malaise otherwise. "Jimmy's so sensible." Her tone was admiring. "If we'd been all together, I'm afraid it wouldn't have worked out so well." Her look was shadowed. "There's too much sadness and anger. But Jimmy's always calm and kind and he made it absolutely clear that Sophia is terribly sorry and truly wants to make amends. We all have to go on. That's how life is. It will be so much better for the children if they can put bitterness behind them, start all over. Everyone knows Sophia has the best of intentions. It's too bad she's never felt closer to the children." A quick sigh. "Well, it doesn't help to dwell on these things."

It was uncannily close to Sophia's disclaimer at the dinner.

"But"—Evelyn brightened—"tomorrow in St. Petersburg after we visit the Hermitage, we're going to Rossi's Restaurant at the Grand Hotel Europe for dinner. It's a famous place and very elegant. Tchaikovsky once stayed at the hotel." She gave a little laugh. "And Elton John. That's fun, isn't it, to think about their music together? Sophia's called ahead and made the reservation. Jimmy said you are invited, but I wanted to ask you specially just in case you might have felt awkward."

"That's lovely." I smiled. "And very kind of you, Evelyn. I'll look forward to seeing the hotel and enjoying dinner."

She clapped her hands together and beamed at me. "That's wonderful. We'll all go together to the museum and on to the hotel."

After our tour bus returned to the ship, I went to the pool deck and ordered a hot dog and french fries. I piled the hot dog high with relish and onions, added generous splashes of ketchup and mustard, and settled at a table in the open area near the pool. Most of the deck chairs were occupied by glistening, darkly tanned sun worshipers. The prevalence of skin the shade of mahogany made me wonder at the lack of awareness of skin cancer.

"This chair free?" Rosie Riordan nodded toward the opposite seat.

First Evelyn. Now Rosie. "Yes. Please join me."

Rosie unloaded her tray, a cheeseburger with everything and fries. She grinned. "Gotta eat American at least once a week. Actually, I've had a burger every day."

We talked about the latest news—more bombs in the Middle East, a rock star dead of a drug overdose, the dip in the stock market—and all the while she watched me covertly.

We were sipping iced tea before she looked resolute, spoke briskly. "You made it clear at the outset that you are Jimmy's friend."

I nodded, my face studiously pleasant and uncommunicative.

"I'd like to ask a favor. Did you know he's schmoozed Sophia, persuaded her to give us all another chance to show our party manners?" The words were light, but her gaze was bleak.

"Evelyn told me." I was tempted to ask Rosie if she preferred that Jimmy leave them on the outside looking in. But it wasn't up to me to destroy the détente. "I'm glad everyone is in accord." That wasn't true, of course. Sometimes there is no point in being absolutely accurate. At least for the moment, the Riordans were in a state of truce with Sophia.

Rosie's smile was rueful. "I wish. Anyway, Evelyn and I want to try and hold everything together until we get home, keep everything calm. It doesn't matter about the money."

I pictured a crashing boulder. The money didn't matter?

"The problem is that it was a big deal to Jimmy to talk to each of us directly and privately. I told him Val was sick this morning—"

I wasn't surprised. Val was likely struggling with a devastating hangover.

"—and I said I could speak for her." A frown creased her face. "Jimmy made it clear he wants to talk to her, give her Sophia's apology in person. That's a bad idea. A really bad idea. Val's shaky and upset and it took me and Evelyn both to persuade her to come along on Thursday. I'd talk to Jimmy about it, but Val would be furious if I did. Would you explain to Jimmy that the best thing he can do with Val is back off?" She looked at me hopefully.

"I'll do what I can." I smiled. "I think he'll understand." I hesitated, then spoke because I thought I should. "Is alcohol Val's way of dealing with sorrow?"

Rosie's face was wary though her answer was smooth and quick. "Oh no. That was my fault. Yesterday was a hard day. I thought a drink would make her relax. I didn't think." Too smooth. Too quick.

I saw the pain in her eyes and defensive, dogged desperation. No wonder she didn't want Jimmy to talk to Val today, not while she was trembling and haggard and only too clearly recovering from a drunk. Rosie knew Jimmy was perceptive. She didn't want Jimmy to talk to Sophia about Val and alcohol. What price, then, the dissolution of Val's trust?

I found an envelope slipped beneath the door when I returned to my cabin and realized it was a reply to my e-mail from Margaret. There was no hurry about opening it. Last night Val had scraped away the dirt from those bones, revealing Sophia's interference, however well meant, in Kent's love affair.

The message light blinked on my telephone. I reached out a hand, let it fall. I wanted a moment more of peace before I responded, reluctant to be drawn deeper into the Riordan family distress.

I poured a tumbler of water, added ice from the bucket. I settled on the balcony, admired once again the brightness of the pitched red roofs in the medieval town, knew this was a sight to savor that I would never see again. A tender maneuvered alongside, bringing the pilot. The *Clio* sailed in less than an hour, en route to fabled St. Petersburg. For a short while we would be visitors there, transient beings in a transient world, but possibly there might be reconciliation for a struggling family at an old hotel that must have known dramas beyond measure.

For now, I basked in the sun and looked across the harbor at the graceful steeple of the Church of St. Olaf. I would long remember Tallinn. I smiled as I recalled the old building on the town square that has housed a pharmacy within its walls since 1422. Long-ago patients quaffed hot red wine and were prescribed lamb's wool, fish eyes, and ground rubies. I wondered what effect a mixture of hot wine and ground rubies would have on the digestive system. Was it the ancient equivalent of bicarb of soda?

I wondered how Val was feeling. She was so young and, I feared, so lost.

I finished the water, was still reluctant to hear the waiting message. I wanted to distance myself from Sophia's world even though I knew I could not. The *Clio* docked at noon tomorrow at St. Petersburg. I picked up the cruise booklet provided by the ship and read: ". . . Tsar Peter founded St. Petersburg in 1703 in an unappealing physical site, subject to floods and cursed by a humid, foggy, rainy climate and six months of winter. Despite its location, the efforts of Peter and his daughter Elizabeth and most particularly Catherine the Great created the loveliest neoclassical city in the world . . ."

I closed the booklet and dropped it on the small table. Drawn to duty, I stepped into the cabin and picked up the telephone. Yes, I wanted to distance myself from Sophia's world, but I was caught up in the currents of her stepchildren's lives and not quite able to swim free.

I punched up the message:

"Henrie O"—Jimmy's voice was robust, upbeat— "good news. It looks like everything's going to work out. I've persuaded Sophia to drop the idea of these breakfast meetings and instead we'll have a bang-up dinner at one of the fine hotels in St. Petersburg. She'll announce that the trusts will be dissolved. You know how Sophia is. She can never resist a dramatic flourish. She's out on the balcony now, putting together a tribute to Frank. So"—his relief was palpable—"from now on, we can relax. I want you to have fun, forget about all of this. We hope you'll have dinner with us. Sophia appreciates your efforts." A pause. "Thanks, Henrie O, for coming. For being my friend. And Sophia's."

I replaced the receiver. I was Sophia's acquaintance. Not her friend. But I wished her well. I felt an instant of sadness for brilliant, well-meaning, imperceptive Sophia. She would, perhaps not even realizing it herself, expect Frank's children to shower her with gratitude and appreciation. I doubted the dinner could possibly rise to her expectations. I only hoped the Riordans would manage to tamp down their enmity for this very important—to them—gathering.

It was kind of Jimmy to thank me, although I hadn't contributed to the rapprochement. Jimmy deserved that credit. I was delighted to resign from the Take-Care-of-Sophia Committee and devote myself to sightseeing. I was turning to step back onto the balcony when I saw the envelope with Margaret's e-mail.

I scooped it up, took it with me, and settled again in the

comfortable chair to soak up the afternoon sunshine. I slipped out the printed e-mail.

The message was pure Margaret.

You got any other easy jobs for me? Took a half day to run down any info, find out that Kent's girlfriend was Heather Bennett. I won't bore you with the travail required to discover her best friend Angela Rodriguez. Angela works in a travel agency. I got her on the phone and pitched a tale about being in the bar recently— Heather works at the Red Carousel—and I was worried about Heather, thought she looked so thin, and whatever had happened to her and was there anything I could do? It didn't take much to get her started on the world's biggest slimewad Kent Riordan.

If you've missed the soaps on your trip, I've got a dandy for you. How do you like this: rich young man dallies with girl from blue-collar background, swears undying fealty, then, apparently seeing the error of his ways—how will his preppy friends receive this charming but uneducated waif?—sends his stepmom with a check to spring him free. Brokenhearted orphan girl, holding down two jobs to keep food on the table for herself and younger brother, whom she rescued from their abusive uncle, accepts check because it is the wish of her beloved but donates money to local homeless mission. Spurned girl despondent. Still working, but shadow of former self, friends worry she will fall ill.

So is truth stranger than fiction? You betcha. Sad story, Henrie O. Next time you ask me to dig up the dirt, try for some happier circumstances. Riordan is a world-class jerk, according to Angela Rodriguez. Angela's definitely Heather's champion. They both have younger brothers in a neighborhood basketball league.

Angela's really bitter about Kent, says he told Heather
he loved her, wanted to marry her, and Angela says
Heather adored Kent but didn't think she was good
enough to marry him, and when the breakup came,
blamed herself, said she wanted him to be happy.
Heather's twenty-two, mother died when she was eight,
dad left the kids with his sister, her husband a drunk,
Heather lit out with her little brother Buddy when she
was sixteen and he was twelve, been working ever
since, managed to keep them afloat without getting into
drugs or prostitution, which means a gold-star effort.
Here's the stats, fyi . . .

Margaret included Heather's address, cell number, apparently no landline phone, which wasn't unusual for young
people, as well as work, home, and cell numbers for Angela Rodriguez.

I heard the piercing whistle and the ship began to move,
sliding away from the shore. I looked at the clock. Three
o'clock in the afternoon. It was—I figured for a moment—in the middle of the night in California. I should
wait until evening to place a call, hope to catch Angela
Rodriguez before she left for work.

If I decided I should place that call.

I climbed to the sundeck to watch Tallinn recede in
the distance, next stop St. Petersburg. The railings here
and on the pool deck below were lined with passengers,
some taking pictures, some waving farewell to the small
boats following alongside. The pale blue sky was clear,
the sunshine warm. I felt curiously separated from my
fellow travelers. I wished my every thought could be focused on this lovely moment on a luxurious ship en route
to one of the world's greatest cities. Instead, I had to

decide whether to try to find out the truth about Heather and Kent and Sophia.

Whatever I did, lives would be affected.

If I hadn't contacted Margaret, I could have left well enough—or ill enough—alone. But now I knew too much and could not pretend ignorance. Someone was lying. Angela. Kent. Heather. Or Sophia.

Did Kent ask Sophia to buy off Heather?

Did Sophia tell Heather the check was from Kent? Was that a lie?

Did Heather believe the check was from Kent or did she lie to Angela?

Did Angela accuse Kent without knowing any facts?

I lifted my hand to wave at the occupants of a gleaming mahogany speedboat.

I recalled the conversation I'd overheard at Tivoli between Kent and Rosie. The pain in his voice had been genuine. I believed Kent loved Heather, that he wanted her on any basis, that he grieved for her.

If that was true, he had not asked Sophia to offer Heather a check in his name.

So the question remained: Had Sophia lied to Heather or had Heather or Angela created the fiction that the check came from Kent?

I didn't have to know to satisfy my own curiosity. I had to see if I could find out the truth because if Sophia lied to Heather, Kent must be told.

I had an after-dinner coffee in the main lounge and listened to Latin rhythms. A handsome couple, her white ruffled dress swirling, danced a dramatic tango. I love to tango. Richard was a wonderful dancer, not a usual skill for a newspaperman. I smiled in remembrance. It was almost as if Richard were there with me, short blond hair with reddish glints, quizzical eyes, a loving smile on his broad open face. We'd had fun, Richard and I. We laughed. We loved. We lived. There is no better epitaph.

At eight o'clock I said good evening to two sisters from New Jersey with whom I'd shared a table. The ship was ablaze with lights and good cheer, men in dinner jackets, women in elegant gowns. It seemed inordinately quiet when I closed my cabin door behind me.

I sat at the small desk, my hand resting on the receiver. Once I placed this call, there would be no turning back. I met my own gaze in the mirror. I looked solemn despite my festive peony-bright dress and gold-plated necklace with dangling azure crystals.

I picked up the receiver, dialed. I tried Angela's home number first and triggered the answering machine. I clicked off. It was too early for her to be at work. I dialed her cell.

True to her generation, it was answered on the second ring. "Angela Rodriguez."

I liked her voice, fresh, firm, pleasant, crisp. As we all do, I formed a picture in my mind of a young woman I likely would never see: raven-dark hair, intelligent gaze. She sounded forthright and capable.

"Angela, I'm calling from a ship on the Baltic Sea." I hoped this fact, surely intriguing to a travel agent, would buy me a few minutes of her patience. "My name is Henrie O Collins and—"

The interruption was swift. "What ship?"

"The *Clio*. We've just left Tallinn en route to St. Petersburg." I hurried to forestall a disclaimer that her agency had no travelers aboard. "I need help on behalf of Heather Bennett. I may have information that will be important to her."

"What connection does Heather have to a cruise in the Baltic?" Her voice was wary. "I had a call yesterday from somebody who wanted to know about Heather. What's going on?"

"Kent Riordan did not instruct his stepmother to offer money to Heather. He knew nothing of that offer until he was told Heather accepted a check to drop him." I held tight to the receiver, hoping she wouldn't sever our connection. "Kent and his family are aboard the *Clio*. At a dinner, it became clear that his stepmother acted on her own initiative to end their relationship."

I heard a quick-drawn, derisive breath. "And pixies turn beer green on St. Pat's Day."

"I'm calling you at great expense to find out the truth." I kept my tone pleasant. "Why are you positive Kent provided the money?"

Her exasperation was clear. "That's what happened. He's a jerk. And Heather's still crazy about him. I keep telling her he's good riddance but she gets thinner and thinner. She's lost hope. If it weren't for Buddy, I don't know what might happen. She keeps on for him. She's sweet and gentle and not tough, not at all tough. I keep telling her she's beautiful, I know a lot of nice guys, I'll fix her up. She shakes her head. She has really soft brown hair and a thin face—awfully thin now—and deep purple eyes like an iris in the spring. They say nobody dies of a broken heart. I don't know if that's true. She gets thinner every day. She told me what happened, how Kent's stepmother brought a check and said Kent wanted her to have it because he thought the world of her but knew they weren't right for each other. Heather said she understood"—there was a sob in Angela's voice—"she knew she wasn't good enough for him but it showed how good and kind he was to send her money, and she didn't want to take it but she couldn't say no because that would be mean. She didn't want to be mean to him!"

"She took the check." The cashed check was all that had been needed to convince Kent that Heather didn't love him.

Angela's reply was swift, uncompromising. "She gave every penny to the mission. I can give you the phone number. Call and ask."

I wanted to be certain I had it right. "Heather told you specifically that his stepmother said the check was from Kent?"

"Yes."

"You're sure Heather was telling you the truth?"

"Bitter truth. I'll never forget that day, the only time she's missed work. I found her in her apartment, sitting there, staring at nothing. Hurting. Why would Heather lie? Make it worse than it was?"

Why indeed? I didn't think Heather had lied. I didn't think Angela was lying. I didn't think Kent had lied. That left Sophia. "I see."

"Do you honestly believe Kent didn't know?" Angela's voice was thoughtful.

Once again I was in Tivoli, the long-ago music boisterous and happy, hearing Kent's anguished voice.

"Angela"—I was crisp—"I'm positive Kent had nothing to do with his stepmother's offer. He only knew Heather accepted a check."

She drew her breath in quickly. "That's horrible."

Sophia's interference, even if well meant, was altogether too clever and, ultimately, cruel.

"Why would she do that?" There was a trace of disbelief yet in Angela's tone.

"To be fair to Sophia, she felt it was in Kent's best interest. I imagine Sophia told Heather the check was on behalf of Kent, perhaps knowing that Heather would assume Sophia meant Kent sent the check." Sophia would never lack for subtlety of expression. If taxed, she could reply that certainly she had made the offer on his behalf, for his protection. If she had been misunderstood, that was yet another indication of Heather's lack of suitability. "I doubt if Heather inquired deeply."

"You're sure?"

I had a sense of inexorability. My answer would unleash events beyond my control. But I had to answer. My voice was grave but definite. "I am sure that Kent did not know or authorize the offer of a check."

"That's wonderful." Angela's voice was soft. "I can't wait to tell Heather. She's out of town until tonight. Buddy got a camp scholarship and she's gone to pick him up. I'll tell her as soon as they get back." Angela was joyous. "It will mean the world to her."

I felt like a lion tamer in the performance ring. "Let me tell Kent first. He'll want to call Heather. For reasons that have nothing to do with Kent and Heather, it would be better if I spoke with him tomorrow night. Thursday night." After the dinner. After Sophia was publicly committed.

Angela was silent.

"Please let me handle it. After all"—I tried to put a smile in my voice—"I'm the one who discovered the mix-up."

"Not a mix-up." Angela was firm. "That woman deliberately lied. Somebody should tell her in no uncertain terms—"

I was equally firm. "It's Heather and Kent that matter. There's no point in making matters worse between Kent and his stepmother. He's very angry now. If I wait until tomorrow night, there won't be any reason for Kent to be in contact with Sophia." If I was as adroit as the most skilled mediator, perhaps Kent would focus on his reunion with Heather, understand that an explosive scene with Sophia would be unwise and unavailing.

"Tomorrow night. Okay. There's the time difference." A travel agent had no difficulty making the adjustment between California and Russia. "That's morning here. It will be a great way to start Heather's day."

I felt limp when I hung up. I remembered a long-ago visit to Niagara, watching the incredibly swift current sweep toward the edge. If a boat came downstream un-aware of the falls, there would never be time to make for shore. I hoped I'd kept a tight grip on the tiller of a frail craft and avoided utter disaster.

## thirteen

THE *Clio* docked in St. Petersburg at noon, gliding up the fabled Neva river to her berth at the Old City Harbor. I looked forward to the drive through the city to the Hermitage, where Catherine the Great housed her ever-growing collection of masterpieces. I also looked forward to the dinner at the Grand Hotel Europe.

The announcement of their forthcoming inheritance should please the Riordan siblings. They would never be fond of Sophia, but possibly they might be more inclined to be agreeable. After we returned to the ship, hopefully in a glow of bonhomie, I'd invite Kent to join me in Diogenes Bar. Mahogany and teak and nautical paintings combined with Oriental rugs and muted piano music to create an ultracivilized environment. I'd ask Rosie as well. Between the two of us, surely we could convince Kent that getting home to Heather was more important than confronting Sophia. I'd suggest he talk to the purser, see about arranging a flight home from our next port, Helsinki.

As I strolled toward the breakfast buffet line Thursday morning, I saw Jimmy and Sophia at their usual table. I was reaching for a plate when Kent Riordan strode into the breakfast area, handsome face twisted in a furious scowl. He'd not yet shaved. He wore a T-shirt and shorts and espadrilles.

It didn't take a crystal ball to figure out what had happened. Heather came home and Angela told her of my call. Angela owed me nothing and I understood her eagerness to share good news. But there was no trace of excitement and joy in Kent's face. He headed straight for Sophia and Jimmy.

I moved fast, skidded to a stop in front of him. He tried to sidestep me, not recognizing me or not caring.

I grabbed his arm. "Kent." I spoke sharply, trying to pierce the anger that enveloped him. His arm was rigid beneath my fingers. "I called Angela, found out the truth."

He stared at me. His breath came in quick, short spurts. "Sophia lied." His gaze fastened on Sophia. "She lied to Heather. She lied to me. I could kill her."

"Come with me." My voice was loud, demanding his attention.

"Get out of my way." Kent yanked his arm free, tried to go around me.

I moved too.

His only recourse was to pause or knock me down. He grabbed my arm, his hand like steel. "Get—"

"Heather loves you. You would not know that"—I paused between each word for emphasis—"except for me. You would never have known if I hadn't made inquiries. That has to be worth something to you. You owe me a few minutes of your time. Now."

He looked at me, saw me.

I pointed toward the deck. "Five minutes. That's little enough for me to ask."

"Five minutes." They might have been words in another language. He loosened his grip. His hand fell away. "Sorry." He swallowed hard. "I didn't mean to be rude.

But—" He twisted toward Sophia. His face was hard again with anger and bitterness.

"Please." I spoke quietly. "Come out on deck with me." There was no point in his railing at Sophia. She would never understand the injury she had inflicted.

He hesitated, shot another furious glance toward Sophia, then turned and we walked toward the door. On deck, we went to the stern and stood by the railing.

I welcomed the fresh sea-scented air. The *Clio*'s massive wake spread a ruffle of white against the dark blue water. Gulls squawked. In the distance, another ship's deep-throated horn gave greeting. It was high season in the Baltic and gleaming cruise ships passed us every hour or so.

I talked slowly, hoping time would diminish some of his anger. I traced my efforts, contacting Margaret, Margaret's e-mail, the discrepancy between what she had learned and Val's revelations at dinner, my talk with Angela.

I held his gaze. "You understand that you would have no future with Heather if I had not intervened."

His face creased in despair. His big hands bunched into fists. "Heather won't come back to me."

I was jolted. "Even though she knows that you didn't ask Sophia to give her a check?"

He lifted one fist, rubbed his knuckles against his bristly cheek. "She has the sweetest voice." His eyes were soft, filled with love and longing. "I was still asleep when the phone rang. It was like a miracle to answer the phone and hear her. I couldn't believe it. On the Baltic and Heather talking to me. I've dreamed about her so much, I thought it was a dream. She talked fast, much faster than she ever really does. She said Angela had found out I had nothing to do with Sophia saying I wanted to be free. She wanted me to know she took the check because she thought I was good and kind and it would hurt my feelings if she turned it down, but she couldn't ever have used any of it. She gave the money to the mission. She said she still loves me, but she knows we weren't meant to be, that my world is too different, and if my family didn't want her, then it would be a bad thing for her to take me away from them. She said she'll always love me"—his voice was hoarse—"but I should find someone who was right for me. She hung up. I called and called and there was no answer. She'd turned off the answering machine. I couldn't even leave a message. I know she was sitting there, hearing the phone ring and crying. Do you see what Sophia's done to us? I'm going to tell her—"

"That she interfered when she shouldn't have? That's true. Berating Sophia won't get Heather back. And"—I was emphatic—"you can get Heather back. The minute you get home, you can take Rosie and Val with you and they'll sweep Heather in their arms, make her welcome. It may take time, but it can be done. It can and will happen, but it can only happen because I made it possible. There's a quid pro quo, Kent, and I'm calling it due right now."

The hardness of his face eased. He stared at me, brows bunched, eyes questioning. "What do you want?"

"Promise me you will keep away from Sophia this morning, take the afternoon Hermitage tour with the family—"

He took a step back, scowling.

"—and come with us to the hotel for dinner. Don't talk to Sophia. When dinner is over"—I couldn't reveal the announcement Sophia planned to make—"keep your mouth shut, come back to the ship, go to your cabin. That's what I want."

He stood with his shoulders hunched, hands jammed

into the pockets of his shorts. Obviously the thought of spending time with Sophia galled him. But slowly, reluctantly, he nodded. I saw grudging acceptance in his eyes. He wanted desperately to confront Sophia, but he understood he owed me a debt.

"Do I have your promise?" I held out my hand.

Solemnly he shook it.

Disaster was averted. At least for now. Perhaps I could distract Kent enough that his initial boiling fury would drain away. "Meanwhile, there are a bunch of things you can do to fix up your future with Heather. Wire flowers. Rent a billboard near her apartment, put up a message: 'Heather, will you marry me? Kent.' See if you can get a flight out of Helsinki to go home. Send telegrams. Have Val and Rosie send telegrams. Does Heather have a computer? Go up to the Internet lounge, e-mail her—"

"You think she'll come back to me?" Hope struggled against fear.

"She will come back." There was no doubt in my mind. To someone in Heather's precarious financial condition, ten thousand dollars was a fortune. She'd given it away. Oh yes, she loved Kent and love has a way of winning out against all odds.

A huge grin transformed his face, making him young, even more handsome, utterly appealing. A big hand gripped my shoulder. "I can get on the Net?"

I pointed toward the stairs. "Deck 10. Forward. Port side."

I watched him go, a man in a very big hurry.

I smiled. Perhaps now everything would go smoothly.

# fourteen

THE bus rolled to a stop in front of the lime green Winter Palace. The guide reminded passengers to leave all umbrellas, coats, bags, and cameras on board. Since the temperature was in the eighties and the sky cloudless, Evelyn and I exchanged a smile.

As the door to the coach opened, Evelyn gathered up her straw purse and smiled at Rosie. Kent was sitting by Val, the two of them in deep conversation. It had not been especially obvious that Kent was keeping his distance from Sophia. Sophia smiled at Jimmy as she pointed to the bronze angel atop the pink granite monolith of the Alexander Column in the huge Palace Square. Madge thumbed through a guidebook. I was willing to bet she wanted to ditch the museum and go to Nevsky Prospect, the main shopping street. I wondered if she wanted amber jewelry or a matrioshka doll. Jewelry, very likely. Alex gestured toward the museum. Madge's face folded in a pout.

As a priest I once knew was fond of saying, all was as it should be, an enigmatic pronouncement that always puzzled me. Perhaps now I'd fathomed its meaning. There was, at this moment, nothing untoward or worrisome. The group was together and there was a semblance of bonhomie.

I felt even more relaxed when we went into the entrance vestibule, jammed with tourists in passels of twenty or thirty with guides shouting in English, German, Italian, Greek, and Japanese. Our guide held up a staff with a red flag on it with the number 14 for our coach and off we went.

Despite crowds thicker than ants on spilled honey, sweltering stuffy rooms, tourists jostling for space, and the melee of languages as guides shouted to their charges, the Hermitage was spectacular.

One dramatic vista was supplanted with another and another. It was a challenge to stay with our group as we sped through galleries, glimpsing glory upon glory. Though I was soon surfeited by the abundance of beauty, some masterworks were especially memorable: Leonardo's luminous *Madonna and Child* and Rembrandt's touching *Return of the Prodigal Son.*

I lost all sense of where we were or where we were going, my mind whirling with facts, my senses burdened by never-ending flashes of gilt, marble, shining wood, and massive pillars. I kept within a few paces of my fellow travelers, determinedly following the guide's hoisted flag, and, truth to tell, was glad when the four-hour tour was almost done.

The red flag bobbed ahead. Our group, surrounded by competing, pushing hordes of tourists, fetched up on a landing near a wide staircase that plunged down perhaps a hundred and fifty steps. This area had a dingy workaday appearance, the steps dull and dirt-streaked, a far cry from the grand Main Staircase where we'd entered.

Anna, our tall, slender guide, waited for a straggler, then shepherded us near the top of the stairs and a stall with postcards and prints for sale. "Ladies and gentlemen, there are free restrooms at the base of the stairs. We will pause here for ten minutes. You may shop and then we shall return to the coach for our drive back to your ship." I was looking forward to escaping from the tour and reaching the hotel.

I looked down the steep, crowded stairs. I considered finding the restroom, knew walking down the long staircase would require climbing back up. I smiled at a rowdy contingent of huge young men good-naturedly bumping and shoving each other at the bottom landing. As they started up the steps, loud shouts boomed, "Hurry up, mate." Two young men, dodging other tourists, raced each other upward, faces red with exertion. I guessed a sports team from Australia and wondered if they played rugby or soccer. They dwarfed ordinary travelers.

I tried to move back from the landing and felt surrounded by poking elbows and brushing shoulders. The world was entirely too much with me. I was hot, tired, thirsty, and ready to leave. As our busload shifted and regrouped near the stall, some looking at the displays, others turning to go down the steps, I was vaguely aware of my fellow travelers, though other visitors were crowding in upon us. I glimpsed Jimmy, taller than most. Evelyn was fanning herself with a scarf she'd loosened from her throat. I shifted my position, realized I was very near the top step, tried to move away, found my progress blocked.

A shrill scream rose above the hubbub. Everyone near the top of the stairs stood frozen, staring down the steps. Sophia tumbled forward, arms flung wide. Cries and shouts rose in the hot sticky air.

"Hey, hey." One of the big young men who had been racing upward abruptly lunged to his right. Massive hands reached up to grip Sophia. As he caught her, he propelled his heavy body forward, managing to turn as he crashed into the steps so that he took the impact.

It happened in an instant.

Jimmy raced down the steps, reached Sophia and her rescuer. He knelt, gathered her in his arms. The guide was right behind him. "Madame"—her clear voice carried—"how did this happen?" Two security guards pounded up the steps.

The athlete's mates hauled him upright. He pushed them away with a loud laugh. "I'm fine, boys. Better than on the field." He reached up to massage his left shoulder. "Let's see to the lady."

A freckle-faced young man turned toward Sophia. "Coo, that was a fine catch Brian made."

Jimmy struggled for breath. "Can you move, Sophia? Be careful. Are you hurt?"

"I don't think so." Her voice was reedy. She held to his arm and shakily came to her feet. Her face was gray-white. She jerked away from Jimmy. "I'm fine." She turned toward her rescuer, who stood there rubbing his shoulder. She reached out. "Thank you."

He tried to shrug, winced, awkwardly took Sophia's hand. "Anytime, ma'am." A flush of embarrassment tinged his cheeks with pink. "Glad to help."

"Brian?" Her voice was stronger. She held to his hand, looked up at him.

"Brian Wheeler. Brisbane. Here for a soccer match. Just kidding around today, running up the steps. Guess it was a lucky thing."

"For me, very lucky." She squeezed his hand, dropped it, then looked at Jimmy. "Get Brian's name and address so I can thank him properly."

The athlete threw out his big hands. "No need, ma'am. My pleasure."

"You saved my life." Sophia took another deep breath.

Some color was edging back into her face. She nodded at the guide. "I wish to return to the ship. Now."

A security guard loomed over her, his wrinkled face in a tight frown. "Madame, can you tell us how this occurred?"

She gazed at him without expression. "I"—her pause was noticeable—"fell. That's all. Thank you for your concern." She took a deep breath, once again swayed.

Jimmy reached out. "Careful, honey. Let me help. We'll get you some water, a place to sit down. Maybe we'd better get a doctor."

Sophia pushed his hand away. She didn't look at him. Her words were swift. "Don't touch me."

Jimmy stiffened. Slowly his hand dropped. He looked at her uncertainly. "Are you in pain?"

I was on the landing, a few feet away. The Riordans clustered uneasily near me. Evelyn was breathing in quick gulps as if she could not get enough air. Rosie curved a supporting arm around her shoulders. Val's face was unreadable, neither shocked nor concerned. She might have been watching a film that held no interest for her. Madge opened and shut the clasp of her linen purse, her bright eyes never leaving Sophia. Alex wiped his forehead with a handkerchief. Kent's frown was dark and intense.

I wondered which of them had pushed Sophia.

Sophia took a deep breath, waved away the security guard. "No harm done." She nodded peremptorily at the guide. "I should like to return to the ship immediately."

That answered one question. There was to be no dinner of reconciliation this evening at the Grand Hotel Europe.

Sophia moved slowly, stiffly up the steps. She stopped opposite the clutch of Riordans, gazed at them dispassionately. "Dinner this evening is canceled. We shall return to

the ship. I expect all of you"—her icy gaze included me—
"to be present in my cabin at eight o'clock tonight."

I'd been in my cabin only long enough to wash my face
and pour a tall tumbler of ice water when a vigorous
knock sounded. I opened the door and was surprised to
see a grim-faced Jimmy. I looked past him, but he was
alone. "I thought you'd be with Sophia."

"I thought so too." The words were quick, clipped.
"She wanted to be alone. She told me to go away, insisted
I leave."

I stood aside for him to enter. He walked to my small
sofa, flung himself down. I perched at the end of the bed.

Jimmy frowned. "Sophia and I have to talk. I understand why she didn't say anything at the museum. She
couldn't prove she'd been pushed, and getting Russian of-
ficials involved would have been a mess. When we got
back and I tried to talk to her about it, it was like clawing
on a rock. I can't get her attention. I guess she's in shock.
But this afternoon proves I'm right. One of the Riordans
pushed her."

Jimmy had to know about Kent. "Jimmy, I didn't have
a chance to tell you this morning. Kent is furious with
Sophia."

Jimmy looked weary. "You'd think he'd get over it.
That's history."

I shook my head. "Not history. Not yet." I told him
what Margaret had unearthed, the whole sad tale of
Heather and Sophia and the check.

He listened gravely. "Sophia lied to the girl?"

I spread my hands. "I imagine Sophia put it smoothly,
said she was authorized to give Heather a generous check
and surely Heather understood that she and Kent weren't
well suited. That's all it would have taken."

Jimmy scowled. "Sophia shouldn't have done that, but I blame Frank. He put Sophia in an impossible situation. She feels she has to do what she thinks Frank wanted and Frank would have been absolutely opposed to Kent marrying a girl from Heather's background."

"I can see that Sophia thought she was protecting Kent." Here I went, once again defending her.

Jimmy frowned, his thoughts obviously unpleasant. "Talk about raw passion! Val is clearly overwrought about the anniversary of Vic's death. Now all this surfaces about Sophia and Heather."

"I'm sorry." I had to take responsibility here.

He almost managed a wry smile. "Hey, I set you on the trail. I wouldn't expect you to ignore facts. Uncovering the truth is all to the good unless Kent pushed Sophia today. In any event, Sophia can't ignore being shoved down stairs. It's a miracle she's alive. If that guy hadn't reached up and got her . . ."

Sophia's rescue had been miraculous. She was the fortunate beneficiary of a superb athlete's reflexes and strength. And smarts. He'd not only managed to catch her hurtling body, he'd had the wit and power to force himself forward and turn as he fell, protecting her from the sharp-edged steps. Sophia owed her life to a snail, to spilled sherry, and now to a strong and quick-thinking young athlete from Australia. Three times she'd cheated death.

"Third time lucky." I stared soberly at Jimmy.

His eyes were haunted. "We have to protect her from another attempt. No one's luck runs that far. I intend to make sure nothing else happens. Sophia's upset now. But if she can't face up to the danger, I'll take charge. I'm going to find out what Evelyn knows. She can't refuse to face facts any longer. I want a witness when I talk to her. Will you come?"

* * *

Evelyn opened her cabin door a scant few inches. Her face was pale and drawn. Alarm flared in her eyes. "I thought it was the steward." She pressed a hand to her forehead. "I have a dreadful headache. How is Sophia?"

"She's sore. Upset. Scared." Jimmy looked at her gravely. "It's time for us to talk, Evelyn."

She made a fluttery gesture of reluctance. "Not now, please. I don't feel at all well. Such a frightening accident—"

His voice was hard. "Not an accident."

Evelyn stiffened. "The landing was crowded, people everywhere, shoving and crowding." She clutched a ruffle of her yellow sundress.

Jimmy shook his head. "Sophia knows someone tried to kill her."

"It was an accident." She reached up, clapped a hand to her face, turned away.

We stepped inside and Jimmy closed the door. Evelyn collapsed onto the sofa. The mirror on the opposite wall reflected a demoralized woman.

Jimmy sat on the side of the bed near the sofa. I took the straight chair from the desk, turned it to face her.

"Sophia didn't fall." Jimmy looked at her steadily. "Help me, Evelyn."

"Of course." She struggled to get up. "Does Sophia want me to come? I'll be glad to stay with her, do what I can."

"I want information." Jimmy sounded stern.

Evelyn's blue eyes widened. She said nothing, pressed her lips together in a thin line. The only movement in the small cabin was the ripple of the curtains from the breeze flowing in through the open balcony door.

Jimmy's look was imploring. "Who poisoned the sherry?"

Evelyn clasped her hands together, made no reply. Her lips quivered. Her breathing was quick and jerky.

"I'm asking you to help me save Sophia. But it isn't only Sophia you will save." His eyes never left her face. "You don't want one of Frank's children to be a murderer."

"No!" Evelyn's cry was anguished. "It isn't true. They wouldn't do anything like that. Never."

Jimmy leaned forward. "Why did you knock down the tray? Why did you wash out the sherry bottle?"

"It's your fault." Tears trickled down her cheeks. "You went storming up the hillside like you were pursuing the devil, and then you came back and you wanted to know where everyone was when the boulder came down. I knew it couldn't be true but it worried me and I kept thinking about it."

I felt this was nearly true, but it wasn't all the truth. Something more than Jimmy's fear triggered her own. Had Evelyn seen someone come down the hillside? Had one of the Riordans claimed to be in a particular spot at the time and Evelyn knew better?

She pulled a wad of Kleenex from her pocket, wiped at her eyes. "You've got to understand, I'm sure now that the sherry was all right. I didn't see anybody near it. I swear I didn't. But when I saw you start up the stairs with the tray, I had this scared, awful feeling. I came down the steps and knocked the tray over. But the boulder could have been an accident. After I knocked the tray down and everything was such a mess, I emptied out the rest of the bottle and washed it. I shouldn't have done it, but you'd made such a fuss about the boulder. I knocked the tray down on an impulse. I realize that was stupid. Now you think I saw someone tamper with it and I didn't."

I did not believe her. She knew more than she would

reveal. That was made clear by the desperate steadiness of her gaze, the tight clasp of her hands, the rigidity of her shoulders. We left her staring after us with frightened eyes.

We were almost to the end of the corridor when Jimmy said bitterly, "I'd like to wring her neck. Maybe every word's true about the sherry, but Evelyn knows something. Or guesses. Maybe she saw something in a face. Or overheard a conversation. Whatever it is, she'll never tell us. I have to warn Sophia. She can't trust any of them."

I wished for a sweater. The early evening air off the sea was chilly. Jimmy and I stood at the railing watching the lengthening shadows envelop St. Petersburg though the sun still hung on the horizon. We'd eaten in the informal dining room, a quick, somber meal. Twice he'd gone to their cabin. Each time Sophia sent him away, and he came back to me.

He scowled. "Why won't she talk to me?" He was irritated, impatient, uncertain.

The Jimmy I knew was almost always equable, rarely discomfited. This was a different Jimmy, his eyes hurt, his voice brusque.

I didn't answer. I didn't know how to answer. I wondered what he was thinking, what possibilities had occurred to him. The answer that I suspected would either shock him mightily or confirm his worst expectations. I hoped I was wrong. Sophia might simply be suffering from shock and trying to deal with fear on her own.

Perhaps.

I glanced at my watch. It was almost eight, time to go to Sophia's suite. "Jimmy, I don't think I should come this evening."

His frown was quick and intense. "Of course you

should. Sophia needs everybody in her corner she can get. I think the three of us can get her safely home, but it's going to take all of us working together. I've been looking ahead. The first thing to do is avoid being around any of the Riordans. That shouldn't be too hard. I want her to talk to the staff captain. He's second-in-command and he oversees security on the ship. Staff Captain Gerald Glenn." Jimmy's face suddenly looked younger, stronger, less burdened. Action was an antidote to fear. "Let's go. I've got a lot to tell Sophia. It's time she listened."

## fifteen

THERE were two doors in the corridor at the stern of Deck 6, Suites 6088 and 6091. Jimmy used his electronic card at the near door. We stepped into 6088 and I caught my breath at the view through the plate-glass windows of the balcony. The sliding door was open. The balcony, perhaps three times larger than mine, overlooked the Neva river, which was streaked with crimson from the setting sun. On the opposite bank the golden stone of Menshikov Palace was bathed in a red glow.

We were in a living room with the bedroom to the right. The furnishings included a blue damask sofa, two rust-colored armchairs, and a round wooden table with four straight chairs. The amber and blue design of the Oriental rug was repeated in the heavy drapes at the windows.

Sophia and a ship's officer stood near a wet bar. Sophia's crisp linen dress was dramatic, the white bateau top a sharp contrast to the black skirt. Golden ringlets framed a pale face. She looked regal. A jet necklace and bracelet accented the skirt. The officer stood with his feet apart in a white uniform crisp as a starched shirt. He was compactly built, perhaps five-ten with short-cut black hair, dark blue eyes, bony nose, and pointed chin. His thin, intense face held no expression.

Jimmy crossed to them, held out his hand to the officer. "Jimmy Lennox."

"Staff Captain Glenn." The officer's tone was noncommittal, as if he reserved judgment. He shook Jimmy's hand, but his glance was appraising.

"Staff Captain Glenn." Jimmy's smile was pure relief. He turned to his wife. "Sophia, thank God. Have you told him everything?"

Her gaze was distant, her expression remote. "We've talked. I'll make everything clear when the others arrive."

"Great." Jimmy clapped his hands together. "This is exactly what I wanted you to do. Staff Captain Glenn, this is Henrietta Collins, an old friend. As Sophia has probably told you, Henrie O's with us to help protect Sophia."

Glenn nodded. If the man had a smile in his repertoire, he was keeping it under wraps.

A knock sounded at the door.

Jimmy swung around, took two strides, opened the door, held it wide.

The Riordans clustered in the hallway. Evelyn was the first to enter. She'd changed from the wrinkled yellow sundress into a summery and cheerful cornflower blue V-neck silk blouse and a swirling skirt with huge white polka dots against a matching blue background. I suspected the stylish outfit had been a gift from Rosie. Despite her untidy red curls, Evelyn might have been the picture of holiday fashion except for her staring blue eyes and anxious face. Rosie was gorgeous in a bright pink cotton top and white cropped pants with a twining red rose design. Coppery hair glistening in a streak of sunlight, she swung into the room as if she hadn't a care in the world. Val moved sedately. Her hair was pulled back into a sleek knot, emphasizing her fine bone structure. She had the fixed look of a mannequin on a runway. Her herbal green linen tunic and cropped green linen trousers were decorated with an occasional modest daisy. The dark circles beneath her eyes were the only hint of a whiskey-drenched night. Alex was scrawny in a too-big blue polo. White shorts hit him mid-knee. He stepped inside with a reluctant frown. Madge was beautifully dressed in a pink floral embroidered sheath, perfect for her ice blond hair and fair complexion. Her bright blue eyes darted to Staff Captain Glenn, her gaze wary.

Evelyn reached out to pull the door shut.

Sophia looked at her sharply. "Where's Kent?"

Evelyn's gaze skittered away. "He wasn't able to come."

"I asked for everyone to be here." Sophia was imperious, her face cold and hard.

Evelyn's hands fluttered. "It . . . he . . . he's sick. Let's not make an issue of it. Please. I'll tell him everything that happens."

Glenn looked toward Sophia. "I'll step out and speak with him."

Sophia held up a hand. "That's not necessary. I'm sure Evelyn will accurately report back to Kent."

There was an instant of uncomfortable silence.

Evelyn bustled forward. "Sophia, we're all terribly upset about the accident this afternoon. Thank God you're all right."

"I'm a survivor. I intend to be a survivor." Sophia's words were clipped, her face bleak. She gestured at Jimmy. "You and Henrie O sit on the sofa. You should be together." It was a command, not a request.

I looked at Sophia sharply. Enmity flashed in her eyes.

Jimmy's brows drew down in a frown. He stood very still, head bent forward, face questioning.

I touched Jimmy's arm and moved toward the sofa. Reluctantly, Jimmy followed. I leaned back against a cushion. I kept my face pleasant, but I felt tightly strung as a guy wire. Sophia was proceeding with a well-thought-out, tightly controlled campaign, one she had neglected to share with Jimmy. I had no doubt that a storm was about to break and somebody was going to get hurt. I desperately hoped it would not be Jimmy.

"Evelyn, you and Rosie take the easy chairs." Sophia waited until they took their places as ordered. "Alex, Madge, and Val at the table." There was not a single if-you-please. The director had spoken.

When her audience was settled at her direction, Sophia glanced at each of us in turn, her stare measuring. She stretched out the moment, heightening the tension. I had a clear sense of her capabilities and an understanding of her success as a filmmaker. She knew how to structure a scene.

"One of you tried to kill me this afternoon."

Her quiet tone emphasized the enormity of her accusation.

Evelyn jumped to her feet. "Sophia, that's dreadful. You don't know what you're saying."

"Sit down!"

Evelyn's will was no match for Sophia's. Evelyn slowly sagged into the chair.

A thin smile curved Sophia's lips. "That's revealing. Only Evelyn objects. No one else said anything. How many of you know who is trying to kill me?"

Rosie folded her arms, her face sardonic. "Come off it, Sophia. We know you're a drama queen, but that's over the top."

Sophia walked toward the table. "Nice try, Rosie, but this afternoon can't be brushed away. When something stinks, there's a rotten egg somewhere. The boulder missed me. Evelyn"—Sophia's head swiveled toward her—"knew I shouldn't drink a particular glass of sherry. This afternoon, one of you, and I'm not forgetting our curiously absent Kent"—she pointed at each of us in turn, me, Jimmy, Evelyn, Rosie, Alex, Madge, and Val— "poked me in the back as I started down the stairs. I fell. I should have died. I was saved by sheer chance. Otherwise, I would be in a coffin in the ship's hold. I was pushed by one of the Riordan family, Evelyn, Alex, Madge, Rosie, Kent, Val." Her cold eyes rested on Jimmy and me. "Or my attentive husband. Or his lover."

Jimmy slowly stood. "Sophia." His face drained of color.

"I am including everyone who had the opportunity to kill me." There was no apology in her voice. "Sit down." She might have been speaking to an annoying guest.

Jimmy remained on his feet, face grim, hands clenched tight, staring at Sophia.

Sophia looked away first.

I would have given the world to take his hand, hold it in mine, tell him not to care so much, not to be wounded beyond healing. He was a good man, a decent and giving man, and Sophia had announced to the world that whatever she felt for him, it could not masquerade as love. Love believes and hopes and trusts. Sophia had taken his love and deemed it worthless.

I could not comfort him. Sophia would see that as a gesture of possession. I remained seated, troubled and increasingly angry.

Staff Captain Glenn stepped forward. "As I told Mrs. Lennox"—his deep voice was stern—"the incident should have been reported to the police in St. Petersburg. I understand her reluctance to involve the Russian authorities, both because of our limited time in port and because of the language barrier. However, I will pursue the matter with the full authority invested in me as second-in-command aboard the *Clio*. I intend to assure Mrs. Lennox's safety both on board ship and ashore. With that in mind, I expect every passenger to offer full cooperation."

No one spoke.

He looked at each of us in turn. "We will re-create the moment before Mrs. Lennox fell. Mrs. Collins, if you will be kind enough to bring me the throw cushions from the sofa."

I picked up two tasseled cushions and carried them to Glenn.

He took the cushions and placed them in a line in the center of the floor. "The cushions represent the edge of the staircase." He looked at Sophia. "Mrs. Lennox, stand where you were when you were pushed." He pulled a small notebook from his pocket and a pen.

Sophia stepped up to the cushions.

Glenn moved to one side, leaving a large space open behind Sophia. He gestured toward us. "Please position yourselves as you were when Mrs. Lennox fell."

There was a general flurry of movement.

Val stopped and stood with her hands on her hips. "The crowd was huge. It was worse than a subway in Tokyo. All kinds of people were jammed up next to me and that booth where they were selling stuff. I wasn't paying any attention to Sophia. How should I know where I was?"

Glenn was patient. "Surely you remember hearing her cry. Where were you?"

Val lifted her shoulders, let them fall, picked her way daintily as a cat past Sophia and stood near a tall blue pottery vase. "I was looking at the guidebooks."

I stopped a good ten feet behind Sophia. On the landing, I'd been part of a packed crowd. Even if I'd been watching Sophia, I doubt I would have been able to see who was near her. Or behind her.

Evelyn bustled close to Val. "There was a table with guidebooks and another with prints. I'd picked up a print of El Greco's *The Apostles Peter and Paul*. He painted both of them with narrow faces. Thin faces. I always think of Peter as being big. With a big face."

Madge pulled Alex farther behind Sophia. "We were together and we weren't even close to her. There were bunches of people between us."

"Where was Kent?" Sophia looked at each of the Riordans in turn.

Rosie lifted her hands, let them fall. "I think he was leaning on one of the big columns."

Jimmy moved slowly, his expression brooding. He took his place a little behind and to the left of Sophia as she faced down the stairs.

Glenn folded his arms, looked at Jimmy. "You were nearest Mrs. Lennox."

"I was." Jimmy's glance never wavered.

"Almost at her elbow?" Glenn's tone was sharp, suspicious.

"That's right. Very near." Jimmy spread his hands perhaps a foot apart.

Glenn stepped toward Jimmy. "Why didn't you see what happened to your wife?"

Jimmy's eyes narrowed. "Like Val said, the landing was jammed with tourists. Sophia told me she was going down to the lavatory. I'd already turned away when I heard her scream."

I walked past Jimmy and Sophia. "Mr. Glenn, the landing was packed. There wasn't exactly pushing and shoving, but you couldn't move without coming up against someone. I don't know that any of us could say where anyone else was. It wasn't possible. I can tell you what was possible. Any one of our group"—I gestured to include the Riordans—"could have stepped close enough to poke Sophia. It may have been a quick decision when someone saw her turn to go down the stairs. Sophia"—I watched her carefully—"can you describe what you felt?"

"A thump." Her eyes narrowed. "It was as if I'd been hit in the back by a broom handle."

I had a quick memory of the milling throng on the landing and the long table crowded with tourists scanning books and prints, buying, moving in and out. There were three or four clerks busy answering questions, taking money, sacking up purchases. Anyone with a quick hand could have filched a desired object.

"Or a cardboard mailer for a print?" I suggested.

I sensed an instant of shock on someone's part. My guess was correct. A mailer had been grabbed and used and dropped to be crushed beneath the feet of the milling crowd.

Sophia looked at me intently. "Clever of you. Possibly you already knew?"

"No." My reply was crisp and definite.

Sophia shivered. "That is exactly how it felt, something rounded and hard."

Staff Captain Glenn finished his sketch, marking us down. "I've recorded the positions. Does anyone have anything helpful to add?"

Evelyn fluttered a hand. "This is silly. Sophia fell. Probably one of the tourists bumped her accidentally."

"With a cardboard mailer?" Sophia's tone was sharp and she glanced again at me.

No one spoke.

Glenn waited an instant longer, nodded. "Very well. If anyone later remembers anything helpful, contact me at once. Please return to your seats. Mrs. Lennox wishes to speak." He remained standing near Sophia.

I didn't like the feeling of being herded into an audience, rather like schoolchildren in detention, but I moved to the sofa.

Jimmy looked at Sophia.

She ignored him.

Lips pressed together, Jimmy joined me on the sofa.

Sophia stood straight as an arrow, her face somber. She looked haggard yet beautiful and desperately alone. "Despite someone's best effort, and it must be quite disappointing for one of you, I am alive. At this very moment"—she glanced at her watch—"we should have been finishing dinner at the Grand Hotel Europe. Had that occurred as scheduled, I would now be announcing that I had decided to approve dissolution of the trusts Frank put in place."

Everyone stared at Sophia.

She stood, eyes cold, face hard, as remote and unworldly as the statue of a goddess. "That is no longer my plan." She looked at each of the Riordans in turn, one by one. "The trusts shall remain in effect. Moreover, the income from the trusts will no longer be distributed but returned to the trusts to be held. The status of the trusts will not be reconsidered for ten years. I shall have the papers drawn up and ready for my signature upon my return. So those, including Kent, who had hoped to profit from your father's acumen will have to be patient. Perhaps in the next ten years—"

Alex jumped up, his freckled face flushing. "That's rotten, Sophia, and damned unfair. I didn't shove you down any stairs. None of us did. That's crazy. Can you see

Rosie or Val hurting anybody? Or Kent? And I can tell you for sure it wasn't Madge or me. Some klutzy tourist poked you in the back with an elbow and you lost your balance. That's all that happened, and now you want to make it a big deal, use it as an excuse to rip us off. Like Kent says, it's our money, not yours."

"I never claimed the money was mine." Sophia was unperturbed. "I have never used a penny from your father's estate for me. But the money you are so willing to claim belonged to your father and I intend to fulfill my promise to him. He knew none of you was ready for responsibility, and everything that has happened on this trip confirms his judgment." Her gaze at Alex was cool. "You are a fool waiting to be fleeced. Madge has the cupidity of a chorus girl. Rosie chooses jobs that throw her in with seedy people. Kent wanted to marry a girl without any background. Val obviously has a problem with alcohol. If your father were here, he would be appalled."

Evelyn lifted a pleading hand. "Sophia, please. You're upset and—"

"I am not upset." No one ever looked more composed than Sophia. "I am simply making it clear that I intend to fulfill my responsibility to Frank. The proposal to dissolve the trusts was not a good one. I was encouraged to do so on the spurious basis that I would then be safe from attack." She looked at her husband. "I have to wonder why you made that proposal, Jimmy."

Jimmy rose and faced Sophia.

I have never been more proud of him. He stood straight and slim, a distinguished-looking man with a kind face, furrowed now in a thoughtful frown. He looked like what he was: stalwart, forthright, and reasonable. "I advised you to give Frank's children what belongs to them. From the first, I thought it was foolish—and, more than that, dangerous—to bring them together to decide on the future of the trusts."

Sophia folded her arms. The jet bracelet on one wrist gleamed. "You keep emphasizing danger." She arched a sleek eyebrow, her face demanding. And skeptical.

"I've been proven right." Anger hardened his voice.

"Yes, I've definitely been in danger. What is the source of that danger? Frank's children?" Her gaze touched them without pleasure. "Possibly. Possibly not. If I were to die a suspicious death without any suspects available, your position would be quite unenviable, wouldn't it, Jimmy?"

Jimmy's mouth twisted in a sardonic smile. "We all know the surviving spouse is the first to be suspected. However, you have nothing I want." The message was harsh. "In any event, if I wanted free of marriage, divorce is a good deal easier."

"Though not nearly as profitable." Her tone was silky.

He looked as though he'd been struck. "That is unforgivable, Sophia."

Madge's shrill voice cut it. "This makes sense." She pointed at Jimmy. "No wonder he runs around accusing us of everything under the sun. If anybody pushed her, it's him!"

Alex grabbed her hand, tugged, but she shook free.

Staff Captain Glenn stepped forward. "Why did Miss Riordan dump the tray with the sherry?" Obviously Sophia had informed Glenn of everything. "Miss Riordan, were you protecting Mr. Lennox?"

"I wasn't protecting anybody!" Evelyn sounded close to hysteria. "I was upset. I told them"—she gestured wildly toward Jimmy and me—"it was because he'd made such a thing about that boulder. I looked at the sherry and I felt scared and I hardly even thought what I was doing. Sometimes I have a feeling something bad is going to happen. Before Vic died, I kept dreaming she was gone and I was running after her, trying to bring her back—"

No one moved or spoke, but the emotional barometer shifted. A dark and ugly anger pulsed, overriding tension and uneasiness. It was as if we stood at the entrance to a cavern where something terrible awaited within.

"—but I couldn't find her. I had to find her or she'd be gone forever. I should have gotten up and gone to her." Tears spilled down Evelyn's cheeks. "It was probably already too late and she'd left the house, running down—"

"Stop!" Val's cry was harsh, desperate.

Evelyn's face crumpled. "Val, I'm sorry. But that's what happened and now whenever I have that feeling I do something about it and that's why I spilled the sherry."

Madge's eyes were bright and excited. "Evelyn picks up on things. I'll bet he"—Madge pointed at Jimmy—"poisoned the sherry and Evelyn had this subconscious warning."

"Jimmy did no such thing." Rosie's voice was sharp. "That's as silly—"

"I'm not silly!" Madge's voice was high and angry.

"—as saying one of us pushed Sophia today."

Sophia's face was grim. "One of you did."

Rosie looked contemptuous. "Sure, you were pushed. Alex got it right. It's a wonder all of us didn't get bumped down the stairs in that crush."

Jimmy's hands folded into fists. He looked at Sophia. "You made a serious mistake tonight. Change your mind before it's too late. Relinquish the estate to its rightful heirs."

"Still harping on that?" Sophia eyed him as she might a stranger.

Jimmy spoke slowly. "If you restrict the income and

maintain the trusts, the heirs receive nothing. If you die, they receive everything."

Her lips trembled. Her eyes were filled with heartbreak. "If I die, you will be free. You will inherit my estate."

"I have no interest in your estate." His voice was brusque.

Evelyn made little clucking noises, her kind face crinkling in dismay. "Sophia, Jimmy, all of this has been upsetting. We all need to get some rest. Everything will be all right. Jimmy wouldn't hurt anyone and neither would any of us. It's a terrible misunderstanding and I think we've talked enough tonight."

Staff Captain Glenn cleared his throat.

Faces turned toward him as if recalling his presence.

"I call upon each one of you"—his voice was somber— "to consider any information you may possess as to the truth behind these events."

Madge shot Rosie a sullen look. "You can make fun of me all you want. But Sophia's nobody's fool." Once again Madge pointed at Jimmy. "She's onto him. Ask him why he paid for Mrs. Collins's cabin. Ask him how well he and Mrs. Collins know each other. Ask him if he wants out of his marriage with Sophia."

Jimmy looked toward Sophia. "I asked you to marry me because I wanted us to be together. Always. I wanted to take care of you. For better or worse . . ."

Sophia wavered. Her eyes held hunger and emptiness and hope. Faith and despair hung in the balance. Then she lifted her chin and said mockingly, " 'Til death do us part?"

Jimmy stiffened.

Sophia spoke almost without a tremor. "Mr. Glenn has arranged another cabin for you."

Glenn reached into his pocket, pulled out a small black rectangular electronic key folder. "Cabin 6048 is ready for you, Mr. Lennox."

Jimmy took the folder, jammed it into a front pocket of his slacks.

Sophia gestured toward the bedroom. "Your things have been packed. The bags have already been taken there. You won't be needing the key to this cabin." She held out her hand, palm up.

Slowly he nodded, his eyes never leaving her face. "I don't suppose I will." He reached to his back left pocket. He yanked out the folder. "You're all alone, Sophia. I hope you can handle it." He turned away, pausing only long enough to toss the black leather folder into a green ceramic bowl on the coffee table. He opened the door, looked back. "You're very efficient, Sophia. You have a talent for organization. It's too bad you aren't as smart about people."

She folded her arms. "I'm smart enough to understand marriage is meant for two. Not three."

"Don't be a fool." I was angry. I moved toward Sophia. "Once Jimmy and I were lovers. Before that and after that, we were and are good friends. I came on this trip because Jimmy was afraid for you and wanted help to keep you safe. I've tried. He's tried. Now you've pushed away the two people who want you to live."

Rippling notes of Gershwin accompanied muted conversations in Diogenes Bar. Earlier I'd made plans to spend time here. I was in the bar this evening, but not as I had hoped. Jimmy was my companion instead of Kent and Rosie. There was to be no celebration for the Riordan clan. Sophia's proclamations tonight had changed the course of many lives. She'd accused Jimmy of adultery and attempted murder. She'd plucked a fortune from the grasp of the Riordans.

Jimmy upended his glass, gestured to the waiter for another.

My own glass was still almost full. "Jimmy, alcohol isn't the answer." My tone was mild.

"I know." But when the fresh drink came, he took a deep swallow, his eyes hurt and angry. "Stupid to drink when your world goes to hell. I don't usually. I guess getting drunk is better than thinking. It's taking the edge off. You know what?" He drank again. Too much. Too quickly.

"What?" I'd spent my life with words, fine, crazy, beautiful, wonderful, haunting words, yet sometimes the right word doesn't come. To tell him Sophia was incapable of love was to tell him he'd given his name and heart to an illusion. But wasn't that what Sophia had made starkly clear?

He cradled the glass in his hands, graceful, gentle, generous hands, and looked into the depths of the golden whiskey. "It's not supposed to be all about me. Maybe that's what I'm realizing. What rubs me raw is that Sophia would think I'm capable of murder, not to mention unfaithfulness. That's all wrong. I ought to be devastated that I've lost her, wild to get her back." His stare was open, sad, chagrined. "I don't give a damn. What hurts is not losing her, it's losing the idea she cared for me. That's not what marriage is supposed to be. I know what a good marriage is. Margaret and I believed in each other. Always. Just like you and Richard. Good times, bad times, we knew we could count on each other. There are going to be bad times, times that tear your guts out. That's when you have to know the person you love will be there beside you. So"—he tossed down the rest of the drink—"maybe I deserve to be as damned as Sophia."

"Jimmy, give it a rest. Tomorrow I'll talk to her—"

His face abruptly turned hard and cold. "About me? Thanks, Henrie O, but no thanks. Sophia and I are finished. I'll get reservations for you and me out of Helsinki. You'll be home, back to your world, by Sunday."

I had a quick memory of Val's cry when Evelyn recalled the dream of Vic that she had not acted upon. I still carried with me a dark sense of foreboding, an awareness of a pulsating anger that had not been sated. I was fearful for Sophia.

"Sophia's still in danger." I felt it deep inside.

Jimmy rubbed one temple. "The ravening Riordans? I don't think so. Tonight spiked their chances. Sophia's on guard. Even though she's picked me as suspect number one, she'll be careful. She won't take a chance with any of us. I doubt she'll be near them for the rest of the voyage. She won't open her door to any of us, and when she's on an excursion or wandering around the ship, there are plenty of people everywhere."

I took a sip of my drink, scarcely tasted it. I still felt worried. "I suppose that's true."

"She'll be careful. The only good thing that came out of tonight is the fact that Sophia not only knows somebody wants her dead, the thwarted murderer knows there's no chance of popping her off in an accident. As for Glenn's investigation, he had to do something, show up tonight, warn us off, but he knows damn well he can't pick out the guilty one. If he had anything up his sleeve, he'd have hauled us in for questioning tonight. Short of a confession, he's not going to figure out the truth."

I didn't feel as sanguine as Jimmy.

He looked at me, read my thoughts. "Relax, Henrie O. Sophia's safe. For now. When she gets home, there won't be any Riordans there except Evelyn. Now"—he looked unutterably weary—"I'm going to take a walk on deck. Maybe I'll find a wreath, toss it in the sea."

## sixteen

THE fiery red brick Church of Our Savior on the Spilt Blood is one of the most dramatic sites in St. Petersburg. The onion domes dazzled with bright coverings of gilt or glittering glazed tiles. The brightly hued domes gave the cathedral a fairy-tale quality. The church commemorates the murder of Alexander II, but the cathedral's beauty transcends its bloodstained origin. As I gazed at the crowning dome, dramatic with swirls of white and blue and green topped by a delicate golden spire, a shadow fell in front of me.

Kent Riordan was obviously American, from his backward navy ball cap to his loose blue polo, casual khaki slacks, and worn running shoes. Dark curls poked from beneath the cap. A backpack hung casually from one shoulder. He'd picked up a touch of sun during the excursion, his cheeks faintly pink. "I understand you got a good dose of Sophia last night."

I shaded my eyes. "I gather you've heard all about it."

"Rosie gave me a blow-by-blow, from our relegation to poverty for the next ten years right through Jimmy tossing his room key into the bowl. High drama. Turn the orphans out into the storm and hand out a scarlet letter. To hell with us and Jimmy, too."

I looked at him curiously. "Why didn't you come?"

His face twisted in a dark glower. He could have doubled for a brooding Heathcliff. "Lady, if I'd come, I would have killed her. I've e-mailed Heather. I've called her. I've called her friend Angela. Rosie's called Heather. So has Val. No luck." He was suddenly forlorn, his eyes filled with misery. "You said she'd come back to me."

"She will. It may take time, but it will happen. Rosie and Val are your secret weapons. And Evelyn. They'll persuade her."

"You believe that?" He was a man hungry for hope.

I smiled. "I do."

He unzipped his backpack and delved inside, bringing out a red-lacquered matrioshka doll, her painted features perfect and elegant. "Twenty-four dolls. They fit one inside another and the tiniest one's just this big." He pointed to the tip of his little finger. "It's for Heather. Do you think she'll like her?"

"Heather will like her." I believed the world would come right for Kent and Heather.

His brief enthusiasm subsided. He put the doll into the backpack. "I want to give it to Heather and see her smile. If it doesn't happen, I swear to God I'll kill her." He meant Sophia and he meant every word.

Good advice usually falls on deaf ears, but I had to try. "Stay away from Sophia. Be glad you know that Heather loves you. Let time help."

"Time." His voice was bitter. "Sophia stole part of our lives."

"But not forever. Think about it, Kent." I hoped his heart was listening. "It could have been forever."

Suddenly he smiled, a sweet, gentle smile. "You found out. You told me. I feel like I've been let out of prison. I feel like the sky is blue and I can be happy if Heather will come back to me. You made it possible."

"I'm glad. I had to tell you when I knew." That was an absolute. I had no choice, no matter the repercussions. "Truth matters, Kent. Your truth. Mine. Jimmy's. You know that Sophia's wrong in accusing him. So was Madge."

"I know that." Kent looked disgusted. "But Jimmy's wrong, too. Nobody's trying to kill Sophia. She got bumped yesterday because the landing was crowded and somebody moved too fast. As for Evelyn, I love the hell out of her, but she's a nutcase sometimes. Knocking over the sherry proves that. She didn't have bad vibes. She obviously thought one of us loosened the boulder and she freaked out when she saw Jimmy with the sherry. That's totally stupid. Evelyn should know better. Sophia's done us a lot of dirt, but nobody's trying to kill her. Not even me, though I don't make any promises if I don't get Heather back. But Alex or Madge or Rosie or Val? Alex would have been so nervous he would've spilled the whole bottle. Madge likes money, but she'd never do any dirty work on her own. They're the only ones who really need cash. Rosie doesn't care about money and Val's eaten up with her work. That's all Val ever does. If she lets herself think, she remembers Vic and she can't function. As for me, all I want is Heather. So I can tell you what's going to happen to Sophia."

I looked at him expectantly.

"Nothing." He punched a fist in the opposite palm. "Nada. Sophia's going to glare whenever she sees us. That won't be any too often. I don't intend to have any-thing to do with her, now or ever. She'll sail all the way to London, high and mighty, treated like the queen bee and secure as gold bars in a safe. Maybe that sour-faced ship cop will figure out this doesn't amount to anything. Anyway, I'm flying home from Helsinki and I'm going to camp on Heather's doorstep. I've already got it set up for a big billboard across from the bar. It's going to have a gold ring and a wedding cake and it will read: 'Dear Heather, I love you. I'm going to marry you. Love, Kent.' That's neat, isn't it? I can't wait to get off this boat. I'll bet you and Jimmy blow ship in Helsinki, too. Am I right?"

"Jimmy's checking into reservations." I'd not turned down Jimmy's offer, though I wondered if we shouldn't stick it out for the duration of the trip. But Sophia wasn't looking to us for help.

"Happy trails." Kent gave me a thumbs-up. "I'm going to find a phone, try again with Heather. Maybe she'll take a call from St. Petersburg."

The message light on the cabin phone was blinking. I tossed my straw hat on the bed, stepped into the bath to splash cool water on my face, then retrieved the message.

"Henrie O." Jimmy sounded tired but determined. "I've booked seats out of Helsinki to London." There was a long pause. He sighed. "This isn't a good time to talk about us. I don't know if there will be a good time. Don't worry. I won't ask anything of you until my situation has changed. I won't even ask you to have dinner with me. The *Clio* sails at seven tonight. We arrive in Helsinki at seven-thirty in the morning. Meet me for breakfast at seven."

There was silence, but the line was still open.

Finally, sadly, he said, "I've been a fool. Do you know what I'd give to roll back the years, be leaving you the kind of message I used to? I'd give the world. But it doesn't work that way."

The connection closed.

I replaced the receiver, felt the sting of tears on my cheeks.

I balanced carefully as I moved around the cabin. We'd sailed at seven. The ship was rolling a bit, nothing extreme, but after two days in port I needed to adjust to the movement. At dinner, I'd managed a pleasant conversation with strangers and excused myself quickly after dessert.

I took a restless walk on the promenade, spent forty-five minutes in the lounge listening to a reprise of the Sinatra years. It was about nine-thirty when I got back to the cabin. I started packing, a listless exercise. Once I paused, frowning, and considered calling Jimmy. I didn't think we should abandon Sophia, but he'd already made the reservations. Slowly I folded clothes, placed them in my larger suitcase.

I zipped shut a bag to be checked and was getting my carry-on ready when my fingers brushed stiff cardboard. I looked down at the mailer containing the information sent to me by Jimmy. Surely anyone reading this material—especially Jimmy's letter—would see his obvious concern, his genuine fear. Everything was dated. In fact, I'd kept the letter in its original overnight envelope. Here was proof of everything Jimmy claimed.

Sophia should see this. I should have taken the folder to the meeting in her cabin last night. I looked at the clock. A few minutes before ten.

I put the mailer on the desk and stretched, standing on the balls of my feet, trying to ease the tension in my back, the restlessness in my mind. I stared at the mailer. It might as well have been blinking neon. I reached for the phone, let my hand fall. It's too easy to hang up on an unwanted caller. I was still dressed, a red and white silk blouse, beige linen slacks, red leather sandals. It would only take a few minutes to go to her cabin.

If I knocked on her door, would she answer?

Twice I kept my balance by catching the railing along the wall of the long hallway. Swells lifted the ship up, eased it down. I didn't see another passenger all the long way aft. The early-to-bed crowd was already tucked in and the revelers were just getting started.

When I reached the stern, I stood for a moment outside Sophia's suite. I had a quick conviction I'd come on a fool's errand, but I'd come this far and I would see it through. If Sophia opened the door, even for a moment, I would hand her the mailer, tell her it contained a letter from Jimmy, a letter she would want to read. She might throw the mailer in my face. I didn't think so.

I knocked three times, loudly, waited a moment, knocked again.

The door swung in. As always, Sophia was strikingly attractive, her eyes a light bright blue, her makeup understated, her golden ringlets a marvel of hairdressing skill. Delicate embroidery added an elegant accent to a pale blue Irish linen shirt. The embroidery was repeated at the hem of the long matching skirt. Her expression was irritated. "I told you I—oh. It's you." She looked at me with distaste. "You have quite a nerve coming here. What do you want?"

I thrust the mailer at her, pushed it into her hand. "Please read Jimmy's letter. Look at the effort he's made to keep you safe."

Her mouth twisted in a sardonic smile. "More of his campaign against Frank's children? What's the point? To convince me to trust him?"

"You'd better trust him. There's a killer around you

and it isn't Jimmy." I remembered Kent's anger at the Church of Our Savior on the Spilt Blood. He had been angry with Sophia for a long time, but now his anger was newly rekindled. He insisted none of the Riordans pushed Sophia. He claimed none of them cared about the money. That might be true, but the depths of feeling against Sophia were about more than money. Much more.

"Don't be fooled, Sophia. One of them—one of the Riordans—wants you dead. Think back. You and Jimmy were happy until they came to your house. Everything was fine."

She looked down at the mailer, then at me, her gaze searching, testing, wondering. "Does Jimmy know you've come to me?"

"No. I was packing and I saw the mailer. If you'll read the materials in it, you'll see that everything we've told you is true." She hadn't slammed the door in my face. Was she going to listen and hear what I was telling her?

"Jimmy doesn't know you're here." Her voice was thoughtful.

I was puzzled. What earthly difference could it make?

Abruptly, she held the door wider. "Come in." It was the old Sophia, imperious and in charge.

As I came through the door, the ship went up and down again and I reached out to brace against the lintel.

Sophia fetched up against the sofa. She gestured for me to sit opposite her.

I sank into the comfortable easy chair, welcomed the fresh breeze that came through the open sliding door to the balcony.

Sophia pulled the material from the mailer, dropped it on the coffee table. She read Jimmy's letter slowly, read it again, then scanned the printed sheets, lips pursed, toe tapping. She radiated energy as she flicked swiftly through the pages. No wonder Jimmy found her fascinating. Being in her presence made anyone feel more alive and vital. She tossed the sheets on the table, kept the letter in her lap. She lifted her eyes. Her gaze was sharp, demanding. "You and Jimmy were lovers. I thought he'd brought you here, that he was tired of me."

"So he tried to kill you? Jimmy? That's crazy." My tone was scathing. I was beyond tact. How could she have spent time with him and have so little understanding of his character?

She brushed fingers through her curls. "Jimmy." She touched the letter, looked at me forlornly. "Sometimes I move too fast. I wasn't thinking straight. I guess I wasn't thinking at all. I was in shock after that fall. The last thing I heard was his voice. He was right beside me on the stairs. That's all I remembered, telling him I was going to the lavatory and hearing him say he'd wait and then I was falling." Remembered fear made her voice thin. "He was right there and he'd been so insistent that I was in danger." She touched the mailer. "But he never knew I'd see this." Her tone was thoughtful, considering. "That's why he was so honest in the letter. It sounds just like him. I can hear him." Her eyes gazed into mine. "There's no point in your coming here if you want Jimmy for yourself. If you wanted to connive at my murder, here you are and here I am and I suppose you could try to kill me if you wished. So you're innocent. And Jimmy . . . Do you know"—she took a deep breath—"I'd never even seen him angry until last night when I accused him. So, not you. Not Jimmy. But to think one of Frank's children . . ." Her voice trailed off.

I understood her distress. She'd not been a mother to them, not ever, but she'd known them as children, watched them grow to adulthood, uncertain Alex, insouciant Rosie, appealing Kent, disconsolate Val.

I looked into her eyes. "Jimmy told you the truth. I'm telling you the truth. I came on this ship only because he is my old friend and I wanted to help him. I wanted—and want—to help him protect you."

"Old friend . . ." Her eyes were a brilliant, piercing blue. "Did he ever ask you to marry him?"

How much reassurance did she need? "Several years before you and he came together. I refused him." It had not been an easy choice. Now I regretted that choice. Jimmy had it right when he remembered the love he and Margaret shared. With love, it is all or nothing. I would have gone to the ends of the earth for Richard. *Whither thou goest* . . . I'd chosen not to go with Jimmy, but I wanted his happiness. I wanted it enough to do my best for his marriage.

She touched the mailer with a shaking hand. "I love him. I've never loved anyone as much. I know"—there was sad certainty in her eyes—"that he loved Margaret more than he'll ever care for me. I've never had anyone who loved me the most. Frank's heart really belonged to Anna. No one's ever loved me with all their heart." Sophia's broken voice spoke truths I knew she'd never revealed to anyone, certainly not to Jimmy.

She clasped her hands tightly together. "Jimmy was kind and caring and generous. I know I wanted more than he could give, but what he gave me was wonderful." She gave me an open, honest, direct look. "I've been a fool. Do you think he'll forgive me?"

Jimmy was as fair a man as any I'd ever known. At this moment, he was hurt deep inside, angry and bitter. If I'd told him I wanted to talk to Sophia, he would have objected.

Now I had to hope he would understand. "I don't know. Call him. Tell him you're sorry."

She held the letter tight, then gently placed it on the coffee table. She rose swiftly, graceful as always, moved to the wet bar, picked up a bottle. "Will you have a drink?" Her voice was steady, but tears filmed her eyes.

I supposed Sophia was prolonging the moment before she dialed Jimmy, a call that would be difficult for her. How do you tell a man you are sorry you accused him of adultery and murder? How do you rebuild shattered trust?

I rose too, moved toward the door. "No thanks." I paused with my hand on the knob. I'd said all I knew to say. "Good night, Sophia."

As the door closed behind me, I carried with me the picture of a vulnerable woman splashing whiskey into a glass.

I turned into the starboard corridor and had passed perhaps five or six cabins when I heard a click behind me. I swung around but the corridor was empty. I saw no one, yet I was sure of the sound. A cabin door had closed.

Someone had stood in a doorway, watched me walk forward. All the Riordan cabins were here in a row: Evelyn, Alex and Madge, Kent, Rosie, and Val.

The corridor stretched long and narrow fore and aft. I saw no movement, heard no sound. I felt defenseless.

I whirled and walked fast, listening all the while for pursuit. I scarcely realized how uneasy I'd been until I came to a cross hall and stairwells. If I continued forward I would reach my cabin. Instead I plunged down the steps. I wanted the gaiety of Diogenes Bar.

## seventeen

THE pianist played "Some Enchanted Evening." The mirror behind the bar reflected lights and clusters of passengers around the shining wooden tables. Laughter and voices sounded pleasant and carefree.

I settled at a small table not far from the piano. By the time the waiter brought a club soda, I felt foolish. I had no cause to be uneasy. I wasn't a threat to anyone. Yet I'd sensed a malignant presence. Slowly I relaxed, immersing myself in the normalcy of the bar with its soft lamplight and comfortable dark leather chairs and nautical watercolors.

I took pleasure in the occasional bursts of laughter, lively yet restrained. I sipped the soda and admired attractive women in lovely dresses as they smiled at attentive companions, everyone enjoying a holiday. I concentrated on the elegance of my surroundings, determined to force my thoughts away from Sophia and the muddle she'd made of her relationships.

I'd enjoyed many happy holidays over the years, most of them with Richard. Richard . . . The pianist slipped into the familiar notes of "September Song," banal yet nonetheless poignant with its haunting evocation of loss and farewell. My thoughts are never far from Richard. It strengthens me to recall his steady gaze, his robust laughter, his sturdy presence, to remember when I could reach out and touch his hands, welcome his embrace. Perhaps it was inevitable that I would feel close to him tonight, a night when I'd spoken of love. Whenever I did, Richard was in my heart.

I don't know how long I sat, sipping the soda, accepting another, immersed in a world that no longer existed. Yet for this moment my and Richard's long-ago world lived in my memory: sun-drenched days at Acapulco, starry nights in Mexico City, amorous afternoons in Paris. Oh, Richard, if only you'd not gone to Kauai. But he had gone, and his life ended in a brutal fall down a mountainside. He had been murdered. I'd gone to Kauai, trapped his killer. But Richard was dead and I was left with memories.

I was no longer aware of my surroundings, my mind and heart far away, when a hand pushed at my shoulder.

Startled, I looked up.

Val Riordan clung to the back of a chair with one hand, pushed at me with the other. She peered down, blue eyes bleary, lipstick smeared, face slack. Her dark red hair, long and loose, framed an accusing face. "Where's your companion in crime?" She looked around. "What's Jimmy doing now? Plotting poison?"

"Val." My tone was forbidding.

She clapped an unsteady hand to her lips, made a moue of simulated chagrin. "Oops. Cat out of the bag?" She pushed away from me, wavered unsteadily, then pulled the chair back, sank into it. "Trouble is, you two missed your chance. Now you've loused it up for us, put the bitch in a monster mood. If you'd waited until tomorrow, she'd have divvied up the money. Our money. Now everything's all screwed up." She spoke with the careful diction of a cunning drunk. "There is a bright side. Bright, bright side. See, I don't care about the money. Did you know I make a lot of money? Buckets of it. I don't even spend it." There was a note of regret, as if she would have liked to spend money but there wasn't anything she wanted.

Drunks reveal more than they ever realize. Val was so cut off from feeling that she had no desires to fulfill.

She thumped the table.

My glass slid, a little soda slopping over one side.

Val squeezed her eyes, gazed owlishly at me. "You want to know the bright side?"

"The bright side?" I mopped up the soda.

"When you pushed her—"

"I didn't push her." It's pointless to argue with a drunk, but I wasn't going to let the accusation pass.

Val waved a hand. "Okay, okay. Maybe not you. Jimmy then. Anything for his lady love." She pointed an unsteady finger. "That's you." She laughed and it turned into a hiccup. "Anyway, Sophia got pushed. You like that better? Okay, that's the good part, she got pushed and she started to fall. She had to be scared, right?"

I remembered Sophia's shrill scream.

"Scared as hell, right?" Val's eyes glittered. Her lips parted in a hurtful smile. Her lips began to tremble. "That was good. I wish she'd fallen all the way, screaming and scared just like Vic must have screamed that night and no one heard her. Vic . . ." Val stopped, tears streaming down her cheeks.

I gestured to a waiter. He was there in an instant. "Some napkins, please."

He brought them and helped me get Val to her feet. I thrust the napkins in her hand. "We're going to take a walk, Val. This way."

I slipped an arm around Val's waist, smelled the faint

but unmistakable scent of vodka, the favorite of heavy drinkers who like to believe it is odorless. She leaned on me, murmuring to herself. The roll of the ship was more pronounced. Our progress was erratic. I caught snatches of her rambling monologue as I guided her to the lift: ". . . hope you get her next time . . . wish I had the guts . . . too bad she didn't die . . . Vic died . . ."

When we reached Val's cabin, I propped her against the bulkhead, reached into the pocket of her loose jacket, found her electronic key in its dark leather folder. Val waited docilely, eyes almost closed, dark lashes stark against her fair skin. I opened the door, led her inside.

She looked around blankly.

An empty vodka bottle lay on the floor. I wasn't surprised. Room service wouldn't hesitate to bring alcohol, but I doubted she would have been served anywhere on the ship in her drunken state. I wondered if she'd wandered up to the bar because the bottle was empty.

She took three steps forward and almost fell as the floor rose with a swell. I caught her, moved her closer to the bed. "Lie down now, Val."

She pulled away from me, scowling. "Don't want to lie down." Swaying, she managed to reach the little sofa, sank down, looked up at me. "Want a drink. That's what I came up to the bar for." She looked around. "Got a bottle somewhere. You can fix me a drink."

There was ice in the bucket. I used tongs, dropped cubes into a glass, poured it three-quarters full with water, took it to Val.

She gave me a brilliant smile, took the glass, lifted it.

I was at the door when she called out. "Damn dirty trick. Don't want water."

"You've had enough for now. Try to get some sleep." I opened the door and stepped into the hall, heard her querulous call. I hoped she would stay put. Tomorrow I would talk to Rosie. Val needed help. Out in the hall, I pulled the door shut, heard its quiet click.

Just so had a door clicked as I walked forward after leaving Sophia's cabin. Again the corridor was empty, but this time I didn't feel uneasy. I was, however, fatigued. I glanced at my watch. Half past eleven. I'd spent almost an hour in the bar and seeing Val to her cabin.

I walked briskly, several times catching the handrail for balance. In my cabin, I looked toward the phone. The message light was dark. I'd half expected a call from Jimmy, either pleased that Sophia had contacted him or angry that I had gone to see her. Perhaps the lack of a message was a very good sign. Perhaps even now, Sophia and Jimmy were quietly talking, remembering their happiness, excising her folly. All of us make mistakes and need forgiveness.

I prepared for bed, deciding to finish my packing in the morning. I slipped into my favorite yellow cotton gown, but as I turned down the spread, I was too tense to try to sleep. Tense and worried. I moved away from the bed, settled on the small sofa. Why did I feel so uneasy? Surely Sophia wouldn't be foolish enough to open her door to any of the Riordans tonight. She was safe so long as she kept her door locked.

Perhaps she'd called Jimmy and was no longer alone. I hoped he'd been receptive, but I had done all I could do, for him and for her. It was up to them to reconcile or not. In any event, Jimmy would likely rethink his plan to leave the ship in Helsinki, although he seemed to think Sophia was no longer in danger since Staff Captain Glenn was aware of everything that had happened.

Maybe that made Sophia safe. I wasn't sure. Actually, until Sophia and Jimmy were publicly reunited, the shadowy figure who had now attempted murder three times would find the prospect of Jimmy as a scapegoat too appealing to resist.

I suddenly found it hard to breathe. I remembered Kent's smiling face and his casual words: . . . *I'll bet you and Jimmy blow ship in Helsinki, too.*

I had answered as casually. Now the import of those words staggered me. I had told Kent that most likely Jimmy and I would disembark after the ship docked tomorrow morning in Helsinki. What Kent knew, all the Riordans very likely knew. If Jimmy were to be suspected of Sophia's murder, she had to die before morning.

Before morning . . .

I jumped up and hurried to the desk, grabbed the phone, dialed Sophia's cabin. The phone rang, rang again, a third time, a fourth. The automatic voice mail system came on, inviting me to leave a message. I hung up. I stood uncertain, my thoughts frantic. Was I semihysterical, seeing danger where none existed? Almost viciously, I jabbed the numbers again. The result was the same. If Sophia was in the cabin, she slept too deeply to rouse. Or—

I dialed Jimmy's new cabin. Please God he was there and Sophia too. The phone rang. My chest ached from want of breath. It rang until the automatic voice mail was triggered. I spoke quickly: "Jimmy, call me when you come in." I glanced toward the clock. Twenty minutes to midnight. Where could he be? "Jimmy, I'm afraid for Sophia. I've called her cabin, received no answer." I was stymied and ever more frightened. "I'm going to call Staff Captain Glenn."

I cut the connection, dialed Operator.

"Yes, Mrs. Collins?" The voice was young and smooth with only a trace of wariness. I doubted calls were common at this hour.

I didn't hesitate although I knew I might end up looking foolish. "Please contact Staff Captain Glenn. A passenger is in danger."

The demand was swift. "State the problem."

"Passenger Sophia Lennox in Cabin 6088 doesn't answer her telephone. I have reason to believe she is in danger. I will meet Mr. Glenn at her door." I heard the sharp voice as I slammed down the receiver. It took only seconds to slip out of my nightgown, pull on a blouse and slacks, and step into sandals, and I was on my way, running down the long empty corridor.

When I reached Sophia's door, I knocked, kept on knocking. My breaths came quickly, my chest ached. My hand ached from the peremptory blows. Finally, I let my hand fall. I leaned against the bulkhead. In a moment I heard the faint ring of a telephone. I looked at Sophia's door. Yes, the ring was from her cabin. The telephone rang and rang and rang, continued to ring, the voice mail in abeyance. I knew Staff Captain Glenn had ordered this call.

It was still ringing when Glenn arrived. There were two young crew members with him, a slender thirtyish woman and a red-bearded giant. I supposed Glenn had dressed hurriedly, but his uniform was immaculate. The only indication of irregularity was the bristle that covered his cheeks. He gave me a quick, searching glance but moved straight to the door, knocked: booming, impossible-to-ignore, crashing knocks. Four of them. He pushed an electronic key into the lock. The door swung open to lights and silence and the silky movement of air flowing in from the balcony.

"Mrs. Lennox?" His call was loud, brusque. He moved into the hallway, cocked his head, listening.

I started to follow Glenn. The massive redheaded

crewman stepped in front of me, held up a restraining hand. "Ma'am."

I stayed where I was, craning to see past him. I glimpsed the elegant living area, chintz-covered sofas, wooden table with a book and half-filled glass, open door to the balcony and the darkness beyond. There was no sound but the rustle of the balcony curtains blowing in the breeze and the distant shush of the *Clio* cleaving the sea.

"Mrs. Lennox?" Again his deep voice was loud, but Glenn was moving as he spoke. He veered to his right to enter the bedroom. It seemed he was gone only an instant before returning to the living area. He gave it another quick scan, then strode out onto the balcony, flipping on the exterior lights.

When he returned, he walked straight to me. His dark eyes were cold, skeptical, and suspicious.

"Sophia?" But I looked at him without hope.

"Mrs. Lennox is not present. We will go to my office, Mrs. Collins." He gestured toward the young woman. "Officer Watkins, secure the premises until further notice. Touch nothing. No one is to enter. If Mrs. Lennox returns, contact me immediately." He turned to the young man. "Officer O'Reilly, call up assistance, organize a search of all public areas. Mrs. Lennox is in her fifties, five feet two inches tall, approximately eight stone, short blond hair in tight curls, blue eyes, narrow face."

Before O'Reilly moved, I added, "At ten o'clock tonight, she was wearing a light blue linen blouse and skirt, matching blue sandals."

Glenn's eyes narrowed. "Thank you, Mrs. Collins. If you'll be kind enough to come with me . . ."

## eighteen

THE reception area on Deck 4 was dimly lit. No one was on duty at the counters for the purser's office and the ship's information office. Glenn walked to an unmarked door, punched a keypad, held the door for me. The minute we stepped through, the character of our surroundings changed. There was no trace of the opulence surrounding the Clio's passengers. The cream walls might have been in any modern office building. He led the way to the fourth door on the right, held the door for me.

Naval maps were posted on one wall. Three metal file cabinets sat to the right of a gray metal desk. The desk was clear except for an old-fashioned walnut clock and a leather trifold picture frame of a smiling woman with brown curls, a teenage boy, and a younger girl. A computer screen glowed green. He gestured toward a straight chair, took his place behind the desk in a leather swivel chair.

Glenn picked up a telephone, dialed. He spoke quickly so the call must have been answered on the first ring. "Sir, we possibly have a missing passenger, Sophia Montgomery Lennox, American, last seen in Suite 6088 at—" He glanced toward me.

I reconfirmed the time. "A quarter after ten."

"—at twenty-two fifteen by passenger Henrietta Collins. Mrs. Collins raised an alarm at twenty-three forty-one. I met Mrs. Collins at Suite 6088. It is empty. A search of the public areas is under way." A pause. "Yes, sir. I will keep you informed." He hung up, lifted a pen and pad from the desk drawer, looked at me, his dark eyes intent. "All right, Mrs. Collins. Why did you call for me?" His tone was uninflected, neither hostile nor supportive. Despite the hour and his unshaven cheeks, he looked alert and decisive.

I welcomed his no-nonsense demeanor. I doubted he often dealt with serious crime aboard the luxurious cruise ship, but in today's world, terrorist attacks are possible anywhere at any time. The *Clio*'s staff captain as second-in-command oversaw security. Glenn had demonstrated he knew how to handle the unexpected and could be counted on to proceed with intelligence.

Most important was the search for Sophia. I wished I believed she would be found. I remembered the open doors to Sophia's balcony and the undulation of the drapes.

I put it baldly, knowing I would have much to explain. "I was getting ready for bed when I suddenly realized that Sophia might well be in danger tonight because her husband plans to disembark in the morning in Helsinki."

His brows drew down in a tight frown. "What's the connection?" His cool eyes studied me intently.

"Last night Mrs. Lennox included her husband among the suspects in her fall at the Hermitage. Clearly, you believed he could have pushed her."

Not a muscle moved in his alert face.

"If Mrs. Lennox were murdered tonight, he would be a prime suspect. If, however, he left the *Clio* in Helsinki and flew to London, there would be no convenient scapegoat. The only persons with a motive for her death would be the members of the Riordan family. Unfortunately, I told one of the Riordans—Kent—that Jimmy planned to leave the ship in the morning." I looked at the walnut clock on Glenn's desk. Already a quarter past midnight. "This morning. As I was getting ready for bed, I remembered that conversation. I thought it very likely Kent told the others. That meant tonight was the last opportunity to kill Sophia and hope Jimmy would be blamed. I called her cabin. There was no answer. I called Mr. Lennox, thinking she might be with him. I did not reach him. I called for you."

"You interest me." His eyes narrowed. "Why did you think Mrs. Lennox might be with her husband?"

"She hoped for a reconciliation." Poor Sophia. Too hasty in her judgments, unable to understand hearts and feelings, seeking a love that wasn't possible. "I spoke with Mrs. Lennox tonight in her cabin." That sounded calm and reasoned, yet both of us had struggled with emotion. "I wanted her to have some materials her husband sent me before the cruise. They prove his fear for her safety was justified. I felt certain that she would agree after she read his letter. I'm glad to say that she did agree. She realized she had been distraught at the Hermitage and that she must have been pushed by a member of the Riordan family. She planned to contact Jimmy—Mr. Lennox—and tell him she was sorry."

He wrote quickly, flicked me an inquiring glance. "Did she do so?" His tone was neutral, his eyes suspicious.

"I don't know. I left her cabin then." Had Sophia called Jimmy? Had she had time to call? What happened after I left? She must have answered a knock at the door, admitted someone. The list was short: Evelyn, Alex, Madge, Kent, Rosie, Val.

I looked at the ornate face of the clock on Glenn's desk. I could picture the clock in a Victorian drawing room and wondered to whom it had belonged and what it meant to Glenn that he brought it to travel the seas with him. The time was 12:18. Did time matter now to Sophia?

I leaned forward. "We have to find Mr. Lennox. He must be told."

Glenn ignored my plea. "When did you last see Mr. Lennox?"

I felt a terrible impatience to reach Jimmy. He had to know that Sophia was missing. "Thursday night. What difference does it make?"

"You didn't see him Friday? How did you know he planned to leave the *Clio* in Helsinki?"

"He left me a message Friday afternoon, but I already knew he was going to make reservations. We talked about it Thursday night. I told Kent Riordan Friday morning."

Static crackled. Glenn turned to a radio set.

"Officer Watkins, sir." She sounded stiff and formal. "Passenger Lennox is here. He demands to know why I am in the hallway. He knocked on the door." Her voice gave no hint of the swift search that was under way or the circumstances that brought her to Sophia's door. "He wants me to open the door."

I wished I were there to catch Jimmy's hands, help him. I heard his voice in the background, sharp and worried: "Where's Sophia? Where's Mrs. Lennox? She left a message for me. Dammit, where is she?"

Glenn's face furrowed. "Let me speak to him."

The young woman's voice was polite. "Mr. Lennox, Staff Captain Glenn wishes to speak to you."

Jimmy's voice boomed into Glenn's office. "What's going on? Where's Sophia?"

Glenn frowned. "Mr. Lennox, I am sorry to report that

Mrs. Lennox's whereabouts are currently unknown. Come to the reception area, please." The staff captain's tone was curt.

"Unknown . . ." Jimmy drew in a harsh breath. "She's not in the suite? Have you looked? Maybe she's sick. For God's sake, have this woman open the door."

"We have checked the suite, Mr. Lennox. It is empty. Officer Watkins will bring you to my office. Please give her the walkie-talkie."

There was a fumbling sound. Officer Watkins spoke. "Sir?"

"Bring Mr. Lennox to my office."

"Yes, sir." There was a click.

A crackle of static sounded. Glenn turned toward a shortwave radio, bent his head to listen. "Officer O'Reilly, sir. All public areas have been checked, including lavatories. No trace of Mrs. Lennox has been found. A search is now under way in restricted areas."

Glenn's face tightened. "Very well." His voice was grim. The likelihood that Sophia was in an area restricted to ship personnel was remote. Glenn picked up the phone, dialed. "Sir, the search parties found no trace of Mrs. Lennox in the public areas. Staff areas are now being searched." He listened. "Yes, sir. Immediately."

He hung up, turned to a public-address system, pushed several buttons, spoke with calm authority: "Attention all passengers. This is Staff Captain Glenn. I regret to interrupt your rest but a passenger is being sought urgently. Passenger Sophia Lennox is requested to report immediately to Staff Captain Glenn. Anyone with information about Sophia Lennox's whereabouts should contact Staff Captain Glenn. Passenger Lennox was last seen at shortly after twenty-two hundred in her cabin. She is in her fifties, American, blond, petite, slightly built. When last seen, she was wearing a pale blue linen jacket and skirt. Anyone sighting Mrs. Lennox after twenty-two hundred is asked to contact Staff Captain Glenn immediately." After a pause to let disoriented passengers shocked to wakefulness hear and understand, he repeated the announcement twice, concluding, "Thank you for your assistance."

I thought of the balcony to Sophia's suite. In daylight it offered a magnificent view of dark blue water and the white froth from the *Clio*'s wake. Below the surface, the propellers churned, massive and inexorable, creating suction that pulled down and down and down.

When Glenn clicked off the PA speaker, I pointed aft. "Could Sophia survive if she went over the railing of her balcony?"

His eyes met mine and I read Sophia's death sentence there. "We don't know what happened. If Mrs. Lennox is not aboard, we have to assume she went overboard. We don't know where or how that might have occurred."

He didn't refute my conclusion. If Sophia fell or was pushed or jumped from her balcony, Sophia was dead.

Glenn's door opened. Jimmy pushed past Officer Watkins. "I heard the announcement." His steps were unsteady as much from shock as from the wallowing movement of the floor as the ship plowed through big waves. "Have you looked everywhere?" Jimmy's hair was tousled, his face pale. He looked rumpled in a navy sweatshirt and worn jeans.

"We have checked the public areas, Mr. Lennox. We are now searching restricted areas. Sit down, please." Glenn was courteous, but his look at Jimmy was brooding and thoughtful.

"She has to be somewhere. Maybe she fainted.

Maybe . . ." The ship rose and fell. Jimmy struggled to keep his balance. I gripped the edge of the desk.

A tinny voice sounded from the radio. "The search has been concluded. Mrs. Lennox was not found in staff areas. Unless she is in a passenger cabin, she is not on board."

"Break out a larger search party. Recheck the entire ship."

I pictured crewmen moving swiftly through the night, looking one more time.

Jimmy's eyes were blank. "Sophia . . ."

I stood and reached for his hand. It felt cold in mine. Jimmy never looked at me. His face was anguished.

Glenn ignored both of us, once again speaking into the telephone. "Sir, no trace of Mrs. Lennox. Staff areas have been searched as well." He bent his head forward, listened intently.

Jimmy jerked free of me, took a step forward. "I've got to go look. I've—"

Glenn held up his hand.

Jimmy broke off, waited. He clenched and unclenched his hands, impatient and desperate.

Finally Glenn said, "Very well, sir. I will proceed."

Jimmy moved toward the desk, slammed his hands upon it. "She has to be on the ship." His voice shook. "She must be on the ship. Somewhere."

Glenn slowly shook his head, his face grim. "The entire ship has been searched, Mr. Lennox."

Glenn's grim face made his conclusion clear. Sophia was not on board. He gazed at Jimmy. "Where were you this evening, Mr. Lennox?"

# nineteen

THE bar. On deck. Everywhere. Nowhere. When I got
back to my cabin, I had a message from Sophia."
Jimmy's eyes were anguished, his tone wooden. "She
asked me to come and see her."

Glenn asked quickly, "What time was the message recorded?"

Jimmy rubbed his temple. "At ten-eighteen, but I was
out on deck. I couldn't stand being in the cabin. I had a
drink in the topside bar, then went up to the sundeck."

Glenn's stare was neither believing nor disbelieving.
"Was anyone else on the sundeck?"

"I had it to myself." Jimmy's tone was somber, a man
who'd stood alone in the darkness grappling with failure,
the worst kind of failure: the end of caring. "I don't know
how long I stayed. A long time. I had no reason to go below. Finally I went down to my cabin, and that's when I
got Sophia's message."

"What time was that?"

Jimmy's shoulders lifted, fell. "Late. Maybe around
eleven."

Glenn frowned. "Did you go immediately to Mrs. Lennox?"

Jimmy pressed his lips together, was long in answering. He stared at Glenn with pain-filled eyes. "No. I was angry. I almost called and told her she was too late. Instead, I fixed myself a drink. I was getting ready for bed when the phone rang. I thought it was Sophia again. I didn't pick it up. Oh God, maybe if I had—"

I shook my head. "That was me. I'd just called Sophia. When she didn't answer and you didn't answer, I contacted Mr. Glenn."

"I should have answered. I didn't. I sat there and stared at the phone until it stopped. I didn't pick up the message, but I kept hearing Sophia's voice in my mind, what she'd said earlier. She said she was sorry. She said she loved me too much and she"—Jimmy glanced toward me—"was jealous and that's why she was stupid about her fall. I kept thinking about what she said. Sophia never apologizes. She's always right. It's part of the structure that keeps her world intact. For her to apologize was unbelievable. That's when I decided to go and see her. I knew what I had to do. She was—she is my wife." There was a strange bravado in his voice. He wasn't giving up. "I had to go and tell her . . ."

"Tell her what, Mr. Lennox?" Glenn's glance flicked from Jimmy to me and back again.

I had a sense of impending disaster. "Jimmy, Sophia knew she'd made a mistake. She wasn't thinking. She was upset."

"Let Mr. Lennox finish, Mrs. Collins." Glenn was abrupt, irritated at my intervention.

Jimmy blinked, stared at me as if just now fully comprehending my presence. "Henrie O, how did you know something was wrong?"

I told him quickly, my decision to give Sophia the packet he'd prepared before the journey, my talk with her, Sophia's understanding that the danger she faced came from the Riordans, her decision to call him, and finally, reluctantly, I described that dreadful moment in my cabin when I'd realized the Riordans likely knew Jimmy planned to disembark in Helsinki. "Don't you see? If you left the ship, none of them would dare attack her. I was sure that put her in terrible danger tonight. But I can't believe she opened the door to any of the Riordans. It doesn't make sense."

Glenn watched us, his eyes thoughtful. "If your visit progressed as you describe it, Mrs. Collins, it is unlikely Mrs. Lennox would have been so foolish." His voice was uninflected. Clearly he was skeptical of everything I'd told him. Skeptical of me. Skeptical of Jimmy.

Glenn turned toward Jimmy. "What were you going to tell Mrs. Lennox when you went to her cabin?"

Jimmy's face might have been carved from stone, but he looked directly at Glenn. "That I was going home. Without her. I'd realized we couldn't go on." He took a deep breath. "How do you think that makes me feel? She needed me and I wasn't there. If I'd come straight to her when I got her message, maybe she'd be safe. I didn't go to her." Jimmy struggled to keep his composure. "But nothing matters now except Sophia. What are you doing? Where are you looking? She's got to be somewhere."

"We have not given up, Mr. Lennox. The ship is being searched again, everywhere. The ship is turning now. The *Clio* will return to her location at twenty-two hundred. At daybreak, we will mount a search. The captain has already alerted the authorities in both Russia and Finland. Air rescue units will assist in our search."

Another swell lifted the ship. Jimmy stared at Glenn. "The seas are rough."

Glenn didn't answer. Instead, he stood. "We are doing everything possible to find your wife, Mr. Lennox. I suggest you and Mrs. Collins attempt to rest. There is nothing either of you can do tonight to help."

Jimmy looked combative, face hard, hands balled into fists. "How about the Riordans? Have you checked them? Found out where they were tonight? If anything's happened to Sophia, one of them is responsible." He glared at the telephone. "That announcement went into every cabin, right?"

Glenn nodded, his face thoughtful.

"Where are they?" Jimmy demanded. "Why haven't any of them responded? I know they hate Sophia, but you'd think one of them would be decent enough—"

The phone rang.

Glenn bent, lifted the receiver. "Staff Captain Glenn." He reached over, punched a button.

Evelyn's voice, high and strained, filled the small office. "Mr. Glenn, this is Evelyn Riordan." She took a breath as if air were hard to find. "What's happened to Sophia? She hasn't been herself at all, short-tempered and upset and really angry with—well, you heard her last night. Making family decisions in public. That wasn't like her at all. And I couldn't believe it when she made you give her husband another cabin. That shows she wasn't herself, suspecting Jimmy of trying to hurt her. Where's Jimmy? He will be frantic. What can we do to help? I talked to the children. None of them saw her tonight. Please, tell us what's happening."

Glenn's glance at Jimmy was faintly ironic. He spoke soothingly. "A search for Mrs. Lennox is in progress. We have been seeking her since shortly before midnight. She is not in her suite. She has not been seen since twenty-two hundred. Are you certain no one in your party spoke with her after dinner?"

"Oh yes. That's the first thing I asked everyone. Oh, if

only I'd gone to her cabin. I knew she was upset, but I didn't feel well." Evelyn sounded tearful.

"So none of you know anything that will aid our investigation?" Glenn's question seemed perfunctory.

I looked toward Glenn and knew that in his own mind the search for Sophia was now an investigation into the circumstances of her disappearance.

"I'm sorry. I wish we did." Evelyn sounded sincere. "We want to help. We'll do everything we can. Should we come to your office? Can we help look?"

"That will not be necessary. I will speak with each of you tomorrow. Thank you for your call." He reached down, clicked off the speakerphone. "Good night, Miss Riordan."

When he replaced the receiver, he looked at Jimmy.

Jimmy scowled. "Evelyn's clinging to a dream world. She refuses to face reality. She's going to convince herself that Sophia jumped or fell."

Glenn's voice was patient. "At present, Mr. Lennox, we have yet to exhaust the search for your wife. When—if—she is deemed lost, we will mount a thorough investigation and consider all possibilities. Accident. Suicide. Murder."

I clung to the railing to keep my balance. The *Clio* had picked up speed, breasting swells. Stars blazed in magnificent splendor, bright as diamonds spattered on black velvet. Twin searchlights beamed down from the bridge toward the dark water.

Jimmy gripped the railing, looked out at dark water. "Even if she's there, we wouldn't see her."

Narrow beams of searchlights illuminated a swath of water. It was an effort, the best that could be managed in the deep of the night.

"Jimmy, I'm sorry." I wished I could give him encouragement. I couldn't. Sophia had to be in the cold, dark sea, somewhere along the *Clio*'s course.

He was long in answering. When he did, his voice was flat. "Sophia's gone."

"Yes." Reality trumps desire. We might wish with all our hearts that Sophia would once again brush back golden curls with an impatient hand, give her quick, bright smile, move fast, always in a hurry, with thoughts to think, love to give, demands to make. Wishing wouldn't make it so.

"It's my fault." His voice was deep in his throat. "If I'd gone to her—"

My fingers clamped hard and tight on his arm. "Stop there. You thought Sophia was safe because Glenn knew what happened at the Hermitage. You thought she'd be careful, keep her door closed. I'd swear she was fully aware of the danger she was in when I left her. I can't believe she was foolish enough to open her door to any of them. When we know why she did that, we'll know everything. As for blame, if it's anyone's fault, it's mine. I might as well have engraved an invitation to murder. You see"—I looked toward him, tears streaking my cheeks— "I told Kent we were leaving the *Clio,* flying to London from Helsinki. You know he told the others. It's my fault."

Jimmy slipped an arm around my shoulder, drew me close. "That's not true. You did your best to protect her. You went to her, told her the truth. She knew who threatened her. But I should have been there." He stood apart from me, moved back to the railing, gripped it. "I was her husband. I should have protected her."

"Jimmy, come below. Go to your cabin. Get some rest." My head ached. My eyes were grainy, my legs leaden from fatigue. We needed sleep, both of us, fitful and uneasy and haunted as it would be. The living must do as the living do, no matter how hard and painful the moment.

He didn't answer.

I left him at the railing, staring out into the night.

# twenty

I found a pair of binoculars in the cabinet of the bedside stand and carried them with me through the silent corridors. I took the lift to Deck 10. The pool was empty and looked uninviting in the dim beginnings of dawn. Every step up the white metal stairs to the sundeck was an effort, weary muscles protesting. Three hours of sleep was woefully inadequate, but I was determined to be on the sundeck at daybreak. I shivered in the early morning chill, the breeze tugging at my windbreaker and my cotton knit slacks.

The *Clio* might have been a ghost ship, shadows slowly melting as rosy streaks threaded the eastern sky. She rode quietly at anchor and I knew we were near the point in her route where I'd said good night to Sophia.

Jimmy was there, slumped in sleep on a deck chair, head pillowed on one arm. I let him sleep, walked to the railing. Silver, rose, and gold spilled over the horizon. The sea was calm with only a trace of whitecaps. The dark water was lovely, immense, forbidding. I lifted the binoculars, scanned the surface.

As the ship came to life, other passengers ranged along the railing here and on the pool deck below, many of them also equipped with their binoculars. A helicopter hovered near the ship, the sound of its rotors loud in the early morning quiet.

Rubbing his eyes, a haggard, unshaven Jimmy joined me, reached for the binoculars. Other ships came into view. A small gray cruiser with a Russian flag and Cyrillic lettering on her bow curved around the *Clio* and began a slow progress toward Finland. When the light was bright, the sea sparkling, the *Clio* too began to move, retracing our journey westward. Crew members stood at the bow, well-trained eyes scanning the sea. Other cruise ships, perhaps ten miles to our port and starboard, kept pace.

Everything was being done that could be done.

I wrapped cold fingers around a coffee mug, welcoming the warmth. The coffee was not strong enough for my taste, but it was coffee. The informal dining room was almost full. It might have been my mood, but it seemed to me that the customary decorous good cheer was absent, that passengers too often glanced seaward, their faces concerned, uneasy, wondering. Imagining.

I took a last bite of a ham and cheese omelet. I had two sweet rolls on a paper plate and a Styrofoam cup of coffee to take up to Jimmy. I'd chosen raspberry, his favorite, knowing he would never notice, exhaustion obliterating taste. I glanced at my watch. A few minutes past nine. The *Clio* had been under way for almost three hours. When we reached the point where the graceful vessel had curved in a half circle to retrace her route, the search would be done.

The PA system crackled. "Staff Captain Glenn speaking. Passengers James Lennox, Henrietta Collins, Evelyn Riordan, Alexander and Margaret Riordan, Kent Riordan, Rosemary Riordan, and Valerie Riordan are requested to report to the Captain's Conference Room forward on Deck 8. The *Clio* has resumed passage to Helsinki. As passengers are aware, a search has been under way for a missing passenger. Anyone with knowledge of the whereabouts of Sophia Lennox after twenty-two hundred last night is asked to report to the ship security office on Deck 4. The *Clio*'s search will conclude at ten hundred hours. Search and rescue helicopters will continue to fly over the area during daylight hours. The *Clio* berths in Helsinki at approximately twelve hundred hours, four and one half hours later than scheduled. Passengers holding tickets for morning shore excursions will find excursions available this afternoon. The *Clio* departs Helsinki for Turku at nineteen hundred hours. Thank you."

Carrying coffee and sweet rolls, I walked forward, took the lift on the forward side of the pool, punched 8. I stepped out and looked about with interest. This was my first visit to Deck 8. More expensive cabins ran from this point to the stern. Staff Captain Glenn waited in front of a single door in a smooth wall decorated with maps. He was clean-shaven, his white uniform crisp, but his face was puffy with dark circles beneath his eyes. Beyond that unmarked door would be the heart of the *Clio*: the captain's office, the bridge, and the radio, computer, and radar equipment that kept the ship in motion.

I was the third of the summoned passengers to arrive. Evelyn and Val perched on the edge of a dark blue settee. Evelyn looked even less collected than usual, frizzy hair sprigging in all directions, blue eyes darting nervously around the foyer. Her oversize mauve blouse was an odd choice with a striped orange and green skirt. Val slumped gracelessly beside her. Val's eyes were bloodshot in a swollen face. She'd pulled on the white top and navy linen slacks she'd worn yesterday. She kept her hands clamped tightly together. I wondered if they were trembling.

Glenn greeted me. "Good morning, Mrs. Collins. We'll wait here until everyone arrives."

Jimmy came next, still in his sweatshirt and jeans, a sandy bristle covering his cheeks. He walked up to Glenn. "No trace." It was a grim statement, not a question.

"No trace." There might have been a glint of sympathy in Glenn's dark eyes.

Jimmy turned away, faced the wall, his shoulders slumped. He looked old and defeated, drained of energy.

I came up beside him. "I've brought you breakfast."

He tried to smile, failed. "Thank you, Henrie O." His voice was dull.

I handed him the cup. He took off the lid, drank, accepted a sweet roll, ate mechanically.

Rosie stepped out of the lift. As always, every eye turned toward her, and as always, she was striking, wind-stirred Titian hair in a cloud of curls, finely chiseled features exquisitely lovely, strawberry blouse a perfect match to tropical floral print slacks. Rosie's gaze swept us. She walked straight to Jimmy.

Rosie reached out, gently touched Jimmy's arm. "This is horrible. I can't imagine what happened to Sophia. I know you may find it hard to believe, but I wish like anything she was here now. Sometimes I hated her, but she made Dad happy. I wish things had been different."

"Made Dad happy?" Val struggled up from the settee. "She killed—"

Evelyn cried out, her voice loud, cutting off Val. "None of that has anything to do with what's happened here!" She clamped an arm tight around Val's shaking shoulders.

Rosie swung toward her sister. "Let it go, baby."

Glenn watched, his gaze sharp.

The lift door opened. Madge strolled toward us, her expression carefully relaxed but her eyes darting nervously around the hallway. Alex's red hair stood on end as if he'd just awakened. His frown was querulous. He had yet to shave and orange bristle covered his cheeks. Kent ambled behind them. His dark curls were damp as if he'd splashed water on them, pulled a comb through. He too was unshaven, his T-shirt and shorts wrinkled, espadrilles slapping as he walked.

As the lift door closed, there was a moment of awkward silence. I looked from face to face. Jimmy was sunk in a dark reverie, his eyes blank, absorbed in thoughts too grim to share. Evelyn picked nervously at her knitted purse, her expression worried and uncertain. Val pressed trembling fingers against her mouth. Rosie watched her sister. Madge held tight to Alex's arm. Kent slouched against the wall, frowning.

Glenn's face was somber. "I regret to inform you that Mrs. Lennox is believed to be lost overboard. It is Captain Wilson's duty to investigate the circumstances and prepare a report for the authorities. We will appreciate your cooperation in our inquiry."

Evelyn clutched at her throat. "All of us can tell you, Sophia wasn't herself, not at all. I hate to think about it, Sophia so upset and all alone. If only I'd gone to be with her, but I had no idea she might harm herself."

Jimmy's head snapped up. "Not suicide. Not Sophia."

Glenn didn't change expression. His voice was smooth. "The investigation will consider all possibilities. The captain is expecting us."

Rosie reached out, took Val's elbow.

Evelyn bustled to her feet. "All of us will do everything we can to help."

Glenn turned to the door, rapidly drummed numbers

on the electronic keypad. He held the door for us. We filed into a wide hallway, passed a half dozen closed doors. The hallway ended at another door. It stood open.

We stepped into a huge room that ran the width of the bow. Broad windows on either side offered a magnificent view of the sea. A massive wooden desk sat near the starboard windows. Computer screens glowed. Captain Wilson waited in the center of the room next to a long mahogany conference table with leather swivel chairs. A few feet from the table, a seaman checked settings on a video camera mounted on a tripod.

The captain stood with his hands behind him, feet apart, in a dark-billed white cap, short-sleeved white shirt topped with a captain's shoulder boards, white trousers, white shoes. He looked even more imposing than at the opening reception, radiating authority, the ship's master. His blue eyes scanned us with deliberation.

Glenn introduced us, beginning with Jimmy.

Captain Wilson looked directly at Jimmy. "Mr. Lennox, may I offer you my deepest sympathy." The quiet pronouncement made it clear that Sophia was dead.

"Thank you." Jimmy pressed his lips together.

Captain Wilson was grave. "I know it is difficult for you to be here this morning. I appreciate your willingness to help us. I also appreciate the cooperation of Mrs. Lennox's family. It is necessary for us to gather as much information as possible to provide to shore authorities when we dock in London. The *Clio* is registered as a British ship and we operate under maritime law and British law. A video camera will provide a record of this inquiry. Please be seated."

We took our places, the captain at the head of the table in a heavy brown leather chair with arms, Staff Captain Glenn at the foot of the table. Jimmy and I were on one side with Alex and Madge. Evelyn, Val, Rosie, and Kent sat opposite us.

I wondered if the captain had any inkling of the irony in his description of the Riordans as Sophia's family.

Captain Wilson opened a green folder, glanced down at it. A legal pad and a pen lay to one side. "Mrs. Lennox was seen last night by Mrs. Collins at approximately twenty-two fifteen. No one has admitted seeing Mrs. Lennox after that time. Mrs. Collins called Mrs. Lennox's cabin at twenty-three thirty-nine. There was no answer. Subsequent investigation by Staff Captain Glenn at twenty-three forty-seven proved the cabin to be empty. An exhaustive search of the ship makes it clear she is no longer aboard. Accordingly, it is reasonable to conclude that Mrs. Lennox was lost overboard between twenty-two fifteen and twenty-three forty-seven."

The silence was broken by a choked sob from Evelyn.

The captain nodded toward her. "I understand this is a painful moment for the family. However, we must do our best to determine the circumstances of her disappearance. As the first step in our inquiry, we must seek to discover Mrs. Lennox's state of mind in order to determine whether her death was the result of accident, suicide, or murder."

Jimmy's face creased in a tight frown. "Sophia was well and strong. There was no reason for her to fall overboard accidentally. Suicide is out of the question. Sophia was a fighter. A survivor. Sophia was murdered." His voice was scratchy with fatigue but dogged with conviction. "The murderer is in this room." He stared at each Riordan in turn. "One of them."

Evelyn clutched at her throat. "Jimmy, you've been wrong from the start." She twisted toward the captain. "Jimmy didn't mean to cause trouble, but he did. He convinced Sophia that someone pushed her at the Hermitage, and I know that was an accident. The landing was packed with people shoving and gouging. It's a wonder more of us didn't fall. Then Sophia got all suspicious about Jimmy and his friend"—her glance toward me was apologetic—"and that shows she wasn't herself. Why, Jimmy wouldn't be involved with another woman and flaunt her right in front of Sophia. But Sophia was upset. You ask anyone here. That's what they'll tell you. She was distraught. I think she was all alone and she kept thinking about everything and knew she'd ruined her marriage, sending Jimmy away, and she decided to die."

Jimmy slammed his fist on the table. "Never."

Val stared down at the table, teeth tight against her bottom lip.

Rosie's face was shuttered, but she watched her younger sister.

Kent rubbed at his forehead. "I need coffee."

Madge burst out, "Evelyn's right. Sophia hasn't been herself, not since this trip started."

Alex hurriedly agreed, "That's what happened. She jumped."

Captain Wilson was polite but firm. "Everyone will have ample opportunity to contribute. Miss Riordan, when did you last see Mrs. Lennox?"

Evelyn looked sad. "Thursday evening. She had all of us to her cabin. She was not herself, making serious financial decisions in front of everyone and that certainly wasn't like her. She insisted one of us pushed her down those stairs at the Hermitage, and she seemed to think it was Jimmy. That was absurd. The museum was crowded and she started down the steps and she fell. Anyway, none of us pushed her. No one was close enough."

Captain Wilson's tone was polite. "Despite the incidents of the dislodged boulder and the spilled sherry before the journey began, you didn't believe Mrs. Lennox when she said she was pushed?"

The realization was instantaneous among everyone present that Captain Wilson was aware of Frank Riordan's will, his children's relationship with Sophia, the circumstances of her fall at the Hermitage, her decree that the trusts would not be dissolved, and, of course, her inclusion of Jimmy and me as suspects in her fall.

In the stillness that followed his revealing question, the atmosphere changed from one of cooperation to wary attention. I felt that one listener was shaken by fear, but I saw no trace of fear in the faces I quickly scanned. Evelyn looked befuddled and uncomfortable. Val pressed fingers to one temple, her eyes bleary with pain. Rosie frowned, her glance sliding toward her sister, then away. Kent straightened in his chair, his expression concerned. Alex chewed on his lower lip, the picture of uncertainty. Madge's glare was outraged.

One of the Riordans had a clever mask firmly in place.

Evelyn clutched her silver necklace. "Jimmy upset me with his claims about the boulder. I'll admit I was scared about the sherry, but I know that was silly. I'll never believe anything that has happened was deliberate. Never." She was as convinced of her truth as Jimmy was of his.

Jimmy looked at her sadly. "Evelyn, can't you see?" He gestured at the Riordan heirs. "They inherit millions. More than that, they've been angry for years. They hated the way their father deferred to Sophia, banished them to boarding schools. Val blamed Sophia for her sister's suicide. And Kent"—Jimmy looked grim—"just found out Sophia caused the breakup with his fiancée."

"Back off, Lennox." Kent bunched his hands into fists. "Leave my sister out of this."

"He's trying to blame us. That's all he's done ever since the trip began." Madge's voice was high and shrill. "He's the one Sophia was afraid of."

Captain Wilson was impassive. "Staff Captain Glenn has reported to me the events of Thursday evening. For the record now"—he nodded toward Evelyn—"you state that you last saw Mrs. Lennox Thursday evening?"

"Yes. Thursday evening." Evelyn's lips quivered. "Poor Sophia."

The captain made a note on his pad. "Where were you from twenty-two to twenty-four hundred last night?"

Evelyn looked unutterably tired. "In my cabin. I read until eleven, then I went to bed."

The captain looked at Val. "Miss Riordan, when did you last see your stepmother?"

"Don't call her my stepmother." Val's face was hard. "She was married to my father. My father's dead."

The captain's blue eyes studied her dispassionately. "When did you last see Mrs. Lennox?"

Val slumped in her chair, her sudden energy fading. She brushed back a tendril of hair that had escaped her sleek bun. "I guess it was Thursday night." She looked uneasy and confused.

"Guess?" Captain Wilson frowned. "You must know when you saw her."

Evelyn patted Val's arm. "She's been having trouble with seasickness. Val isn't a good sailor."

"Miss Riordan can make her own replies, please." His eyes never left Val's troubled face.

"Thursday night." Val's voice held no conviction.

"Where were you last night?" He watched her closely.

"In my cabin. I didn't feel good." Val's eyes were huge

and uncertain. I doubted she had any memory of Friday evening. She'd drunk herself into oblivion.

"Did you leave your cabin during the period in question?"

I didn't give her time to reply. Her uncertainty was evident, and I wanted to save her from embarrassment. "Val and I were in Diogenes Bar. I went there after I'd talked to Sophia. Val joined me. I suppose it was ten or fifteen minutes after eleven. I walked with her to her cabin, left her there about eleven-thirty, went on to my cabin."

Val stared at me with haunted eyes.

Wilson persisted. "Where were you before you joined Mrs. Collins?"

Val looked down at the table. "In my cabin."

"Very well." The captain made notes, looked up. "Miss Rosemary Riordan?"

Rosie was brisk, almost casual. "Thursday night was the last time I saw Sophia." She gave an engaging smile. "As you might imagine, Captain, none of us had any reason to spend time with Sophia after that. She made it clear she didn't want to have anything to do with us for about ten years. That suited us fine. We all felt the same." She gestured toward her sister and brothers. "It was a relief to have the show-and-tell exercise over. We didn't come up to Sophia's expectations. So be it. We certainly didn't care enough to plot murder, and that's what we're talking about. I'm with Evelyn. Either Sophia jumped or somehow she fell. Anyway, I saw her Thursday night and didn't have a glimpse Friday night. I was here and there after dinner. I listened to the music in the main lounge. Bossa nova." Another smile. "When they started the movie, I went up and had a drink at the topside bar. I took a walk on deck, turned in around eleven."

"You were alone all evening?"

I wasn't surprised the captain was skeptical. Rosie was not the kind of woman to spend an evening by herself except in the most unusual of circumstances.

Her smile was genuine, the implicit compliment accepted. "Yes, I was." She looked composed and confident.

He wrote on his pad, looked at Kent.

Kent shrugged. "Same song, second verse. I didn't see Sophia after Thursday night, never planned to see her again. I was finished with the lady. She could whistle, but this dog didn't intend to come. Thursday night was my farewell to Pop's insanity. Friday night I wasn't paying attention to time. I spent most of the evening up in the computer bay, sending e-mails." For an instant, his eyes were hot points of anger. "And yeah"—his glance at Jimmy was cold—"Sophia screwed up my love life, but"—he jerked his head toward me—"thanks to Mrs. Collins, I think I can straighten everything out. You can check what time my e-mails went out. I don't know that it matters. I took some breaks, got a couple of beers, went to the john. I got back to my cabin around eleven, must have just missed seeing my sis. But I never saw Sophia after Thursday night."

"None of us saw her after Thursday." Madge Riordan looked at Captain Wilson with her blue eyes wide. "It's like Kent said. We didn't have any reason to talk to her. Friday night Alex and I watched the movie *Calendar Girls*. You know, the funny one about the ladies who pose nude for a calendar to raise money. Alex and I loved it."

I was looking at Alex. His expression was tense.

Madge rushed on. "There's a scene where—"

Captain Wilson was brisk. "Yes, Mrs. Riordan. You watched the film. And then?"

She looked at him earnestly. "We stayed for the whole

thing. We didn't get back to our cabin until eleven-thirty. We must have just missed all the excitement when you started looking for Sophia."

The lounge was darkened for the showing of a movie. It would be easy to slip out unnoticed and return. I suspected Madge and Alex would have no difficulty describing the plot, the funniest scenes. Movies shown in the lounge were also repeated throughout the day on cabin television.

Madge relaxed back in her seat. Was it the relief of an innocent person or was she hiding something?

Captain Wilson turned to me. "Mrs. Collins, you are the last person to have seen Mrs. Lennox."

"I am the last person who admits to seeing Mrs. Lennox." I wanted the distinction to be made.

"Indeed. Describe your meeting with her." His gaze was intent, his blue eyes speculative and thoughtful.

I intended to go about it in my own way. "I took Mrs. Lennox materials I received from her husband prior to the trip. I was convinced that once she read Jimmy's letter and the information he had sent to me about the Riordan family and the trust funds, she would understand that her husband was trying to protect her and that the danger to her came from a member of the Riordan family."

"That's what they've claimed all along." Madge's voice was shrill, her glare was venomous.

I ignored her. "As I expected, once Mrs. Lennox read the letter she realized she had been mistaken in suspecting her husband. In fact, almost her last words to me were her hope that he would forgive her. She intended to call and ask him to come and see her."

Captain Wilson's eyes narrowed. "Describe the materials you took to her cabin."

The request surprised me. "I left them on the coffee table. You can read them, add them to the record."

"Describe them, please."

I was puzzled. "An overnight mailer, a letter from Jimmy, biographical data about each of the Riordans, pictures of Sophia and the Riordans."

The captain's voice was measured. "No such materials were found in Mrs. Lennox's cabin."

I stared at him, bewildered. "I left everything with her. The letter and the dossiers were spread out on the coffee table." I realized as I spoke that neither Jimmy nor I could prove the existence of any of the papers. Captain Wilson and Staff Captain Glenn could conclude that Jimmy and I had engaged in an elaborate charade, our final objective Sophia's murder with the Riordans as suspects-in-waiting.

"There were no such papers." His voice was decisive.

Evelyn looked shocked. Val sat in quiet misery with no apparent interest in her surroundings. Rosie frowned. Kent gave a low whistle, raised an eyebrow. Madge hissed in Alex's ear.

Jimmy and I had no proof that anything we'd reported was true. There was no way we could prove—suddenly, I felt almost giddy with relief. "Sophia called Jimmy. She left him a message."

"I told Glenn last night." Jimmy's voice was weary. "I found Sophia's message when I came down to my cabin. Sophia said she was sorry for even thinking I might have pushed her, that she wasn't thinking straight, that she"— he took a breath—"was jealous. She said Henrie O had brought my letter to her and now she understood. She asked me to forgive her."

Captain Wilson watched Jimmy intently. "Would you say that the tenor of her message was emotional?"

Jimmy's face was abruptly ridged with lines of distress. He was long in answering. "Yes."

"Yet"—and the captain's eyes were cold—"you did not save that message. If your description of the message is accurate, why did you erase it? Wouldn't the recipient of such a message have been inclined to save it, perhaps to listen to it again? Instead, you erased that message. Why, Mr. Lennox?"

Jimmy slumped back in his chair. He stared toward the windows giving onto the sea, his face heavy with sorrow. "I was furious. I didn't see anything beyond the way she'd treated me. God forgive me, I didn't help her."

I leaned forward. "Is there a record of a call from Sophia's suite to Jimmy's cabin?" Even as I asked, I knew an electronic record was no help. As far as the captain and Glenn were concerned, every word I'd uttered could be a lie. I could have gone to see Sophia, possibly Jimmy and I together, killed her, pushed her overboard, then called his cabin and left a message which, of course, he later deleted.

Captain Wilson glanced at his notes. "A call was made from Suite 6088 to Cabin 6048 at twenty-two hundred eighteen. If it was made by Mrs. Lennox, that is the last indication that she was alive." He turned to me. "Where did you go when you left Mrs. Lennox's suite?"

"Diogenes Bar. I was there until I left with Val Riordan about half past eleven." I was sure the waiter would remember helping me with Val, but my presence there was no proof of innocence.

Captain Wilson folded his hands, gazed at Jimmy. "Mr. Lennox?"

Jimmy met his stare with a trace of anger. "I've already told Glenn. Topside bar. Sundeck. Down to my cabin around eleven."

"You claim that you did not enter Mrs. Lennox's cabin

last night?" There was a heavy finality to Captain Wilson's voice.

"I did not." Jimmy's face was set in hard, defiant lines.

Captain Wilson folded his arms. His gaze was steely. "Mr. Lennox, your key was used to enter Suite 6088 at precisely twenty-three oh-three Friday evening. Every time an electronic key is inserted into a cabin lock, the code on the back of the key registers which key was used. The key that opened the door at that moment was one of two keys issued to that suite when you boarded. Mrs. Lennox's key was in her purse."

Jimmy looked stunned. "That's impossible. I left that key in the bowl on the coffee table Thursday night." He looked at Glenn. "You saw me leave it. Sophia kicked me out, asked for my key."

"No folder was found in the bowl. Neither the folder nor the key within it." Glenn's eyes narrowed. "To be precise, Mr. Lennox, I saw you toss a key folder into the bowl. If you recall, you accepted a new key folder from me, placed it in your right trouser pocket. Mrs. Lennox asked for your key to her cabin. You reached into your left hip pocket, but it is possible that you edged the card loose in your pocket and threw the folder—without the key card—into the bowl."

Across the table, Kent flipped open his key folder, edged the key from behind its plastic sheath. He looked at Jimmy, his gaze wondering.

I wanted to cry out that Jimmy could not possibly have managed such a sleight of hand, but it could have happened. I knew it had not. I knew Jimmy. There were many Jimmys, but never a crafty, wily, dangerous Jimmy.

Jimmy's face was bleak. "You give me credit for incredibly quick thinking. Murderous thinking, I take it."

Captain Wilson held up a hand. "I am not implying

murder, Mr. Lennox. However, we have to consider the facts as we find them. The key must be explained. It would be understandable"—he picked his words carefully—"if you came to see Mrs. Lennox and if you told her that your differences were irreconcilable, she might have been so distraught after you left she decided upon suicide."

"In a word, no." Jimmy was emphatic. "It didn't happen. If there had been such an exchange with my wife, I can assure you suicide would never have been her choice. Moreover, I accept responsibility for my actions. I'm guilty for not responding when she reached out to me. But that's all I'm guilty of. I didn't see Sophia. I didn't quarrel with her. I never hurt her." He swallowed hard. "I've told you everything I know. I did not keep the key, nor did I use it last night. If anyone entered the cabin with that key, it wasn't me."

## twenty-one

NO one spoke as we filed out of the bridge area into the public foyer. Glenn accompanied us. He remained in the doorway and looked toward Jimmy and me and Kent. "The captain requests that all passengers who traveled with Mrs. Lennox complete the voyage and disembark when the *Clio* reaches the port of London. However, you may join shore excursions if you wish." His meaning was clear. We might have some freedom of movement, but we were to continue as passengers for the duration of the voyage. He didn't wait for an answer. He turned back and the door closed.

Kent scowled. "That makes one more week before I can see Heather. Sophia is as much trouble dead as she was alive."

Jimmy took a step toward him, his fists doubling. I grabbed his arm, then stepped toward Kent. "You told everyone Jimmy and I were leaving in Helsinki."

Kent's gaze slid away. He didn't answer.

Rosie was crisp. "He told us at lunch. We all heard it. Everybody hoped things would go better for Jimmy. But none of us harmed Sophia. I know Jimmy didn't either." She looked at him. "She either fell or jumped. Nobody pushed her. Not you. Not us."

Jimmy's face softened. "Thank you, Rosie. But we have to find out about that key. Somebody opened Sophia's door. Who?"

Evelyn clapped her hands together. "I know."

We all looked at her, waited.

"Maybe Sophia decided to go out for a while and that's the key she picked up." Evelyn's voice was eager. "The key was right there in the bowl. It saved her from finding her purse, getting out her folder." Evelyn looked excitedly at Jimmy. "Maybe Sophia went to your cabin to bring you the key. When she didn't find you, she came back, used that key to get in. It makes all kinds of sense. I'll tell Mr. Glenn. It just shows they aren't so smart. No one even suggested Sophia using the key." Her voice lifted with confidence. "I'll call him when I get back to my cabin. Anyway, there's nothing we can do about any of it now. The ship people will make out their report, and we have to see the trip through. But"—her look at Jimmy was kind—"I know you wouldn't hurt Sophia. It had to be an accident. Accidents happen." Her tone was stubborn. "I for one am sure it was an accident. In any event, we'll want to arrange a memorial service for Sophia."

Jimmy was touched. "Thank you, Evelyn. I'd appreciate your help."

Evelyn's smile was pleased. "We'll all work together."

I suddenly felt uncertain. Jimmy insisted Sophia wouldn't fall, must have been pushed. But at this moment I had trouble imagining any of the Riordans as dangerous. Evelyn was the epitome of a frowsy traveler, no more threatening than a water beetle. Val stared blankly at the lift door, withdrawn, self-absorbed, nursing her hangover. Rosie looked as though a weight had been lifted from her shoulders. Kent rocked back on his heels, nodding in agreement. Alex beamed at his aunt. Madge's face was inscrutable, but she slowly nodded.

"Sophia could have picked up the key from the bowl." Jimmy's weary face wrinkled in thought. "If she didn't find me, she'd have come back to the cabin, used the key."

Evelyn rushed ahead. "The sea was rough. Maybe she went out on the balcony. She could have fallen."

I watched Jimmy, saw his face smooth out into unreadable blandness. I knew that look. He didn't believe Sophia had fallen, would never believe she'd jumped, but he was an old and savvy reporter who was smart enough to listen without tipping his hand. "Maybe," he said slowly.

"That has to be what happened. I know Mr. Glenn will agree." Relief lifted Evelyn's voice. "Now, Jimmy, you better get some rest. You've been up all night. I'll get busy, send word to some of Sophia's friends." Evelyn moved toward the elevator, her nieces and nephews following. "Jimmy, let us know if there is anything we can do."

I wandered restlessly about the *Clio* throughout the afternoon, watched the excursions depart and return. We sailed from Helsinki at six-thirty. I heard nothing from Jimmy. I knew he was dealing with e-mails and phone calls. I hoped he was too busy to feel, too numb from exhaustion to grieve. I ordered soup and a sandwich to my cabin for an early dinner, then stumbled to the bed and fell into a deep but uneasy sleep.

I woke to unpleasant memories: my last glimpse of Sophia, the long wearing night and longer day with no news, the strangely polite yet devastating inquiry, and Glenn's bombshell: Jimmy's key had opened the door to Sophia's cabin at three minutes after eleven.

I propped up on my elbow, gazed toward the balcony door, realized it was bright outside. I'd slept for a long time. The key. . . I wondered if Evelyn had contacted Glenn and if it had possibly already occurred to him that it might have been Sophia who used the key.

I showered and dressed, walked up to Deck 9 for breakfast. The *Clio* docked at Turku, Finland, at eight o'clock. After the excursions were done, the *Clio* departed for Stockholm in midafternoon. I carried my tray to an outside table though it was still cool. I spread cream cheese on a bagel, added a slice of salmon.

We passed small fir-crowned islands, part of the archipelago. As I ate, I thought about the key. Was it as simple as Evelyn believed? Had Sophia reached for the nearest key? That was plausible.

If Sophia had not used the key, whose hand held it? How had it been obtained? Would Glenn seek to answer these questions or was the investigation done, the conclusion reached that Jimmy had managed to slip the electronic card free and kept it for his own use?

Yet surely the missing material that I brought her was proof that someone other than Sophia had been in the cabin. She had no reason to throw away the folder. Jimmy had no reason to destroy the information. Only one of the Riordans had reason to get rid of the letter and dossiers. But, of course, Glenn might not believe the material had ever existed.

There was another possibility. Sophia opened the door to a visitor, the visitor overpowered her, pushed her overboard, and took Jimmy's key. Sophia's murderer then stepped out into the hall, closed the door, and used Jimmy's key to reopen the door, a deliberate effort to incriminate him. That would explain why the key wasn't in the ceramic bowl. It had not been used by Sophia to enter the cabin. It had been used to make it look as though Jimmy had kept the key.

There was one impassable barrier to this solution. If the visitor was not Jimmy, Jimmy for whom Sophia had called, and was instead a member of the Riordan family, Sophia would not have opened the door. She knew she was in danger. She had no doubt about the incident at the Hermitage. She had been pushed, deliberately and hard. Sophia was confident and cool, but she was not reckless. It would have been foolish indeed to open her door late at night to one of the Riordans.

I did not believe Sophia opened her door.

I knew Jimmy didn't palm the leather folder.

I doubted Sophia used the key. Why wouldn't she have dropped it into the bowl upon her return? Wouldn't that have been natural? Of course, Sophia could have opened the door and slipped the key into the pocket of her linen slacks and the key went with her to her watery death.

Perhaps, but I had a bone-deep feeling that if we ever discovered who used the key, we would know everything.

I had a ticket for the excursion into Turku, but I had no intention of going. I wondered if the Riordans were among those disembarking. I hoped Evelyn had encouraged them to take the excursion. Activity helps relieve stress. None of the Riordans, with the possible exception of Evelyn, were fond of Sophia, but her loss was shocking.

I would have been glad to be free of the *Clio* for a few hours, but I wanted to satisfy myself that I'd done everything possible to help Jimmy. I didn't call him, tell him what I planned. I debated calling Glenn, asking him what he'd discovered from the stewardess who serviced Sophia's cabin. There was no good reason why he should tell me anything. Also, I'm like most old reporters. Don't take handouts. Find out for yourself.

When the last party of sightseers departed, I stepped out of my cabin. The ship had a feeling of emptiness. Our stewardess was midway up the hall. I started toward her. Monika was tall and thin, with a gentle face. Her short-sleeved white blouse was topped by a blue half apron that matched her skirt. I heard the sound of vacuuming from one of the cabins.

I stopped in front of her. "Monika, what hours do you work?"

I suppose it was part of her training to reply politely no matter how odd the question. She replied quickly in slightly accented English. "I am on duty from ten to fourteen hundred and from sixteen to twenty-two hundred, Mrs. Collins. If you need me at any other time, I will be available."

"Thank you." I smiled and walked on. My smile slipped away. Stewardesses went off duty at 10 P.M., too early to be of help. Still, it never hurt to ask. I kept on toward the stern. I spotted a service cart in the hallway near the Riordan cabins.

As I recalled, Evelyn was in the cabin next to Sophia and Jimmy. I came around the cart. I was at the conjunction of the long hallway from the bow to the stern and the short hallway from starboard to port. I could see the door to Sophia's cabin as well as the row of cabins belonging to the Riordans.

I waited until the stewardess stepped out into the corridor. She was humming a cheerful tune. She stopped when she saw me. "Ma'am, may I help you?" Her nameplate read INGRID. She was younger than my stewardess, Monika, likely not much over twenty. Her round face was framed by thick blond hair. Her complexion was rosy and flawless, her features attractive. She was a pretty girl with a full figure. Likely she'd tend toward plumpness when she was older.

I wasn't especially hopeful. Staff Captain Glenn was smart and capable. I was confident he would be careful, thorough, and persistent in making inquiries, but it wouldn't do any harm to try.

"Ingrid"—I gestured toward Cabin 6088—"I'm sure you know that Mrs. Lennox disappeared Friday night. I'm a friend of hers, and I'm hoping you can help me."

"Oh, ma'am, I'm sorry." Her eyes, a clear bright blue, clouded in sympathy. "What can I do?"

"Staff Captain Glenn asked you if you saw her that evening." I made it a statement, not a question.

"Yes, ma'am. I turned down the covers at twenty-one hundred. I didn't see her again. I go off duty at twenty-two hundred."

That should have been that, but her response was so glib, so quick, that I looked at her intently. There was the tiniest flare of wariness in her eyes. Her expression was open, frank, and honest. Too honest. There was something she didn't want to reveal.

"What did you do when you got off work?"

The question caught her by surprise. She hesitated a fraction too long. "I went to the second showing of the movie."

"I'll bet that was fun. Did you go with a friend?" She was a very pretty girl. I didn't doubt that some young man aboard ship had noticed.

She looked uncomfortable. "Oh no, ma'am. I went by myself."

Did she resent being asked a personal question? Or was she unable to claim a companion at the movie because she hadn't been in the lounge? "I was hoping you might have seen the person who entered Mrs. Lennox's cabin a few minutes after eleven."

"Entered it? But—" She broke off, looking puzzled, then shook her head. "I wouldn't know. I go off duty at twenty-two hundred." Her expression was bland.

"Perhaps you forgot something, came back to this area."

"No, ma'am." Her gaze didn't falter. "I went to the movie."

Jimmy took a sip of Scotch. His face was pale and drawn, but his blue eyes were no longer glazed with fatigue. We sat at a secluded table in the topside bar. The wide windows were dark and the *Clio* churned steadily southwestward en route to Stockholm. A trio played Caribbean music, the notes of the marimba soft and evocative.

He listened intently as I described my inconclusive interview with Ingrid. ". . . and I don't believe for a minute she went to a movie. She looked at me with wide-open eyes and an angel's face and lied." I paused. "She's a pretty girl."

"Yeah. She is." Jimmy picked up the tall slender dish in the center of the table, rattled peanuts into his hand. "That's probably the answer right there. She's probably having an affair with some guy and she doesn't want anybody snooping into where she was after she got off work."

I didn't know much about the inner workings of a cruise ship, but I doubted staff had the free time and, much more important, the privacy to pursue too many amorous delights while at sea. I suspected private quarters were only for high-ranking officers. A dormitory arrangement was probably the rule for service personnel.

I felt dissatisfied. "Do you think it would do any good for me to talk to Glenn, ask him to see her again?"

Jimmy looked thoughtful. "If she's lied to him once, she'll cling to that story no matter what." He popped peanuts in his mouth, said indistinctly, "Don't rile up Glenn. I'll give it a try, see if I can get anywhere with her. If I offer her a reward, maybe she'll cooperate. If she actually knows anything. But"—he sounded discouraged—"I can't see any reason why she'd be near her duty station an hour after she got off work. Probably the lie had to do with going to the movie. She was up to something that she wants to keep hidden."

"I suppose so." I was oddly reluctant to give up on Ingrid. I was sure that she was hiding something, but Jimmy was probably right. Her secret likely had nothing to do with Sophia, and if she had indeed lied to Glenn, she could not afford to change her story.

"The hell of it is"—Jimmy looked grim—"I don't see what more Glenn can do. He's interviewed the passengers in nearby cabins and the service staff. Nobody saw Sophia Friday night or anyone in the corridor. He thinks Evelyn may be right and Sophia herself used that key."

"Then where is the key? And where are the papers I gave her?" That was the sticking point to me.

Jimmy's hand tightened around his glass. His voice was strained. "Glenn thinks she was so upset when she got back she went out on the balcony and jumped. If that's true, she must have had the key and papers with her." He looked at me with tortured eyes. "I know that's not true, but he won't listen. He thinks I don't want to believe it because I blame myself. I can't get him to understand that it doesn't matter how distraught Sophia was, she would never have killed herself. That leaves it up to me to figure out what happened." His voice was low and hard. "Evelyn wants to believe it was an accident. I let her think I agreed. I have to be able to talk to the Riordans. I'd agree to anything."

I'd correctly read Jimmy's suddenly bland expression yesterday.

Jimmy rubbed his face. "Evelyn's crazy about those kids. In her heart she must know one of them did it. She has to know. Or maybe she wants to believe in them so bad she's convinced herself that Sophia jumped. But I know one of them killed Sophia. I'm going to keep after them. I'll find out the truth. Somehow. Some way. I owe Sophia."

I woke early and watched the sun rise. After breakfast, I sat on my balcony as the *Clio* glided to her berth in Stockholm. At the last minute, I decided to go on the excursion into the city, hoping to divert my thoughts from their endless, fruitless effort to figure out who took the key from the ceramic bowl.

In the sumptuous Golden Hall of Stockholm's city hall, a trim, energetic guide described the grandeur of the annual Nobel Prize banquet: the elegant dress, magnificent music, the congregation of the world's greatest minds. Names drifted through my mind of past winners in literature, Octavio Paz, John Steinbeck, Albert Camus, Ernest Hemingway, Sinclair Lewis. I tried to envision them as living writers. Did they feel overwhelmed by the opulence of this huge gleaming gold room? I wondered if Alfred Nobel, who invented dynamite and left a fortune to fund awards to those deemed to have most benefited mankind in the previous year, would have been pleased by the kingly presentation of the prizes in his name.

I enjoyed seeing the Golden Hall and the wooden sculpture *St. George and the Dragon* in Storkyrkan Cathedral, and all the while I worried at the questions I couldn't answer. Who took the key? What happened to the papers? What could Ingrid have seen?

I skipped the afternoon excursion to Drottningholm Palace, knowing I would once again be among the few passengers remaining aboard. This time the service cart wasn't on the port side. I expected Ingrid was even now working her way forward, servicing the starboard cabins. I had no wish to encounter her. Not at this moment.

Once again, I stood at the conjunction of the passageways, the door to Evelyn's cabin to my right, Sophia's door in the cross passage about ten feet to my left. Clearly, Evelyn could see Sophia's door every time she stepped out of her cabin. But—I backed up a few feet—when the other Riordans came into the hallway their view was obscured. The center portion of the *Clio* was devoted to storage and service areas.

I walked aft into the cross hallway. The two great suites occupied the space at the stern. Opposite them, at the end of the central service block, there were two cabin doors, 6090 and 6093. These were small interior cabins with no outlook to the sea. Less desirable, they would be considerably less expensive. However, anyone opening one of these doors had an unobstructed view of Sophia's door.

And so? I shook my head in discouragement. Glenn told Jimmy he'd checked with all nearby passengers. He certainly wouldn't have missed these cabins. Yet it was clear that Ingrid could only have glimpsed Sophia's door by looking out of one of four cabins: Evelyn's, the matching cabin on the starboard side, or the two interior ones opposite the suites. There were no storage doors with the necessary vantage point. Even if Ingrid had been in the area long past her duty hours, she could not have opened a service door and seen anyone at Sophia's door.

Disappointed, I turned and walked slowly forward. Sophia was gone and there didn't seem to be any link to her murderer. The days of our cruise were growing ever shorter. Today was Monday. We would leave Stockholm shortly before dinner, sail through the night, and anchor tomorrow afternoon off the Swedish coast for excursions by tender to Karlskrona. Wednesday the *Clio* reached the German harbor of Travemünde at noon for afternoon excursions to Lübeck. Wednesday evening the *Clio* began her final leg of this cruise, leaving Travemünde to be at sea for two and a half days before arriving in London at noon on Saturday, where we would disembark.

Would a murderer walk free?

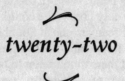

# twenty-two

I leaned against the railing on the promenade deck. Preparations were under way for the *Clio* to sail. The pilot's boat rode nearby. Seagulls scolded. The dark blue water looked placid. The last excursion group had returned almost an hour ago. Soon the hawsers would be loosed and the *Clio* would sail southwestward from Stockholm to anchor off the old naval village of Karlskrona tomorrow afternoon.

"Hi, Mrs. Collins." Rosie Riordan wore sunglasses. Her red hair was tousled and her cheeks pink from sun. "Did you go on an excursion?"

I gestured toward the city, time-stained copper domes glittering in the late afternoon sun, graceful church spires punctuating the soft blue sky. "This morning. I stayed aboard this afternoon."

Rosie placed her elbows on the railing, looked out at the deep blue water. "It didn't feel right to go. But it doesn't do any good to stay. We did the city tour this morning and Drottningholm Palace this afternoon." She turned toward me, the light reflecting from the dark lens of her sunglasses masking her eyes. Her face looked drawn and tired. "Everything seems unreal. This was

Sophia's trip. It's crazy that she's gone. I can't believe it even though I know it's true."

"I understand." Sophia had been gloriously alive, overwhelmingly dominant. Now she didn't exist.

"If only—but there's no point in thinking how it could have been different." Rosie sounded sad. "Anyway, you were nice to speak up and tell the captain that Val was with you in the bar."

I raised an eyebrow. "I'm always pleased to be considered nice, but I was simply reporting a fact."

Rosie shook her head. "You knew she didn't remember. To have everyone realize that would have been devastating for her. She's scared enough as is. She's—well, she's promised to go into treatment when we get home. This is the first time she's had blackouts. Now she knows she was with you from about a quarter to eleven to eleven-thirty." She sounded relieved.

I wished I could see Rosie's eyes, know whether she was anxiously watching me. I stared at the dark lens, my gaze steady. "I can't say exactly when Val got to the bar, but it was after eleven, possibly as much as ten minutes after the hour."

"Oh, it was sooner than that." Rosie was insistent. "I rang up her cabin about a quarter to eleven. I was up in the top deck bar and I thought she might want to come up and join me. There wasn't any answer so she was already on her way down to Diogenes. She's pretty fuzzy on everything that happened Friday night, but she thinks she went straight from her cabin to the bar. She wanted another drink and her bottle was empty. So if Val asks you, tell her she was with you from ten forty-five on." She took a deep breath. "You saw her. She was too drunk to—" She didn't have to complete the sentence: —*push Sophia*

*overboard.* "Anyway, please, if she asks you, tell her everything's fine, that she was with you. She's scared because
she doesn't remember what happened and it freaked her
out when they said somebody used Jimmy's key to open
Sophia's door right after eleven. It's better if she thinks
she was with you."

Rosie turned away, walking swiftly, head down, shoulders hunched.

I stared after her. Rosie was afraid. Desperately afraid.
I would have gone after her, demanded to know what she
feared, but she'd never tell me.

The message light flickered on my telephone. I sat at
the desk, picked up the receiver, punched 7 for the
message.

Jimmy sounded irritated. "Ingrid's either stringing me
along or too dense to understand what I'm asking her. I
told her that it was important to find out who entered Sophia's cabin right after eleven, and if she could be of any
help, I'd be glad to pay her a reward. I offered her a thousand dollars. That got her attention. She said she couldn't
help me, then asked if it was worth a lot of money to
know who was in the hall then. I told her if she knew
anything she had to tell me. I guess I got too excited. I
promised I'd try to keep her out of it when I talked to
Glenn. That's when she started backpedaling, protesting
that she didn't mean she knew anything, that she was nowhere near the cabin at eleven and she had to get back to
work, and she turned and pushed the cart down the hall
so fast she almost crashed into an old lady coming out of
her cabin a few doors down, one of those dowdy but regal
English passengers. She looked at me like I was a serial
rapist, then sailed by with her eyes flashing and her mouth
pursed. I feel like I struck out all the way around." A

pause. "I'm running out of ideas. Look, you always help me think. Let's have dinner in the main dining room at seven."

Waiters in white jackets and shirts and black trousers moved deftly among the white-clothed tables. The *Clio* was under way, cruising through the dramatic Swedish archipelago, the shadowed portions of the fir-crowned islands so darkly green they appeared black. The archipelago is made up of twenty-six thousand islands, many uninhabited. Occasionally we passed a small island with a weathered dock and a single rustic wooden house on a bluff with smoke curling from the chimney. I wondered at the owners. Was the house a vacation retreat? Did anyone live year-round in such a remote place?

The dining room was almost full. I looked from table to table, women in cocktail dresses, men in suits or tuxedos. Most faces were smiling. The buzz of conversation was a melding of deep voices with the higher tones of women. The mood seemed lighthearted, as befitted the elegant surroundings.

Jimmy dashed salt into his soup. "Why don't you talk to Ingrid again, see if you can get her to open up."

I forked a piece of watercress. "I don't believe Ingrid could have seen anything useful. I checked out the passageway by Sophia's cabin this afternoon. I thought Ingrid might have been in a storage room after her duty hours, opened the door, and seen someone at Sophia's door. That won't work. There are no storage rooms in the cross corridor. There are two interior cabins opposite 6088." I was getting all too familiar with that portion of the ship and easily recalled the numbers. "Cabins 6090 and 6093. Of course," I added perfunctorily, "Sophia's door is also visible from Evelyn's cabin and from the cabin opposite Evelyn's on the starboard side. Will you ask Glenn again just to be certain that he checked with the occupants of all the nearby cabins?"

"He said he did. He's thorough. If he'd come up with anything, I think we'd know." Jimmy's expression was puzzled. "I'd swear there's something there with Ingrid, but I don't know what it could be."

The waiter cleared away the first course.

I took a sip of wine. "I wonder if Glenn's checked to see what time keys were inserted into the doors of the Riordan cabins Friday night. Your key opened Sophia's door at eleven-oh-three. I called Sophia at eleven thirty-nine. If a Riordan cabin was entered after eleven-oh-three, that might be a link. I left Sophia at ten-fifteen. She called you at ten-eighteen. That's the last indication that she was alive. I wish I knew what time Val came down to the bar. If Sophia answered her door, let Val inside, there may have been time for her to have killed Sophia and come upstairs, pretending she'd had too much to drink. It may have been five or ten after eleven when she got to the bar." It was possible that Val's interlude with me had been calculated, her apparent lack of memory pretense. Was Rosie worried about what Val might remember? Or terrified about what Val might have done? "All the Riordans were vague about when they turned in."

Our entrées arrived, lamb chops for me, veal for Jimmy. When the waiter was out of earshot, I looked soberly at Jimmy. "The murderer's sitting pretty. Glenn may have suspicions, but there isn't enough proof to tie anyone to Sophia's disappearance, much less prove she was murdered. Besides, he seems to be inclined toward suicide. If we can't come up with something specific, her death will be passed off as suicide or an accident."

"Everything is nebulous." Jimmy sounded discouraged. "None of the Riordans can prove where they were after ten-eighteen. That's the critical period: ten-eighteen, when Sophia called me, to eleven thirty-nine, when you called her."

I looked at Jimmy with a deep sadness. He was convinced that one of the Riordans had committed murder and desperate to see justice done. But there was the heartbreaking possibility that Sophia might have grabbed up the key from the bowl, gone to hunt Jimmy, and used it to reenter the cabin at 11:03. If she were despondent at not finding Jimmy and assumed his lack of response meant he was unwilling to forgive her, she could have gone out on her balcony, key in her hand, clutching the envelope with his letter and the dossiers, and jumped to her death. I did not speak of this to Jimmy. He would never believe Sophia committed suicide.

I know better than ever to say never.

"I don't know what else to do." Jimmy's face creased in misery. "I have to admit Glenn's done everything he can. He told me he talked to every passenger within twenty cabins either way of Sophia. The only fact he's certain of is that my key opened her door right after eleven. Everything else is what we've told him or the Riordans have told him. It all comes out to nothing." He looked at me with despair in his eyes. "I'll never forgive myself if Sophia's death isn't avenged." Then he added, so softly I scarcely heard, "Sophia will never forgive me."

I reached across the table, caught his hand, wished I could help him bear his weariness and despair. "Sophia would never blame you."

It was almost as though Sophia were there with us, blue eyes glinting with intelligence, vibrant face inquisitive, golden curls tight against her head. I remembered her that last evening and knew I had to tell Jimmy what she'd said. I hoped it would be of comfort.

"Sophia told me she'd been a fool, that you were kind and caring and generous. She loved you very much, Jimmy." Then and now I'd not been certain whether Sophia truly loved or desperately sought love.

"I wasn't there when she needed me." His eyes were haunted.

I stood on my balcony, gripped the railing. Far below, the white froth of waves glistened in the moonlight. Stars blazed with a magnificence not seen on land except atop remote mountains or in secluded valleys, far from the brightness of cities. The *Clio* plowed steadily southwestward through the velvety August night.

I felt quite alone, though an occasional splash of light through a balcony door illumined several adjoining balconies. The balconies, of course, were connected, running the length of the ship, each balcony separated from its neighbor by a chest-high railing. Had the traveler next door chosen to enjoy a nightcap on the balcony, we could have exchanged greetings, shaken hands. I smelled the distinctive, to me unpleasant, odor of a cigar. Someone was on a nearby balcony.

I spent almost an hour on the balcony, looking out into the night, thinking and figuring and planning. I didn't have much hope, but I'd learned as a very young reporter that if you want to know, you have to ask.

## twenty-three

I ate an early breakfast Tuesday morning, keeping an eye out for any of the Riordans, but none passed by. I went down to Deck 4 at shortly after eight o'clock and asked to see Staff Captain Glenn. I waited only about ten minutes before I was shown into Glenn's office.

He looked more rested this morning, though his eyes were grave and his face somber. "What can I do for you, Mrs. Collins?"

"I'd like to know the status of the inquiry. I know you have investigated everything pertaining to Sophia's whereabouts on Friday evening. Was she seen anywhere on the ship after I said good night to her?" I was careful to keep my voice pleasant without any trace of confrontation.

He pulled several folders from a drawer, spread them on his desk, but he didn't refer to them. "She was not seen. However, that doesn't preclude her having walked from her cabin to her husband's and returned."

At eleven o'clock, the long hallways could easily have been empty except for Sophia.

He gave a small shrug. "It would have been helpful had she been seen. As it is, we can only surmise what must have happened from the facts we have. The most important fact is that Mr. Lennox's key opened her suite door at twenty-three oh-three. There are three possibili-ties. Mr. Lennox retained the key Thursday evening, leaving the empty leather folder in the bowl. Mrs. Len-nox admitted someone to her cabin Friday evening and that person took the key, stepped into the hallway, closed the door, then used the key to reopen the door. Mrs. Lennox picked up the key from the bowl and carried it with her when she left the cabin, then used that key to open her door.

"In the first instance, if Mr. Lennox entered the cabin, there may have been a quarrel and Mrs. Lennox commit-ted suicide after her husband departed, or she was killed and thrown overboard. In the second, Mrs. Lennox ad-mitted her murderer and was dead by the time the key was used. In the third, Mrs. Lennox was so distraught upon her return to the cabin she jumped from her balcony or, in the most benign interpretation, accidentally fell as a result of her distress and the rough passage."

I couldn't tell if Glenn favored one theory. "Do you expect to reach a conclusion before we arrive in Lon-don?"

His brows drew down in a frown. "We don't have enough evidence to indicate with any certainty what hap-pened. We will present the results of our inquiry to the authorities in London. The likelihood is that Mrs. Lennox will be officially deemed missing at sea and the investiga-tion will remain open. As the facts now stand, I believe there would be a presumption of suicide or accident be-cause there was no disarray in her cabin, no evidence of a struggle, no traces of blood."

The lack of disarray in the cabin was an argument against murder. "Mr. Glenn, I hope we can discover the truth." I waited as the soft bong of his walnut clock marked the half hour. "It would tell us a great deal if someone saw Sophia use that key to enter her cabin at eleven-oh-three."

He picked up a pen, softly tapped the desktop. "It seems unlikely that anyone observing her would have failed to mention the fact." His tone was faintly sardonic.

"It could be"—I picked my words carefully—"that someone might have done so but doesn't want to admit seeing Sophia that late." Val's memory of Friday night might well be spotty.

He looked alert. "On the idea that such an admission puts the observer too close to the point when Mrs. Lennox disappeared?"

"Exactly." I pushed away an image of Jimmy and said words he certainly would have been astonished to hear. "Mr. Glenn, it may be that the solution is sad but understandable. If Mrs. Lennox herself used that key at eleven-oh-three, the likelihood is that her death was suicide. If she was seen by a member of the family, that person must have entered his or her cabin after that time. If I knew when each Riordan cabin was last entered Friday night, I would have an idea whether there was a possibility that Sophia was seen."

He studied me, his gaze thoughtful. "It isn't customary to reveal information about passengers."

I met his gaze directly. "It isn't customary for a passenger to disappear in mid-cruise."

"Granted." There might have been a spark of approval in his dark eyes. "So your idea is that any passenger who returned to a nearby cabin shortly after twenty-three oh-three might possibly have glimpsed Mrs. Lennox. However, you should realize that the locks only register when a cabin is entered and which key was used. There is no record when someone exits a cabin. For example, it would have been possible for Mrs. Lennox to have left her cabin after twenty-three oh-three and theoretically she could have gone to another deck and fallen, jumped, or been pushed."

I understood that Glenn was being precise, but I was looking for a link to a murderer. I had no belief in accident or suicide. I wanted to know who among the Riordans had the opportunity to insert Jimmy's key in Sophia's door. It could only have been someone who entered their cabin after three minutes past eleven.

"That's possible, but it doesn't do any harm to check with passengers who could have been in the hallway when Jimmy's key was used. Several of the Riordans said they entered their cabins around eleven."

Glenn tapped his pen against the desk. "Is it your hope that one of the Riordans might confide in you if Mrs. Lennox was seen?"

"It's a possibility." I foresaw other possibilities, but I didn't intend to mention them. "And, of course, there are the interior cabins directly across from Mrs. Lennox's suite." I had no interest in the occupants of those cabins, but it might convince Glenn I wasn't focusing simply on the Riordans.

He waved a dismissive hand. "Those two cabins are not occupied on this voyage." He looked down at a sheet in the folder, jotted notes, pushed a sheet of paper toward me. "Keep me informed, Mrs. Collins." It was a command.

I took my precious sheet of paper up to Deck 9, found a comfortable deck chair near the pool. Glenn was thorough. Under the heading "Last Cabin Entry Friday Night" he'd listed each of us:

*James Lennox—2309*
*Henrietta Collins—2332*
*Evelyn Riordan—2152*

*Rosemary Riordan—2306*
*Kent Riordan—2309*
*Alex Riordan and/or Mrs. Alex—2328*
*Valerie Riordan—2332*

I went through, changed the times to non-naval usage: Jimmy, 11:09 P.M.; Evelyn, 9:52 P.M.; Rosie, 11:06 P.M.; Kent, 11:09 P.M.; Alex and/or Madge, 11:28 P.M.; Val, 11:32 P.M. The times marked the last entry into any of the cabins Friday night. Only Evelyn was safely within her cabin before the earliest moment when Sophia could have died. The rest of them remained possibilities.

I'd found out what I needed to know, but it wasn't the times that burdened my thoughts. Instead, I wondered if Jimmy and I were wrong. Perhaps Sophia *had* fallen or jumped. Otherwise, why was there no sign of a struggle? Even though Sophia was not a large woman, she would have fought an attacker. Any one of us, some easily, some with effort, could have tumbled her dead body over the balcony railing. But how could she have been taken by surprise and overcome without leaving behind some indication of a struggle? If she had opened her door to one of the Riordans, she would have been facing that person. She would have been wary and alert because she knew she was in danger. Any attack would surely have resulted in a struggle. Moreover, none of the Riordans appeared scratched or bruised. No blood . . . That ruled out a knifing. The screening of passengers and luggage almost precluded a gun. Again, gunshot wounds bleed.

I pushed away my uncertainties. What happened to Sophia hinged on the truth about Jimmy's key. Perhaps if I was clever indeed, I could find out.

It was midmorning when I sighted Evelyn in the fitness center. It was my fourth circuit of the ship's public areas.

One of the lovely aspects of shipboard life is its quicksilver quality. A wanderer occasions no attention. After all, when the ship is under way, unless passengers are in their cabins, they are likely to be drifting about and there are only so many possibilities: the cafés, deck chairs on Deck 5 or near the pool and Jacuzzi, card room, fitness center, beauty salon, spa, library, promenade, Internet room, tearoom, and sundeck. I'd spotted Alex and Madge drinking mai tais near the pool and Kent hunched over a computer keyboard, but I wanted to start with Evelyn.

Evelyn rode an Exercycle. Her back was to me. Her hair frizzed with dampness beneath a calico bandanna and her skin was flushed, indicating she'd been working out for a while. Apparently, she was fit despite her bulk and generally frowsy appearance. Jimmy had said she was an accomplished dancer and that's why he was suspicious of the supposedly accidental spillage of the sherry. Now we knew she'd deliberately bumped into him. She'd told the captain she'd been afraid the sherry might have been poisoned. She insisted to Jimmy that she hadn't seen anyone tamper with it. Perhaps that was true and she was simply fearful without any evidence because of the boulder that fell so near Sophia.

I didn't intend to discuss Sophia's death with Evelyn. Instead, I hoped she would make it easy for me to join the Riordans on a casual basis.

I climbed on the Exercycle next to hers and looked across with a smile. "Good morning, Evelyn."

"Good morning." She was puffing from effort. "How are you?"

"I'm ready for some exercise. It helps, doesn't it?" I set the timer, began to pedal.

"Oh yes." She was definitely short of breath. "I hope

Jimmy is bearing up. I know he's working hard on the memorial service." She slowed her effort, wiped her face with a towel. "We'll do everything we can to help." Her look at me was earnest. "Now is the time for all of us to remember Sophia's gifts—"

I kept my expression pleasant and marveled at the ability of the human mind to recast reality. Evelyn was a sorrowing former sister-in-law.

"—and we all know she did her best. I'm sure it was a dreadful accident. But now"—she stopped pedaling—"we have to look forward. That's what Sophia would want us to do. I've persuaded the children to take the excursion into Karlskrona today. It's much better to keep busy, don't you agree?"

I felt like I'd scored a bull's-eye. I'd expected the Riordans would take today's excursion since they'd traveled into Stockholm yesterday. "That's a very good idea." I looked at her eagerly. "May I join you?"

There was only a hint of hesitation before she nodded. "That would be lovely. I understand there is a museum with a glass tunnel and we can see the remains of a shipwreck."

"Just the sort of thing Sophia would have enjoyed." I doubted Sophia was ever attracted to the distant past. She would have been much more interested in talking to vendors on the square, finding out if their goods were handmade, exploring the impact of the European Union on their lives.

Evelyn's smile dimmed. "It might be as well if we didn't talk about Sophia this afternoon."

"Certainly. But"—I stopped cycling, dropped my voice to a confidential note—"don't you keep trying to figure out what could possibly have happened?"

"She fell." Evelyn's voice was stubborn. She pulled off the bandanna holding her flyaway hair, dabbed it against her throat.

"If she fell—or jumped—from her balcony"—and the bleakness of my voice wasn't simulated as I pictured Sophia plunging toward the roiled sea—"wouldn't she have screamed?" The wash of the ship's passage was distinct, but anyone on a nearby balcony should have heard a cry. I remembered the quiet on my balcony the night before. Evelyn had retired to her cabin early. Was there any chance . . . "Were you out on your balcony Friday night?"

"Balcony?" She looked at me as blankly as if I'd spoken Sanskrit.

"Friday night. If Sophia screamed—"

"I was reading in bed. You saw her after that." She wadded the bandanna in a ball.

"Yes." I had indeed. Evelyn couldn't be of any help. In fact, she probably wouldn't have heard anything even if she'd been awake and on her balcony. I'd already realized a cry would likely only have been heard by someone standing on the huge balcony next to hers at the ship's stern. Evelyn's balcony was the first around the corner on the port side. Probably sounds from the stern wouldn't carry there.

I frowned, envisioning the occupants of the cabins in order: Evelyn, Alex and Madge, Kent, Rosie, Val. None of the cabins except Evelyn's was occupied during the critical period.

Evelyn thumped to the floor. "That was good. I'm off to shower. And perhaps I should check with Jimmy, see if there is anything else I can do. You don't suppose he'll be upset that we are going on the tour?"

"Not at all. He'll understand. I'll be down at your cabin

about two-thirty. I know Karlskrona will be interesting. It will be fun to take boats into shore rather than dock. Thanks for including me."

"Of course." Her smile was genial.

As she turned away, I lifted my hand in a farewell wave and resumed cycling, simply a lonely traveler seeking companionship.

## twenty-four

THE sixteen-passenger tender bounced in a choppy sea, plunging up and down as it crossed a half mile of white-capped water to Karlskrona, Sweden's original naval supplies base and now a UNESCO world heritage site. The island was an appealing mélange of dark green trees and multihued historic buildings, the colors bright and vivid in the clear northern summer light.

I sat with the Riordans on the back benches. Evelyn clamped a hand on the wooden back of the bench in front of her. "I had no idea it would be this rough." She looked with concern at Val.

Val slumped on the bench next to me. Sweat beaded her upper lip. She breathed lightly, her eyes glassy, her face drained of all color.

"Look at the island, Val." I pointed toward Karlskrona. "We'll be there in just a few minutes." I pulled a plastic bottle from a side sling. "Splash some water on your face."

Val held out shaking hands.

I poured an ounce or so. "There's nothing quite so refreshing as cool water." If I could keep her mind engaged, she might make it to shore without getting sick.

Val lifted her hands, patted the water onto her cheeks.

Kent leaned toward his sister. "Hey, Val, I got an e-mail from Angela this morning. She said when Heather saw the billboard, she cried. Do you think that's good?"

Val focused on her brother. "I think"—she swallowed—"she's coming around. We'll call her again this afternoon. I've been thinking. The wedding ought to be outside. We'll have an arch of roses. I can see the pictures now, you and Heather, framed by roses. All kinds of roses." Some color came into Val's cheeks. "Pink and red and cream and salmon and magenta."

Rosie beamed at her sister. "You're a genius. Lots of flowers. Do you remember when we used the language of flowers for a code? We found an old book of grandmother's and it was full of all this stuff about flowers. That was so much fun."

Val suddenly looked younger, eager. " 'I have a yellow acacia and can't resist an apple because cedar leaf.' "

Rosie whooped with laughter. "It's coming back. It's coming. 'I have a secret love and can't resist—' " She frowned in thought.

" 'Temptation.' " Val managed a weak grin.

" '—because I live for thee.' " Rosie was triumphant.

Kent stared at them in bewilderment. "I don't get it."

I chimed in. "In Victorian times, a young man could communicate with his lady love, no matter how well chaperoned, through the flowers he sent her."

Madge sniffed. "Sounds awfully artsy." She jangled the gold bracelet on her arm.

"Kind of fun, though." Kent looked at his sisters. "What's some more?"

Rosie's eyes sparkled. "I remember some of them. African marigolds represented vulgar minds. That was a favorite. Rendezvous was chickweed. We'd write notes saying, 'Let's chickweed at the soda shop.' "

Val brushed back a straggle of auburn hair. "Bachelor's buttons meant celibacy. We had a great time with that."

Rosie patted Kent's knee. "We'll fix up the prettiest arbor you ever saw. Because my name is Rosemary—for remembrance—I memorized all the meanings of roses. Rose itself means love. Let's see: white rose—transient impressions, Carolina rose—love is dangerous, red rosebud—pure and lovely, bridal rose—happy love." She smiled at Kent. "Cabbage rose—ambassador of love. There's lots more. It's going to be fabulous."

Alex poked his brother. "As long as there is plenty of champagne, the girls can drape roses over their ears and we won't care."

The tender thumped alongside the quay.

Evelyn surged to her feet despite the uneven motion of the boat. "Here we are." Her voice was hearty.

We were among the last to disembark. By the time we climbed the steps to Fishing Square, Val looked queasy again. The broad cobblestoned square overlooked a harbor teeming with tour boats. Sailboats, white sails bright, slipped gracefully past. The *Clio,* riding at anchor, looked small in the distance, her dark blue hull glistening in the sunlight.

The cobblestone square was crowded with families, children squealing as they raced toward water's edge. Evelyn studied a self-guided tour. She looked comfortable and at ease, stylish today in a ribbed peach blouse that matched the flower pattern on her white slacks. A matching peach hair band tamed her often flyaway locks. Madge looked almost too elegant for her surroundings in a beige silk blouse and trousers and sandals with rhinestones. She tugged on Alex's arm, pointing at the vendors' stalls. Alex shaded his eyes with his hand, looked toward the booths.

His dark blue polo was overlarge, his khaki shorts mid-knee length. Rosie, of course, was spectacular as usual, her lovely hair fiery in the bright sunlight, her green cotton top and white capris both flattering and comfortable. She gestured to Kent, her words drifting toward me. ". . . I'll keep calling Heather . . ." Kent's handsome face was eager, at great variance with his sour expression earlier in the trip. True, he'd not bothered to shave, his blue cotton shirt was frayed at the neck and his khakis old and worn, but women from eight to eighty would notice him with pleasure. The Riordans made up such a genial group, their natural and wholesome demeanor quite in keeping with their holiday surroundings.

Except, of course, for Val.

Val walked like an old woman, head down, shoulders slumped, to a stone bench not far from the Erik Höglund statue *The Fisherman's Wife*. I quietly followed, slipped onto the hard bench next to her. Several strands of dark red hair had slipped loose from the bun at the nape of her neck. The vagrant strands made her look disheveled, emphasized her pallor and the bluish smudges beneath her eyes. She hadn't dressed with her usual care. Her blouse and slacks matched in color but the blouse had a spot near the shoulder.

"Here, Val. Take the water." I held out the bottle.

She took it docilely, looked at me with a forlorn expression. "I don't feel good."

"I know. Drink some water. You'll feel better. Rest here for a while. You don't have to go on the tour."

"I don't?" She uncapped the water.

"No. I'll stay with you. It's a lovely view." I gestured out at the harbor. "The air is fresh. We can watch the children."

Her smile was tremulous. "You're very nice."

The words twisted within. I wasn't nice. I was as pred-atory as a tiger. I forced a smile. "Oh"—my tone was careless—"I like to sit by the sea."

Rosie was suddenly beside us. She looked down at Val, her gaze questioning. "You okay, baby?"

Val lifted the bottle. "This is all I need. I'm going to sit here with Mrs. Collins, enjoy the view."

Evelyn rounded up the group. "It isn't far to the Mari-time Museum. I want to see the glass tunnel." She stopped beside the bench. "Come on, Val. You'll be sorry you missed it. Mrs. Collins won't mind."

"I don't ever want to move again." Val drank deeply.

After they left, Rosie with one last worried glance back toward us, I remained silent, letting Val garner strength, sitting in peace on the hard bench in the mild sunlight, cooled by the brisk breeze.

"I wanted to get away from the ship." Val's words were abrupt. "But it doesn't do any good. I can't forget. I hated her. I wanted her to die. And now I can't remember"—her hands came together, twisting, twisting—"anything about that night. Every time I try to remember, I have a terrible feeling, an awful feeling. I needed a drink. I didn't have anything to drink, the bottle was empty. I came out into the hall and I didn't know which way to go. It was like a nightmare when your feet get stuck in slime and you don't know where you are, nothing's familiar. I started off and the floor kept moving. I don't know which way I went. I wanted to run and I couldn't run."

I sat as still as the bronze statue of the fisherman's wife, one hand forever linked to her cart. The timing had to be so close. It was possible that Val, woozy and disoriented, turned toward the stern. If she reached the cross hall just as someone unlocked Sophia's door, she might have seen the back of a familiar figure. If she could remember . . .

Val shuddered. "I try to remember, but I don't want to remember." She looked toward me. "It couldn't have been me, could it?" Her eyes, filled with foreboding, stared into mine.

I wished I knew. What memory did she fear? Was it what she did? Or what she saw? Or was her foreboding the product of an alcoholic haze, peopled with phantasms of her own making?

I temporized. If Val was sincere, I couldn't deepen her misery. If she wasn't, it didn't matter how I responded. "I'd try not to think about that night. Perhaps in time the memories will come back."

Val gulped in a deep breath. "I can't stop thinking about it." She looked at me hopefully. "Rosie said I came up to the bar and I was with you. Was I okay?"

I saw terror in her eyes. I was glad I could offer some comfort here. "You'd had too much to drink, but you acted quite normal." If it was normal to obsess over the death of a sibling.

She gave me a tremulous smile.

I patted her hand. I liked Val, felt enormous sympathy for her. I hoped that she was what she appeared to be, a distraught young woman burdened by anger and guilt, frightened by alcohol-induced memory lapses, not an accomplished film director with the skills of a consummate actress.

As I stepped into my cabin after our return from Karls-krona, I saw the envelope that had been slipped beneath the door. My name was on the outside in Jimmy's familiar script.

I fixed an icy club soda, settled on the small sofa, opened his sealed note.

*Henrie O,*

*Glenn asked me to pack up Sophia's things. They're finished with the cabin. Glenn said I could get into the cabin at nine-thirty in the morning. I'd be glad of your help, but if you'd rather not, I understand.*

*    Hope the afternoon in Karlskrona offered some respite.*

*    Please join me for dinner at seven in the main dining room.*

*Love—Jimmy*

I felt cold, knew the chill wasn't from my icy drink. This time last week Sophia had laughed and loved, been angry, felt chagrin, enjoyed the caress of silk against her body, reached out for Jimmy's hand, knowing it would be there. Now her husband steeled himself to touch clothes that bore her impress, carried her scent. To be in that silent suite, look toward the balcony, would be terribly difficult for me. Yet those moments would be much harder for him.

I didn't want to go. I would go.

Now it was time to shower and dress for dinner. The living sit down to meals no matter the turmoil in their minds and hearts.

All through my shower, I pictured Sophia's suite, the small sofa where she'd faced me and told me how much she loved her husband. Jimmy must now rid the cabin of her belongings. On the next cruise, new occupants would enjoy its elegance, stand on the balcony looking out at the sea, unaware that death had preceded them by only a few days.

I toweled quickly, used the hair dryer, brushed my hair. As I pulled on the comfortable terry-cloth robe, I heard the telephone. I steeled myself, moved quickly to answer.

But it wasn't Jimmy.

"Henrie O." Evelyn talked fast. "I'm glad I caught you. I thought it would be a good thing for all of us to have dinner together tonight. I've already talked to Jimmy and he's agreed."

That didn't surprise me. Jimmy would grab any opportunity to be with the Riordans.

"We'll meet in the main dining room at seven. I think we should—well"—an uncomfortable pause—"we can't bring Sophia back and we need to remember her"—Evelyn's tone was an odd mixture of uplift and gravity—"but we can't let ourselves get mired in grief. Don't you agree?"

I had difficulty picturing any of the Riordans overcome by grief. Fear. Worry. Relief. Even elation. The disliked stepmother gone, their father's fortune theirs to share. There were many possible emotions, but not grief.

"I certainly do." I saw my wry expression in the mirror.

"Good. We'll see you then. Oh, and thank you for being so kind to Val. She's much more herself now. We're so glad."

I put down the phone. All was right with Evelyn's world, a world Sophia no longer inhabited.

I liked being outside on my balcony in the darkness, swept by sea-scented air beneath the canopy of stars. I'd settled there to watch the *Clio*'s departure at nine. We were on our way to Travemünde, the port for our visit to Lübeck and our last stop before we spent two and a half days at sea en route to London, where the cruise ended.

I felt worn and worried. Dinner had been a strain, a long meal studded with awkward pauses. We'd eaten together in the main dining room, everyone who began the journey with Sophia.

I realized before the first course was done that Evelyn simply wanted to make everything appear as normal as possible, underscoring her belief that Sophia had been the victim of an unfortunate accident.

I watched distant lights glide past, another cruise ship heading north, and pictured the Riordans at dinner. Evelyn had been alternately vivacious and quiet, chattering to her family, looking anxiously at Jimmy. Rosie smiled steadily and covertly watched her sister. Val's hands trembled, but she'd drunk only water with the meal. Madge burbled happily to Alex that she wanted to stay over in London, do some shopping, she'd seen an article about the most wonderful jewelry shop on Regent Street. Alex nodded agreement with his wife, eagerly discussed investment plans with Kent. Kent had been on his best behavior, freshly shaven, dark curls well brushed, wearing a blazer. He'd managed small talk though his face in repose was creased by uncertainty. So, no contact yet with Heather. If Kent had any thoughts about Sophia, they were well hidden.

Jimmy was quiet, though he responded to conversation. His eyes moved from face to face around the table. He was seeking answers. He hadn't found any. Nor had I.

I rose and walked to the railing of my balcony, knew I should turn in. I placed my hands on the damp wood, looked down at the froth marking the *Clio*'s passage. Tomorrow the ship docked at Travemünde. Tomorrow night it departed, en route to London. Time was running out.

## twenty-five

THE sea was pond-smooth this morning. There was scarcely a hint of motion as I hurried toward the stern. I didn't want to keep Jimmy waiting, but he was there before me, standing by Sophia's door. He looked thin, his white polo sagging over khaki shorts. He managed a weary smile.

I reached out, touched his arm.

For an instant, his eyes lightened. "I'm okay."

He wasn't okay. Time passes, wounds close, but scars remain.

The young woman who'd guarded Sophia's door on Friday night came around the corner. She looked at us, light blue eyes curious as a cat's. "Good morning, Mr. Lennox, Mrs. Collins." As with all the *Clio* staff, whether service personnel or security or deck hands, courtesy was ingrained. "I've brought a key. After you complete the packing, you may leave it with the luggage or bring it to the security office. If you will leave the luggage in the foyer, it will be unloaded in London."

She handed the key to Jimmy, turned away.

Jimmy hesitated briefly, then abruptly shoved in the electronic key card. He held the door for me.

When we stood in the center of the living room, the

door soughing shut behind us, I felt as if Sophia might come through the bedroom doorway any moment. Her aura was everywhere, from the indentation in the sofa cushion where she'd sat, to the casual heap of an open magazine on the coffee table, to the straw purse lying on a sideboard, to the tumbler filled with amber liquid, whiskey diluted by melted ice.

The balcony doors were open. I looked at them in surprise.

Jimmy followed my gaze. "I guess nothing's been touched since Friday night. They're supposed to be kept shut but Sophia liked them open, liked the way the air felt, liked hearing the swish of the water. Let's keep them that way." He turned toward the bedroom, stopped in the open doorway, staring.

The bed was turned down. A lacy white nightgown was tossed near the foot. Brocaded house slippers, mandarin orange with a black design, lay on the floor. A guidebook rested on the night table. A pair of wire-rim glasses were folded near the lamp. There was a faint scent of orchid, possibly from perfume or bath powder. The doors to the balcony were wide open in the bedroom, too. The pink fringe on a lamp shade moved in the breeze.

I didn't look at Jimmy's face. There is nothing that reaches out to the living with as much impact as ordinary, everyday belongings that no longer matter. Sophia had looked ahead to her night's rest, assumed without giving it any thought that she would step into the nightgown, throw back the sheet, settle against the downy pillows.

Head down, he strode to the closet, yanked open the door, began to pull out suitcases. I crossed to the bed, picked up the negligee, felt its silky softness, folded it into a neat square.

Jimmy began with the dresses hanging in the closet,

taking them out one by one, folding them neatly, packing them in the largest case.

I started with the top drawer of the dresser. Both of us had spent many years traveling to far-flung destinations and packing quickly and efficiently was second nature, but I had never dealt with such an extensive wardrobe. It took a good half hour for us to finish with the closet and the dresser, filling two large suitcases. That left the vanity.

Jimmy set a small cosmetic case on the satin-cushioned bench. He gestured helplessly at the array of potions, makeup, perfumes, oils, and powders. "Would you take care of these?"

"Of course." I slid onto the bench, put the case in my lap. Jimmy walked out into the living area. The beauty products didn't take long. I opened the drawer and found a slim, elegant black-lacquered box. I slid it out, lifted the mother-of-pearl-decorated lid. My eyes widened. I'd not paid a great deal of attention but I'd noticed that Sophia had jewelry that matched every outfit. The array of lovely and expensive pieces ranged from diamond earrings and necklace and bracelet, to jade pendants, to silver bracelets and golden chains. There was a spectacularly lovely old-fashioned amethyst necklace. I carried the jewel box into the living room.

Jimmy stood by the blue damask sofa, staring down at the cushions where Sophia had sat. He heard my step, looked around.

I came up to the back of the sofa, which faced the balcony, held out the jewel case. "You'll want to take this with you."

He took the case, opened it. His lips pressed tightly together.

I came around the end of the sofa and scanned the room. Nothing was out of place. The four chairs around the small dining table were perfectly placed. The coffee table sat squarely in front of the sofa. The easy chairs were on a diagonal slant facing the sofa. The drapes hung straight, though billowed a bit by the breeze through the open doors to the balcony.

Jimmy closed the case and moved to my side. He, too, looked around the luxuriously appointed living room, at the blue sofa and rust-colored chairs, the shining oak table and matching chairs, the glass coffee table, the drapes gently stirred by the breeze from the balcony. "Nothing's out of place. It doesn't make sense."

I glanced at him. We'd always been attuned, our minds working through circumstances to the same conclusion. Now we grappled with the incongruity of this serene room as the site of murder, the murder of a woman fully alert to danger, a woman who was not feeble, a woman who'd always been a fighter.

I pointed to the wet bar. "When I left, she was standing there, fixing a drink." I pictured Sophia with glass in hand walking across the room to use the telephone, call Jimmy. "We know she called you. Then . . ." I glanced at the sofa. "If she sat there again, she was facing the balcony. But if someone came to the door, knocked, she would have gotten up, gone to the door, and when she opened it, she definitely would have known if it was one of the Riordans. Jimmy"—I balled my hand, thumped it into the opposite palm—"I don't believe Sophia would have opened the door without looking through the peephole. Sure, she'd have hoped it was you knocking, but she would have looked.

"If she didn't open the door, the person who came in must have obtained your key." Perhaps Ingrid might have noticed whether the key folder was still in the bowl when she serviced the cabin on Friday morning. "Even if someone had the key, Sophia would have heard the door open and twisted around, seen someone entering. There would have been time to scream. Evelyn was in her cabin and she didn't hear anything." Evelyn had made it clear she hadn't been on her balcony, but a scream of terror should have pierced the cabin walls. "Most of all, if Sophia saw her attacker, there had to have been a struggle. The only possibility is if her visitor got behind her, struck her down. But why wouldn't there be bloodstains?" I looked down at the floor, at shining wood parquet and Oriental rugs.

Jimmy's face ridged into lines of misery. "She couldn't have screamed if someone grabbed her by the throat . . ." He broke off.

I could see the dreadful picture in his mind: Sophia struggling, flailing, slipping into unconsciousness, her limp body dragged to the balcony and tumbled over the railing.

"Only a man would be strong enough." His voice was heavy.

Alex or Kent. Alex wasn't big but he was wiry, a rock climber. Kent was physically imposing, lithe and muscular.

I shook my head. "Scratches." It was summer. Everyone wore short sleeves. Sophia was athletic, and a woman fighting for her life would scratch and kick.

Jimmy's face creased. He was remembering, as I did, Sophia's tanned, capable hands with red nails, pointed nails, and the Riordans, all of them with unblemished faces and arms.

"Somehow"—I turned away from the balcony, moved slowly to the door—"Sophia was caught by surprise."

Jimmy shook his head. He gave a last somber look toward the balcony and I wondered if he was struggling against the horrific conclusion that Sophia had flung herself from the ship. He put the jewel box on the coffee table, carefully did not look again at the sofa. "I'll bring the cases out." His voice was gruff.

We were done, Sophia's lovely dresses packed away, all trace of her personality removed. I walked to the door, opened it, and stepped into the hall.

The service cart stood at the end of the hallway on the port side. Ingrid was stepping out of Evelyn's cabin, her arms full of bed linen. I hurried toward her, thinking once again of the electronic key case Jimmy had tossed angrily into the pottery bowl. "Ingrid."

She stopped pushing the sheets into a laundry bag and looked up. She smiled, the automatic pleasant response to a passenger, then abruptly her round face froze, eyes wide, lips parted, the look of a schoolgirl expecting to be chastised. "Ma'am?" One hand lifted to touch the throat of her white blouse.

I gestured toward the cabin. "Mr. Lennox and I have been packing away everything in Suite 6088."

She looked past me, her gaze uneasy. Her hand dropped, nervously adjusted her blue apron. "I need to get the cabins done."

"I'll only keep you a moment." I kept my tone casual. "You serviced Cabin 6088 on Friday morning as usual, I suppose."

"Yes, ma'am." Some of the tension eased out of her shoulders. Clearly there was nothing stressful about recalling Friday morning.

"When you serviced the suite, did you dust the furniture?" I pointed to a feather duster tucked next to cleaning cloths on top of the cart.

"Yes, ma'am. We always dust." She looked puzzled.

"That would include the green pottery bowl that sits on the entryway table?"

Ingrid nodded and her thick blond curls bobbed.

"What was in the bowl?"

Her eyebrows drew down into a frown. "In the bowl? There was a key folder. Nothing else."

"Did you pick up the folder?"

"No, ma'am." She was emphatic. "I moved it aside, used the duster."

"Did you leave the folder in the bowl?" I watched her closely.

"Yes, ma'am." She was comfortable now.

That answered one question, one very big question. Sophia's attacker didn't gain access to her cabin with the key. Either Sophia herself used the key after a fruitless search for Jimmy and the key was in her pocket when she went over the railing, or Sophia was dead when her attacker took the key from the bowl, stepped into the hall, closed the door, and used the key to reenter the cabin in an effort to make it appear that Jimmy had kept the key.

Behind me, I heard the door to Sophia's suite close. I was turning to tell Jimmy what I'd learned when Ingrid gasped. Her eyes widened. She grabbed the cart and fled up the hallway. Jimmy and I stared after her.

## twenty-six

I poured a handful of pepitas, welcomed their salty crunch. Night pressed against the windows as the *Clio* steamed toward London. We would be at sea for two and a half days. I was a few minutes early to meet Jimmy for an after-dinner drink. I'd taken the excursion into Lübeck and stayed for dinner, a welcome respite from our failed effort to determine the truth behind Sophia's disappearance.

I hadn't joined the Riordans on the tour. I deliberately chose another bus. What good would it do to look at them once again, see their now-familiar faces, try to imagine one of them stepping into Sophia's cabin with a murderous heart? I didn't sightsee with them, but I caught occasional glimpses, once in the famous marzipan store, again at the Gothic city hall. Evelyn clutched shopping bags. Rosie clowned with a lion's-head hand puppet, making Val laugh. Alex ate a big pretzel. Madge shrank away from a dancing bear and his accordion-playing owner. Kent carried a porcelain doll. Everywhere he went, he shopped for Heather. Perhaps that was his way of clinging to the hope that love would win out.

I'd tried to persuade Jimmy to come with me, lose himself for a while in wandering about the old city, which played such a major role in the Hanseatic League, but he was involved with e-mails about Sophia. He'd fielded calls from the media. He'd prepared a release with a summary of Sophia's career and the enigmatic pronouncement: "Sophia Montgomery Holbrook Riordan Lennox was last seen on the evening of Friday, August 20. After a search of the *Clio* and the surrounding waters, *Clio* staff captain Gerald Glenn officially deemed her missing at sea."

Jimmy would face intense media questioning in London. I doubted that he cared. If he reached London with Sophia's loss still a mystery, he would have failed. I wished I could reach the frozen core deep inside him, make him see that he'd done everything possible from beginning to end, that Sophia's loss could never be blamed on him whether it was the result of suicide or murder. I didn't think we would ever know what happened.

The pianist segued into a sprightly version of "Tennessee Waltz." Voices murmured, occasional laughter sounded. The mood in the dimly lit bar was mellow. Most of the tables were occupied, passengers enjoying their last days of carefree delight as the cruise neared its end.

Jimmy paused in the doorway, looking for me. I raised a hand. He came quickly, dropped into the opposite chair, saw the Beck's beer I'd ordered for him. He touched the frosted bottle. "Thanks."

I lifted my glass, a gin and tonic. "To you." I hoped he understood what I was telling him. *You've done your best. Remember and grieve. Don't blame yourself.*

"I can't stay long." There was a ripple of excitement in his voice. "I'm going to break it open." He poured the beer into the frosted glass. "In fifteen minutes Ingrid's going to meet me on the sundeck, tell me what she saw Friday night."

I looked at him in amazement. "This morning she acted terrified." Ingrid had turned the service cart and pushed it forward as if the hounds of hell were nipping at her heels. Jimmy had wanted to follow and confront her, but I'd persuaded him to let it go.

Jimmy lifted the glass, took a quick drink, wiped foam from his upper lip. He was excited. "Who's to know? I thought she'd done something that would get her in trouble with Glenn and was afraid I'd mess everything up for her. I'd decided she didn't know anything useful about Sophia. I still don't know where she could have been. Like you said, there are no supply closets in the stern corridor. But tonight when I got back to my cabin after dinner, there was a phone message from her."

"Are you positive it was Ingrid?" I felt uneasy.

"Not a doubt." His smile was wry. "She told me to bring the money. Nobody else but you knows I offered her a thousand dollars. So she's got something to sell."

I leaned forward. "Jimmy, I don't like this. Call Glenn, tell him."

His smile fled. His sandy brows drew down in a thoughtful frown. "Tell him what?"

"Your contact with Ingrid. Mine. The fact that it looks like she knows something and is willing to speak up for cash." I reached across the table, caught his wrist.

"I can't do that. When I offered the reward, I promised her I'd try to keep her out of anything I told Glenn." He twisted his hand, caught mine in a tight, reassuring grip. "Don't worry, honey. This is the break we need." He loosed my hand, grabbed his glass, his face upbeat once again.

The endearment pulled me back to other days, days when we had found such pleasure in each other.

He drank half the glass, checked his watch. "I'm going

on up. If all goes well, I'll have something definite for Glenn."

I crumpled my napkin, tossed it on the table. "I'll come with you."

He held up a hand. "I have to show up alone. She insisted. If anybody's with me, it's no deal. She'd spot you near the stairs to the sundeck. It's okay, Henrie O. Relax, finish your drink." The old vitality was back in his voice. "What can go wrong? I'll tell you what, I'll come by your cabin after I've talked to her." He paused. "If I find out something big, I'll take it straight to Glenn, then call you."

I took my time finishing the gin and tonic. I didn't want another. I signed the check, strolled up to Deck 6. It was a good twenty minutes after Jimmy headed for the sundeck that I reached my cabin. I glanced at the phone. No message light. I was puzzled. It was almost ten-thirty. I wouldn't have thought Jimmy and Ingrid would still be talking. Perhaps he'd persuaded her to go and see Glenn, promising that he'd intercede to help her keep her job.

I sat on the vanity bench, removed my gold filigree earrings. They were old favorites. Richard had given them to me for a long-ago birthday. I looked in the mirror. When I'd first worn them, my skin was smooth and unlined, my dark hair untouched by silver. I balanced the earrings in my palm, looked dispassionately at my silver-streaked hair, the smudges beneath my dark eyes, the lines of laughter and sadness on my face. I felt caught between past and present. Perhaps the truest sign of age is when the heart stubbornly looks back instead of forward. If Richard had lived . . .

I opened the drawer, dropped the earrings into my satin-lined jewel case. I had a quick vision of Richard, broad open face kind but chiding. He'd always embraced the old Protestant hymn "Work, for the Night Is Coming." I no longer had work as my mainstay, but I still had tasks to complete. Jimmy needed my support.

Abruptly my eyes sought the clock. I'd slipped into a reverie but time, as time does, had inexorably passed. A quarter to eleven and no word from Jimmy. I rose, walked toward the closet. I slipped out of the beige silk dress I'd worn to dinner, hung it up, placed the sling pumps on the floor. I hesitated, then reached for a blue T and white cotton slacks, pulled them on. I stepped into sandals.

I settled on the balcony, left the door open so I'd hear Jimmy's knock. I still felt uneasy, although Jimmy was probably right. What could go wrong? Why would Ingrid talk to Jimmy unless she was willing to offer some kind of information? Still, her invitation to meet him on the remote and dimly lit sundeck seemed surprising after her frantic flight this morning. However, a thousand dollars was probably a goodly sum to Ingrid, though I wouldn't have thought enough to make her jeopardize her job. If she saw Sophia Friday night long after she'd gone off duty, she had subsequently lied when Glenn spoke to her. I didn't think Glenn would be pleased if an employee lied.

I pushed up from the chair, moved to the railing, looked up at the star-spangled sky. The brilliance of the stars and the luminous glow of the August moon and the darkness of the water were a reminder not only of the puniness of human affairs but of the reality of how far we were from land. The *Clio* churned steadily through the night. I understood Jimmy's desperation, but I wished—

The telephone rang. I felt a surge of pleased surprise. Jimmy must have found out something important enough to share with Glenn so he was calling rather than dropping by. I hadn't expected this outcome. I was thrilled for him. Perhaps it had taken Ingrid time to understand the importance of what she had seen. If she saw anything that mattered, it had to be the person who used Jimmy's key. Had it been Sophia or was the answer darker than that?

I hurried into the cabin, reached for the receiver. "Hello." I heard the uplift in my voice. I was smiling.

"Henrie O." Jimmy's voice was stiff and strained, a man grappling with shock. "Ingrid didn't show up. I waited almost an hour. Finally, I gave up. I came back to my cabin and she's here. She's dead. I've called Glenn. Don't come. It's ugly."

## twenty-seven

I found it hard to breathe. Ingrid had been lively and bouncy and foolish and now she was dead. I was already moving as stark thoughts streamed through my mind. I tucked my key folder in the pocket of my slacks, plunged out into the corridor, running lightly. I came around the corner at the cross hall amidships, swerved to avoid a cheerful couple stepping out of the elevator, darted past them to the starboard corridor.

Jimmy was standing by his door, face stricken, body rigid, still wearing the navy blazer and soft-collared shirt and gray slacks he'd worn in the bar, everything the same except he looked unutterably weary.

I skidded to a stop beside him.

"You shouldn't have come." His voice was gruff. "Nobody can do anything. She's dead as hell. God, she was just a kid." He took a deep breath, looked at me in misery. "I should have gone to Glenn the minute I got that message. Maybe she'd be alive. First Sophia, now this kid."

I gripped his arm. "Stop it. She must have tried to blackmail—"

Then the corridor was alive with movement, Glenn pounding toward us, his security officer and subordinates following. Suddenly Jimmy and I were surrounded.

"Stand aside." Glenn gestured for us to move out of the way.

A security officer, hands encased in plastic gloves, poked a key in Jimmy's lock, pushed the door in.

"You'll see her. She's in the closet. I'd opened the closet door . . ." Jimmy's voice trailed away.

Glenn nodded toward the two security officers waiting a step behind, the same young people I'd seen outside Sophia's door on Friday night. "Escort Mr. Lennox to Office 8." He glanced at me. "It would be helpful, Mrs. Collins, if you returned to your cabin. I will ask you not to reveal any information about this evening to anyone other than ship personnel."

Time dragged past, the minutes moving as slowly as a funeral cortege. I kept dialing Glenn's office. The phone rang to no answer. I moved restlessly from my small sofa onto the balcony and back again every few minutes, wild to know where Jimmy was, what was happening, what had happened to Ingrid, berating myself for not asking Jimmy. *She's in the closet . . .* How could Ingrid have been murdered in Jimmy's cabin?

Finally I got out pen and pad, scrawled desperate conclusions:

*Ingrid's murder proved Sophia was murdered.*

*Ingrid saw the murderer use Jimmy's key.*

*Jimmy's offer of a reward suggested to Ingrid that the information she possessed might be worth a great deal more than a thousand dollars.*

*Ingrid approached the murderer. The murderer persuaded Ingrid to call Jimmy, promise to meet him on the sundeck. Then . . .*

I tossed the pen down, walked back out to the balcony, caught the scent of a cigar. Someone nearby was smoking, basking in the beauty of the night while Jimmy faced sharp, hard questions and struggled with the death of a foolish young woman.

I whirled back into the cabin, tried Glenn's number again. No answer. I poured a glass of water, ignored the throbbing ache in my temples.

Ingrid had contacted the murderer. Had she demanded money? Or was it more innocent than that? Possibly Ingrid said, "I saw you at Mrs. Lennox's door Friday night and Mr. Lennox has been asking me about that and he's offered me a thousand dollars and I don't know what to do."

The murderer, caught by surprise, must have come up with something to satisfy Ingrid, had somehow gained Ingrid's trust.

I pressed my fingers against my temples. The murderer must have convinced Ingrid that Jimmy was involved in his wife's death. That would account for Ingrid's obvious panic this morning. Maybe the murderer told Ingrid that when she or he opened the door, Jimmy was with Sophia. Obviously, whatever tale had been spun was adequate for the murderer's purpose, and that purpose was to set Jimmy up to take the blame for Ingrid's murder.

That had to have been the decision, right from the first: Ingrid must die, but her death had to be linked to Jimmy. Perhaps the murderer suggested the family might offer a substantial reward, more than the thousand offered by Jimmy, if Ingrid would help bring the crime home to Jimmy. Thinking fast, the murderer crafted a clever plan. The murderer instructed Ingrid to call Jimmy and set up a meeting on the sundeck, but when it was time, the murderer persuaded Ingrid to open Jimmy's cabin—I was willing to bet that her key was used for their entry—and once they were inside, Ingrid was killed. It must have been easy, perhaps the suggestion that it might not be safe for Ingrid to meet Jimmy on the sundeck, that instead they would go to his cabin and wait inside, the murderer perhaps hidden in the bath, ready to step out and face him down.

I called Glenn's office. This time he answered. It was a quarter to two.

"Mrs. Collins." His voice was cold.

"Where is Mr. Lennox?" Jimmy had looked so old, so defeated as he waited in the corridor only feet away from Ingrid's body.

"Mr. Lennox is in custody. He will be turned over to the authorities when we reach London."

"So you've made up your mind. You aren't going to investigate." My voice was cold, too.

Glenn's pause was heavy with anger. I felt his anger without a word being said.

"Mr. Glenn"—I talked fast—"what prevented Mr. Lennox from pushing Ingrid's body over his balcony into the sea? Had she disappeared without trace as Sophia did, there could have been suspicion of murder but never proof. If Mr. Lennox is the killer you assume him to be, why would he call and inform you that Ingrid's body was in his cabin?"

The reply was immediate. "Guilt, Mrs. Collins."

"No. Never." I held the receiver so tightly my hand ached. I wanted to shout my certainty. I tried to keep my voice even, reasonable. "He called you because he is an innocent man. If he were guilty, no one would ever have known what happened to Ingrid."

"I'm sorry, Mrs. Collins." Glenn sounded regretful. "I know that you and Mr. Lennox are old friends. I understand that you believe in him. But the facts are incontrovertible. Mr. Lennox's key was the last used to open the door to his wife's suite and she was never seen again. Ingrid Shriver—"

Ingrid Shriver. Now I knew her name. Ingrid with her round face and golden curls and blue eyes, a pretty girl who looked seductive and voluptuous even in the sexless stewardess's uniform. Ingrid who had been promised money and received death instead.

"—was strangled in his cabin with a towel from his bathroom. It appears she was taken by surprise, a rolled towel dropped over her face, twisted at the back of her neck. She apparently went down on her knees. There's a massive bruise in the small of her back. The murderer jammed a knee there. She never had a chance. There is a message on Mr. Lennox's telephone. In it, Ingrid asked him to meet her on the sundeck, bring the money he had promised. That's—"

I interrupted. "She didn't die on the sundeck. Why not? He's a strong man. He could have killed her there, thrown her over. No one would ever have known."

"Perhaps someone else was there." Glenn was impatient. "You can be assured we'll try to find out tomorrow. We know that she came down to his cabin with him—"

Again I broke in. "Not with Jimmy. Ingrid never showed up on the sundeck."

"That's what he claims." Glenn's disbelief was evident.

"Mr. Glenn, please listen. Jimmy came down to his cabin and found Ingrid. Tell me this: What key opened that lock before his was used tonight?"

There was a slight pause. "Ingrid's."

"When?"

"Twenty-two ten."

"Jimmy had just left the bar on his way up to the sundeck. Yet you have suggested that Jimmy met Ingrid on the sundeck and asked her to come down to his cabin. There wasn't time. And why would her key have been used to open his door?" Surely Glenn would understand this made no sense.

"Mrs. Collins, we may never know the exact circumstances. Perhaps they'd spoken in the hallway, he'd asked her to wait for him in his cabin, explained he needed to meet you—"

"That's nonsense. Jimmy told me about their appointment on the sundeck. He was excited. When he left me, he went up there. He thought he'd soon know who was in the corridor outside Sophia's cabin. He hoped he'd have information to bring to you."

"That's what he told you." Glenn spoke with finality.

"Knowing all the while that Ingrid was waiting in his cabin?"

"It's one possibility. Likely we'll never know exactly what happened. We certainly have a sound reason to hold him and turn him over to the police. Mrs. Collins, you may make whatever arrangements you wish with a solicitor in London. We will present the authorities with the information we've gathered. Until then, Mr. Lennox will remain in our custody."

## twenty-eight

MY mood at breakfast was savage. I felt as helpless as a skier in the path of an avalanche. This was Thursday morning. When the *Clio* sailed up the Thames Saturday morning, Scotland Yard would take Jimmy into custody. I ate quickly, tasted nothing. I had two days and then the Riordans would return home, safe and rich. Very rich, the overseeing stepmother wielding power no longer. I speared a sausage, paused to listen as the PA system sounded: "This is Staff Captain Glenn. Any passengers near or on the sundeck last night between twenty-two and twenty-three hundred are requested to contact my office. Thank you for your assistance."

I put down my fork. The announcement was interesting. Very interesting. This was Glenn's effort to see if anyone had observed Ingrid with Jimmy on the sundeck. But what intrigued me was what he hadn't said. There was no announcement that a crime had occurred and that ship officers had, in their judgment, apprehended the criminal. I picked up my coffee, drank, welcoming the strong dark brew, the infusion of energy, and the burgeoning of an idea.

I was at the ship's information desk at precisely 0800. I wouldn't have been surprised if Glenn had declined to see me, but in a moment the trim young woman at the desk nodded at me, her dark eyes curious. "Mr. Glenn will be out in a moment."

As she spoke, the door opened and Glenn stepped into the lobby, ramrod straight in his white uniform. His dark hair was neatly brushed, but his narrow face was pale and lined.

I moved quickly toward him. I was careful to appear conciliatory. "Mr. Glenn, I appreciate your seeing me. I will only take a few minutes of your time."

He looked as immovable as a mountain. "Mr. Lennox will not be permitted to see visitors."

"I understand. The matter I wish to discuss is entirely different." I glanced around the lobby with its thick red carpet and urns filled with fresh flowers. There was the usual clutch of passengers clustered at the purser's office, some paying up accounts, others changing money.

An imperious woman with a mound of snowy hair and piercing blue eyes stared down at a harried clerk at the information desk. "Since I've decided on the Phoenician cruise, I must insist upon Cabin 7005. If it is already booked, you must move them to another cabin."

I gestured at the eddy of passengers. "If you don't mind, Mr. Glenn, I would like to speak with you privately." Once again, my voice was pleasant.

I don't know whether it was my nonconfrontational demeanor or whether Glenn simply was exercising the courtesy to passengers which is so much a part of luxury cruising. Whatever the reason, he looked at me gravely and nodded. "Of course, Mrs. Collins."

Once again I stepped through the unmarked door from the elegant passenger center into the beige-walled, functional world of the ship's interior. I knew the way to his office now.

His small square domain looked as it had on my last visit, with nothing to hint at the loss of lives, the intense effort that had been made to search for Sophia, or the painstaking investigation of Jimmy's cabin.

When I was seated, he settled behind his desk. His dark eyes were not encouraging, but neither was his gaze hostile.

I kept my face pleasant, my hands relaxed in my lap. "I heard the announcement at breakfast asking passengers near the sundeck last night to contact you."

He made no response.

I looked at him inquiringly. "There was no announcement of Ingrid's murder."

His face was grave. "That is correct. It seemed unnecessary to alarm the passengers. There is, of course, no danger to them or certainly they would have been alerted. May I ask if you have mentioned her death to anyone?"

"I have not." I looked at him steadily. "Mr. Glenn, will that information remain confidential?" Here was my prayer, my hope, the linchpin of my campaign to free Jimmy. As long as the murder was not revealed, the Riordans would have no way of knowing. One of them, of course, knew only too well. Surely official silence would seem odd and ominous. Surely the murderer would wonder and worry.

Glenn's long face was impassive, but his eyes considered me warily. He was trying to determine why I wanted to know, what I sought. "We do not plan an announcement."

I didn't change expression, though this was what I desperately wanted to hear. "Is the crew generally aware of what has happened?"

He spread out his hands in a gesture of defeat. "Very likely most of the crew know by now, although we asked those involved not to discuss the matter. But . . ." He shrugged.

I understood. Too many people had been involved last night for Ingrid's murder to be kept secret from the crew. There were the security officers, the ship's doctor, whoever carried poor Ingrid away from the cabin. "Mr. Glenn, Jimmy Lennox had nothing to do with Ingrid's death. I have every intention of trying to find out who committed the crime."

His fingers moved in a soft tattoo on his desktop. "Your course of action is entirely your decision."

This was not the moment to try to convince him that Jimmy was caught in a trap of another's making. I'd told Glenn last night what I was sure had happened, what must have happened. I hoped he'd think through the circumstances and realize that Jimmy, if guilty, could easily have escaped detection by throwing Ingrid's body overboard. Jimmy, if guilty, would never have notified Glenn.

"If any member of the Riordan family inquires about Ingrid, will you inform me?" Would the murderer feel compelled to find out?

His gaze was somber, but I saw sympathy and understanding in his eyes. "I'm sorry, Mrs. Collins. I can't discuss confidential inquiries made by other passengers. However, I believe"—he spoke slowly, picking his words with care—"that it would not be inappropriate to decline to discuss ship personnel with any passenger. Any inquiry about a change in service staffing would be explained by saying that the staff in question was unable to perform duties at the present time."

I wondered if he saw the glint of tears in my eyes. He'd given me what support he could, but more than that, much more, I felt he was telling me that he had reflected on the oddly law-abiding actions of a man who

was suspected of committing two murders, that he too
had doubts about Jimmy's guilt, that he would let me do
what I could do.

The *Clio* was encountering a choppy sea. The lift and
plunge as I held to the handrail in the corridor outside Sophia's door was eerily reminiscent of Friday night. I'd
knocked on Sophia's door at about ten o'clock Friday
night. I'd seen no one, certainly not Ingrid. But it was
later that Ingrid must have been here. To be precise, Ingrid must have observed the opening of Sophia's door at
11:03. In his investigation, Glenn had asked all the occupants of nearby cabins if they'd seen Sophia or anyone
entering her cabin. The answer had been no.

I looked toward the two small interior cabins. Glenn
had said they were not occupied this cruise. Not
occupied . . .

I looked from the empty cabins across the corridor.
Sophia's door was fully visible from either of the unoc-.
cupied cabins. Ingrid must have been in one of the cabins
that night. She opened the door and saw someone unlock-
ing Sophia's door.

Why didn't the murderer see Ingrid?

Because Ingrid didn't want to be seen, couldn't afford
to be seen. I felt as elated as if I'd pulled a slot machine
lever and three red cherries locked into a row. I knew I'd
hit the jackpot. Ingrid opened the door, saw the figure at
Sophia's door, and immediately closed her door. She didn't
want to step into the corridor and be seen. That meant she
was somewhere she shouldn't be, that she felt constrained
to hide her presence in the empty cabin. So it wasn't work
that brought her to that cabin late on Friday night.

A pretty girl in an empty cabin . . .

I whirled away from the corridor with its ghostly images of a distraught Sophia and a deceptive Ingrid and walked fast.

I rang the bell for my stewardess at shortly after ten. When I opened the door, I said pleasantly, "Monika, please come in for a moment." I held the door.

It never occurred to her to refuse. "Yes, ma'am." She stepped inside. Her gentle face was pale and strained, her eyes red-rimmed.

I moved to stand in front of the door.

She looked at me, puzzled, her kindly face attentive, ready to be of service.

I gently touched her arm. "Was Ingrid a good friend?"

Her face puckered into grief, tears sliding down her cheeks.

"Here." I gently led her across the cabin to the sofa. "Please, sit down." I handed her a box of tissues, poured a glass of water, held it as she struggled for composure.

"I'm sorry." She swiped at her face, started to get up. "I mustn't stay."

"Take a moment, Monika, please." I handed her the water. "Tell me about Ingrid."

She held the glass tightly in both hands. Her green eyes blinked nervously. "We aren't supposed to talk about what happened."

"I don't want to talk about last night. I want to talk about Ingrid. Had you known her long?"

Monika sniffed. "I was the one who helped her come to work on the *Clio*." Tears welled again. "We grew up on the same street in Hamburg."

"I'm sorry." There is a special place in our hearts for childhood friends. Old friends are best friends. "I hope you can always remember the happy days. Ingrid was very pretty."

Monika's lips trembled. "The prettiest girl on our street, always. When she was in school, she always had a boyfriend, but her mother and father were so strict. If a boy wanted to go out with Ingrid, he had to have dinner with the family, meet her grandmother."

I smiled. "I imagine she had her pick of boys even so."

Monika nodded jerkily. "She laughed so much. She always had a special friend." There was no jealousy, only pride in her voice.

"I'm sure she had a lot of admirers on board."

Monika brushed back a dark curl. "Gustav adored her. She thought he was going to ask her to marry him. And now . . ."

"I'm terribly sorry." For Monika, for Gustav, for stricken parents in a small house in Hamburg. "I'd like to give you some money for her family. To help with the funeral expenses." I reached for my purse, slipped a hundred-dollar bill from a zippered pocket. "I want to speak with Gustav, also. Perhaps I can give him a donation for flowers for the funeral."

She looked at me in wonder. "You are so kind."

I wasn't kind, but perhaps ultimately I could offer those who grieved for Ingrid the justice that should be hers. "I want to help." I did in a way that Monika couldn't imagine. "How can I speak with Gustav?"

"He works in the purser's office. I can tell him you want to see him."

"I'll meet him when he gets off work. Have him call me, please."

When the call didn't come by late afternoon, I knew Gustav was either too grief-stricken by Ingrid's death or suspicious of uncommon generosity from an American passenger he'd never met.

I gathered up assorted currencies and set out for the purser's office. When a young woman with strawberry blond curls greeted me with a smile, I looked past her. "Is Gustav here? He helped me the other day."

"Yes, ma'am. Just a moment." She turned away.

In a moment a tall thin young man moved to the counter. He looked gangling and not quite fully grown. He'd likely manage another inch or two in height and a good thirty pounds. Thick horn-rim glasses rode a beaked nose beneath a widow's peak of bushy black hair. He looked at me politely. "Ma'am?"

"Gustav, I'm Mrs. Collins."

He scowled. "I don't want—"

"I must talk to you or I will have to tell Staff Captain Glenn you were in the unoccupied cabin on Deck 6 Friday night with Ingrid Shriver."

"Nobody can prove I was there." His voice was defiant, but his hands clenched into fists.

"I can prove it." My voice was hard. "Your fingerprints are in the cabin. You had no legitimate reason to be there. If you don't want me to tell Mr. Glenn, you are going to talk to me. I have to know what Ingrid saw, what she told you. I won't tell Glenn where I found out." I hoped this was a promise I could keep. Gustav's eyes were filled with misery. I didn't know his schedule but I picked a time that likely was his to spend. "Be on the sundeck at nine o'clock tonight."

## twenty-nine

THE flaming sun hung just above the horizon, painting crimson streaks on the darkening sea. I clung to the railing, steadying myself as the *Clio* lifted and dropped. Wind fluttered the standards on the pole behind me, tugged at my clothes, turned the air cool. I turned up the collar of my jacket. If Gustav didn't come, I would once again call on Glenn, hope that he would listen. Gustav's fingerprints were sure to be in one of the cabins opposite Sophia's door. His fingerprints should not be there, had no cause to be there except for the fact of a lovers' tryst. Surely Ingrid had shared something with Gustav. He might even know who Ingrid approached, the Riordan who maneuvered her into the quiet of Jimmy's cabin and death.

A footstep sounded behind me. I turned.

Gustav stood a few feet away. His features were hard to make out in the twilight, but grief was evident in the hunch of his shoulders, the slump of his body. When he spoke, his voice was empty. "If you tell Mr. Glenn, I'll lose my job. But I don't care. It doesn't matter anymore. We were going to get married in October."

I moved toward him. "I am sorry, Gustav."

His voice was ragged. "I told her not to have anything

to do with him. I told her to stay with the lady, but it was so much money. I don't know what could have happened. They were supposed to go together, wait for him in his cabin. Ingrid shouldn't have been there by herself."

"Ingrid wasn't by herself." The lady. I was so close I found it hard not to grab him, demand more. Rosie, Val, or Madge. One of them. Oh, Ingrid, how safe it must have seemed, how easy. Why would she fear another woman?

Gustav stepped close. "She must have been alone. That man killed her."

"Mr. Lennox didn't kill Ingrid. She was killed by the woman who persuaded her that Mr. Lennox was guilty."

His jaw jutted out. "They arrested him."

An arrest would be made in London. But that didn't matter to Gustav. "Yes, they took Mr. Lennox into custody. Do you know why?"

"He killed her." Fury made Gustav's voice rough.

"No, he found Ingrid's body and called Mr. Glenn. He would not have done that if he was guilty. He would have pushed her body into the sea. No one would ever have known."

"He called Mr. Glenn?"

"Yes."

"How do you know that?" He bent toward me.

"Mr. Lennox called me after he called Mr. Glenn."

"They arrested him." He came back to the information that had spread among the crew: Ingrid dead in a passenger's cabin, the passenger arrested.

"She died"—I saw him flinch, hated his pain—"in his cabin. He wasn't there. He'd gone up to the sundeck. Ingrid left Mr. Lennox a message, asked him to meet her there. While he waited—and she never came—she and the lady went into his cabin and she killed Ingrid."

"A woman?" He didn't believe it. "Ingrid was strong."

"She took Ingrid by surprise. She used a rolled-up towel, dropped it over Ingrid's head and twisted, then jammed her knee—"

"No." It was a guttural cry.

I stopped, reached out, gripped his hands in mine. "Help me find out the truth, Gustav."

"If he didn't—" He struggled with the horror of how Ingrid had died, unable to say the words that evoked her death. "If it wasn't him, it had to be the woman, didn't it? She's the only one who knew Ingrid was going to be in his cabin."

"The only one. So please, Gustav, tell me everything that you know. What time did you and Ingrid go into the cabin Friday night?"

"I came right after ten. That's when she got off work and she made sure no one was around and slipped into the cabin. I tapped three times on the door and she opened it and let me in. She had a bottle of wine for us and cheese sandwiches and a strawberry torte. We pretended we were passengers and going around the world. We had our meal like we were kings and then—" He bit his lip. "She was so beautiful with her hair loose on her shoulders. Her lips—" It was as if he were speaking to himself, remembering warmth and love and life. Tears slid down his cheeks. "Later, after we'd dressed, she opened the door and then she pushed it shut real quick and whispered we had to wait, someone was coming out of the cabin across the way."

Coming out? "What time was it?"

His shoulders lifted and fell. "I don't know exactly. Around eleven."

At 11:03 Jimmy's key was used to open Sophia's door. Coming out. . . Coldness touched me, moved over me. Ingrid opened her door as the murderer came out of So-

phia's cabin and turned to pull the door shut, making sure
it was firm, then used Jimmy's key that was taken from
the green pottery bowl to open it. Ingrid didn't see the
murderer go back inside because she'd drawn back quickly
to avoid notice.

"What did Ingrid whisper?"

Gustav massaged one temple. " 'We have to wait.
Someone's coming out across the hall.' We stood there,
and in a minute or two she eased the door open just a tiny
bit and peeked and said, 'She's gone.' I went out first. Ingrid was going to wait a few minutes and then leave."

*She's gone.*

I scarcely dared to hope. I spoke in as level a tone as I
could manage. "Did Ingrid describe the woman?"

He shook his head. "She just called her 'the lady.' "

"I'm sure you talked about it later. Did Ingrid ever describe her?"

"No. She didn't have any reason to."

"When did you last see Ingrid?"

He jammed his fingers together, looked down at them.
"Last night. In the cabin. Our last night."

I gave him a moment, but I had to keep pressing. Gustav knew that Ingrid was supposed to be in Jimmy's cabin
with the lady. What exactly did he know? "What did Ingrid tell you about the lady?"

He took a deep breath. "Ingrid said she had wonderful
news, that she was going to help solve the mystery about
the passenger who'd disappeared from the ship and she
was going to get a big reward, ten thousand dollars. I
asked her what she could do to earn that kind of money.
She said she was going to help the lady she'd seen coming
out of the cabin Friday night. Ingrid said it was the lucki-
est thing"—Gustav's voice shook—"that she'd decided to
talk to the lady. She almost hadn't because she was afraid

for Mr. Glenn to know she'd lied about not seeing anybody in the hall. But she said it wasn't really a lie because he'd asked about Mrs. Lennox and it hadn't been Mrs. Lennox and that's what she'd tell Mr. Glenn." Gustav hunched his shoulders. If Ingrid had told Mr. Glenn . . .

Gustav took a deep breath. "Ingrid was making up the lady's cabin, and Ingrid told her about Mr. Lennox wanting to know if she'd seen anyone in the hall and how he'd promised her a thousand dollars but she didn't think she'd tell him because it might get back to Mr. Glenn and she'd lose her job, and a thousand dollars wasn't that much money.

"The lady said it was a good thing Ingrid hadn't had anything to do with Mr. Lennox, that he was dangerous and everybody knew he'd thrown his wife overboard, and it would be wonderful if Ingrid would swear she'd seen the lady in the hallway because then she could speak up and tell about how she'd seen Mr. Lennox with Mrs. Lennox but she'd been afraid no one would believe her if she couldn't prove she was there. She told Ingrid that the family would pay ten thousand dollars, and all Ingrid had to do was come with the lady to see Mr. Lennox."

Gustav's face twisted in pain. What was a thousand dollars or ten thousand when life was gone?

"What else did the lady say?"

Gustav stared at me with teary eyes. "She told Ingrid she'd have Mr. Glenn ready to come in and help and she promised she'd be right there with Ingrid. Ingrid said she called and left a message for Mr. Lennox to meet her on the sundeck, but that the lady said he'd come on down to his cabin when Ingrid didn't come and the lady would be hidden and he'd be surprised to see Ingrid and she could ask him about being in Mrs. Lennox's cabin."

Gustav's face was bitter. "The lady promised she'd tell Mr. Glenn that she'd asked Ingrid to bring her a snack late and that's why Ingrid was in the hall and there wouldn't be a word about Ingrid being in the cabin. I told Ingrid to let Mr. Glenn worry about what happened to that passenger. But Ingrid said she ought to help if she could, and when we got to London we'd have ten thousand dollars for ourselves."

A lady with quick wits had spun a plausible tale to a credulous young woman and dangling in the background was more money than Ingrid could have dreamed of having.

"Ingrid didn't say anything else about her?"

The ship rose and fell. As I reached out to grab the railing, Gustav steadied me.

"Just that she was nice."

I looked out at the dark water. I knew a great deal, but I didn't know enough. Tomorrow was our last day at sea.

# thirty

THE atmosphere was different Friday morning, the last day of the *Clio's* journey. Inveterate shoppers crowded the gallery of stores. Discreet signs indicated last-minute sales, touted the final chance to purchase crafts and *Clio* ball caps at half price. I wasn't surprised to find Madge Riordan at a glass counter with several amber necklaces spread on a swath of black velvet. Not, of course, sale items. She fingered amber beads that had the glow of honey in the sunshine.

"That's lovely." I touched a shiny bead.

"I think I want it. But I like this one too." Madge touched another necklace with larger beads interspersed with jet. "What do you think?"

I thought she was a shopkeeper's dream, eyes glistening with cupidity, the very reach of her hand grasping. Her nails were long and sharp, bright red talons. I looked at her right hand carefully. No scratches, the nails unbroken.

"Maybe you should get both."

Her lips curved in delight. "That's what I'll do." She opened her purse, found her key card, which was also used for purchases on board.

I followed as she moved to the checkout counter. "I

was looking for you and Alex last night around ten for a nightcap. Did you turn in early last night?" The oddity of my seeking them out occasioned not even a ripple of surprise. To one of the Riordan women, ten o'clock would be very meaningful. Madge's focus remained on the necklaces as she scooped them both up.

Her reply was careless. "Early? No, we were in the card room. We played gin rummy until almost midnight. I won thirty-five dollars. It was my lucky night." Her smile was brilliant.

The day was cloudy and cool, the dark water bristling with whitecaps. The *Clio* was in the North Sea, plunging southwestward toward England. Despite the rise and fall of the deck, hardy passengers ignored the gray skies and stretched out on deck chairs near the pool, though some snuggled beneath thick fluffy white towels.

The breeze stirred Rosie Riordan's coppery curls. She was leaning forward, a graceful hand outstretched. The look on her face was so expressive that I paused for a moment to watch. Her eyes were eager. Her lips curved in a soft smile. She looked open and vulnerable and young.

I looked at her companion, sitting cross-legged on the deck chair beside hers. He gave a bellow of laughter, obviously concluding a raconteur's delivery. He was burly with thinning sandy hair and irregular features dominated by a blunt chin. But his laughter was infectious and he obviously was delighted by the woman whose company he was keeping.

I strolled closer. They would never have noticed me, they were so absorbed in each other, but I stopped and called out, "Good morning, Rosie."

She looked up with a quick smile. "Hello, Mrs. Collins. How are you?"

"Fine." Except a murderer walked free. "Are you enjoying our last day?"

She grinned. "Sure. Had to get that last burst of sunshine. Mrs. Collins, this is Harry Jacobs."

He was getting to his feet, his broad face warm and welcoming for Rosie's friend.

We shook hands. "Hello, Harry. I'm glad to meet you."

Rosie smoothed back a tangle of red curls. "I was going to introduce him to you and Jimmy last night in the bar, but we didn't get across the room before you left."

I smiled at him. "So you and Rosie were having too much fun last night to table-hop?"

"Time got away from us. We closed the place down." His look at her was as admiring as a teenage boy's. "It's our bad luck we didn't meet until I damn near knocked her down on the stairs yesterday. But it's our good luck that I've just moved to Santa Barbara."

I slotted times into my mind. If Rosie and her new friend were in the bar when Jimmy and I were there, Rosie could not have been in Jimmy's cabin with Ingrid.

I went to Val's cabin twice. I called three times. I wondered if she heard the summons at her door, listened to the peal of the telephone, sat with eyes staring and body tense, struggling with her murky memories of Friday night. Or was she thinking of years ago, Vic's death made fresh and raw, and grappling with the reality of Sophia's murder. No matter how much she hated Sophia, the violence of murder had pierced Val's careful containment. Val knew Sophia was murdered. I had no doubt of that.

I made one more circuit of the public areas. I found Val finally near the stern on Deck 5 huddled beneath a blanket in the last deck chair. Only two other chairs were taken and none near Val, the day too gray, the sea too rough.

I walked slowly toward her. She didn't look up at the sound of my approaching footsteps. Her pale, set face stared out at the gray water. A green scarf was tied beneath her chin, lending a nun-like severity to her features. She looked tragic, hopeless, and forlorn.

I stopped in front of her.

Her eyes widened. I saw the flash of fear that told me everything I needed to know. "I've been looking for you."

She drew in a quick breath but she made no answer.

I spoke gently. "If you'll tell me what happened Friday night, you'll feel better." The shackles of guilt and fear would loosen.

She lifted a hand, touched trembling fingers to her lips.

I ached for Val, for her pain and the terrible burden she carried.

"I can't." The whisper hung between us in the cool air. Abruptly, she pushed up, flung down the blanket, scrambled to her feet. "I can't." She pushed past me, broke into a run.

It was nearing lunchtime when I returned to my cabin, remembering the slap of Val's shoes as she fled. I knew enough now to be certain that Val was the key to the truth about Sophia.

I glanced toward the telephone. No message light. But there would not be a message from Jimmy, who must be watching the passing time with the frantic helplessness of a condemned man. As for Glenn, he'd done what he could do. I felt claustrophobic in the cabin. I stepped out on my balcony and moved to the railing, gripping it to keep my balance. The breeze ruffled my hair, tugged at my jacket and slacks. I was outside, and Jimmy was locked somewhere, unable to walk free. Tomorrow he would be whisked to jail.

What could I offer Glenn? Ingrid had turned to Gustav and told him they couldn't go out into the corridor because someone was coming out of Sophia's door. Later Ingrid told Gustav about the nice lady and their plan to trap Jimmy. A nice lady had stepped out of Sophia's cabin . . . She was coming out to turn and shut the door, then use Jimmy's key. Sophia was dead at that point, had to be dead. Everything was done. The murderer finished.

I gripped the railing. It was as if I were standing in that corridor on Friday night, watching the door to Sophia's suite open and across the corridor another door open for an instant, then close. The murderer hadn't seen that movement, was perhaps looking down at the precious electronic key card. Then, a turn, the door pulled shut, the key card used, the incriminating key card.

A moment later, Ingrid peeked out and saw no one. No one was in the corridor! But the murderer should have been there, walking away, moving purposefully toward a cabin. Instead, no one was in the corridor. That meant the murderer had stepped back inside Sophia's cabin, closed the door. Why didn't she come out? Why didn't either Gustav or Ingrid, who left only a moment later, see her?

I felt the chill of the breeze on the balcony as facts and suppositions and half-formed imaginings coalesced and I knew.

I knew who pushed the boulder, poisoned the sherry, and crept quietly into Sophia's cabin to commit murder and push Sophia over the balcony. I knew how and why Jimmy's key was obtained and used. I knew whose guileful manner beckoned Ingrid to death. I knew the dreaded memories that Val was fighting.

I knew, but between knowing and proving there was a chasm I had to bridge.

Glenn made notes as I spoke. When I finished, he shook his head. "It's all hearsay, what Ingrid told her friend." His dark eyes plumbed mine. "I need to know who gave you this information."

"If you will let it go for the moment, it may not be necessary." I wanted to keep my promise to Gustav.

He tapped a pen on his desk, finally nodded. "All right. For the moment." He glanced down at his notes. "According to your assumptions, Mrs. Lennox was dead before her husband's key was used."

"That's right." Everything had been done, Sophia strangled and thrown overboard, the files with Jimmy's notes also tossed away, likely in a pillow case weighted with something from the suite. Glenn should check, see if the binoculars were in the bedside table.

"Because of the information Ingrid gave to her friend, you believe that Ingrid approached one of the Riordan women and told her about Mr. Lennox's offer. The woman persuaded Ingrid to call and leave a message for Mr. Lennox, asking him to meet her on the sundeck while Ingrid and the woman waited for him in his cabin and there the woman killed Ingrid." He recited his summation in an uninflected voice, then looked at me, his face grim. "Who?"

I told him.

His reply was immediate. "That won't work. We know—"

I didn't let him finish. We knew what the murderer intended for us to know, but there was a way it could have been done, a way it was done. I described a daring and clever plan, just as clever as her manipulation of Ingrid.

Glenn came right to the point. "There might be finger-prints. I doubt she brought gloves on board."

"She may have carried a hand towel with her and pol-ished as she went, but there's a chance she missed some. As for gloves"—I shrugged—"she may have bought some while on shore."

Glenn turned toward his computer. "I'll send a security officer to get her."

"Wait." My voice was sharp.

He looked at me in surprise.

"That can be done later. Let's not take a chance on alerting her."

He frowned. "What do you suggest? We have to have some proof. Even if we found prints, that's not enough, not nearly enough." He kneaded a bony cheek with his knuckles.

Our adversary was cunning and quick. I did not be-lieve she would break down if confronted, even though she carried a terrible burden of guilt, especially with the death of Ingrid. But Glenn might be persuaded other-wise. "As you promised, there's been no general an-nouncement of Ingrid's death. The murderer knows but none of the rest of the family has any knowledge. Here's what we can do . . ."

He listened with his dark head bent forward, face som-ber. When I finished, he was silent.

I spread out a hand in appeal. "Jimmy Lennox is an in-nocent man." I watched Glenn, saw his frown, felt his tension. In the world of luxury cruising, consideration for passengers and their comfort is paramount. He struggled with the propriety of subjecting the Riordans to a shock-ing confrontation with, in his view, little hope of yielding results. Glenn was a man of method, comfortable with rules and regulations and order. There was nothing orderly or ordinary in my proposal.

He stared down at his desk, his face uncertain.

I spoke in a quiet tone, soft as the whisper of wings. "Ingrid was very young."

He lifted a hand, massaged tight muscles in the back of his neck. "The captain has reposed in me the authority to investigate as I feel necessary. I will summon the members of Mrs. Lennox's family to her suite at twenty-one hundred to offer them information on the conclusion of our investigation."

## thirty-one

I arrived at Sophia's cabin at a quarter to nine. Glenn held the door for me. I stepped inside, saw the two security officers in their crisp uniforms standing near the wet bar, the thin young woman and massive red-haired man.

Jimmy sat in an easy chair a few feet from them. He looked toward me with so much sadness my heart ached. His face was pale and gaunt, his eyes hopeless. He looked exhausted and defeated, deep lines in his face, slumped shoulders, lax hands. He said nothing.

I wished I could run to him, hold him in my arms, tell him he was going to be safe. I knew he wasn't absorbed in his own peril. He grappled with despair because of Ingrid, unable to forgive himself for drawing her into danger.

He looked away, sinking into remote misery.

Glenn's face was somber as he handed me a folder. "As you requested."

I tucked the folder under one arm, steeled myself to focus on the task ahead. There would—I hoped, I prayed—be time for Jimmy, time to help him heal, time to help him accept the truth that Ingrid could have told him what she had seen but had not done so. There would be time if I prevailed tonight.

I looked slowly and carefully around the luxurious room, impersonal now with no trace of previous occupancy. Since Jimmy and I had packed away Sophia's clothes, the luggage had been removed, the balcony doors closed, the drapes closed. I checked the sofa. Yes, it faced toward the balcony with the door to the bedroom slightly behind and to the right.

I moved quickly aft, punched the button that opened the curtains to the balcony, then stepped to the sliding doors, pushed them open. Cool, misty air surged inside, and the muted hum of the ship, the distant susurrus of swirling water.

Glenn watched in silence as I walked past him, twisted the knob on the bedroom door, stepped inside, leaving it open behind me. I was opening the drapes to the balcony when he came close. "Why open the doors to the balconies?"

"I want everything as it was Friday night." I gestured toward the balcony and the silken drapes fluttering from the breeze. "You found the doors open that evening, didn't you?" I was certain the sliding doors to the bedroom balcony had been pushed wide. They had to have been open.

"Yes. All the balcony doors were open."

I led the way back into the living room, closing the bedroom door behind us. Everything was in readiness. I moved to stand near Jimmy.

A knock sounded. I felt tightness in my chest, clutched the folder with sweaty hands.

Glenn opened the door to Alex and Madge. Madge wore a strapless silver georgette gown. Her hair was piled high with an amber comb to one side. One of the amber necklaces she'd admired this morning glowed against her pale skin. Alex pulled at his stiff collar as they moved toward the center of the room. Unlike his sport clothes, his tuxedo fit him perfectly. The difference between a fine tailor and buying off the rack. Madge looked without interest at me and Jimmy, flounced to the other easy chair. "We had to leave the party—"

There was a champagne farewell dance in the lounge tonight.

"—and they're going to play salsa next so I hope this doesn't take too long."

Glenn gave her a level stare. "I assumed the family would find the report to be of interest."

Alex rushed into speech. "Sure thing. Glad to come. Hope everything's worked out." He looked uncomfortable. "I mean, maybe Sophia got dizzy. That's what I think."

Madge covered her bright red lips and giggled. "Can you imagine Sophia dizzy?"

Alex clamped a hand on her shoulder and I wondered how many glasses of champagne she had already drunk.

A hesitant knock sounded. Glenn opened the door to Rosie, Val, and Kent. Rosie had lost her bloom of the morning. Her lovely face shadowed by worry, she walked with a gentle hand on Val's arm, guiding her, promising support. Val's delicate face looked worn. She moved as if every step cost effort.

Kent followed his sisters, once again unshaven, navy polo wrinkled, khaki shorts sagging, espadrilles slapping against the parquet floor. He looked around the living area, his face twisted in a frown. I wondered if he was remembering Sophia, remembering her, hating her still for her interference in his life.

Evelyn came up behind them. She looked as if she'd thrown on whatever came to hand: a fuchsia cotton blouse, green capris, white sandals. Her faded red hair was untidy, too, and she hadn't bothered with makeup. The events of the last few days had left their mark, her face pale, dark patches under her eyes, but she burst into speech. "I'm sorry if I'm late. I was packing and lost track of the time. Oh, everybody's here. Good evening, Mr. Glenn. You're very nice to keep us informed." She nodded toward Jimmy and me. "I suppose you want us to sit down. Girls, why don't you take the sofa. I'm hot as can be. That breeze feels good." She bustled to the table near the open balcony doors. She chose a straight chair and turned it to face the center of the room.

Glenn waited until everyone was seated. He stood with his back to the corridor door, arms folded, legs apart. "Ladies and gentlemen, tomorrow when we reach London I will present to the authorities the result of our inquiry into the circumstances surrounding the loss of Mrs. Sophia Lennox. As you know from our meeting with the captain, Mrs. Collins said good night to Mrs. Lennox at twenty-two fifteen. Until today, that was the last admitted sighting of Mrs. Lennox. However, Mrs. Collins has obtained information from a crew member—"

I was watching our quarry. There was the faintest tightening of lines from nose to mouth, the almost imperceptible flare of guarded eyes.

"—indicating one of you was observed coming out of Mrs. Lennox's suite shortly after twenty-three hundred."

The murderer sat stone still, alert and wary.

"One of us?" Rosie looked at Glenn sharply. "But that was the time"—she looked toward Jimmy—"when Jimmy's key was used to go into the suite. At least, I think that's what you said Saturday." She brushed back a glossy red curl.

"Perhaps it will be clearer if Mrs. Collins explains." Glenn nodded at me gravely.

I stepped forward. "A laminated security information card rests on top of the safe in the closet of each cabin." The Riordans gazed at me in bewilderment, all except one of them. "It contains suggestions and facts, including the information that whenever an electronic key card is inserted into a cabin lock, the provenance of that card registers. In other words, when Jimmy's key was used to open Sophia's door at eleven-oh-three Friday night, that fact registered. The murderer's intent—"

Madge's voice was shrill. "Who's talking about murder? Sophia fell. Or jumped."

"Sophia was murdered." I looked at each Riordan in turn. "Sophia was strangled with a towel—"

My quarry's face was still and brooding. How did I know? How could I possibly know?

"—after she called Jimmy's cabin and left a message and before the door was opened at eleven. By then, Sophia had been thrown overboard. When the murderer stepped into the corridor, she was seen by Ingrid Shriver."

Kent frowned. "Who's that?"

"The stewardess who serviced your cabins." I pointed at each Riordan in turn.

Kent was abruptly irritated. "So why don't you stop this charade? Sure, I remember her. Cute girl. Bring her out. Have her point at the guilty party."

"I would have her here if she could come. Someone else saw the murderer, too. She can tell us." I walked slowly toward the sofa, looked down. "It's time, Val, time to tell us who you saw."

Rosie came to her feet. "Leave her alone. She's sick and frightened."

"She's sick and frightened because she knows who committed murder." My voice was hard and cold, pressing, demanding. "She has to tell us or Jimmy Lennox will go to jail. Val, who did you see?"

It was painful to see the stark despair on Val's face. Tears welled, spilled, streaked her cheeks.

Everyone watched, frozen.

In my peripheral vision, I glimpsed movement, quick and quiet.

Rosie was a flash of fury. "Leave her alone. She doesn't remember."

"She remembers." I stared into Val's desperate eyes.

"I can't." Val was sobbing. "Sophia must have fallen. That's what happened. She wouldn't hurt anyone."

The pronoun did not refer to Sophia, who had, willfully or not, hurt so many over time, not out of malice, not even selfishly, but perhaps most galling of all, through mistaken certainty that she knew best for all concerned.

"She hurt Sophia. Val, tell us."

Val awkwardly came to her feet. She trembled. "Get that girl, the stewardess. Let her be the one who says."

"Ingrid can't be here. Do you want to know why? Ingrid went to the murderer, told her she'd seen her. Let me show you what the murderer did. You can see for yourself." I opened the folder, fanned out the glossy color photographs of Ingrid, face purple and distorted, tongue protruding, neck caught in a tight twist of towel.

Val lifted her hands as if to ward off the sight and then slowly, in an agony of comprehension, turned to look at Evelyn.

Evelyn no longer sat at the table. She stood framed in the open doorway to the balcony, lightly balancing against the motion of the ship.

I pointed at Evelyn. "You read about the electronic keys on the security card—"

Evelyn's face was a frozen mask.

"—and that helpful fact made it possible for you to commit murder at a time when you could point to the electronic record to prove you were in your cabin. I should have known right from the first. When I knocked on Sophia's door, she said, 'I told you—' and then broke off. To whom had she spoken? She knew her life was threatened. She suspected Jimmy and the Riordan children. But not you because you had knocked down the tray with the glass of sherry and gone on to empty the bottle and wash it. You knew the sherry was poisoned—you had poisoned it—but you realized that Jimmy suspected the falling boulder wasn't an accident and Sophia's death from an overdose wouldn't pass as an accident. Then came the attack at the Hermitage. Perhaps that was spur-of-the-moment. You took a chance. It failed."

Evelyn's eyes, eyes filled with despair, never left my face.

"Friday night you tried one more time to persuade Sophia not to close down the income from the trusts. She refused. It wasn't only the money, of course. How long had you hated her?"

Evelyn brushed back a straggle of faded red hair. "When she came into our lives, everything was ruined. The children needed their home and she sent them away and later she insisted Vic go back to the school. I should have killed her then, pushed her over the cliff where Vic jumped. But I never thought about killing her until she summoned the children to see about the trusts." Hot anger glowed in her eyes. "Sophia told me she was going to see how they were doing with their lives, try to decide what would be best for them. She didn't ask me!" Evelyn's hands clenched. "I know them better than anyone in the world. I love them. But she didn't ask me." Years of anger made her voice hard. "I tried to talk to her but she wouldn't listen. I gave her one last chance, but she wouldn't listen."

"You were determined to kill her while Jimmy could be a suspect. You think fast, Evelyn. You knew that if you left and reentered your cabin, there would be a record. But there was another way to get to Sophia's suite. Your cabin's balcony and the side balcony of the suite are joined. You knew Sophia kept open the doors to the balcony, both from the living area and from the bedroom. You are strong and athletic. You climbed over the railing and edged your way to the suite balcony. You stepped over and slipped into the bedroom. You took a towel from the bath and crept up behind Sophia on the sofa and strangled her."

Glenn moved from the doorway. "Miss Riordan, I am taking you—"

Evelyn whirled and ran out onto the balcony. She reached the railing, climbed to the top.

Glenn was moving, shouting.

Evelyn balanced for an instant, then plummeted out of sight, lost in darkness.

## thirty-two

I print out e-mails that matter to me. As I waited for the phone to ring, I looked over the messages I'd received from Jimmy.

September 5—I was touched that all of them came to Sophia's memorial. I wasn't sure they would. The service was on the headland at sunset. She would have been pleased that so many old friends came. Kent brought Heather. As soon as they got home, Rosie and Val went to see her, told her she was the sister they'd dreamed of having. I liked her and she's right for Kent. They have a dozen ideas for the wedding. Val wants it to be outdoors, says the day will sparkle. Kent's got a job. Heather's helping plan a memorial for Evelyn. I wasn't sure they'd want me there, but they do. Rosie told me they know none of it was my fault or yours.

September 22—You'll be glad to know Val's in treatment. Rosie's taken charge for the family. She asked if I would oversee clearing out the house, putting it up for sale. None of them want it. They've taken the keepsakes that matter to them. Rosie chose for Val. I said I would take care of everything. I'm staying in town. I don't want to be there either.

October 14—I've almost finished clearing out the house. I'm not sure what I'm going to do next. I'd like to talk to you. I'll call in the morning at nine. Will you be there?

I pushed up from my kitchen chair, walked toward the counter. It was two minutes before nine. When the phone rang, I reached out for the receiver. "Hello."

*"Bueno."*

I laughed aloud at the old, familiar salutation from our long-ago years in Mexico City, Richard and I, Jimmy and Margaret. It brought back good days and good times and later years when Jimmy and I had laughed and loved. *"Bueno."*

Words tumbled, his and mine: the tribute to Sophia, the progress with the house, the Riordan siblings. "Val's doing really well. Rosie goes to see her every day. And Rosie's talking about a wedding too, she and Harry from the cruise. Alex"—Jimmy's tone was dry—"is wheeling and dealing. It will be interesting to see how fast he can lose a fortune. Of course, Madge may spend it all on Rodeo Drive first. Kent's coaching Heather's little brother and has asked him to be best man. That's one reason I called; Kent told me he and Heather want you to come to the wedding, that it would never have happened except for you."

"They want me?" I'd thought that seeing me again would be the last thing any of the Riordans would ever want. If it weren't for me, Evelyn would be alive. Troubled and burdened, but alive.

"They want you." He took a deep breath. "I want you. Will you come?"

I blinked away tears. "Yes." One simple word and with it I offered my heart.

Available in hardcover

**DEATH WALKED IN**

A Death on Demand Mystery
by Carolyn Hart

BEN Travis-Grant wished he'd brought his ski jacket. He hated cold weather. Too bad Geoff's birthday was in February. It was more fun to come home to the island in July than in winter. He grinned as he thought of women on the beach in bikinis. However, despite Broward's Rock's chilly breezes, not one of them would miss Geoff's annual week-long birthday bash. The entire family rallied round for cake and ice cream and champagne toasts to Geoff's longevity. Still, February was the pits. A damp chill oozed through a crack in the top of his classic '74 MGB convertible.

The house would be warm and cheerful, and Geoff's parties were always fun. Without exception, they all wished him a long life. When Geoff knocked at the pearly gates, the good times would grind to a halt. Geoff had unveiled his testamentary intentions several years ago. Everything went to Chastain College. The college had already repaid the expected boon with a position on the board of trustees and a distinguished-graduate award. Fortunately Geoff wasn't really old, though almost fifty seemed ancient compared to Ben's exuberant twenty-five. Ben brightened. Geoff had married Rhoda a couple of years ago. Sex was good for people. He'd seen a story the other day that even old folks enjoyed sex. He grinned. Why not?

None of them had any right to grouse. Geoff had been generous to one and all, adopting the offspring of his first two wives, giving them his name and helping them through college. He also had a real instinct for what mattered to kids. He'd insisted each kid add his birth dad's name to Grant. It bothered Geoff that Ben hadn't graduated, but Ben was in no hurry. As for the party, Geoff could always be counted on for a thousand bucks at his birthday gathering and a cool five thousand every Christmas.

Ben raised an imaginary glass. "Long live Geoff!"

Slowly his hand fell and his face furrowed. Could he touch Geoff for an extra ten thou this week? He thought of Joey in the hospital in Bangkok. He wanted to help Joey if he could—no money and sick as a dog.

He moved restlessly, almost opened the door to plunge out on the deck of the ferry and pace. He hated being confined, but he also hated the cold wind on the open deck. Earlier, he'd scanned the half-dozen cars waiting to come aboard and hadn't spotted any of the family. He'd hoped to see Kerry, but likely she was already at the house, seated on an ottoman near the fire, watching and listening, dark hair swirling to her shoulders, grave eyes attentive, sweet lips ready to curve into a smile.

Kerry. Kerry. Kerry. Lovely as a dream, elusive as a wisp of cloud, beyond his reach. Of all the women for him to want . . . It made no sense. He'd always rocketed along having fun, but deep inside he couldn't deny his hunger for Kerry. Yet, even if he somehow captured her heart, Geoff would make good his threat. Geoff had always been protective of Kerry. But who wasn't? She was goodness wrapped in beauty. Geoff was tough about some things. He wanted everyone in the family to set a good example to the world. That's what he'd told Ben on a grim day six years ago.

There was one way to forestall Geoff's revelations to Kerry.

Ben's hands clenched on the steering wheel. If he told the truth, he'd be safe. But he couldn't do that. What else could he do?

Rhoda Grant hurried through the statuary garden. She'd felt choked in the overly warm house. The misty February day was chilly, the temperature in the forties. She welcomed the brisk air, the sense of escape.

She stopped at the far end on the lowest terrace, hidden from view behind a reproduction of a nude Aphrodite kneeling. The white marble statue was a favorite of Geoff's. Her eyes flashed, but she pushed away the clamor of angry thoughts that threatened to envelop her. She had only a moment. Rhoda lifted her cell phone, punched a number. It rang without answer. She left no message, clicked off. If he'd answered, what would she have said? She had to make up her mind.

It was all Geoff's fault. If he hadn't sold the plane, she would have been happy. She loved to fly, going up into blueness, far from the earth, exhilarated and free. Would she ever be free again?

Hyla Harrison worked at a table in her room. She welcomed the warmth from the fireplace. She gave the .40-caliber semiautomatic Glock pistol a final swipe with the cloth. The steel-polymer gun gleamed, dark as midnight. She balanced it in her hand. Without warning, the nightmare vision returned, blotting out the dancing flames in the fireplace, wrapping her in shaking horror:

*George called in. "Two-adam-seven." Dispatch responded, "Two-adam-seven, go ahead." "We'll be out of the unit checking a suspicious light in apartment construction at Market and Halliday." "Ten-four, two-adam-seven." George touched the screen, pinpointing their location. They grabbed their nightsticks and, flashlights shining, approached the entrance on opposite sides to avoid being silhouetted. After that, the details were hazy. Shots. George spun around, blood splotching his khaki uniform shirt. She called in. "Two-adam-seven, officer down! Officer down! Market and Halliday." Dispatch: "Confirm Market and Halliday?" "Affirm." As the sound of running steps dwindled in the distance, she knelt beside George. "Jessie . . ." His wife's name ended in a bubble of blood.*

A black-clad figure in thick-soled running shoes slipped down the broad shallow steps of the main stairway. No one else stirred in the silent house. The grandfather clock in the main entryway tolled the hour, once, twice, marking the depth of night when sleep is heaviest, consciousness lost in the labyrinth of dreams and imaginings.

Once in the hallway, cautious steps led to the heavy oak door of the library. The recently oiled—think ahead, avoid trouble—hinges made no sound as the panel swung in. With the red velvet curtains drawn against the night, the room was black as pooled oil. The hall door closed behind the silent figure. A pencil-thin shaft of light danced around the room, touching a basket of potpourri, a dingy suit of armor, settling on the glass display case.

Heart thudding, the figure reached the case. If this were successful, the future would be bright. The plan was foolproof, the contact made with the dealer, a huge sum of money the prize.

Eight quick steps reached the French window to the terrace. A pull and the heavy drapes parted. The pale rays of the February moon fell in a faint path across the room, turning the furniture ghostly. A click and the door opened. The figure stepped outside, eyes nervously scanning crushed-oyster-shell paths, moon-touched sculptures, a trellis covered by winter-browned vines, a dark row of cedars.

The garden should be empty at two o'clock in the morning. There was no movement, only the rustle of magnolia leaves fluttering in a sharp breeze.

The gloved hand reached inside, closed the drapes. It was important that faint splinters of glass be found embedded in the velvet. A thick cloth pad was pressed against the pane nearest the handle. Three sharp blows of a small hammer and the glass cracked, showering inward. The gloved hand yanked the drape out of the way, hurried back to the case. Several more blows, muffled by the pad, and the plate-glass shattered.

The gray fox paused at the clearing. Head lifted, the vixen sniffed into the cool February breeze. She caught a hot, moist, rich scent. She waited, wary for movement or danger, but no sound broke the night calm and her sensitive nostrils detected no trace of dogs.

Satisfied, the fox veered left, padded noiselessly, nostrils quivering. The succulent scent grew stronger, more enticing. The chicken coop lay silent at the back of the modest yard.

The fox's sharp eyes studied the gray wooden structure in a pale wash of moonlight. She circled, nose close to the earth. At the rear of the coop, she found a broken slat and hooked at it with a paw. The wood was old and rotten. The slat crackled as it split. The hens began to murmur and stir. The board ripped free. The fox nosed inside.

Frantic squawks clamored against the night silence.

A slight breeze stirred the curtains. Gwen Jamison slept with her windows raised, welcoming cool fresh air. She moved restlessly in her bed, her sleep fitful. A mother's heart grieves, going back over years and time, wondering what she could have done to make things better. She'd tried, but he wouldn't listen. Robert had been such a beautiful baby—

The shrill cries of the hens woke her. That loose board at the back of the henhouse! She'd asked Charlie to put in a new two-by-four. He'd promised but he hadn't been by yet. He was working so hard to fix up a nursery for the baby. Dear Charlie, such a good son.

She slipped into her house shoes, but didn't take time to get a jacket. As she ran through the kitchen, she grabbed a broom. No fox was going to get her hens. She could count on Buster, the cock, to fight with beak and spurs. Dust and feathers and straw would be whirling about the roost as the terrified hens sought escape.

She plunged out the back door and ran down the path. By the time she reached the henhouse, the hens were quieting. She saw a gray shadow running fast toward the woods. Buster likely had bloody spurs. She doubted the fox would return, but she tugged and pulled an empty rain barrel against the broken slat.

Gwen rested for a moment, breathing heavily. Her back ached. She shivered in her nightgown. She felt cold as frost on a windowpane. She'd fix herself a cup of hot chamomile tea, let her pounding heart slow. As she turned to go back to the house, she heard the squeak of the iron gate at the small, private cemetery nestled among the willows.

Gwen strained to see through the night. Willows screened the cemetery, but she glimpsed a flash of light.

Someone with a flashlight had entered the old family cemetery. The burial ground dated back to plantation days in the late seventeen hundreds. Her mama and daddy's people were buried there. Nobody but her people had any business in that cemetery.

Kids up to no good, that's what it had to be. She'd make short work of them. She walked swiftly toward the willows. When she reached the gate, she stopped and stared.

A figure knelt by Grandpa Wilson's grave. The faint glow from a flashlight illuminated a face she knew. She watched as a hole was swiftly dug, a small packet thrust into it, the dirt replaced.

Gwen stepped deep into the shadows of a willow, held her breath as the figure moved past her and the gate squeaked shut. She stood until there was no trace of the flashlight, no sound, and she was alone with a mournful hooting owl amid old headstones silvered by moonlight.

Gwen didn't need a flashlight to move unerringly in the cemetery. She weeded around the stones, wiped rain-spattered streaks from markers, always knelt by her mama and daddy's graves, remembering laughter and love and long-ago sunny days. She skirted Cousin Amelia's grave and Aunt Thomasina's to Grandpa Wilson's marker. She bent down and moved the bricks that had been placed above soft earth. She scraped away softened earth until her fingers touched the slick surface of a small package securely wrapped in a waterproof trash bag.

Annie Darling rolled over, still in that delicious floating world midway between slumber and wakefulness, eyes closed, one hand reaching for Max. The sheet felt cool to her fingers. She opened one eye. Max was already up. Her smile was sleepy, but content. He was always in a rush these days with so many plans for the remodeling of the old Franklin house. Something special was arriving on the ferry today. She didn't remember what shipment was scheduled to arrive, but Max was excited. Construction and remodeling on a sea island had challenges, not least of which was arranging for delivery of materials. However, she loved their remoteness. To her, Broward's Rock was the loveliest of the South Carolina sea islands, even if it wasn't a hub of commerce and the nearest Home Depot was across the sound in Chastain.

Both eyes opened even though she didn't hurry to wake up. February might not be the island's loveliest month, but the slow, hassle-free pace was welcome after the hubbub of Christmas. She had to handle the store by herself since Ingrid, her stalwart assistant, was out of town for two weeks. She and Duane were visiting her sister in Florida. Going solo wasn't a problem. Tourists were rare in February and she felt comfortable slapping up her *Back Soon* sign whenever she needed to run an errand. Fellow islanders understood about February.

She sniffed. Mmm. Max was obviously fixing something special for breakfast. She popped up and shivered in her mid-thigh-length cotton sleepshirt from Victoria's Secret. Max always approved of lingerie from Victoria's Secret. She slipped into a soft fleece robe and pink fluff flip-flops, gave her tangled curls a quick brush, and ran lightly down the stairs and into the kitchen, the wonderful aromas enticing as an embrace.

Max was lifting a casserole from the oven. He turned, blond hair tousled. She loved his slightly disheveled morning appearance, the stubble of beard on his cheeks.

He grinned. "Why am I not surprised that you arrive at the same time breakfast is ready and the coffee brewing?"

Annie laughed. "Timing is everything."

Max slid the casserole onto the tile table, reached out to pull her close. "Good morning, Mrs. Darling."

Their morning ritual never varied, a smile, a hug, a cheerful beginning to the day. Ever since August, when Max had been jailed for a murder he didn't commit, they held each other extra tight.

Annie pulled out her chair, dropped into it, and looked at him expectantly.

"Just a trifle I put together early this morning. Baked apples stuffed with sausage and cranberries." Max delighted in cooking. All the finest chefs were men, he often exclaimed.

Annie would have pointed out the sexist-pig tenor of the comment, but she wasn't going to discourage creativity. Max's cooking was to die for. She lifted a succulent rose red apple with its mound of stuffing onto her blue Fiesta plate, caught a faint scent of thyme along with the rich aroma of browned sausage.

Max poured coffee. Their newest enthusiasm was Tanzanian Peaberry, strong, brisk, and delicious.

Annie heaped apple and stuffing on her fork. She took a bite. Her eyes widened. "Max! This is the best yet."

Max smiled modestly and served himself.

Annie reached for the paper. Except on Sundays, *The Gazette* was an afternoon paper. They saved each issue to read over breakfast the next day. This morning they looked at the Tuesday afternoon edition. She slid sports and business to Max, kept the front section.

Annie unfolded the paper, glanced at the front page. "Wow."

Max looked over the top of the sports section.

"We had a million-dollar heist Monday night right here on our sleepy island. Marian wrote the lead story." She began to read:

BURGLARY NETS
DOUBLE EagleS
VALUED AT 2 MIL
by
Marian Kenyon

Annie grinned. "I expect Marian came up with the headline. It's too jazzy for Vince." Vince Ellis, the editor and publisher, was much more formal. Marian's salty personality added spice to *The Gazette*.

"What happened?" Max added a dollop of butter to his stuffed apple.

Annie rustled the paper and read aloud:

> Eight twenty-dollar gold coins, including an extremely rare 1861 Philadelphia Mint Reverse Double Eagle, were stolen Monday night from the home of island civic leader Geoffrey Grant, Police Officer Hyla Harrison said Tuesday.

Annie raised an eyebrow. "I guess with Billy and his family on a holiday and Lou in the hospital, Sgt. Harrison's in charge." Lou Pirelli was recuperating from an infection following an appendectomy.

> Sgt. Harrison said Grant estimated the value of the 1861 Double Eagle at more than six hundred thousand dollars. According to Grant's report, the stolen coins total almost two million in value and include a rare Mint State (MS–65) 1850 Double Eagle valued at $200,000.
>
> Sgt. Harrison said Grant called police Tuesday morning when he found the glass display case containing the collection smashed and the coins gone.
>
> Sgt. Harrison said the display case stood in Grant's library. Grant told police he last saw the coins when he locked

them into the case around ten-thirty p.m. Monday night. Grant told police he discovered the theft shortly after seven a.m. Tuesday.

The officer said investigation revealed a broken pane in a French window leading into the study from the terrace.

No one in the house reported hearing a disturbance, Harrison said. The officer declined to say whether any suspects had been identified.

Grant served three terms on the town council. He is a past president of several service organizations and has worked with the Chamber of Commerce to publicize the island as a vacation destination. He is an adjunct faculty member at Chastain College and is an authority on Victorian literature. Grant said, "The stolen coins represent some of the finest American coins. I hope the thief can be found and the coins returned without damage."

Annie turned the front page for Max to see. "Two pix. One of Geoff Grant." Grant wore his black hair a little long. He looked genial and a trifle smug, a man sure of his position in the world. "And a shot of a gorgeous gold coin." Even in a newspaper reproduction, the coin had unmistakable glory. Annie said casually, "Maybe Grant will hire you to find out what happened."

Max retrieved another apple. "I'm too busy to run around looking for a small–time thief."

She was startled. "Since when is two million dollars small time?"

Max added a dollop of orange marmalade to the stuffing. "The thief is small time even if the theft isn't. It's too risky for a sophisticated crook. The only access to the island is by ferry or private boat or plane. You can bet Harrison's already got a line on arrivals and departures. I'll bet she already has a list of every car, truck, bike, or boat that left the island Tuesday morning. Strangers stand out like a sore thumb this time of year. A thief with any savvy would wait until July, maybe July fourth when the island is packed with visitors, and it would be easy to come and go without notice. Here's my prediction: When the police find out why the theft occurred in February, they'll know the whole story."

Tendrils of fog drifted across the island, turning the marina ghostly, trailing over the boardwalk to hover near the plate-glass windows of the shops and stores. Snug in the inner office of Confidential Commissions, Max Darling reclined in his red leather desk chair, head resting comfortably, feet slightly elevated, and gazed at his favorite portrait of Annie in the ornate silver frame provided by his mother.

Come to think of it, he'd never paused to wonder at Laurel's selection. The intricate silver swirls of the frame were dramatic. A no-nonsense, plain silver frame, something on the art deco line, would better suit his delightful and delightfully predictable wife, honest, open, genuine, unpretentious, adorable Annie.

Was Laurel suggesting that the inner Annie—his mother was ever attuned to subconscious—might not be quite so predictable? Certainly Annie was often impulsive. She'd been known to explode when provoked. Sometimes when she plunged directly toward her objective, she was unaware of possible repercussions. Max gave a thumb's up to the portrait.

Annie's gray eyes gazed steadily toward him. Flyaway honey-bright curls framed an open and generous countenance. Her kissable lips were slightly parted, ready to smile.

Whatever, predictable or possibly possessing depths

perceptible only to his perspicacious mother, he was one lucky man and he knew it.

Max's smile faded. He drew in a sharp breath as he grappled with the sudden tightening in his chest that still came, though not so often now. He gripped the edge of the gleaming Renaissance refectory table that served as his desk. The table was one of the few furnishings that hadn't been replaced. Last summer, not long after a last-minute case embroiled him in a murder charge, he'd totally redecorated his office, cypress walls and bookcases, huge framed black and white photographs instead of paintings, spare Danish furniture, carpet in squares of black and white.

He'd never said why. The day the office was done, Annie stood on tiptoe to kiss him. She held him tight. "Don't you think a new desk would be better?" The table had been a Christmas gift from Annie when he first opened the office. "Something in chrome and glass?" That would leave the room completely transformed with nothing to remind him of the day when a sultry, hot-eyed young woman walked through that door and asked for help, all the while knowing that a shadowy figure behind her request intended no good for Max.

Max had touched Annie's lips with a finger. "I only think of you when I see my table." He smiled at the memory, and the tightness eased. He gave a final glance at Annie's portrait and was still smiling as he rose and moved quickly toward the door. He should have left a few minutes ago to meet the finish carpenter at Franklin house. Hopefully, he was ready to put in new cypress paneling in the library. Next stop would be the ferry landing to pick up a shipment of solid bronze sash window fasteners.

Max was eager to get to the house. Yesterday the locksmith had been scheduled to install solid bronze doorknobs with a star pattern in the front and back doors as well as matching plates with upper keyholes which any old skeleton key would open, common to most antique locks, and lower covered keyholes that controlled newly installed interior deadbolts. Of course, there were often delays and complications in getting tasks accomplished. The first shipment of window fasteners had been lost in transit. Stained glass windows with matching peacocks were overdue. If all went well—his grin was wry, the knowing resignation of a householder involved in renovations—they might move in by April. The house had been his salvation throughout the fall and early winter, always a decision to be made, a workman to hire, an elusive purchase needed. The memory of August blurred beneath happy days and nights.

The door to his office swung. His tall blond secretary, Barb of the bouffant hairdo, culinary talents, and generous heart, beamed at him. She held the portable phone tight to her chest, the speaker covered. "Max, a lady needs to talk to you. She says it's urgent."

Barb's voice lifted with delight. To her, urgent spelled trouble and trouble meant Max might soon have an interesting case and Barb could use her Internet skills to come up with information. Max understood her elation. Barb was high energy and though she'd enjoyed helping choose swatches for the office furniture and dealing with the frame shop about the photographs, she often had nothing to do. She blamed Max for the fourteen pounds she'd gained since summer because she said she only cooked when she was bored. Despite the limitations of a two-burner stove with a temperamental oven tucked into a dark corner of the storeroom, she created succulent triumphs. Yesterday's dish had been mustard fried rice seasoned with blackstrap molasses and garlic. It had been . . . interesting.

Ever since August, he'd turned down almost all who came to Confidential Commissions. He'd helped a school teacher struggling with identity fraud, found a missing gray cat, and failed to authenticate a pitcher's mitt alleged to have belonged to Babe Ruth though he and Annie had a swell time in Boston checking out records.

He always insisted he wasn't a private detective, explaining that Confidential Commissions was devoted to assisting clients in solving problems. If in the past Confidential Commissions at times appeared to resemble a private detective agency, Max was determined that confusion would no longer arise. Problems he would deal with. But if anyone came to him with a tale of crime, he would remember the lesson that had been seared into his soul: People lie.

"Max?" Barb's whisper was piercing. "She sounds scared."

*. . . sounds scared.*

Max's face hardened. Last summer a sexy young woman had pretended to be afraid to go to the police. He'd fallen for her story, hook, line and sinker, and he'd almost been sunk. If the caller was scared, she could be scared on her own time or ask a cop for help.

He sidestepped Barb and flung over his shoulder, "Got to go. Man waiting on me. Tell her to call the cops." He plunged toward the front door. On the boardwalk, he gave another thumb's up as he passed Death on Demand, the finest mystery bookstore north of Miami. He didn't give another thought to Barb's disappointed face or to the caller who sounded scared. He strained to see through the fog and hoped the carpenter showed up and the ferry was running on time.